"Erin Duffy is a fresh, funny, and fabulous new voice in literature."
—ADRIANA TRIGIANI,
New York Times bestselling author

on the rocks

A NOVEL

ERIN DUFFY

author of *Bond Girl*

P.S.
INSIGHTS,
INTERVIEWS
& MORE...

ON THE ROCKS

ALSO BY ERIN DUFFY

Bond Girl

ON THE ROCKS

Erin Duffy

wm
WILLIAM MORROW
An Imprint of HarperCollins*Publishers*

This is a work of fiction. Names, characters, places, and incidents are drawn from the author's imagination or are used fictitiously and are not to be construed as real. Any resemblance to actual events, locales, organizations, or persons, living or dead, is entirely coincidental.

A hardcover edition of this book was published in 2014 by William Morrow, an imprint of HarperCollins Publishers.

FIRST WILLIAM MORROW PAPERBACK EDITION PUBLISHED 2015.

Waves provided by StudioSmart/Shuttershock, Inc.

Designed by Lisa Stokes

Library of Congress Cataloging-in-Publication Data has been applied for.

ISBN 978-0-06-220576-6

15 16 17 18 19 OV/RRD 10 9 8 7 6 5 4 3 2 1

For my girlfriends,
who manage to find the fun in everything

ON THE ROCKS

Praise for *On the Rocks*

"With its more realistic and modern ending, this engaging novel offers readers relaxing and light yet thoughtful summer escape."

—*Library Journal*

"Duffy's second novel is tenderly introspective. . . . Abby's attempts to navigate the ever-changing rules of dating are infinitely relatable and will prove to be an ideal beach read for fans of Elin Hilderbrand and Sarah Pekkanen."

—*Booklist*

"Alternately humorous and touching, this novel is a fast, fun read. . . . [Abby] is someone you'd want to friend, freezer full of ice cream and all."

—*Romantic Times* (four stars)

Praise for *Bond Girl*

"A compelling, fun read."

—*Kirkus Reviews*

"Despite financial details that may make your head spin and a workplace that will make your stomach churn, Duffy's fresh take on the single-in-the-city tale does a terrific job of reviving chick lit (not every girl works in publishing or PR, after all)."

—*Library Journal* (starred review)

"*Bond Girl* is . . . witty and very racy. . . . Trust me, you won't be bored with this Wall Street story."

—*Washington Post*

"*Bond Girl* is a sparkling debut, smart and snappy but never weighed down by financial terminology. Who knew Wall Street could be this much fun? A-"

—*Entertainment Weekly*

"Duffy's first novel is a sharp, witty look at the intricacies of the trading floor and the people who populate it. The writing is clever and articulate, and Alex's story of personal growth makes her a sympathetic, likable heroine. Filled with too-good-to-be-true anecdotes and enough of a biting, cynical bent to offset the chick-lit romance angle, *Bond Girl* is a fun read-alike to the canons of Weisberger, Kinsella, and Green. Duffy's acknowledgment of the recent financial collapse and ensuing recession makes *Bond Girl* an entertaining and timely read."

—*Booklist*

"I'm crazy about *Bond Girl.* Erin Duffy is a fresh, funny, and fabulous new voice in literature. Her heroine, 'Bond Girl' Alex Garrett, has moxie and drive—her veins are pumped with Red Bull while her heart is full of hope. At long last, thanks to Ms. Duffy, I grasp the world of high finance, and the hearts and minds that drive it. Great story. Delicious debut."

—Adriana Trigiani, author of *Lucia, Lucia* and *Brava, Valentine*

"Writing with an addictively acerbic sense of humor, Duffy gives readers a sassy new heroine and an unforgettable tour of financial trading."

—*Chicago Tribune*

"Told in first person in Alex's voice—and what an appealing voice it is, one that makes Alex likable from the first page—*Bond Girl* is a smartly written comic novel that's great fun to read."

—*Times-Dispatch* (Richmond, VA)

"If you're looking for a great weekend retreat or a great book for the beach, look for this one. For any woman who's ever had a love-hate-detest relationship with a job *Bond Girl* is truly perfect."

—*Wisconsin Rapids Tribune*

CHAPTER 1

Just Like Instant Cookie Mix, but Slightly More Expensive

THERE HAS GOT to be a reason why they do this," I said as I turned and checked out the back of my dress in the three-way mirror. "I mean, it doesn't make any sense. This is without question the most expensive dress you will ever buy in your life. Explain to me why the sample size is so big you need clothespins to hold it up? You can't even tell how it's going to look when it's the right size!" I stared at the back of the ivory strapless Vera Wang gown, in all its beautiful satin and lace glory, being held up by heavy-duty clothespins that cost two dollars for a bag of three hundred from the corner store. Personally, I thought the wedding dress industry was pushing the concept of shabby chic just a little too far.

"That's not even the worst part, Abby," my best friend Grace said from her perch on the chair in the corner of the room. "You go to a sample sale for normal clothes and the average size barely fits a six-year-old.

The fashion industry is all kinds of screwed up." She downed a glass of champagne. Free cocktails seemed to be the latest trend in customer service for soon-to-be brides and, in this case, their friends. I was pretty sure the booze was the only reason Grace was so eager to follow me to bridal shops all over the city, but I didn't mind. I figured there was no harm in having a few drinks as long as Grace, not me, was the one who got buzzed. The concept of getting love-struck girls liquored up in a bridal salon seemed a bit risky. The last thing I needed was to overdo the bubbly and end up putting down a nonrefundable deposit on a dress with a forty-foot train or something.

Kate Middleton I am not.

"On the flip side, it does make me feel skinny," I admitted.

"You may have just answered your own riddle," Grace said as she finished her glass of Moët. "Do you think we could get some of our other friends to pretend they're getting married so we can keep coming in here for free happy hour?" she asked. Most people would have laughed this off, but I knew Grace well enough to know that she wasn't kidding. These were tough times, and you'd be surprised how creative you can be when you're looking for ways to cut down on bar bills.

"That's got to be bad luck," I said as I shook my head. "Of all the wedding superstitions I've ever heard, pretending to be engaged so you can save money on alcohol has got to be right up there with wearing someone else's ring on your ring finger."

"It's bad luck to wear someone else's ring?" she asked as she peeled chipped pink nail polish off her thumb.

"The worst. Don't ever do that," I scolded her.

"Well, I'm screwed. I've been doing that for years. We've been friends since we were six. Why are you just telling me about this now?"

"Clearly, I've failed you," I said as I piled my bottle-blond hair on top of my head to simulate actual wedding hair instead of the unbrushed mess of frizz that it actually was. "I'm going gray. Look at this," I said as I smoothed the hair around my part. My overgrown, mousy brown roots were now showing random strands of gray. "I need to get my highlights done."

"You spend so much money on highlights! You don't need them. You're not going gray."

"Not all of us have perfect hair."

"I'm a redhead. Not perfect."

Grace's hair wasn't red. It was an ethereal, natural shade of auburn. It was a color that girls spend hundreds of dollars on trying to simulate and never come close to achieving. Grace was a stereotypical Irish girl. She had gorgeous red hair, shocking blue eyes, pale skin, and the ability to guzzle booze like a three-hundred-pound man. When I looked at the thousands of pictures of us from over the years, she always looked the same, while I transformed from the short girl with mousy brown hair and brown eyes to the short girl with bottle-blond hair and brown eyes. I wanted to hate her for her God-given beauty, but I loved her too much. I have, however, stopped standing next to her in pictures.

The annoying perky bridal lady who was helping me popped her bobble-head into my dressing room. "How are we doing in here, ladies? Can I get you anything?" she asked in a voice so high it sounded like she had sucked on a helium tank.

"The bride needs a glass of champagne," Grace said with authority. "She's a little jittery."

"Not a problem, I'll be right back," she said as she pushed her way back through the heavy curtain.

"I don't want a glass of champagne," I said to Grace after the perky lady had left.

"It's not for you, it's for me."

"Why do you need to drink to watch me try on wedding dresses?" I joked, though I already knew the answer.

"I don't. But it's free, so why wouldn't I?" she said with a shrug.

I laughed. I loved Grace for her blunt honesty and her ability to find the fun in any situation—even sitting in the corner of a dressing room wallpapered in satin wedding dresses that more or less all looked the same. "Well, for what it's worth, I do think that dress looks beautiful on you," she said. "You know, assuming you ditch the clothespins and have about fifty yards of fabric removed. Do you want me to take a picture to send your mother?"

I shot her a knowing look. "No. If my mother was at all interested in seeing me in my wedding dress, she'd be here instead of at the day spa, covered in mud or seaweed or some other crap."

"She just wants to look her best for your big day. Don't let it upset you—I'm here!" Grace said, hoping that she'd assuage the dull pain I felt from once again having my mother be absent for a defining moment in my life because she was too busy taking care of herself.

I swished the skirt from side to side, listening to it rustle and trying to picture myself wearing it on the most important day of my life. It was early September, and I didn't have a lot of time until my "Winter Wonderland"–themed wedding in January, so I had no time to waste before buying the perfect gown. I was planning my entire wedding in only six months, which to some people doesn't seem like a long time, but when you're thirty-one and have dated your boyfriend since college, six months might as well be six years. I was ready for my real life to start. And once you're ready for that, you want it to start immediately—as in yesterday. Six months was more than enough time to plan the wedding because I was planning on sticking to the basics: dress, band, church, flowers, guests, add champagne, stir, and bam-o, instant wife. Just like instant cookie mix, but slightly more expensive.

"What's up with Ben?" Grace asked as she typed on her iPad. Clearly tired of looking at the reflection of her best friend in triplicate, she preferred to post a picture of her champagne glass on her Facebook page. The world's obsession with social media completely baffled me. I could think of no reason on earth why anyone would care that Grace was drinking champagne in a bridal salon on a Saturday afternoon, but still, she felt a need to alert people she was "friends" with all over the country that that was what she was doing. Girls these days no longer seemed to value their privacy in the slightest, which I found profoundly sad. I wasn't sure when exactly the shift toward total voyeurism had occurred, but I was pretty sure it was right around the time women started getting bikini waxes on national TV.

"Not much," I said as the lady returned with another champagne flute, smiling another game-show-worthy smile before she left. I handed the flute to Grace and fidgeted with the top of my dress, trying to place it so that my chest didn't squish out the sides. "He's been really busy lately at work. I think he's stressed about the wedding and stuff. It's going to be hard for him to take two weeks off for the honeymoon."

"What does he have to be stressed about? He's not the one people are looking at. You are. He could show up in a stained tux with a rip up the ass and no one would notice. You, on the other hand, better not show up with so much as one hair out of place or people will mock you for the rest of your life."

"That's comforting," I said as I turned to the side for the millionth time to check out my silhouette. "Other than that, he's fine." And that was the truth. He was completely fine; he was just, I don't know, different. Weddings can do strange things to people, so it was a good thing that I was the picture of calm while we finished up this planning process. All he had to do was book our honeymoon in Hawaii, and I'd take care of everything else. The less added stress I put on him the better, and besides, everyone knows that as long as there's an open bar and a good band, guys don't give a damn about anything else. When you think about it, if your fiancé cares about or even knows the difference between a peony and a hydrangea, you've probably got a whole other set of issues you need to deal with. So I was perfectly content with him not caring about anything in any way whatsoever. "I called him this morning before my appointment, but I got his voicemail. Maybe he can meet us for lunch after this or something. I'll call him when we finish up."

"Cool," she said. "I think you need to try on a few more, though. I'm not ready to leave yet."

"I don't need to. This is it. *This* is the one." I could hear the wedding march music in my head just standing in it. The satin gathered perfectly at my waist, the small crystal-encrusted appliqué at the hip added just enough sparkle to make it special without looking cheesy, and the flare of the skirt had just enough volume without making me look like a cream puff. It was perfect. Perfect, perfect, perfect.

I continued to twirl on the circular platform in the middle of the dressing room like one of those ballerinas in little girls' jewelry boxes. I never thought that I was a girly girl, but I was starting to second-guess myself because I could have stood on that platform and twirled until I got dizzy, pitched over, and fell face first off the pedestal and onto the floor.

I heard my phone ring and glanced at it in the corner, lying on the floor next to my purse and the pile of discarded clothes. I ignored it because I was pretty sure it was my mother trying to explain to me for the millionth time why she simply could not miss her microderm abrasion appointment to come with me today. My wedding day, in her mind, was all about her, and the approaching date had turned her into a bigger narcissist than she usually was. If she wasn't having something wrapped, scrubbed, plucked, or lasered, she was popping anxiety medication and lying around the house with cucumbers on her eyelids moaning about how she simply wasn't old enough to be the mother of the bride. Most people wouldn't consider this normal motherly behavior, but anyone who expected my mother to be normal had never met her.

And should consider themselves lucky.

Anyway, I didn't need her to come with me. I had Grace, and Grace had her champagne, so everyone was happy. Things were going great. I loved this dress. I imagined I'd love it even more twelve sizes smaller so I could raise my arms without it falling down around my waist.

My phone beeped rapidly three more times in succession, but I refused to get down off the pedestal. I loved my friends, but didn't they know that wedding dress shopping requires complete concentration and that I shouldn't be disturbed?

"Oh. My. God," Grace said as she stared at me, still clothespinned into the size 22 dress, enjoying, unbeknownst to me, the last few moments of happiness I would have for a very long time. "Oh my God," she said again. The color had suddenly drained from her face, and it had nothing to do with the fact that prison waiting rooms had better lighting than this dressing room, or that she had rapidly consumed three glasses of champagne on an empty stomach.

"What?" I asked, finally able to tear myself away from my own reflection in the three-way mirror. I was beginning to feel a bit vain staring at myself for as long as I had, but I couldn't help it. I looked frea-kin' amazing in this thing.

"This can't be right," she said as she shook her head. "This can't possibly be right. I'm . . . confused."

"What?" I said again as I felt goose bumps rise all over my back and my arms. It was as if my subconscious was ready to admit there was a problem before my brain was, because my brain was too busy admiring the duchess silk satin I was swathed in.

"Check your phone," she said as she snatched it off the floor and handed it to me. I scrolled through my text messages, realizing that I had three from friends and one from my little sister.

What the hell happened?

Are you okay?

Hang in there, Abby!

Hey sis, call me! I need to talk to you!

"Why is everyone telling me to hang in there and asking me if I'm okay?" I asked, confused. "What's this about?"

"Someone is clearly just messing with him," Grace said, forcing a smile so grotesquely insincere I worried for a second that her body had been invaded by a pod person.

"I sound like an echo, Grace. I repeat, What is going on? Answer me," I demanded, my nerves finally detectable in my voice. "What the hell are they talking about? Why wouldn't I be okay? I'm wearing Vera Wang. It's impossible to not be okay in Vera Wang. It's every girl's happy place, a veritable bridal Shangri-la."

Grace stuttered, and sputtered, and coughed, trying desperately to delay saying what she had no choice but to say. "Abby, look at Ben's Facebook page," she finally managed to squeak out as she tentatively handed me her iPad, the Facebook application already uploaded. "And here," she said as she also handed me her champagne flute. "Drink this."

For a second, I didn't see it. I saw the usual pictures of him with his buddies, and wall posts from his friends, and stupid information about the Patriots and the Red Sox, but I didn't see it.

Until I did. Then I realized there were a lot of things I apparently didn't see.

Then everything faded to black.

CHAPTER 2

I Thought He Was the Love of My Life . . . and He Thought I Was a Sock

After I saw Ben's Facebook post changing his status to single and telling everyone he had ever met in his life (except me) that we were over, I did what any red-blooded American girl who had been trying on wedding dresses for impending nuptials would have done: I went directly to his apartment and tried to break down his door with my fists. When that didn't work, I walked halfway down the hallway, took off in a full sprint, and charged the door with my shoulder like they do on TV cop shows, but since I'm only five-two and weighed 110 pounds at the time, all I managed to do was bruise my shoulder so badly I couldn't raise my arm above my head for six weeks. I probably could've tried ringing the doorbell like a normal person, which would have alerted me to the fact that he wasn't home, but adrenaline and shock will make a girl do really stupid things.

I sat in the hallway outside his door for over three hours, calling him again and again and again until the battery on my phone died, with no answer. I had no clue what was going on, but I refused to admit that I had missed warning signs that Ben was about to freak out and tell me he didn't want to get married by changing his Facebook status. Nobody is that stupid. Sure, there was his disinterest in all the wedding details, and the fact that I had to change the date multiple times because the timing wasn't good for him. And sure, he was working really late every night, and we hadn't hooked up in over a month, and then there was that random apartment rental site in Tucson I saw on his laptop that he swore was for a friend. But really, that's not sufficient evidence to prove that your fiancé's about to bolt. I mean, it's not like he put it in skywriting or posted it on Facebook or anything.

Fine. I actually am that stupid.

I heard footsteps and knew it was him. We had been together so long I could recognize the rhythm of his walk, so I didn't even bother to look up. "Oh, Abby," he said when he reached the top of the stairs and saw me sitting on the floor with my head buried in my hands. "How long have you been here?" he asked, like he was oh so very sorry for the huge inconvenience of making me wait in the hallway.

"I don't know. Since I saw you break up with me on Facebook while I was wearing a wedding dress. It seems that time sort of stands still after that."

"Come inside, we need to talk," he said as he extended his hand to help me up. I glared at him before smacking it away and climbing up off the floor on my own, busted shoulder and all. If he didn't want to give me his hand in marriage, I didn't want his hand at all—unless it was to shove up his own ass.

"You think we need to talk? Oh, I don't know, Ben, maybe we could just start talking solely via Facebook posts since that seems to be your preferred method of communication these days. Actually talking to your fiancée must have gone out of style. Did Michael Kors announce that on *Project Runway* or something?" I wiped tears from my cheeks and tried to find the Ben I loved in the one I was looking at. He opened the door, and I followed him inside.

"I don't even know what to say to you," he said, his back turned toward me as he stared out the window. I had been in denial the entire time I was sitting on the floor in the hallway. It had been nice while it lasted.

"So it wasn't some sick bachelor party–type joke?" I asked, my voice shaking so badly it actually cracked like a prepubescent boy's.

"No," he answered flatly.

"You actually wrote that."

"Yes."

This isn't happening. I won't allow it.

"What's the problem, Ben? What in God's name made you spaz out like that?" I felt like if I just kept talking I wouldn't have to deal with listening to him speak. "Are you nervous? Because that's totally normal, I forgive you, but you can't just go around writing things like that on Facebook without thinking them through. Your little freak-out has gone viral. I'm getting condolence posts from people I haven't seen in ten years. How am I supposed to fix this?"

"Abby, it wasn't a freak-out. You can't fix this, there's nothing to fix. I don't know how to tell you this, but I can't get married," he whispered, as if it pained him to say the words, although apparently not to type them.

"Yes, you can. And you will. See this?" I held up my left hand and wiggled my ring finger, the emerald cut stone I had fished out of a chocolate dessert only a few months before, a clear indication to sane people the world over that a wedding was going to happen. "This is the ring you gave me when you asked me to marry you. And when you ask someone to marry you, you don't get to change your mind. This is not like ordering delivery and deciding that you'd rather have pizza than Chinese. This is not up for debate. I don't know what's going on with you, but we are getting married. End of discussion."

"I know this is hard for you to understand," he said as he stared at the floor. "I hate myself for doing this. I do."

Nope. Still not letting this happen.

"No, calculus is hard for me to understand. Quantum physics is hard for me to understand. The Kardashians' fame is hard for me to understand. This isn't hard to understand. This is insane. I mean, where is this even coming from? Did you wake up this morning and think, 'Gee, I'm going to have a bagel for breakfast, and then I'm going to break up with my fiancée?' What planet are you living on?" I was hysterical, and still I thought that if I just kept talking I'd somehow be able to talk him out of it. Not exactly the way I imagined my marriage beginning.

He stared at me, or rather, through me, like I was some kind of apparition and not actually there. "Is there somebody else?" I asked. My breath caught in my chest, figuring that the only way he'd ever leave me was if he had someone else to run to. He didn't even know how to do his own laundry.

"No, I swear to God there's not," he said.

"You're not even leaving me for another woman? You're just leaving?" I shrieked so loudly I was pretty sure people on the street outside could hear me.

"I'd have thought that'd be a good thing," he replied, a bit stunned by my reaction.

"Think again." I wasn't sure why it wasn't either. But it wasn't.

"Thinking is all I've been doing, Abby. It's all I've thought about since the day after I proposed. I don't think I'm ready to get married; there's still too much I want to do with my life. I want to travel. I want to experience life outside of the Northeast. I don't want my Sundays to fucking revolve around Tom Brady."

"Then don't watch the Patriots! What does that have to do with me? Are you listening to yourself?" He didn't flinch. He might have been in the acceptance phase of this process, but I was very much still entrenched in denial, and I was planning on setting up camp there. "Okay, this is completely fixable. This is good, because I can travel. I'll go anywhere you want! I can get a passport. I like hotels. I know how to say hello in, like, three different languages! We're going to Hawaii on our honeymoon; I have no problem with traveling. Aloha." I knew I sounded desperate, and I didn't like it. The problem was, I disliked having my fiancé leave me for reasons that so far made no sense to me whatsoever even more.

He sat down on his large leather man-couch, rubbing his face like he was trying to rip his own skin off. I figured if he was unsuccessful I could just do it for him. My nails were longer.

"I got a great job offer," he whispered.

"Okay," I said calmly, trying to soothe what clearly was just a really grotesque case of nerves. "That's not a problem, I want you to work. I didn't think that was something I had to tell you. We need the money, and hey, I fully support men in the workforce."

"No, Abby, you're not listening to me. I got a great job offer. In Arizona."

"I'm sorry, what?" This didn't help disprove his point that I wasn't listening.

"I'm taking it."

"I'm sorry, what?" I replied. That didn't help either.

"It's a great opportunity, and I need to do this, for me. It will get me out of this rut. I want to live somewhere else, meet new people, experience new things."

"Like, the desert. You don't want to get married because you want to experience the desert." When he'd said he wanted to travel, I assumed he meant somewhere exotic like Bora Bora, or Laos. Not Arizona. *This isn't happening. Not to me.*

"I know you don't understand. I'm not even sure that I understand. I just know that everything inside me is telling me I need to do this."

"Oh, thank God. Now I get it."

"You do?"

"Yes, so you're hearing voices?" I was grasping at straws. Thin, weak, little straws of hope that I could somehow stop this catastrophe from occurring.

"Abby . . . stop."

I didn't recognize this person. It wasn't the Ben I had known and loved for all of these years. It wasn't the Ben I was ready to commit my life to. It was the Ben whose head I wanted to bash in with the large ceramic coffee mug sitting on the kitchen counter.

"I'm pretty sure people get married in Arizona. I'll wear sunblock and turquoise earrings. I'll exchange my satin pumps for cowboy boots. I'm willing to work with you on this. I don't think that's reason to call off the wedding." I had crossed over the border of pathetic and was now so firmly entrenched in crazy town I could've planted a flag.

"Abby, listen to me," he said as he grabbed my hands and pulled me down on the couch next to him. "I need to do this alone. You coming to Arizona with me isn't the solution to our problems. I don't want to uproot you and move you away from your friends and your family. You deserve better than me."

"I'll decide what I do and do not deserve. You don't get to make those decisions without consulting me first. We've been together for ten years, Ben. Ten fucking years. And what problems are you referring to? I wasn't aware we had any problems. Until an hour ago, the only problems I had were trying to pick out a wedding dress, trying to keep Grace from getting smashed before noon, and trying to keep my mother from liposucking herself into oblivion."

"I know you don't want to hear this, Abby, but I've been thinking about this for a long time. Something isn't right with us, and then this opportunity out west came up, and I think it's a sign that we're not meant to be together. I'm too young. I'm not ready."

"You're not ready? Do you think maybe you could've figured that out before you went and bought me a diamond ring? What did you think was going to happen after that, Ben? Usually, a wedding follows an engagement. I thought this was a concept you were familiar with."

"I know. I think I just resigned myself to thinking that we had been together for so long, it was time. But it's not. It's not time for me. I feel like I can't breathe."

"Try loosening your belt. Better yet, take it off so I can strangle you with it." I lunged at him, but he grabbed my hands and clasped them tightly against his chest.

"Abby, I hate hurting you like this, but I don't want to be divorced in a year either. I don't think we're right together, and as much as I don't want to, it's better to admit we made a mistake sooner rather than later."

"Why didn't you break up with me then?" I was sobbing uncontrollably. I finally realized that this wasn't something I was going to be able to talk him out of. My shoulders slumped forward, and I let my hair cover my face, as if concealing it from him would mask the pain I was feeling. "Why'd you let me run around planning our wedding like an idiot if you weren't ready? Why didn't you say something sooner?"

"I was scared, and I was selfish. I didn't want to let you go." He released my hands and rubbed my arm as he continued. "You're kind of like a really old sock, you know? A really, really comfortable sock that you've had forever and love, so you keep it, even though you know it's time to replace it. Do you know what I mean?"

"You didn't just compare me to a gym sock. You didn't," I stuttered, suddenly feeling so very, very tired.

"That didn't come out right," he admitted quickly.

I couldn't speak. I thought he was my best friend, my partner, the love of my life, the would-be father of my children.

And he thought I was a sock.

"I just started envisioning our life together, and I realized that we don't challenge each other enough." He got up and walked back to the window and leaned his weight against the panes of glass.

"I'm sorry, I have absolutely no idea what that means."

"We're too similar," he whispered.

"No. That's not good enough. I don't think we're too similar, as evidenced by the fact that you're a psychotic asshole and I'm a somewhat normal, nice person. You'll have to do better than that."

"You make everything so easy on me, all the time. We're always agreeing on everything, you know? Where's the balance? Your partner in life is supposed to make you whole, but we're two sides of the same coin, Abs."

It seriously sounded like he was telling me we were too compatible. I mean, has any girl on earth ever been dumped for being too compatible with her boyfriend? Are these the same girls who get dumped for being too thin, or too blond, or too rich? I always thought those were urban legends that someone propagated through the single women's circuit to keep the regular girls from killing themselves every time they got tossed away like last week's *Us Weekly.* Now I was beginning to wonder if they were really out there, and if they all had some kind of secret underground sorority where they got together and drank wine and ate cucumber sandwiches and lamented being alone because they were too perfect in one way or another. I wonder if they advertised in the yellow pages.

"So you're breaking up with me because we don't fight enough?" I asked.

"No. I'm saying that you and I see everything the exact same way, and I need someone who can challenge me a little more, open my eyes to new things. And I know if I stay here in Boston that will never happen."

"You've already accepted the job in Arizona, haven't you?" I whispered, trying to figure out how I was going to survive not just without Ben as my fiancé but without him living in the same state. I finally understood how a woman could murder someone in a fit of rage.

"Yes," he said, no emotion detectable in his voice. It was as if this wasn't even affecting him, like once I left he'd move on to more important matters—like packing, or defrosting his refrigerator.

"What the hell am I going to tell my mother? She's insane on a normal day. Do you know what canceling this wedding will do to her?

She's at a spa getting some beauty treatment as we speak. She will go bat-shit crazy if I tell her that the wedding is off. People will be able to hear her screaming up in Maine! Did you ever think of that?"

"No, Abby. I can honestly say your mother was not a factor in my decision-making process."

"When do you leave?" I asked flatly.

He stared at the floor, then at the wall behind my head, then at his gym bag on the table in the corner, anywhere except into my eyes. I knew before he said a word that I didn't want to hear the answer.

"Next Thursday. They need me to get out there."

"And you care more about them needing you there than about me needing you here." It wasn't a question, which was good, because he didn't have an answer.

"I don't know what to say. I love you. I do. That's never going to change."

"If you loved me, you wouldn't do this to me." I wiped my hand across my face, not wanting to give him the power to see me so utterly destroyed, but there was no stopping the tears.

"I'm sorry, Abby. I'm so, so sorry."

"Go fuck yourself, Ben," I said as I removed my ring and threw it across the room. It bounced off the coffee table and rolled out of sight under the couch. I knew I'd never see it again.

I walked over to him, the last time I planned on ever being close enough to smell his cologne, or his soap, or the detergent on his clothes, and with my left hand (because my right side was still throbbing from the attempt to break down his door) cracked him across the face as hard as I could. Then I turned and limped out of his apartment, knowing that in all likelihood I'd never lay eyes on him again. And for the next six months I didn't. Then again, that shouldn't be surprising, since I'd barely left my apartment, never mind the city of Boston, and that makes it kind of hard to run into someone who lives in Arizona.

I found Grace waiting for me on the sidewalk outside Ben's building, or more accurately, she found me when I stumbled sobbing and in excruciating pain onto the street. She took me to the emergency room—where they checked out my shoulder and gave me some much-needed painkillers—and then she brought me home. I slept for twelve hours, but it wasn't nearly long enough, because when I woke from my narcotic-induced sleep I begged her to medicate me again so that I could go back to sleep forever. Grace had called my aunt Patrice, who had served as my de facto mother for my entire life, and told her everything so that she could begin to run damage control.

"What time is it?" I asked when I woke up, my shoulder in a sling and still throbbing from the impact. So was my heart, but there were no painkillers for that.

"It's two-thirty. On Sunday. You've been asleep for the better part of twenty-four hours. You need to eat something," Grace said as she smoothed the hair out of my face.

"Have you been here the entire time?" I asked, though I already knew the answer.

"Basically. I did run out for a bit." Grace placed a white box on the bed next to me and opened the top. Cupcakes. Since we were little, we solved problems and celebrated victories with cupcakes. I appreciated the gesture, but unless these things were spiked with Percocets I didn't think they'd cure much this time. She removed one with colored sprinkles and peeled the paper back halfway as she handed it to me.

"You have to eat something. The doctor said you can't take the painkillers on an empty stomach. Please, for me. Eat one."

"So I wasn't dreaming," I said flatly. I was so empty and exhausted, I felt like I wouldn't have the strength to get out of bed for weeks.

Grace's eyes welled as she gazed at me, but she didn't say anything. What was there for her to say? In all our years of friendship, Grace had never been at a loss for words, and I had never found myself with either a busted engagement or a busted shoulder, let alone both at the same time, so there really is a first time for everything. I licked a small amount of vanilla frosting off the corner of the paper, and then handed the cupcake back to her.

"I can't eat anything."

"I'm so sorry, Abby. If I could do something to fix this, I would."

Before I could answer, my phone rang. Grace picked it up and checked the caller ID before handing it to me. "It's your sister," she said softly.

"Let it go to voicemail."

"Abby, she's probably worried sick. I'm sure your aunt called her. Talk to her."

I took the phone from her, preparing to try and explain to my little sister what just happened. I didn't even know where I'd start. I didn't know myself where or how any of this started—only how it ended.

"Hi, Katie," I whispered, tears streaming down my face just from the effort of talking to someone in the outside world. I realized this was the first of probably hundreds of times I was going to have to relive this for other people, and I wasn't ready to hear the pain in her voice as she watched her big sister's life fall apart on the Internet. She had idolized me for her entire life, always wearing my hand-me-down clothes, following me around after school, copying my hair, my makeup, my hobbies, the way little sisters who are only two years younger tend to do. It used to drive me crazy—copying me like she was some kind of miniature body-snatcher—and I remember wishing the day would come when she'd want to be an individual, not a little sister coming dangerously close to being a single white female–type stalker. I guess that day had finally come.

"Abby! Guess what!" she shrieked, as if this was any normal day and not the day my world and shoulder were shattered. The tone of her voice told me that not only did she have no idea what had happened, she was in a very good mood. The wonders would apparently never cease. "Did you see my text message? I told you I needed to talk to you. Guess what?"

"Katie, have you talked to Aunt Patrice today?" I asked. "Or seen my

Facebook page?" It was becoming very clear that when she sent me a text saying she wanted to talk to me, it was not to offer her condolences. She was clueless. That must be nice.

"What? No, why? I have news! You will never believe what happened! I'm engaged!"

"I'm sorry. What?" I fully believed that I didn't hear her correctly. I squeezed my eyes shut, hoping that when I opened them my head would be clearer.

"Yes! Can you believe it? We're engaged at the same time! We can do all our planning and everything together, isn't that fantastic? And before you say anything, don't worry, I'm going to wait until next summer to get married, so I'm not going to steal your thunder, but isn't this great?"

I opened my mouth to speak, but nothing came out. I wondered for a second if the painkillers were messing with my head and making me hallucinate conversations. I waved my hand in front of my face to see if there was a rainbow trail following it, searching for some indication that I wasn't hearing Katie correctly.

"Abby? Say something?" she pleaded, surprised that she didn't get the reaction she was expecting. In fact, she didn't get much of a reaction at all.

"Ben broke up with me," I said, the words sounding so strange saying them out loud for the first time. "The wedding's off."

"What? What do you mean you broke up? I'm sure it's just nerves. You guys didn't really end things. There's no way."

"It's over. He's moving. It's on Facebook."

"But I don't understand . . ." I could hear the guilt in her voice. She didn't mean to kick me when I was down, but she had, and I couldn't muster the energy to even pretend to be happy for her. And that made me hate myself even more.

"Katie, please don't make me get into it right now."

"Oh my God. Abby, I'm so sorry. I didn't know. I never would have called you like this. Does Mom know?"

"I have no idea, but I'd guess no, since I can't hear her screaming from across town."

"Don't worry about anything. I'll tell her. She's my next phone call. I don't know how I'm going to tell her that I'm engaged and you're not. How do I explain this?"

"All she'll care about is that there's still a wedding to plan. She won't care which one of us it's for."

"Abby, what can I do? I'd come over, but I'm supposed to meet my friends for celebratory drinks. I can't cancel. They're already waiting for me, and well, I did just get engaged, soooo . . ."

"Don't cancel. Go." I wasn't trying to be the bigger person. I was just telling her what she wanted to hear, and what we both knew she was going to do. I didn't want to ruin her moment. One of us deserved to be happy.

"I'll come over first thing in the morning. I promise. I don't know what to say. I thought this was going to be one of the happiest days of my life, and it's the worst of yours. I wanted us to do this together! I'm so bummed!"

"You're bummed?" I was pretty sure my sister had managed to make my rejection ruin her plans for some kind of co-bridal shower she had probably been envisioning where we would wear matching dresses and receive duplicate Cuisinarts. "I want to say I'm happy for you, Katie. I just . . . I can't right now. Please don't hate me." I rolled over and looked at Grace, who had been able to discern what happened from listening to my side of the conversation. She went into the kitchen and returned with a glass of wine, just a sip or two swirling around the bottom of the glass. "I have to go," I said as I threw my phone on the bed next to me, experiencing a virulent self-pity that I didn't know was possible until that moment.

Grace sat on the edge of my bed. The tears that had been brimming before the phone call were now falling down her cheeks. "You don't deserve this, Abby. I wish I could do something to make everything better. I wish I had a way to fix things for you."

"What the hell is happening to me?" I wailed, choking on my breath, my words, and the bile that I felt rising in my throat. "I can't handle this. Katie's engaged now?"

"Do you remember when you were ten and you broke your wrist roller-skating?" she asked. I nodded, though I wasn't entirely sure where she was going with this.

"Yes. You were the one who roller-skated over it. And it was my birthday party."

"Right, and do you remember who came over every day after school and watched TV with you because you couldn't play outside?"

"You did," I replied, burying my face in my pillow.

"And when our class went on that field trip and you couldn't go because your mom forgot to get the doctor's note saying it was okay? Who stayed behind with you?"

"You did."

"Exactly. You weren't alone then, and you're not alone now. You still have me."

"Thanks," I said apathetically. I loved Grace, but I didn't want to marry her, so frankly it wasn't the same.

"I know you're not supposed to drink while you're on these drugs, but a sip or two won't kill you." For the second time in twenty-four hours Grace handed me a glass and said, "Drink this."

And I did. Then I went back to sleep.

Six months and twenty pounds later . . .

CHAPTER 3

Petty Thieves with Eating Disorders

COUGH, WHEEZE, SPIT, SNORT. My lungs sputtered and heaved and spasmed as I tried to run the trail along the Charles River for the first time in months. I struggled to inhale oxygen, while women pushing baby strollers and middle-aged men who probably smoked three packs a day managed to jet past me. My legs quaked as my muscles readjusted to being used for anything other than walks to the grocery store, and when I grew lightheaded I decided it was time to take a little break or risk having a massive coronary while attempting to be healthy. I leaned my hands on my knees while I glanced at the distance display on my newly purchased jogging watch and discovered that I had gone about ten feet. *Great,* I thought as I stretched my quads and pretended to be busy so I could delay starting up again until I could breathe like a normal human being. *This is just absolutely fantastic.*

March is still cold in Boston, but on this particular morning the weather was just warm enough to manage a pathetically slow run in yoga pants and a zip-up fleece. The events of the last six months had rocked my entire world, and let's just say that my mental health wasn't the only part of me that suffered—my ass took the brunt of it as I decided to feed my grief with ice cream, cookies, and anything else that had a high sugar content and wasn't nailed down. Weight gain was really the least of my problems, all things considered, but once your underwear and your shoes become painfully tight, you realize it's time to rein it in a bit.

One hour and one mile later, I returned to my walk-up apartment on Hancock Street, stopping to pick up my mail from mailbox number 3C, my name, Abby Wilkes, written in black pen and taped to the little silver door. I grabbed the stack and flipped through it, throwing the things I didn't want to open, and the things I didn't need to open thanks to the wonders of auto-pay, in the trash can: bill, bill, birth announcement, another bill, bank statement I would most likely never bring myself to open, catalogs, baby shower invitation, and a rent statement. I really, really hated mail. All it ever seemed to do was remind me that people out there were happy or that I owed people money. I know it's selfish to begrudge other people's happiness, and I'm not particularly proud of it. That said, having to send out wedding cancellation cards that say, "Picked the wrong guy, gave him the wrong finger," can change a girl.

I entered my apartment and threw myself despondently on my couch, which is what I did every time I came home these days. This last year had been the absolute worst of my life, and that included the year I read an article in my mom's magazine about eyebrow shaping and thought that meant you were supposed to shave your eyebrows off with a disposable razor. I thought that episode had put my "most humiliating experience" on lock, but it paled in comparison to how embarrassed and ashamed I'd felt lately. That's really saying something. Spending most of fourth grade without eyebrows was a hugely traumatizing experience, as ten-year-old girls don't really have much interest in hanging out with someone who accidentally turned herself into a walking mannequin. Trust me.

As a little girl, I dreamed of getting engaged, though I guess that doesn't make me any different from any other little girl on the planet who used to wear a pillowcase on her head and pretend it was a veil. I don't know why girls dream of wedding days the way boys dream of playing professional baseball, but for whatever reason, I was obsessed with the thought that somewhere in my future a day would come when I'd be able to wear a pretty white dress and look like a princess. Deep down, we all want the fairy tale, and if I have to fault anyone for being able to single-handedly combat all of the progress of the women's movement and still convince little girls that the proverbial dream life begins at the end of an aisle standing next to a man, I blame Walt Disney. Feminism may have come a long way since our grandmothers' time, but Gloria Steinem is no match for Cinderella, which I'm sure is hugely frustrating for her. It has to be painful admitting that your biggest adversary is actually a cartoon wearing one shoe whose only friends are a pack of mice. Whatever. As far as I'm concerned, Cinderella can suck it.

Since everything happened, I had turned myself into a hermit, rarely leaving my apartment for anything other than my walk to and from work. I saw no reason to leave when I could have food, movies, dry cleaning, and alcohol delivered. I had no interest in being out there anymore with normal people who had normal relationships and didn't have to wear a big hat and sunglasses every time they walked by Vera Wang to keep from being recognized by the salesladies. I was pretty sure if they saw me they were going to chase me down the street and hit me with a bill for Grace's champagne. I was fairly certain they didn't appreciate customers who downed their Moët and then left an expensive gown in a heap on the floor while they bolted from the store in tears, but in my defense, at the time, that was not how I saw that afternoon ending.

Fate can be a finicky bitch.

After that I just gave up. I know I probably shouldn't have, but I resigned myself to a life alone, broke, and, apparently, fat. Not exactly how I pictured my thirties starting out. I don't know what I did to anger the universe so much that it felt the need to sucker-punch me the way it did, but I figured there wasn't much point in worrying about it anymore. Instead, I locked myself in my apartment, let my bills pile up, let my friendships wither away, and let myself dry up like a prune. It might not have been the best of coping mechanisms, but the sad truth was, my apartment was the only place left on earth where I felt safe. The only way the universe could screw with me in there was if it put Häagen-Dazs out of business or blew up my cable box.

When Grace called me earlier that week begging me to meet her to do some shopping, I hesitated, much preferring to stay home alone than brave the masses, but eventually I caved. I knew that getting out of my apartment was a good idea, especially since my couch now had a permanent indentation from the excessive amount of time my fat ass had spent on it, and I couldn't afford to buy a new one. It's comical what motivated me to do things these days.

I took a quick shower and left my building, glancing nervously over both shoulders like I was expecting someone to jump out of the bushes and assassinate me. I walked through the Back Bay and met Grace on the corner of Newbury and Dartmouth Streets. As soon as I saw her, I knew she was going to ambush me with something. Maybe looking for assassins wasn't as crazy as it seemed: maybe this was like the mob, and the people who came to kill you were pretending to be your friends. I stared at her, trying to read her mind before she said anything. Grace had no poker face whatsoever.

"What?" I asked as soon as I hugged her hello. "What are you going to do to me?"

"Why do you think I'm going to do something to you? I'm not the enemy, Abby, remember? I want to help you."

"I don't need help," I lied.

"I can count on one hand the number of times you've left your house in the last six months for anything other than work, and you just entered Ben and Jerry's 'Name a New Ice Cream' contest with a flavor called Flabby Abby. You definitely need help," she said as she smoothed her long auburn hair behind her ears.

"I thought it would be cool to name the new ice cream! I know I've been in a bit of a funk, but you'll be happy to know that I went for a mini-run this morning. I'm trying to get back into an exercise routine. And for the record, I tried the frozen yogurt, but it doesn't taste the same. People tell you it does, but it doesn't."

"This has nothing to do with your weight. You'd look great at any size."

"Thanks. I feel all warm and fuzzy inside. Why am I here, Grace? Seriously. I thought we were going shopping." I didn't mean to sound impatient, but I felt like I was being trapped in some kind of half-assed therapy session.

"I've decided you need an intervention. I'm afraid I'm going to come over one day and find you hanging by a bridal veil from your shower rod. I'm not letting you wallow anymore. It's not healthy."

"Neither is housing a pint of ice cream every day, but I'm still doing that."

"Exactly. I want the old Abby back. I don't like this new antisocial, depressed version. If you keep this up, you won't need clothespins to hold up that Vera Wang sample size," she joked, the way only a best friend can.

"In case you forgot, I'm no longer in need of Vera. We had a falling-out. I don't plan on talking to her or her giant dresses ever again."

"I haven't forgotten, but it's time you get over it. You're not the first person on earth to have her engagement broken off."

I stared at the sidewalk and let my shoulders slump forward. "I don't know how," I whispered. "I don't know how to pull myself out of this."

It's funny: you don't realize that you're losing yourself until the day you wake up and look in the mirror and don't recognize the person staring back at you. If you didn't even realize it was happening, how can you possibly know how to stop it?

She removed her hands from her pockets and firmly grabbed my shoulders, forcing me to face her. "I'm not saying it's going to be easy, but it's time you at least tried. You can't beat yourself up like this anymore. I love you too much to let you do this to yourself."

"And how do you propose I do that? Are you going to try to put me in an ice cream eaters anonymous meeting? I already looked online. Oddly enough, I couldn't find one in the greater Boston area." I was getting really tired of people just telling me to pull it together, to move on, to get over it. What the hell did they know? Last time I checked, these people weren't attacked by social media in a bridal salon. I was pretty sure if I asked people on the streets of Boston for a show of hands for who had been through a similar experience, I'd be the only one with my hand up. It was fitting, really. I was living one of the nursery rhymes I sang to the kids in my class every year.

The cheese stands alone.

"Funny you should ask. I have a proposition for you," Grace said.

"I'm listening," I said. And I was. I was planning to listen to whatever she had to say, politely say no, and go home to my *Pretty in Pink* DVD and a canister of Pringles.

"Hear me out before you answer," she ordered, rubbing my shoulders before she released them and put her hands back in her pockets. She looked at me with so much pity, it was all I could do to not run for home. I would have, but the extra pounds on my ass had me running slower than I used to, so she'd have had no problem catching me. At this point, it was a safe bet Roseanne Barr would have no problem catching me.

"I'm scared," I said, well aware that nothing good ever follows that sentence.

"A paralegal I work with was supposed to go down to Newport for the summer, but two of her friends backed out and now she can't afford to do it."

"My sympathies to the paralegal."

"Very funny."

"Chubby girls usually are."

"Would you stop it?"

"I assume there's a point to this story about a paralegal with no friends and no money, because if this is your way of illustrating that everyone has problems, it's not working."

"Not exactly. Apparently, it's too late to get her deposit back, so she offered it to me for half-price. I saw it online, and it's this super-cute beach cottage with a deck, and it's walking distance to all the bars in town, and I think we'd be nuts not to take it. It makes complete sense for you: teachers don't work in the summer anyway. You can spend three months relaxing and figuring out how to resurrect the old Abby, the one who didn't live in elastic pants and find toothbrushing optional."

"You just pointed out that when I'm not at work I live in sweats, and then suggested I do a summer house where normal attire is a bathing suit? Your sales pitch needs works. Thanks, but no thanks."

"Abby, I'm not taking no for an answer. You need this."

"Let's just assume for a nanosecond that I'd be interested. Do I really need to point out the fact that I'm not exactly rolling in cash at the moment? And what will I do out there by myself all summer? Your solution for snapping me out of my depression is to sequester me at the beach in Rhode Island for three months? How does that make sense?" Minor details like my complete and total isolation apparently were not as important as Grace's quest for the perfect tan. Still, I knew she wasn't going to drop it. Grace had a way of pushing until the craziest things seemed to make sense. It's one of the things that made her such a good attorney.

"You can afford it. It's only three thousand dollars for each of us for the entire summer. That's completely reasonable."

"What are you talking about, I can afford it? You're a lawyer, I'm sure you can afford it. In case you've forgotten, I'm a kindergarten teacher.

I don't have three thousand dollars to randomly rent a house in Newport. Three thousand dollars is like, a lot of sessions with a shrink. If I was going to spend that kind of money on anything, therapy would be a better option. No way. I don't want to do it. I'll be perfectly happy sitting in my apartment alone all summer, thank you very much."

"That's a great idea. Sweat to death in your apartment. You don't even have air-conditioning."

"I'll stick my head in the freezer if I have to," I said. I realized that if it did actually come to that, I'd have to move some of the ice cream containers in order to accommodate my head, but I figured if I had to I'd just eat them all in one sitting or something.

Not that I've ever done that before.

"Do you think Ben is sitting around self-destructing like this? Do you?" she asked.

I thought about him again, for maybe the millionth time, and at least the tenth since I'd woken up this morning. I was still so angry about what happened. I was so angry I could barely see straight, and for that I blamed the obvious culprit. Facebook.

"I don't know what he's doing," I whispered. "But I hope whatever it is is causing excruciating physical pain to his reproductive organs." Truth be told, I did kind of know what Ben was doing. I had elevated Facebook-stalking to a science. The Internet made it possible to stay linked to people without ever seeing them, and I admit, I had developed some unhealthy cyber-habits in addition to the unhealthy eating habits. I checked his Facebook page dozens of times per day to see if he had posted new pictures, or changed his status, or written anything that could give me some insight into what he was doing. Unfortunately, I didn't learn much, because Ben was never really much of a Facebook person. You know, except for when he used it to break up with me.

I knew it wasn't healthy to keep tabs on someone who clearly couldn't care less about me, and eventually I realized that the only way to get over him was to deactivate my Facebook account, because even if

I didn't stalk him, I'd definitely follow his friends. Unfortunately, Ben found other ways of staying connected to me, and now we sometimes, on occasion, emailed and texted. I'm sure qualified therapists the world over would say that also was unhealthy—which is precisely why I'd avoided seeing one. He sent me messages every once in a while, asking me how I was doing, telling me he still wanted to be friends, making me laugh and reminding me of what I'd loved about him to begin with, and I answered them. We were broken up but we were still attached, and I looked forward to hearing from him despite what he had done to me, though I had no idea why. It was so pathetic it made it hard for me to look at myself in the mirror in the morning. Truth be told, the extra twenty pounds I'd packed on didn't help with that either.

"So what do you think?" Grace asked.

"What?" I had started to daydream again. Or more appropriately, day-nightmare.

"Are you listening to me?" she asked as she readjusted her bag on her shoulder.

"Not really. I can't hear you above all the screaming in my head."

"Abby, I know your grandmother left you some money when she passed away last year. Since you're still living in your tiny walk-up apartment, I assume you haven't ripped through the cash. I think spending it on a fun summer that you desperately need would be exactly what she wanted you to do."

"I was planning on saving it for a rainy day. Not spending part of it on a beach house—where, coincidentally, rainy days would render it a complete waste of money."

"Umm, Abby? It's been raining on you for the last six months. Think about it."

"I don't think I'm ready," I admitted, rubbing my temples as if I could somehow massage out the dull pain I'd been feeling for what felt like forever.

"Which is exactly why I'm giving you three months to prepare for it.

Look, I don't blame you for being miserable. If I were you, I'd be a million times worse. I don't even know how you go to work and smile and play with those kids all day without losing your mind. Nobody wants to make you uncomfortable, but you can't seem to snap out of this on your own, and I'm afraid you're heading for a full-blown depression."

"Heading for it? I collided with full-blown depression months ago. I think it's okay, though. I'm pretty sure it's one of the stages of grief. Stand back when anger hits, it's going to be ugly."

"That's the point. I know you better than anyone, and I know you're scared, but we need to shake up your routine a little bit, get you back out there, reintroduce you to the dating world. I think you should get out of the city. You need to expand your circle and spend some time in a place not haunted by memories of him."

I sighed.

I felt like the upheaval of my personal life overflowed into every other area of my life and made me question everything I thought I wanted. I didn't even know if I wanted to be a teacher anymore, and that was something that I had wanted since I was old enough to play school with my friends in my basement. Don't get me wrong, I love my job. I take great pride in knowing that I'm helping to mold a future generation of leaders at a prestigious Catholic nursery school in the Back Bay. But after ten years and the reality check that this last year had provided, I was starting to wonder if I made any impact on the kids whatsoever. I mean, it wasn't like I was teaching chemistry or economics or calculus. I was teaching kids not to eat glue. Most of them would be able to figure that out on their own, eventually. The last week of February I caught a girl stuffing extra Oreos into her kneesocks at snack time. So much for molding future generations of America's leaders. Apparently, the only thing I was molding was a future generation of petty thieves with eating disorders.

And that wasn't even the worst of it.

To add insult to oh-such-severe injury, my little sister Katie's wedding was fast approaching. There really ought to be some kind of written rule that says little sisters are not allowed to get engaged while their big sisters are dealing with the utterly fantastic destruction of their own relationship. Now, I'm not one of those people who have an issue with a younger sister getting married before them, I swear, I'm not. I do, however, have a really big issue with wearing a pink taffeta dress and opera-length gloves in July, or anytime, really. There should be written rules against that too, but I don't think Emily Post ever got around to tackling this specific wedding dilemma in any of her books. So all has not been quiet on the home front either, and fighting wars on two fronts is never a good idea.

Just ask Napoleon.

Grace snapped her fingers in my face, forcing my wandering mind to focus on the conversation instead of on the image of myself walking down a church aisle looking like a giant stick of cotton candy. "If you won't do it for yourself, then do it for me. I have to get out of the city on the weekends or I'll go crazy. Please come with me. We both need to get away, and you know it."

"Sorry, what?" I asked as I shook my head, hard, as if thrashing my skull would get the image of myself in that dress out of my head like it can get water out of your ear. For the record, it didn't. All it did was make me look like I had a serious mental problem.

Awesome.

Grace, despite being one of the smarter girls I know, was in a very sticky situation at work. Actually, "sticky" probably wasn't the right word to describe having an affair with a married colleague. I have no idea how you describe that. Don't get me wrong, I love *Working Girl* just as much as the next person, but I really didn't think that this love affair was going to end with her sitting in a corner office while "Let the River Run" played through a loudspeaker at her law firm. It was hard to be supportive of something that could single-handedly ruin every aspect of her life, but she was my best friend, and I would never turn my back on her. I hated what this relationship was doing to her and feared that she was on a collision course with disaster, but I was in no position to judge. I mean, I was basically having an affair with the frozen food section of the grocery store. For smart girls, both of us were pretty stupid when it came to handling relationships with the opposite sex. In fact, we sucked at it.

"So you want me to dip into my savings so that you can keep yourself busy while Johnny is home with his family?"

"No. You should dip into your savings because you're too young to give up. If that's not enough of a reason, then yes, you should do it because I'm your best friend and I need you and I would do the same for you."

"I work with nuns. If I was having an affair with one, we'd have a shitload of other problems."

"You know what I mean. It will be fun. My friend Bobby from law school is out of work right now. He's living at his parents' beach house for the summer with a friend while he looks for a job. I'm sure he has other friends he's known forever bouncing around down there too. Some of them have to be cute and interesting, right? And since you're very much single, and you clearly won't be meeting a guy at work, I think it's a great opportunity for you to start over. How many straight guys teach at your school anyway?"

"Zero."

"Exactly. Which is why you should come to Newport and spend some time with normal adults. Get a tan. Drink some cocktails with umbrellas. Go for walks on the beach that will help your mental health and get you exercising again. Hang out with me and meet some new friends. And quit acting like you have so many more appealing options."

Clearly, I didn't. That being said, I still had some reservations.

Summer rentals are infamous for throwing disparate groups of people together who would otherwise never speak. Sometimes real friendships develop. But since I had no interest in meeting anyone new in my current mental state, I was pretty sure I was going to hate everyone. I had no doubt that Grace's friend was a nice guy. At least, I really hoped that was the case, because the last thing I needed was to be forced to hang out all summer with another sociopathic male. The old me would've loved to be at the beach, but the new me was really worried that this random combination of people was going to cause more stress than anything else, and I wasn't sure that I was going to be able to make it through three months without spearing someone to death with barbecue tongs. Of course, the alternative was going home to my mom's house to escape the brutal summer heat and living with my wedding-obsessed sister and intolerably psychotic mother. So maybe hanging out with a bunch of strange dudes and risking a lifetime sentence in a women's prison somewhere was worth considering. Life has its trade-offs.

"Please don't make me beg," Grace added, looking at me with an expression that I had seen only a few times before, and then she was usually giving it to her father when she was trying to convince him to give her the car keys or let her go out with the captain of the football team in high school. No wonder he always gave in.

"Even if I did spend some of my savings on this, it doesn't change the fact that you'll be in the city all week. What will I do by myself? I don't think spending that much time alone is necessarily good for my mental state either, ya know?"

"I told you. That's what I think is great about this. You'll be no more alone out there than you would be if you stayed locked in your apartment in the city. Get a job, hang out with Bobby and his friends. I'll be working during the week one way or the other, so who will you hang out with if you stay here? I think getting a summer job is huge. It will give you extra money so you can stop bitching about the cost of the house, and it will get you away from your laptop and that toxic cyber-relationship you're clinging to like a security blanket. He's gone, Abby. He's not coming back. Answering his messages is an epic waste of your time and only makes him feel like less of an asshole."

I knew she was right. Once again, my mind drifted back to Ben.

Damn. Make that eleven times since I woke up. I was so hoping that today would be better.

"Okay," I sighed. "I'll come. You're right. I have to do something."

"I'm so happy!" Grace squealed as she clapped her hands together and wrapped her arm around my waist. "You know, even on your worst day you're still the best. I just want you to have a little fun, remember how to laugh, be social. You have to stop punishing yourself," she whispered as she gazed in the window of Chanel, adoring the clothes neither of us would ever be able to afford. "I think we both could use a little break from reality."

"True." I nodded. I really didn't want to go, but I was tired of feeling depressed and rejected and unworthy. I wanted to feel better, and sadly, that was never going to happen if I hung around Boston and the memories the city held. I needed a change of scene, some excitement, some racy X-rated encounters with impossibly tan guys in some exotic hot spot with limitless possibilities and countless opportunities for personal growth.

Like Rhode Island.

Grace was right, getting out of my apartment and going somewhere else wasn't a bad idea. I needed to stop cyber-stalking. I needed to stop answering Ben's stupid, pointless texts. I needed to remember who I used to be and at least try to make some positive changes in my life before it was too late. My decision was made. Summer at the beach would be great for me. Clean air, soft ocean breezes, new friends, flip-flops, and cocktails made in blenders. If that doesn't help a girl's mood, well then I just don't know what will.

CHAPTER 4

Khaki Folders

Ughhhhhhhh! Hurry up, you enormous idiot!" Grace leaned on her car horn and gave the middle finger to the driver of the red convertible Mercedes in front of us. She pressed her bare foot on the gas pedal and inched up to within a hair of the Mercedes's bumper before slamming the brakes again, causing the car to lurch forward. My seat belt locked across my chest, keeping me from having to brace myself against the windshield.

"Grace!" I screamed as I rubbed my right clavicle, where the strap had burned my skin. "Would you please calm down? It's not like we're going to get there any faster if you kill us!" I readjusted my seat belt and smoothed the fabric strap across my chest to keep it from wrinkling my silk shirt. I turned to stare at Grace and sighed. We had been friends for as long as I could remember, and I anxiously awaited the day when I wouldn't envy her for her looks. Today wasn't the day. She looked like goddamn Jessica Rabbit.

"Seriously, who the hell designed this stupid highway? What asshole thought it would be a good idea to narrow the entire thing down to one lane?" Grace gripped the steering wheel so tightly I thought she might tear the leather with her bare hands.

Beach traffic, in a word, is a bitch.

"What's the big rush? The bars will still be there when we get there," I said, smiling out the open window and breathing in the crisp air. If someone had told me a year ago that I'd be spending the summer in Rhode Island in an attempt to redefine myself and incite some kind of personal growth, I never would've believed them. Go figure.

"Well, aren't you all calm and collected? I like it, you seem like you're in a good mood."

"I am. You were right, this beach house was a great idea."

"I know it is. I'm more curious as to why you now think it is. I feel like I had to drag you into this, and now you're all Zen about it?"

"Zen might be a stretch, but I am excited. I feel like this is the first positive thing I've done for myself in a very long time. I think this may be what I need to turn things around. At the very least, it's a nice change of scenery and the ocean is calming. I think it will go a long way toward helping me get centered."

"Have you been doing yoga or something?" she asked, sounding a bit suspicious.

"No, I just realized when I was packing up and leaving that little sweatbox I call an apartment that this is probably good for me, and I'm really looking forward to it."

"I'm so proud of you! So you're not nervous or anything? It's been a while since you've been out and about."

"Let's not get crazy. I'm terrified. But it's a good feeling, not sad. I like that the sadness has been replaced with something else."

"You're very welcome. Now if these other morons would get out of my way so we can get there before midnight, maybe I'd share your newfound calmness," Grace said as she turned her attention back to the cars inching along in front of us and slammed her hand on the steering wheel for the second time in as many minutes. Granted, traffic is infuriating, but Grace seemed a bit too upset for that to be the only thing bothering her.

"Are you going to tell me why you're so fired up? That steering wheel never did anything to you, you know."

"Sorry, I'm a little jumpy. Johnny and I had a fight yesterday before I left the office," she said.

Grace had been seeing Johnny for about nine months. They were friends who worked closely together, and after innumerable late nights and bad office take-in, their relationship had developed from friendship into love. The way Grace tells it, she became a confidante when things started to go wrong in his marriage, and somehow the lines became blurred and then obliterated entirely. They kept up the charade of being just friends for as long as they could, and then over drinks after work one night he confessed his true feelings for her. It would've been a great thing to have happen if he wasn't married, and while he promised her that he was going to leave his wife, as of yet, it hadn't happened. The stress of the constant sneaking around and the knowledge that she was dating a man who belonged to another woman had worn on Grace over time, but she loved him. And for now, the hope that he would eventually man up and make an honest woman out of her was enough to keep her hanging on.

"Do you want to tell me what happened?"

"It's nothing new. That's the worst part. We keep having the same arguments over and over about when he's finally going to walk away from his sham of a marriage. When things are great, they're just so great, but only having him part-time is killing me. Anyway, I'm sorry. I know we've talked this to death. I don't know how you even stand to listen to it anymore."

"That's what friends do. Listen to their friends talk about the same guys ad nauseam. You do it for me all the time. I know this is hard, but you signed up for this."

"I know I did. And for what? What kind of future do we have? We see each other once a week outside of work, and I now carry a portable hair dryer and a toothbrush in my purse. Thank God hobo bags are in style since that's basically what I am."

"I do love a good hobo. You're being too hard on yourself. This isn't a normal relationship, it hasn't been from the beginning. You can't expect it to function normally. Stuff like this comes with the territory."

"I thought leaving on the weekends, and being busy, and meeting new people would force him to realize how close he is to losing me, you know?" she said.

"He's not worried about losing you. You're not going anywhere, not that that's your fault. Look at it realistically. You work with him."

"True, but I'm going to Newport. That's somewhere."

"Grace, do you really think he will leave his family? How do you see this all ending?"

"I think we're meant to be together. I know if I say that to anyone else, they'll think I'm delusional, but I do."

"Then I hope that it happens. But until then, I think you need to work on your life outside of him. It's something I didn't do while I was with Ben, and look how badly I'm paying for it. You can't be defined by a guy because, if he leaves, you will have nothing except your couch and cookie dough ice cream, and I promise you, you don't want that. Learn from my mistakes."

"I know. Why does it all have to be so complicated?"

"He's married, babe. It's complicated by definition. I guess all relationships are."

"And everyone is judging me. Everyone but you, and even you judge me a little."

"No, I don't!" I replied, trying to defend myself. "I just hate seeing you upset all the time. But I don't judge. I'm in no position to criticize anyone's relationship."

"Speaking of, are you still trading emails with Ben?"

"Occasionally," I admitted.

"I don't know why you even acknowledge he exists. You're so smart when it comes to other people's relationships."

"I'm working on it. Actually, can you do me a favor?"

"Try me."

"I don't want your friend to know what happened with Ben. Did you tell him already?"

"No. I just told him that you were fun and that you recently broke up with someone, so you were single. Why?"

"I just want to escape it, you know? And I don't want him to know me as the girl who had her engagement canceled online."

"It's nothing to be ashamed of."

"I'm not ashamed, but I am embarrassed, and then I have to explain what happened and relive the whole thing over and over and over again. It's bad enough I was the talk of the town at home. If I'm going to meet some new people, I'd like to leave that part of me in the past. I want a fresh start. Okay?"

"That makes sense. Okay, I won't say anything about the engagement. We'll keep that our dirty little secret." She reached over and locked her pinky finger around mine.

"Of course, the downside of that is that then I just look like I'm fat for no reason."

"You're not fat," she answered reflexively.

"I gained twenty pounds and I'm short, Grace. I know love is blind, but you don't love me enough to not have noticed. It's okay. I'm working on that too."

"So you gained a few pounds. Who hasn't?"

"Seeking comfort in Betty Crocker and Sara Lee seemed like a good idea at the time. Then again, so did marrying Ben. I apparently have horrible decision-making skills."

"Well, you keep good company.".

I smiled as I stared ahead at the seemingly endless traffic. Leaving the city at 3:30 P.M. on the Friday of Memorial Day weekend had also seemed like a good idea at the time, but since we were still sitting in traffic almost three hours later, we were starting to rethink our plan. The weather reports said that it was going to be seventy-five degrees and sunny this weekend, perfect beach weather, so it was unfortunate that we were not the only people who apparently read accuweather.com. We had packed up our summer clothes and all other warm weather essentials—our bikinis, beach towels, sunblock, and enough Coronas to get the entirety of Mexico hammered—and headed out.

I looked out the window as we drove, my mind flitting back and forth between the dream life that I wanted and the real one I was currently living. I thought about the storied mansions on the Newport cliffs and how at one point people actually kept them solely as summer homes. I'm sure that the old adage that money can't buy you happiness is true, but as someone whose checking account was pathetically low, it was hard for me to believe that it hurt anything. I mean, maybe money can't buy happiness, but it can buy you plenty of other things to distract you from your misery. Which is more than I could say for myself. All I'd had these last few months was Grace and sugar in all its many wondrous forms.

"I need you to read these to me," Grace said as she handed me a white napkin with blue ink scribbled illegibly on it. There were only two lines written on it, and for a second I was nervous that maybe Grace had been bombed when she attempted to write down the directions and passed out halfway through.

"I don't see a beach," I said, wondering if this had all been some giant ruse and she was really about to drop me off at a fat camp in the middle of nowhere.

"The house is close to Gooseberry Beach, but it's a drive. Before you freak out, the house is literally a two-block walk to town, the piers, and all the bars. I figured we'd care more about being able to walk to the bars than we would about walking to the beach. Oh, and there's an ice cream parlor too, in case you keep talking to Ben and fall off the wagon again."

"I resent that. I've been doing so well."

"It's been two hours."

"You're impossible to please."

I felt my phone vibrate in my pocket. I pulled it out hesitantly, sensing that it was Ben, knowing that I shouldn't even bother to read it, and not caring about that in the slightest. I really hated when Grace was right.

I read on Grace's Facebook page that you guys were going to Newport for the summer. I'm jealous. I miss the beach. Actually, I miss you.

I replied:

Just getting here now. I'm not the one who told you to land lock yourself.

I know. One of many decisions I regret. Have fun.

What does that mean?

When twenty minutes passed and I hadn't heard back, I realized that I wasn't going to. I knew better than to give Ben the ball, to let him be the one who determined when and how our conversations ended, but for some reason, time and time again, I did. There were freakin' lab rats that learned faster than I did.

"Abby," Grace yelled as she snapped her fingers in my face. "Put that thing away or I swear I'm going to rip it out of your hand and throw it out the window."

I returned my phone to my bag and tried not to obsess over what Ben had said, which was clearly impossible. Find me a girl who doesn't try to decode even the most straightforward of messages from a guy, and I'll show you a girl who's lying.

"Read the directions. I know we have to make a right somewhere up here," Grace yelled.

"It says make a right on Thames Street."

"Where the hell is that?" she asked as she slowed to avoid pedestrians.

"How should I know? I have no idea where we are, and I think that's what this says, but I'm not sure. I can't read your writing!"

Before Grace had the chance to defend herself, the street sign appeared in front of us. We made a right and continued to head south, parallel to Newport Harbor and the bustling piers. We drove through the town, teeming with bars and restaurants, the sidewalks overflowing with seemingly happy couples, all of them smiling and laughing. Who could blame them? If I had actually managed to make it down the aisle, if I'd been able to afford a charming little house in Newport and live there for the summer with my loving husband, I'd be laughing and smiling too.

If only I didn't have "if" in front of all of those things.

We passed by Bowen's Wharf, Bannister's Wharf, and a bunch of other wharfs that all seemed to have one thing in common: waterfront bars and restaurants. We continued through town before making a right onto Grafton Street and immediately pulled into a narrow driveway running along the side of a pale yellow shingled house. A small flight of stairs led from the front lawn to a large porch—complete with a barbecue and patio furniture—that wrapped around the first floor.

"If this is home for the summer, it was worth the four hours in the car," I said as I stared at the quaint but adorable piece of real estate in front of us. It wasn't just walking distance to the bars. It was spitting distance. It was perfect.

"Told you! Welcome to your new home until Labor Day, Abs. Don't waste it!"

We grabbed our bags out of the back of the car and raced inside. The house was airy and calming, decorated with white wicker furniture and in shades of blue and green. Large glass jars filled with seashells were placed decoratively on the coffee table, and framed pictures of sunsets, dunes, and boats hung on the walls. The hardwood floors throughout the house were immaculately polished, sheer white, gauzy drapes hung from the windows, and the sliding-glass door opened up onto an expansive back deck. I left my bag in a small room at the end of the hall on the second floor and returned to meet Grace in the kitchen.

"Well, now what?" I asked. "Did you call your friend Bobby?"

"I texted him. He said to meet them at a bar down on the water called the Landing. His parents' house is actually just down the block, which is awesome. It's going to be like living in a dorm with cute boys at the end of the hall and no bunk beds. They're here all summer, Abs, so you'll have boys to play with."

"You mentioned that already. I agreed to come to the beach, Grace. I didn't agree to let you play matchmaker. I don't want you trying to set me up with one of your friends, okay? I'm not ready, and I already know I won't like him."

"How do you know that?"

"He's male."

"Lighten up, Abby," Grace said. "Let's get going."

I shrugged reluctantly, grabbed my purse, and followed her out into town.

Ten minutes later, we pushed through the crowds of the bare-bones seafood shack on the wharf. It was so crowded you could barely move, but everyone was happy and wearing sunglasses and their bathing suits, so it was hard to mind. "Hey, there's Bobby," Grace said as we squeezed our way up to the bar and the whirling blenders that promised frozen drinks and margaritas.

"Which one is he?" I asked as I eyed the preppy crowd, interested to see who Grace none too subtly was trying to set me up with. She was still very much involved with her boss, despite the fact that she threatened to break up with him on a weekly basis, so she clearly wasn't interested in meeting someone. She was, however, very interested in helping me meet someone. In fact, it was beginning to look like her sole mission for the next three months.

Good friends who have no problem interfering with your personal life are so hard to find.

"He's right there. The guy leaning on the railing."

I eyed the waifish man slugging a beer and smoking a cigarette over by the bar, flirting mercilessly with girls who walked by. He looked like he weighed about a hundred pounds, like I could carry him around in my beach bag. You could almost see his ribs through his button-down as he slugged his beer, and for a minute I wondered how he didn't pull his bicep from the effort. I mean, I'm not a snob or anything, but Grace had talked this guy up so much I was expecting someone who looked like he fell off the pages of *GQ,* not a man-child who looked like he'd get blown over by a strong wind. He was cute the way puppies are cute. You wanted to pet him and muss his dark hair and then lock him away somewhere so he didn't get in your way or eat your shoes.

"He's a little thin, no?" I asked, still staring at him while he chatted up some younger girls at the bar.

"So what if he's not built like a lumberjack? He's still cute."

"Sure he is. Kind of like those hairless cats like Dr. Evil had in *Austin Powers.* Some people find them cute too."

"Stop finding flaws with everyone because you're too afraid to move on. Maybe you guys will hit it off, who knows?"

"No way," I said as I shook my finger in Grace's face. "You can never hook up with a guy who weighs less than you. It throws the whole power structure off. Next thing you know you'll be the one responsible for jumping car batteries and killing spiders. Plus, how is that good for a girl's ego? You don't want to be known as "the big one" in a relationship. No way. I'd rather die alone."

"You will die alone if you keep up these ridiculous parameters you have put in place for potential boyfriends. Do I need to remind you of Ben's flaws?"

"What parameters?" I asked defensively. "I just want a guy who's employed. Even though I realize those guys are fewer and farther between these days."

"And that he weighs more than you do," she added.

"And that he does not need a green card," I countered.

"Is that all?" Grace asked in a tone laced with skepticism.

"Well, there might be a few more small things, but nothing major."

"Such as?"

"Well, I mean I don't think I could date a guy who chews with his mouth open. I have no patience for guys with bad table manners. I won't be able to handle anyone who eats like a Neanderthal. Oh, and he can't be a Jets fan. God, I could never date a Jets fan," I said as I feigned a shiver just thinking about the New England Patriots' most hated rival. "And he needs to have good teeth. This day and age, there is no excuse for an overbite." I didn't care if Grace thought that was hypercritical. I like a nice smile. Sue me.

"That's all, huh? Yeah, you're right, that's completely normal," she said as she pushed her sunglasses up on her head.

"Oh, and he needs to not be a khaki folder. But I think that's it."

"What the hell is a khaki folder?" Grace asked in disbelief.

"You know, the guys who stop mid-hookup to make sure their khakis are folded and not getting wrinkled on the floor. Those guys have issues." I stared at Grace for some kind of validation, but Grace was looking at me like I was some kind of alien life form. Apparently, I was on my own on this one.

"You have serious issues," Grace said as she flagged down her man-orexic friend.

That was hard to argue with considering the list I'd just spewed out.

We approached the bar, and Grace, despite her size, was able to elbow guys who were three times bigger than her out of the way. She ordered us beers and waved enthusiastically for Bobby to come join us. He crushed the butt of his cigarette with his flip-flop and ambled over, a big smile on his face. I felt a thought creep into my head that wasn't the kind of thought I should have been having if I wanted to make new friends and start to enjoy my life again: maybe this was a very big mistake.

CHAPTER 5

Damaged Goods

I ALTERNATED BETWEEN staring at Bobby and staring at my flip-flops, afraid that if I made eye contact with him, my nerves would show. He gave Grace a big hug and shook my hand when he introduced himself. As Grace handed me a lukewarm beer, I scanned the crowd for anyone interesting, but the bar seemed to be filled with guys who neglected the gym, their hairlines, and, in all likelihood, the girls they dated. I wondered if it was too late to look into houses on the Cape.

"Hey, you must be Abby," he said as I shook his impossibly small man hand.

"I am. Nice to meet you, Bobby. Grace told me a lot about you."

"You're a kindergarten teacher, right?" he asked, as if my profession was somehow more important than my name.

"Yup." I realized that I was more out of practice than I'd thought. I didn't even know how to make small talk with guys. I was screwed.

"Single?" he asked.

"Yup."

"Interested?"

"Nope."

"Apparently, you share the verbal communication skills of the kids that you teach," he quipped with a laugh.

"Only when talking to people who share their maturity level," I shot back.

Well, this was off to a stellar start.

"Abby!" Grace said as she elbowed me in my side. She turned to Bobby with a smile. "You'll have to forgive her. Abby is now one of those people whose initial instinct is to dislike everyone she meets until they prove they don't want to somehow ruin her life. Be nice, Abby. He doesn't bite."

Nice. I could do that. It had been a while since I had tried to make friends of the opposite sex. Truth be told, it had been a while since I had really spoken to members of the opposite sex. I hoped it was like riding a bicycle—which I was never particularly good at now that I thought about it.

"Sorry," I said, and I meant it. I didn't want him to mistake my nervousness for bitchiness, and it was a very fine line.

"Ahh. I get it. So, who's the guy?" he asked smoothly, as if it wasn't an entirely too personal question to ask someone he'd just met.

"What makes you think it's a guy? How do you know that I'm not just someone who likes to know people before I'm overly friendly to them? If more girls were like me, there'd be a lot less need for pepper spray in this world."

"It's always a guy. Do you want to tell me about him?" Bobby asked. He seemed genuine, but I'd come here to get away from Ben and the stigma of being his jilted fiancée, not to tell everyone I met about what happened. I might as well have stamped "damaged goods" across my own forehead.

"Not really. Why do you even want to know?"

"I'm just trying to get to know you. I don't mean to pry, but since we'll be hanging out all summer, we might as well cut to the chase, don't you think? What'd this guy do to make you so defensive?"

"Why do you assume we'll be hanging out all summer?"

"How many people do you know in Newport? Including me and Grace, who's only here part-time?" It wasn't a question so much as a challenge, like he was saying I simply had no choice but to be his friend or be alone. Little did he know that I was quite comfortable with being alone, so it wasn't a hard choice at all.

"Two," I admitted, hating to concede he had a point.

"Exactly. But okay, I get it. You like to keep your life private. I can respect that."

"Thank you." I sighed, feeling the tension leave my shoulders.

"Eventually you'll fill me in. I'll be patient."

"That's your way of respecting my privacy?"

Before he could answer, a very tall man made his way over to our group. He gently slapped Bobby on the back and said hello, betraying a thick European accent I couldn't place. Then again, I'd never been to Europe, and my familiarity with accents was confined to what David Beckham sounded like in fast-food commercials, so that wasn't all that surprising. He waved to Grace and me as he energetically introduced himself.

"Hi there, I'm Maximillian Wolfgang, but everyone calls me Wolf. It's so nice to meet you guys."

"Your name is Wolf?" I asked as I stared up at him. He was probably six-five, and standing next to Bobby, he looked like André the Giant. Thank God he was friendly because otherwise I'd have been terrified of him.

"Yah, I know it sounds a little strange, but it's a common name where I'm from."

"I'm Abby," I said as I found myself relaxing a bit after Bobby's forward introduction. I liked Wolf. I already could tell he would never probe into a girl's personal life within a minute of meeting her. Kind of sad that that's how low the bar was to impress me.

"So, Wolf, where are you from?" I asked, feeling comfortable talking to a guy for the first time in a long time.

"Munich, but I've been living here for about a year now. My dream is to one day get my citizenship and be proud to be an American," he said, excited, the way I sound if I find a pair of boots on sale or read something scandalous in one of the gossip rags.

My priorities are apparently very screwed up.

"That's great, congrats. I've actually never been to Germany," I admitted, without confessing that I'd never even left the continental United States.

"Oh really? You should definitely go, it's a ton of fun. I go back to the tents at Oktoberfest every year. You should check that out at some point! People get super-drunk, but it's one of the best weekends in Europe, and all the girls wear dirndls. I'm sure you'd love it."

"What's a dirndl?" I asked, not entirely sure I wanted to hear the answer. Then again, Ben had said he wanted to travel, so maybe it wouldn't kill me to learn a few things about foreign cultures, just to give Ben another reason to wish he'd never broken up with me.

"Traditional German garb," Bobby informed me. "Think Heidi. Or the girl on the Swiss Miss box."

Since we'd just met, I gave Wolf a pass on being sure that I would enjoy dressing up like one of the von Trapps or seeing a grown man of any kind wearing lederhosen. I figured if nothing else he had just informed me that my first trip to Europe would not be for Oktoberfest. I'd stick to countries where people wore normal clothes that actually fit and didn't parade around half-naked in public.

Like the south of France or something.

"How did you and Bobby meet?" I asked Wolf.

"I'm a caddy at the Newport Country Club," he answered. "Last summer Bobby was playing a round, and he kept losing his balls. I helped him find them, and I carried his bag. It was such a fun day for me. Most of the guys who play aren't that nice to the caddies, but Bobby was super-cool! We've been friends ever since."

"Wolf is a rare breed of Newport guy. He doesn't own a pair of top-siders, and he knows how to read the greens on the ninth hole like a pro. He's the man," Bobby said.

"Yes. I'm the man!" Wolf echoed, somehow managing to sound charming and not pompous in the slightest.

"Okay then, if I decide to take up golf this summer, you'll be my first call," I said, knowing full well that I would not take up golf this summer, or any other summer for that matter.

"Okeydokey!" Wolf answered.

The four of us stood in an awkward circle trying to make small talk and pretending that we had a lot in common when in reality the only link we had to each other was through Grace, and she was spending most of her time texting on her cell phone while pretending to listen to the conversation. I had a feeling that the summer was going to end up like this: me with a bunch of strange guys and Grace glued to her phone so she could talk to her boyfriend. I'd just have to remember it was one of the reasons why I had agreed to get a job. Without one, I'd have way too much free time on my hands to think about the course of my life, and worse, I'd be idly making electronic small talk with Ben. I could think of no sane reason why I would want to do that.

When I finished my beer, I headed back to the bar for a refill and some quiet, which I quickly realized was impossible in a beach bar in Newport on Memorial Day weekend. As I stood and waited for the bartender to peel his eyes away from the fake blondes in bikinis with fake boobs, fake tans, fake nails, and fake personalities, I suddenly found myself confused. When did the East Coast turn into southern California? I was terrified that if I turned around I'd bump into one of thirty cameramen filming a completely unscripted version of *The Real House-*

wives of Rhode Island. Then I'd have to figure out how to turn a bottle opener into a weapon I could use to put myself out of my misery once and for all just in case the Mayans were wrong and the world wasn't about to end on its own.

Bobby sidled up next to me as I waited for my change. I had a distinct feeling that Bobby was one of those guys who liked to push girls' buttons for no reason other than he liked to watch them squirm. He was probably the kid who poured salt on slugs to watch them die too. Hanging around a guy like that is never a good idea.

"Sorry, do you mind if I at least take your space at the bar since you didn't bother to ask if I needed a drink before you ran over here?"

"I'm sorry. I didn't mean to be rude."

"You didn't? In that case, I hate to see how rude you can be when you're actually trying," he said with a smile. I stared at him, not entirely sure how to respond. "Relax, I'm just kidding."

I sighed. I had gotten so used to having my guard up I had no idea how to take it down. "The truth is, these days, I could teach a course. I'm not entirely proud of that."

"We've all been there. I think those of us who are in our thirties and still dating are all a little worse for wear, so don't be too hard on yourself. That said, don't be too hard on me either," he joked.

"Fair enough. So you and Grace went to law school together?"

"Yup. Good ole NYU. We had a great time living in New York. I stayed there after graduation, got a job, lived downtown, and did the whole hipster thing for a while. Grace told me then that I should get out of the city before it ate me alive, but I was having way too much fun."

"Why'd you leave?"

"My law firm downsized, and I found myself unemployed. Little-known fact: New York is a very expensive place to live if you don't have an income."

I laughed, just a little. "Good to know."

"Anyway, that was back in January, and I realized that if I had to start looking for a new job, it was time to leave New York. I grew up in Providence and decided to move back to New England. I've been coming to Newport since I was a kid. My parents have owned their house here forever, so it worked out okay for me. I don't have a job, but I also don't have to pay rent, and I get to relax here for the summer."

"So you're living with your parents?"

"I didn't say that."

"Except I think you just did."

"I said I'm living in my parents' house. They retired and moved to Florida. They kept the cottage here for when they come back, but they spend most of their time playing golf and eating oranges down south."

"Ahh, I see."

"Yes, but thank you for pointing out that I probably shouldn't lead with that in conversation. Being thirty-three, unemployed, and living with my parents probably isn't what the babes are looking for in a guy," he mused.

"Probably not, no."

"So what are you looking for, kindergarten teacher? A guy who clears five feet and doesn't sleep with a night-light?"

Before I could respond, a tall blond guy who I had spotted working the crowd earlier for what I assumed was the goal of finding the drunkest girl to separate from the herd, take home, and ultimately destroy, accidentally bumped my arm, causing my beer to slosh all over my wrist.

"Hey, sorry about that," he said.

"Not a problem," I replied. And it wasn't. My watch was waterproof.

"Why don't you let me buy you another one?" He leaned over the bar and waved his arm in the air trying to get the bartender's attention. The bartender was busy with other people and was able to ignore him. I didn't have anywhere near as convenient a reason to ignore him.

"I'm fine. Really, I don't need another beer." I felt the small chink that Bobby had put in my armor start to heal.

"Okay. What do you need?" he asked, flashing a smile that he probably practiced in the bathroom mirror.

"A stun gun apparently." And just like that, it was back.

"Huh?" he said, taken aback by my attitude. Little did he know, he hadn't seen anything yet, but he was about to.

"Look, buddy, I'm not interested, okay? I don't want you to buy me another beer, I don't want you to ask me if I come here often, I don't want you to talk to me at all, so do us both a favor and find someone drunk enough to want to talk to you, because you struck out over here."

"What the hell is your problem?" he asked, understandably surprised at being attacked.

"She's off her meds, sorry about that," Bobby interjected, in what I assumed was an attempt to defend me.

Blond guy walked away, and Bobby stood staring at me with that same goofy grin on his face that I was beginning to think was some kind of genetic mutation. "What?" I asked. "I told you that I'm a little guarded. I didn't feel like making small talk with that guy."

"You know what's interesting? I'm kind of offended that that guy had no problem hitting on you in front of me. I mean, how did he know I wasn't hitting on you?"

"Maybe because I wasn't twirling my hair around my finger or suggestively sucking on a straw or something. Isn't that what girls do when they flirt?"

"Not past the age of sixteen typically, no."

"Good to know." I had so much to relearn. Or maybe learn for the first time. I decided to go home and order as many romantic comedies from Netflix as I could.

"That guy completely broke the guy code. You don't do that. I don't think you had to destroy the poor guy, but still, he was out of line."

"I'm sorry, 'the guy code'? Someone invented a code for you? I wasn't aware of that."

"Yes, honor among gentlemen. You don't go after another guy's girl."

"What is that, some kind of territorial thing? Why don't you just pee on me and get it over with?"

"Nah, not my thing. Hey wait, is that what the other guy did to make you so mad? I know some dudes are into it, it's really not all that strange. Have you looked on the Web? There's all sorts of stuff on there that . . ."

"What happened to you respecting my privacy?" I asked.

"I did. For the first ten minutes of our getting to know each other. Will you tell me now?"

"Good-bye, Bobby." I wove through the crowd and grabbed Grace's arm as she chatted with Wolf. "I'm going to head home," I said loudly so she could hear me over the crowd. I chugged my beer and handed her my empty cup.

"What? Why? Aren't you having fun?" she asked.

"I am, I just . . . I don't know. I'm a little overwhelmed. I need to break myself in slowly, and I think I've had enough for one afternoon. Am I too old to develop social anxiety problems?"

"I don't think you have social anxiety. You just need to go slowly, that's all. You haven't been out in a while. I totally get it."

"Are you sure you won't mind?" I asked, fidgeting with my watch as if I had somewhere to be.

"Not at all. I'm happy you're here, and you came out, and you met the guys. That's all I asked for. Do you want me to come home with you?"

"No. You stay. I'll be fine. Thanks again for forcing me to do this."

" 'Force' is a nasty word. 'Encouraged.' "

"Strongly encouraged."

"Just don't email Ben, okay?"

"I won't," I replied. I wasn't entirely sure I believed me, but I wanted to.

"Good girl. Go relax, I'll see you in a bit."

I hugged her and waved good-bye to Wolf as I headed for the exit. I had just hit the sidewalk when I heard someone call from behind me. It was Bobby, trotting down the road, his awkward gait revealing that one thing Bobby was not was an athlete.

"Hey, Abby," he called. "Why don't you stick around?" He gestured over his shoulder back at the bar.

"I have to get home." It was only a partial lie.

"No, you don't," he challenged.

"How do you know that?" I was never a good liar.

"Because unless you have some sort of emergency unpacking problem, you don't need to be in an empty house right now. I think you're avoiding me," he teased. He crossed his arms across his chest and smiled at me. Bobby was charming in a strange way. In the way that made me want to keep talking to him, but to not really be nice when I did. I'm pretty sure that's not how you go about getting guys to like you as a friend or anything else, but it was the only way I knew how to be.

"Why would I avoid you? I don't even know you," I replied with a shrug.

"Oh, so you want to come back to the bar and talk to me? I'll tell you all about myself."

"Maybe next time. I'm just a little tired."

"I'm starting to get the feeling that you don't like me."

"I didn't say that."

"Then you do like me."

"I didn't say that either."

"Can I buy you a beer?"

"No thanks."

"Please?"

"Well, in that case . . . no."

"Okay, suit yourself. I'm just trying to be friendly here and make you feel at home since you don't know anyone, but if you'd rather be alone, that's fine. I'm sure I'll see you around." He shrugged, finally giving up on breaking me down. Little did he know that someone had beaten him to the punch a long time ago.

"What makes you say that?" I asked before he walked away.

"What?"

"That you'll see me around?"

"I live down the block for starters," he said.

"Oh yeah, I forgot. Look, I really just want to relax for a little. It was nice to meet you. I'll see you later," I said as I waved him off.

"As you wish," he said as he turned and headed back to the bar, leaving me on the sidewalk.

When I got to the house, I walked in, went into my bedroom, removed my laptop from its case, and set it gently on the bed in front of me. I turned it on and opened my Gmail account, waiting to see if the little dot next to Ben's name turned green to let me know he was logged in. When it did, I opened a chat box and stared at it for a full five minutes, knowing that I shouldn't write him, but I couldn't stop myself. We had been together for ten years, and had been friends for a year before we started dating. I could no more keep myself from writing him than I could keep myself from swallowing. It was like muscle memory, and that, like my other memories, would take time to fade. My hands started typing before my brain knew what they were doing. I didn't want to be his friend, but I didn't want him to be out of my life either. I didn't know what I wanted. And that was the problem.

I typed slowly.

Hi. Just got back from the bars. How are things going out there?

Hey yourself. Going okay, had a busy day and just relaxing now with a beer. How was the bar scene?

Crowded. Met some of Grace's friends.

Preppy guys?

Yes.

Not happy to hear that. You always liked the preppy guys. One in particular.

Once upon a time, yes.

Be patient with me Abby. I'm working things out.

What does that mean?

Sorry, got to run, I'm taking a friend to the movies.

What? I stared at the conversation, brief as it was, and could swear that Ben was telling me that he wanted me to wait for him, that he didn't want me seeing other guys, and that he was taking another girl to the movies. I read and reread and read the conversation again to see if I'd missed something, but there was nothing there to miss. The dot next to his name turned gray when he signed off. I threw myself back on the bed and buried my head in the pillows. It was unreal how quickly one person could make me feel so inadequate. I closed my laptop, not only because I couldn't stand the mental torment for another minute, but because I was exhausted. What was I doing? I was not this person. At least, I didn't want to be this person anymore. It was time to make some changes.

CHAPTER 6

This Is Like Zagat's—No One Gets a Perfect Score

I WOKE UP early Saturday morning and went for a run to better learn the area and try to get the summer started on a healthy note. As much as I needed Newport to be a reboot for my mental health, I needed it to kick-start my physical health as well, and I figured the best way to fix both was to get set in some kind of exercise routine. I ran in a small circle from the house up toward Cliff Walk and back through town, slowing down to catch my breath by pretending to window-shop at the stores along Thames Street. Dark storm clouds began to roll in when I was a few blocks from home, and I turned onto Grafton Street two minutes before the skies opened up in a vicious summer storm. I hopped in the shower, and when I changed and went back into the den, I found Bobby, Wolf, and Grace seated in a circle on the floor around the coffee table. Apparently, they had come up with a way to spend the morning that didn't involve being outside—Scrabble and Bloody Marys.

Made perfect sense to me.

An hour later, the four of us were still sitting around our Scrabble board on the floor in our tiny living room with beer and a bowl of Tostitos while the summer storm continued to pound the windows so hard I was afraid they would shatter. Otis Redding played off the speaker dock, and I had to admit, I was enjoying getting to know my new friends and I was having a good time, if for no other reason than playing Scrabble with someone whose first language wasn't English was almost reality-show material.

We waited for Wolf to place his letters on the board, and when he did, he spelled out BMW.

"BMW is not a word, it's an abbreviation for British Motor Works," Grace said.

"It's a German company," Wolf countered. "Don't tell me it's British, silly American girl. The B stands for Bavarian. Like me!"

"Even if that's true, you can't use abbreviations," I said. "No one gave you a hard time when you played U-BOAT last round, and don't even get me started on you using the word STRUDEL. You should be using this game to help develop your English skills, not to insert German words all over the board."

"These are words. The little book with the definitions says so. And BMW is *not* British. You're all wrong." So we checked.

Damn it. He was right on both counts.

The argument had momentarily distracted me from what I'd been thinking while running earlier. I hesitated to bring it up, if for no other reason than I didn't know the boys that well and didn't want them to think I was crazy. Then I realized that if we were going to be hanging out all summer, they'd find out sooner or later anyway, and it was probably better to let them know who they were dealing with. Besides, those earlier thoughts were ruining my Scrabble concentration, and I had just lost the chance to play the word QUICHE for thirty-seven points.

"I was thinking while I was running this morning."

"About?" Grace asked.

"Ben. Or I should say, how to get over him for good," I admitted, without bothering to look up at the skeptical expression that I knew was on Grace's face.

"The guy's name is Ben. Got it," Bobby said. "I knew it was a guy!"

"Fine. There was a guy, and yes, his name is Ben, and our breakup was, what would I call it . . ."

"Horrifying?" Grace offered.

"I was going to say messy, but sure, let's say horrifying and leave it at that. Anyway, I've been thinking about what I need to do in order to get back out there and let people know that I'm available."

"If you're trying to come across as available, then yeah, you probably need to revamp your strategy," Bobby said.

"Why do you say that?"

"For starters, the guy at the bar yesterday was hitting on you and you didn't give him the time of day," Bobby said.

"What guy?" I asked.

"The guy who offered to buy you a drink when we were at the bar. You not so subtly told him to go kill himself."

"Oh please, he wasn't hitting on me. He was just drunk and being stupid, and I might add, he was entirely too forward considering he didn't know me."

"Are you seriously so dating-impaired that you don't even recognize the act of being hit on?" Bobby turned to Grace with a bemused expression I wanted to smack off his face with my tennis racket. "Grace, is she kidding me?"

"No. She's that clueless," Grace said as she stared at her Scrabble letters.

"Thanks, Grace," I said.

"Hey, it's not a bad thing. You're just out of practice is all," she replied.

"He was most certainly hitting on you. When was the last time you went on a date?" Bobby asked. Suddenly, no one was interested in the

Scrabble board, which was a shame, because I had a monster word to play.

"She hasn't been on a date with anyone in like, twelve years," Grace so nicely offered up. The guys gawked and stared at me like I was some kind of circus freak.

"Really?" Wolf asked. "I've been on more than that, and I'm still learning English."

"Yes, well, I was in a long-term relationship, and it's been a long time since I've been on a real date. And that's my point!" I said, getting excited about sharing the details of the plan I'd concocted in my head somewhere around mile two before I started to see spots.

"That you need help in the dating department?" Bobby said as he clapped his hands together to get the Tostito dust off his fingers.

"Yes. I hate to say it, but I do," I said.

"Okay," Grace said, finally devoting her full attention to me and not to the letters in front of her. "What kind of help?"

"I was thinking that maybe I should move. I mean, I can teach anywhere. Maybe a fresh start outside of Boston would force me to come out of my self-imprisonment."

"Oh, this is fantastic," Bobby said. "You think you'll be better at dating in other cities, huh? Okay, hotshot, let's play this game. Where would you go?"

I hadn't really thought about it much. But now that everyone was wondering, I guess I had a few ideas. "How about New York?"

"No way," Grace said. "It's crazy expensive. Aside from that, it's too high-maintenance. In order to survive in New York, you need to have a session with your personal trainer, a resurfacing facial, a full body wax, a manicure, a pedicure, $500 highlights, and a designer wardrobe just for most people to deem you acceptable to walk on the sidewalk. Too much pressure. Bobby and I both lived there, and we are both back. You'd never last."

I wasn't sure if that was an insult. I decided not to find out.

"DC?" I offered.

"Nope," Bobby said. "Everyone there is in politics, i.e., they're game players, they know how to play them, and most importantly, they actually recognize them when they see them. Besides, half the guys in that city think emailing naked pictures of themselves to people they meet on MySpace is a normal way of getting to know someone. Are you up for that?" he asked. I sensed sarcasm.

"What do you think?" I answered. "What about Chicago?"

"Too windy," he said. "Boston may be just as cold, but the wind in Chicago will kill you. Plus, then you'd have to be a Cubs fan."

"Funny."

"You need to do some research if you want to move. You need to go somewhere where there are a lot of guys and not a lot of good-looking girls," Bobby offered.

"I can't believe I'm going to ask you this, but why is that?" I asked.

"Because guys who live in those cities don't know what really pretty girls look like. Their scale is all screwed up, so a seven on the East Coast is like a nine in some places. You'd definitely be a nine in some cities."

"Really? You couldn't just give me a ten?" I asked. I was oddly insulted . . . again.

"No, this is like Zagat's. No one gets a perfect score," he said flatly, as if his explanation somehow justified his insult.

"I see."

"This exercise is pointless," Grace said as she scooped salsa out of the dip bowl with a chip and then walked into the kitchen to add a bag of salt-and-vinegar potato chips to the Scrabble picnic. "You and I both know you aren't going anywhere, and besides, moving won't solve anything. You'll have the same problems in any city anywhere in the world, so let's take geography out of the equation and figure out what you can do to change your situation *here*."

"Okay, how do I go about changing my situation here? How do I go about being proactive?" I asked, thinking that in this case maybe four heads were better than one malfunctioning one.

"Would you go online?" Wolf asked. "The Europeans love Internet dating. I bet you'd be popular with them."

"I don't think that's for me. I thought about it at one point, but then I chickened out."

"Oh, you got wet feet," Wolf said, nodding sympathetically. "I understand."

We shook our heads in unison. "The expression is 'cold feet,' Wolf," I said.

"Why would cold feet keep you from doing something? Wet feet are way more annoying than cold feet. I'd change my plans if my feet were wet, not if they were cold," Wolf said in a no-nonsense tone.

He had an interesting point.

"Anyway, I don't want to go online. I want to meet someone live and in person. I know that's a crazy concept in this day and age, but I guess I'm just old-fashioned that way." I sighed. My reluctance to let go of the concept of fate and being in the right place at the right time was probably going to be the end of me.

"Times have changed," Bobby said. "If you don't want to change with them, then you need to get aggressive, and since that's clearly not something you're comfortable with, you're going to have to think outside the box."

"What does it mean to think inside the box?" Wolf asked.

"No one says 'Think inside the box'!" Grace said.

"If you don't know what's inside the box, then how do you know when you're outside of it?" Wolf asked, confused.

It was quickly becoming clear that idioms in the English language didn't make a whole lot of sense.

"I don't know. I'll get back to you on that," I answered him as Grace and Bobby laughed.

Wolf appeared bemused as he continued. "When I first came here, I didn't know anyone. I had to force myself to go out and meet people! I didn't want to, it was scary, Americans talk way too fast. It's hard to understand you. Girls especially, because you squeak a lot when you talk. You sound like birds chirping."

Bobby laughed as Grace and I stared at him. "We don't squeak!" Grace, well, squeaked.

"German isn't the easiest language to understand either," I added.

"It is for me," Wolf answered. "Anyway, I pretended it was my job, and I had to go. It helped me make my new friends. Maybe it will help for you too."

"So what are you saying? That the only way I'm going to get my head back in the game is if I treat dating like it's a job?" I asked.

"It worked for me. I have a lot of friends now," he pointed out.

"Wolf is right," Bobby said as he finished his beer. "Dating is not fun. First dates by and large suck, but they're a necessary evil if you want to get a boyfriend, right?"

"Yeah, that sounds about right," I admitted.

"This is genius. Why hasn't anyone ever thought of this before?" Bobby asked as he scratched his head, frustrated that Wolf had come up with this idea and he hadn't.

"I don't know. Most people don't listen to me, I guess," Wolf said with a shrug.

"I mean, it's just so obvious! Relationships are hard, exhausting, soul-sucking work. Everyone knows that," Grace mused.

"It's a job, basically, yeah," I said, becoming more and more intrigued by this idea.

"I really need one of those," Bobby said.

"A relationship?" I asked.

"No. A job. Law is also exhausting, soul-sucking work. You just made me remember that I'm unemployed."

"I'm liking where you're going with this, Wolf," Grace said. "How would Abby go about dating like it's a job? I'm not entirely sure I get it."

"You know how some days you wake up and you really don't want to go to work?" he asked.

"That's *every* day," Grace answered.

"Right. But you still make yourself go, yes?"

"Yeah," I said hesitantly.

"Well, sometimes you have to go on dates you don't want to go on, but you still have to go. Pretend you don't have a choice, and you don't have the option to call in sick."

Bobby stood and addressed us with authority. He really did need to get a job, because he was about to turn our living room into a courtroom. "You need to make yourself available, ask people to set you up, talk to the guys at the bar who offer to buy you drinks, and maybe even give them your phone number."

"I think I could do that," I said, even though I wasn't sure I believed myself.

"That's the complete opposite of what you did yesterday. You know that, right?" he asked.

"Yes. And I recognize that that was stupid."

"Wow, what a difference a day makes."

"So while you're out here this summer, make it your goal to go on at least two dates a week, minimum," Bobby suggested as he continued to pace around the living room.

"You totally need to do this," Grace agreed.

"That's great practice, plus no doubt there will be some major catastrophes in there and that will give us something to laugh about. Just make sure you don't end up on the Walk of Shame website. While I'd personally love it, I don't think you'd ever recover."

"What Walk of Shame site?" I asked, shocked that there was now a website dedicated to capturing embarrassing situations on film and broadcasting them on the Web for all the world to see. Once again I found myself dumbfounded at how technology had changed the way we all interacted. It used to be that people had to actually know you in order to humiliate you. Man, I missed the nineties.

"There's some guy who drives around the island in the morning and takes pictures of people walking home in their clothes from the night before. It's amazing. I've busted my friends on that thing more times than I can count," Bobby said.

"That's disgusting," Grace said. "I'd never let that happen to me. I'd kill the guy first."

"You'd have to find out who he is. No one knows who does it, but I have to say, whoever he is, the guy's got talent."

"Is no one listening to me anymore?" Wolf asked, hurt that he had lost our attention to an anonymous blogger.

"No, I'm listening to you. You're saying she should have a dating project!" Grace squealed as she sat up on her knees. "I like this. I like this a lot."

"I do too," Bobby said.

"I think this is just a little bit ridiculous," I replied, even though I knew that I was outnumbered and that no one cared what I thought.

"It's kind of a ridiculous idea, but that doesn't mean that it won't work or that it won't be good for you," Grace said.

"I have a hard time accepting the fact that nothing seems to happen organically anymore, you know?" I said, pulling my hair into a messy bun on the top of my head. "Is this what a girl needs to do now to meet people?"

"Look, Abby," Grace said, "I'm your best friend, and I love you, but you have to face the facts. You're a smart girl and a great friend, but for whatever reason you have terrible—and I mean *terrible*—taste in guys. Your instincts are miswired for some reason, because there is no other explanation on earth to account for the fact that you won't let go of this loser."

"True, but I'm not the first girl on earth who's had a hard time letting go of someone who deep down I know is toxic. I mean, you and Johnny aren't exactly the model for highly functioning relationships."

"Hey, I thought this wasn't about me."

"The rules have changed."

"Look, I never liked Ben, and you know it. He was a jerk from day one, you just didn't want to admit it. And let's not forget the gem you dated in high school."

She may have had a point. As bad as Ben was, he was nowhere near as big a loser as my high school boyfriend. I was pretty sure he might actually still be in high school unless he had found someone else's papers to copy.

"I was sixteen! Every guy is an idiot at that age."

"Most of us are still idiots in our thirties, to be fair," Bobby added.

"I don't think I'm an idiot. Maybe only sometimes," Wolf said, looking hurt that he was lumped into the category of all men when it was very clear that he was a different breed of male.

"All I'm saying is that what you've been doing isn't working. So let's do the opposite of what you would normally do and see what happens! What's the worst possible outcome? You go on ten bad dates, summer ends, you go back to the city, and you've had some practice."

"No. The worst possible outcome is that I end up with a stalker or with mouth herpes or something. This plan comes with its fair share of risks."

"It's time you took some risks," Grace scolded.

"I know. I guess desperate times call for desperate measures."

"I'd totally leave the word 'desperate' out of this," Bobby suggested. "It's just not a good word for a guy to hear from a girl's mouth."

"I think the fact that this entire idea makes you uncomfortable is good. You need to get out of your comfort zone," Grace said.

"My comfort zone is my couch. So I've already done that."

"I think there was a *Seinfeld* episode on something like this once," Bobby said. "Opposite George."

"Seinfeld was a smart man, see?" Grace added.

"I don't remember if it worked," Bobby said as he stared at the ceiling as if trying to remember how the episode ended.

"Who's Seinfeld?" Wolf asked.

We ignored him. It was simply too ridiculous to address.

"I think you should do it," Bobby said. "I'll be your consigliere. I'll be here to offer advice and help you along the way."

"That's supposed to be a selling point?" I asked, not entirely sure how Bobby had gone from not knowing my name to wanting to serve as my mentor in the span of twenty-four hours.

"Yes. Don't be so defensive and admit that you could use some guidance in the guy department."

"Can Wolf be my guidance counselor?" I asked.

"Okay!" Wolf shouted. "I'd like that! What's a guidance counselor?"

"You can have both of us," Bobby answered. "Come on, I'll help you lose some of your inhibitions, which is exactly what you need. No offense, but you're wound tighter than a mattress spring."

"Just as long as it's not in your bed," Grace joked.

I licked salt from the potato chips off my index fingers and thought about their points. They were right. In fact, Wolf's suggestion very well may have been the single best piece of dating advice I had ever heard, and that's saying something. I watch a lot of *Dr. Phil*.

"Okay, maybe you guys are right. I can do this. I'm smart, I'm cute, how hard could it be for me to get a few dates at the beach?"

"Don't get cocky," Bobby said. "Guys don't like girls with attitudes."

"You don't know what you're talking about. Guys like girls with confidence," I countered.

"Where'd you read that?" Bobby asked curiously.

"*Cosmo,*" I admitted, realizing how stupid that sounded.

"Stop reading *Cosmo.* They don't know what they're talking about either."

"Who made you the authority on dating? You're single too!" For some reason, I felt the need to point that out.

"This is *not* how you get me to be your wingman."

"I didn't ask you to be my wingman." I felt the need to point that out too.

"Can you two please just get a room or something," Grace said as she stood.

"Okay, Abby, you put your big girl panties on and do this all by yourself. If you change your mind, you know where to find me," Bobby said, finally returning to the floor with the rest of us. Apparently, he was done holding dating court.

"Yeah, probably stealing beer from our fridge," Grace joked.

"I overheard some girls in town talking about a ton of people going to 41 North tonight," Bobby said, clearly forgetting that he had just told me to fly solo. I guess he *was* my wingman, no matter what either of us said. "Let's start there. Your job is to talk to five different guys and let at least two of them buy you a drink."

"I don't know what 41 North is," I said, though that wasn't strange since I had only been in Newport for a day.

"It's one of those places called a bar," Bobby said sarcastically. "See, that's where guys and girls our age go to meet each other. Do you need a dictionary before we release you on the social circuit? Oh wait, that would entail me helping you. Never mind. I can't wait to see you on the dance floor. You *do* know the funky chicken is passé, right?"

I responded by sticking my tongue out at him. I guess I did employ the same communication skills as my students.

"Then it's settled," Grace said. "I'll pick out your outfit. You blow-dry your hair and put on makeup and do all the things that girls do when they're happy and single and ready to meet someone normal. It will be fun, and I'm not taking no for an answer."

"Okay, I'm game. And Grace, you'll be happy to know that I also decided I'm going to get a job. When I was jogging through town this morning, I saw a HELP WANTED sign in one of the store windows. I'm going to go up there later and see what the deal is."

"Look at you!" Grace said as she applauded me. "A plan to start dating *and* a plan to get a job. You've done more to help yourself in the last hour than you have in the last six months!"

"I told you I was ready to make some changes. The extra cash won't hurt either."

"With this new attitude, finding a nice rebound guy will be like shooting fish in a barrel."

"Americans shoot fish in barrels?" Wolf asked.

"No, it's just an expression. It means that it's easy," Bobby answered, growing frustrated with Wolf's completely reasonable questions.

"Why wouldn't you say that it's easy to shoot fish in the tank then?"

"I actually have no idea. Don't ask me questions I don't know the answer to, dude!" he said.

"That means don't ask Bobby anything," I quipped.

"Now can we finish this Scrabble game? Wolf, no more abbreviations. Deal?" Bobby said as he turned his attention back to his Scrabble letters.

"Okay," Wolf said, still proud of himself for proving that BMW is in fact a marvel of German engineering. "Abby, I know a guy here I can set you up with. He's super-nice, I think you'll like him. Why don't I give him a call? Maybe you can meet him for a drink or something."

"A blind date? I don't know how I feel about those," I admitted.

"Stop it," Bobby snapped. "Blind dates are awesome. You think Wolf is going to set you up with a freak? You should go. You need to explore as many avenues as you can."

"What's his story?" I asked Wolf. I figured I was fully within my rights to get some details on this guy before I agreed to meet him. Considering what guys were doing these days to vet girls before they dated them, a few simple questions seemed completely reasonable.

"What do you want to know? His name is Paul. He's thirty-five and girls love him. He hasn't had a real girlfriend in a while, but I think he wants one. I'll call him and set it up. I want to help!"

"You know what? You're right," I said, realizing that I'd be stupid not to accept his help. Wolf was one of the nicest people I'd ever met. If he thought his friend was a good guy worth meeting, then I had no doubt he was. "Okay, Wolf, let's do it. If you set it up, I'll go."

And just like that, I had a plan. I couldn't focus on the rest of the game because I was too busy mentally running through the entire contents of my closet and trying to quell the excitement I was feeling. I was ready for the great dating project of 2012 to begin.

CHAPTER 7

If You Can't Join 'Em, Eavesdrop on 'Em

A FEW HOURS later, after two more rounds of Scrabble, multiple rounds of drinks, and an hour-long nap, the four of us walked down Thames Street heading for the bars. For the first time I realized something horrid: I was old. Not *old* old, but bar scene old. I stared at some of the girls walking ahead of us, shrieking and laughing, already sufficiently drunk and speaking at a decibel level that alerted everyone within a three-block radius to that fact. At some point while I was dating Ben and staying blissfully unaware of what was happening on the social circuit, a change had occurred. Girls started leaving the house practically naked. Don't get me wrong, I'm not saying anyone had to dress like the nuns I worked with, but let's just say, if a normal person owns a dish towel larger than your skirt, you're probably a bit scantily clad. If this had been Vegas, it wouldn't have surprised me, but this was Rhode Island. How was I going to compete with half-naked twenty-three-year-olds who knew all the cool places to hang out and what style of jeans were in and what it meant to have a tumblr account?

When we arrived at 41 North, I immediately approached the bar and asked the bartender for a cocktail list. He was tan and muscular, his white uniform making him look like he belonged on an episode of *The Love Boat* instead of making watered-down cocktails that cost fifteen bucks a pop at a bar in Newport. But the recession was causing everyone to take a shot at reinvention, so really, who was I to judge? I ordered Dark 'n' Stormys for Grace and myself, but when I turned around to hand her drink to her, she was scurrying off into the corner of the room.

"Where are you going?" I asked, almost panicked at the thought of being left alone at the bar.

"Sorry, I have to take a quick call from work. I'll be right back," she said casually.

"Please don't leave me!" I joked, looking around at all the strangers and knowing that I was terrible at making small talk. I didn't want to be the girl standing alone in the bar, hoping that someone would talk to her. I had thought that by the time I hit thirty I'd have outgrown the fear of being alone in a crowd, but apparently I was a late bloomer. "Who am I going to talk to?" I whined.

"I'll be right back, and you'll be just fine. Go mingle. You can talk to people, Abby. I have complete faith in you," she said as she walked off.

"Sure. I'll just mingle. Because I'm good at that." I sipped my drink and glanced nervously around the room. Bobby wasted no time invading the dance floor with his ridiculously uncoordinated dance moves, and Wolf stood to the side saying "Guttentag" to every pretty girl who walked by. I took my drink and stood next to Wolf. While I watched people dance with each other, I couldn't help but have the same thought I'd had on the walk over: *I'm getting old. When did that happen?*

"You know what's funny, Wolfie?" I asked with a sigh.

"The girl in the corner dancing with the wall?" he asked. We both turned to stare at the very intoxicated girl in a short spandex dress slow-dancing with the wall. That was one I hadn't seen before.

"Yeah, but other than her. There was a time when I would've been leading the pack on that dance floor. I would've been the life of the party. Now all I can think about is what movie I'm missing on TV. I can't compete with these kids and their miniature outfits."

"Abby, I think you look very nice. Don't worry about those other girls, just relax and have fun. There are plenty of people our age here," he said, bobbing his head to the music, smiling at everyone who walked by.

"They're staff," I said with a sigh.

"Not just them. You're prettier than those drunk kids anyway."

"Thanks, Wolf." I reached over and patted his arm, happy to have a genuinely nice guy as a friend.

"I mean it," he said with a smile, instantly putting me at ease. "Any guy here would be lucky to have you."

"Why aren't you dating anyone? Haven't you found any nice American girls to go out with?" I asked, hoping that I wasn't intruding on his personal life the way I felt Bobby continually intruded on mine.

"Not yet, but I'm having fun looking."

"That's the attitude I should have," I said. He was right. I needed to relax.

"Hey, can I ask you a question?" Wolf said.

"Sure."

"What's that over there?" he asked, pointing to the other side of the bar.

Oh God.

There were more than a few things I didn't know about Newport nightlife. I didn't know which bars were popular on which nights, I didn't know which places had the good bands or the bartenders with the heavy pours, and I was fine with that. What I wasn't fine with was no one bothering to tell me that Newport was apparently a hot spot for bachelor and bachelorette parties. I scanned the crowd and discovered you couldn't swing a bat (which I had unfortunately neglected to throw in my clutch before leaving the house, though I won't be making that mistake again) without smacking a girl wearing some kind of accessory letting the world know that she was about to be married. Stepping into the middle of the bachelorette party mecca of the Northeast wasn't really how I'd envisioned the first night of my project going. I knew I'd remember this night forever, just not for the reasons I had hoped. You can only watch so many girls swing pink feather boas around like spastic Vegas showgirl outcasts before the image is permanently imprinted in your cerebral cortex. Right next to the part that stores vital information like your name, your age, and the number of fat grams in a pint of Chunky Monkey ice cream.

I wove through the crowd, found Grace, and grabbed her by the arm as she stood with Bobby on the edge of the makeshift dance floor, singing along with the music. "You didn't tell me this place was going to be like a *Girls Gone Wild* episode."

"What, the bachelorette parties? It's a beach destination in the dead of summer. You can't go anywhere and *not* run into bachelorette parties. What's the big deal?"

"This isn't exactly helping to take my mind off of things. How am I supposed to be perky and pleasant when I'm standing in the middle of a bridal carnival? Is the entire summer going to be like this?"

"I sure as hell hope so," Bobby said as he adjusted the collar on his striped shirt and smoothed his dark hair out of his eyes. "I love bachelorette parties. Girls who are secretly jealous that their friend is getting married before they do are the easiest scores on earth. You guys are on your own tonight, there are lonely hearts everywhere. It's time I find one to help cheer up." Bobby darted away from us, very much a single guy on the singles circuit. I wished I could be more like Bobby, but I actually cared what people thought about me. I felt deflated.

"I'm going to sit down over there," I said, pointing to a cluster of small cocktail tables dotting the periphery of the bar. I collapsed in one of the metal chairs and took out my lip gloss. There was an exceedingly large group of girls gathered around the table next to me, squealing and laughing and doing exactly what girls were supposed to be doing on a Saturday night in summer: getting drunk. I glanced in their direction and realized with horror that they weren't just a large, rowdy group of girls. They were members of one of the bachelorette parties—one with a T-shirt-wearing ensemble cast and a very drunk, boa-clad bride. Apparently, no place was safe.

I placed the bride's age somewhere around twenty-five by virtue of her wearing purple nail polish with sequins attached to each thumb and extremely pink lip gloss thick enough to make her hair stick to it like flypaper. I reapplied my lip gloss and figured, if you can't join 'em, eavesdrop on 'em.

"Okay, ladies!" the maid of honor said as she clanked her fork on her nearly empty champagne flute. I wasn't using woman's intuition or my razor-sharp detective skills to deduce that she was the maid of honor. I simply read it off her T-shirt. Apparently, being a maid of honor now warranted your own T-shirt, like you were the most special of the nonbrides in the group. I wondered if this little tradition would snowball until the entire wedding party was wearing T-shirts denoting their place in the wedding caste system. I felt bad for the girl who got stuck wearing the shirt that said OBLIGATORY BRIDESMAID SO AS TO AVOID PISSING OFF FUTURE IN-LAWS. It was only a matter of time before the bridal T-shirt people stopped being polite and just put the truth out there like Letterman. And Joan Rivers. And Taylor Swift after some guy pisses her off.

"It's time to play the question game!" the maid of honor sang as the rest of the girls clapped and oohed and aahed. The maid of honor turned to the bride, sitting on her throne at the head of the table, her blinking, battery-operated tiara lights making her look like a malfunctioning Christmas tree ornament. "We emailed Connor a bunch of questions about you, and I have the answers right here!" she said as she waved a sheet of paper in the air. "Every time you answer a question wrong, you have to drink!"

Everyone oohed and aahed and clapped again, like drinking was some kind of exotic punishment that no one had ever heard of. The maid of honor, being the head bridal groupie, was ready to begin. So was I. I had a full beer, I was good for a while.

"What did you do on your first date?" she asked, saying every word slowly, lest one of the monosyllabic words confuse the contestant. Wow. Scandalous stuff.

"We went for pizza and a movie, and then he walked me home to my apartment and kissed me on the sidewalk. I knew right there that we'd be together forever," the bride gushed, proud of herself for knowing her own personal history so well.

Bullshit. I thought. *You probably got drunk and don't even remember going home. Then you sat by the phone for two days wondering if he was going to call you and you know it.*

"Okay, that one was too easy!" the maid of honor said as she handed the paper to the girl sitting to her right. "Where's the strangest place you've ever had sex?" girl number two, a non-T-shirt-wearing member of the wedding party, asked.

"The Dumpster behind my parents' house in Florida," the bride said without hesitation.

What? I thought as I choked on my beer, spattering foam onto my dress. *Seriously?*

"No," the girl replied, stifling a giggle.

"The parking lot of the ferry in Hyannis?" the bride guessed again.

"No," the questioner shrieked, the girls at the table laughing so hard it was a wonder one of them didn't fall off her chair.

How are you getting these wrong? And why aren't you hooking up indoors?

"The swing set in my neighbor's backyard?"

"No!" the girl yelled as the table erupted into laughter. "Drink!"

Oh God. I'm more out of my league than I thought. Apparently people didn't even have sex inside anymore. When did that happen?

The printout was passed to the next girl, who was drinking a margarita through a straw like it was last call in a women's prison, but my spy session was interrupted when I heard the screech of metal chair legs on pavement as the chair next to me was pulled out. "Hey," an amazingly stoned guy said as he sat down and began making conversation with me as if we were old friends. Which was interesting, since I had never seen him before in my life and was pretty sure that he was seeing three of me at once.

"Hey, yourself," I said as I turned my attention back to the bridal party and tried to hear the next question.

"How are you?" he asked, his eyes darting from side to side as if he was afraid someone was going to jump out from behind the potted plant and murder him. You know, because that happens all the time.

"I think you have me confused with someone else," I said politely. I know I said I'd be open to meeting new people, but maybe I should've stipulated that that didn't include guys who were very clearly drugged out of their minds.

"Oh, no, I know. I was wondering, do you happen to have any blow?" he asked in a hoarse whisper.

"Huh?"

"Blow. Cocaine. Do you have any?" he repeated.

I wasn't a drug user, dealer, or connoisseur of any kind, but I knew enough to know that this guy didn't have a clue what he was doing. I looked down at my white halter sundress and flip-flops and wondered if eyelet was now some kind of signal to the narcotics-using underground that you were a drug mule. If so, someone needed to alert J. Crew immediately, because I really don't think that was what they were going for when they put out their spring line.

"Dude, don't worry. I'm not a cop. I swear. It's my buddy's bachelor party, and he wants to get high," he said, as if that explanation somehow made his question more normal.

"I can't help you," I said as I stood to leave. He stood and attempted to walk with me, reaching out to grab my forearm before I had a chance to pull away.

"You have two seconds to let go of my arm before I scream," I hissed. This night was not going the way I wanted it to.

"Sorry, sorry. Seriously, I'm not a cop."

"That's great. And I'm seriously not a veterinarian, and now that we're both aware of what we're not, this conversation is over. And in case you were wondering, I won't have any coke, crack, or crystal meth on me when I get back either, so you should find someone else to buy drugs from."

"Okay, yeah, but seriously, it's just my buddy, it's his . . ."

"Yeah, I know. It's your buddy's bachelor party, so he wants to do cocaine. I don't know what getting married has to do with your friend wanting to snort drugs up his nose, but hey, whatever floats your boat. Now move."

I pushed him out of the way and took a deep breath before diving into the mosh pit that occupied the space between me and the ladies' room on the other side of the bar. I waited on line in the hallway behind a few of the members of yet another bachelorette party and various other women who, like me, didn't care that anyone was getting married. The only thing we cared about was that there were only three stalls and thirty women waiting to get into the ladies' room.

As I washed my hands I looked in the mirror to see exactly how much mascara had melted onto my face since leaving the house, when yet another bride-to-be exited a stall. She smoothed her T-shirt, readjusted her sash, and finger-combed her hair. Whoever had glued on her fake eyelashes didn't have a steady hand. They were crooked and made her look like a psychotic drag queen. Oddly enough, it was obvious that she thought people were staring at her in awe or envy, but I knew that no one felt like pointing out that it looked like someone had glued shoe tassels to her eyelids. (We nonbrides were entitled to a little fun too.)

As her maid of honor approached her the bride proceeded to scream loudly enough to blow out my eardrum and scare another unsuspecting woman into dropping her purse on the sludge-covered floor.

"I'm getting married!" she yelled as they grasped hands and jumped up and down. I guess she figured she should make that announcement just in case her friend was confused as to why she was wearing a maid of honor T-shirt and a glow-in-the-dark dick necklace.

"I know!" (See, I knew she'd figure it out.) "In just a few weeks you're going to be Mrs. Joseph DiLuca."

"I'm so excited! I mean, I really love him, you know?" she said slowly, like she was trying to explain nuclear fission to her friend. "I do, I mean, when you know, you just like, *know*."

"You guys make the best couple, you really do," the friend gushed as she dabbed her lips with more gluelike gloss.

"Did you see that cute guy in the corner of the dance floor wearing the jeans and the royal blue shirt?" the bride asked as she gently elbowed her friend in the ribs.

"Yeah. He's a total smoke show."

"I'm going to ask him to dance with me. I saw him looking at me before, and it's my bachelorette party, I'm allowed to have a little fun."

"Oh totally, the actual wedding ring isn't on your finger yet! Your bachelorette party is a get-out-of-jail-free weekend, everyone knows that." The friend smoothed her shirt and winked.

I smoothed my dress and gagged.

"You're the best friend ever," the bride said as she hugged her friend to say thank-you for giving her permission to cheat on her fiancé. It was a good thing that they didn't think that a bachelorette weekend meant you were free from all rules and regulations or they probably would have knocked over liquor stores and wreaked havoc on the great state of Rhode Island like a real live Thelma and Louise. I wondered how their "but everyone knows you can do whatever you want without repercussions as long as you're wearing a bride sash" defense would go over in court.

It'd probably depend on how many married women were on the jury.

The bride pulled out of her friend's drunken grasp and began to sing

"Going to the Chapel" as she spun and twirled and knocked unsuspecting women into the walls. She spun again, but this time she tripped, flew forward, and smacked her head on the mirror over the sink. She screamed as she grabbed her head on impact. For a second, I was worried she'd cut her head or given herself a mild concussion.

"Oh my God, did I break my tiara?" she asked her friend in horror, as if there was no fate worse than being forced to suffer through the rest of the night without her bridal tiara.

Well, that answered that. This chick's mental malfunction clearly started long before she head-butted a mirror.

"No, Missy, it's totally fine, don't worry."

"Thank God, my whole night would have been ruined!"

She straightened her headpiece, and then, without batting a tarantula-esque eyelash, proceeded to projectile-vomit all over the floor, her platform espadrilles, and her mint green pedicure.

That Joey DiLuca is one lucky guy, I thought as I exited the ladies' room and left the girl who no longer felt so lucky to be wearing that maid of honor T-shirt to clean up after the bride.

I wove in and out of the drunken people grinding each other on the dance floor, the guys looking to prey on any girl who had had one too many John Dalys, and the guys in the bachelor party who for some reason equated their drunkenness with how many buttons on their shirts they should undo, and ran for the street. I was about to hit the sidewalk when I heard Bobby call after me. "Where are you going? You can't leave yet. You promised to talk to five people!" He caught up to me at the door.

"I did," I lied. "I talked to lots of people. I just didn't like any of them, and I didn't want them to buy me a drink. I've had enough."

"You talked to the two bouncers at the door, the bartender, and the gay guy who told you he liked your earrings. For the record, he wasn't all that into you."

"Shows how much you know," I said smugly. "I also talked quite a bit to a cracked-out dude who thought I was a coke dealer. So there."

"I'm sorry, what?" Bobby asked, unable to hide his amusement.

"I'll tell you about it tomorrow. I'm going home. Have fun."

I hit the sidewalk and walked away quickly, afraid that Bobby would chase after me and try to pressure me into staying. I crawled into bed twenty minutes later without bothering to wash the makeup off my face, trying to not let my first night out ruin my optimism about the dating project and my hope for a summer of personal growth. The bitch of it was, someone, somewhere, who incidentally was about to be cheated on, thought that that girl in the ladies' room was marriage material, a girl worth spending the rest of his life with. I tried very hard not to focus on the fact that if this night was any indication, the only thing anyone thought I was good for was an eight ball of cocaine.

CHAPTER 8

Leave It to Me to Stump *Webster's*

TUESDAY MORNING, at the beginning of my first official week in Newport, I worked up my courage and walked into the store with the HELP WANTED sign in its window. Grace had gone back to the city for the workweek, and I was feeling at loose ends. It was time to get my life back in gear. I stood outside for a few minutes watching ladies enter and roam around the store, buying candles and straw handbags and other essential summer items. After about ten minutes of standing on the sidewalk, I pushed open the screen door and entered the store. I was immediately overcome by the smells of scented beach candles and potpourri. I wanted this job badly. I felt like somehow it was so much more than a job. It was the fresh start that I desperately needed.

I walked up to the register, sidestepping a wicker basket overflowing with striped throw blankets. I smiled at the woman sitting behind the counter, flipping through papers in a navy blue folder. She was classically pretty, with long blond hair and deep blue eyes. She was wearing khaki shorts that all but hung from her thin frame, a loose white T-shirt, and canvas sandals.

"Hi," I tried to say, but my voice caught in my chest. I cleared my throat and tried to speak clearly. "My name's Abby, and I'm here about the HELP WANTED sign," I said nervously. I hadn't applied for a job in a very long time. I forgot how much I hated it.

"Oh hi," the slight woman behind the register said as she extended her hand to greet me. "I'm the owner, Lara Richards. Nice to meet you."

Lara Richards? I stared at her a second longer than I should have, trying to figure out if she was the person I thought she was.

"I'm sorry, this is going to sound crazy, but did you go to Milton Academy?" I asked. She was understandably taken aback by a reference to high school. We were in our thirties now. At some point you don't want to be recognized for who you were fifteen years ago.

"I did. I'm sorry, do we know each other?" she asked curiously.

To say we knew each other would be a stretch. Lara was the most popular girl in our high school. She was the head cheerleader, in the National Honor Society, and drove a super-cool red Saab. She was one of those annoyingly fit, blond, and naturally jovial girls who might as well have jumped off the pages of a Sweet Valley High book. She was three years older than I was in school, so I admired her from afar—and by "admire" I mean I was so insanely jealous of her that I couldn't even bring myself to be in the same room with her. Which was a good thing for me, because for all of high school she pretended that the underclassmen didn't exist. So no, the short answer to her question was, she didn't know me.

"Not really, sorry, I don't mean to sound creepy. I went to Milton too. I was a few years younger than you were, but I recognized your name. I'm Abby Wilkes."

"Oh, what a small world. It's nice to meet you, Abby," she said with a smile.

"You too, Lara. You haven't changed at all since high school."

"High school," she sighed as she stared vacantly out the window overlooking the street. "How much would you give to have your biggest problem be that you didn't finish your math homework?" she said, her smile helping to break the ice.

"Or lost a field hockey game?" I suggested.

"Or ripped your friend's favorite sweater?"

"Who told you?" I joked.

Her eyes suddenly grew cloudy as she continued. "Unfortunately, things these days are a lot more complicated than they used to be."

"I hear you, believe me." We stood in awkward silence for a moment as Lara's mind drifted off somewhere else, before she shut her eyes tightly and returned to reality. I immediately liked Lara. Why was it so easy to find women you clicked with in an instant and thirty-one years on this earth wasn't enough time to find a guy who didn't have a severe mental problem?

"So this is your store?" I asked, hoping to return the focus of the conversation back to the fact that I needed a job and she needed help.

"It is. I knew the previous owner, and when I heard she was selling it, I jumped at the opportunity. My husband, Mark, and I were living in Atlanta, but then he had a great job opportunity in Boston, and I really wanted to move back north. My parents live in the area, so it sort of worked out perfectly."

"Congratulations, the place looks great. A perfect spot for all your beachy needs," I chirped, trying a little too hard to convince her I was the girl for the job.

I found myself intrigued by her decision to move home. It seemed odd (to me at least) to give up the yearlong warmth and sunshine of Georgia to be buried under snow and wearing roll-neck sweaters until April in Rhode Island. I looked at her again and was struck by how little she had changed from how I remembered her. She had the same blue eyes, the same perfect nose, the same friendly look, and even now, a twenty-six-inch waist. Just in case I needed another reason to envy her.

"Yeah, I like to think so. It's not much, but I love it." She looked at a display piece that was overflowing with starfish coasters, nautically themed linen napkins, and huge chip-and-dip trays decorated with multicolored flip-flops. The store had everything you'd need to entertain, every knickknack you could ever want in a beach house.

"So what brings you to Newport? Just escaping the city for the summer?" she asked.

"Yeah. I thought it'd be a nice change of scene. I'm getting over a breakup and thought getting out of town would be a good idea."

As soon as the words came out of my mouth I wanted to take them back. I'd gone to Newport so that people wouldn't know what had happened to me. Not so I could tell people within five minutes of meeting them. I didn't want to be one of those girls who couldn't shut up about her relationship problems. The problem was that I'd been one of those girls who couldn't shut up about her relationship problems for the last six months. I needed to add that to the list of habits that needed breaking as soon as was humanly possible.

"Ah, a breakup escape hatch," she said as she once again stared blankly out the window and fidgeted with the wedding band on her left ring finger.

"Kind of. Anyway, I don't want to harp on it. I'm happy I'm here, and if I can help you out with the store, I'd like to."

She stared at her hand and started to slowly twist her wedding ring around in clockwise circles. "Well," she said with a slight smile, "I think that sounds like a good plan. Anyway, this is great! How funny that our paths would cross again like this."

"I think it's a sign," I said somewhat awkwardly. "We Milton girls need to stick together."

"You're not going to start singing the fight song on me, are you?"

"No," I admitted. "Probably only because I don't remember it."

"You're lucky. All those years of cheerleading has it burned into my brain. So I really need help organizing the store. It's small, but we carry a ton of stuff, so I'm going for a shabby-chic, overcluttered type of look. How are your organizational skills?"

"Well, I teach kindergarten for a living, and since the kids in my class don't seem to care too much about being orderly, I've sort of mastered it," I laughed.

That was only partially true. I was a highly organized person, but it had as much to do with my profession as it had to do with my breakup. After everything happened, I had tried to restore some kind of order to my life by becoming obsessively neat. I color-coded my closets, folded all the clothes in my drawers, even my socks, and actually went so far as to alphabetize my spice rack. None of it really helped to ease the pain of losing Ben, but it was kind of comforting to know that I could locate the cinnamon right next to the cloves should some sort of spontaneous bake-off erupt in my apartment.

"Great! I need help unloading the inventory and marking all the prices, plus I'll need some help working the register and with the occasional gift wrap. Things like that. Obviously the store is small, so I only need someone part-time. Ideally I need someone to work Wednesdays, when our new inventory arrives, and Saturdays to help with the weekenders. Does that work for you?"

"That sounds perfect."

"Good! The pay isn't great, but it's more than you'd make babysitting." She told me the hourly rate, which wasn't much above minimum, but I didn't care. I just wanted the job. "So if you're still interested, I have a shipment coming next Wednesday that I'll need help unpacking. Do you think you could start then?"

"No problem, I'll be here at nine o'clock, is that okay?"

"That would be perfect."

"Okay," I said. "I'll see you next week." She waved good-bye as I slowly pushed open the screen door and let it close quietly behind me.

I put my hands in my pockets and turned to walk back to the house, feeling pretty good about myself for taking a step, even a small one, into my new life without Ben. It felt strange, having a part-time job be such a big step for me at this stage of my life. I thought about why the relationship road was so easy for some people and, for reasons unknown, so exponentially harder for others. Now that I was in my thirties, I worried that I was going to be one of those people who never really knew true love. I was pretty sure the dictionary would not call my relationship with Ben true love, or it wouldn't have ended the way it did. I actually don't think the English language could possibly define whatever the hell that was.

Leave it to me to stump *Webster's.*

I was deep in my "time to face the music 'cause the fat lady is singing" thought when my phone beeped, displaying a text message from Wolf.

> **Hey little Abs, me and some European friends are heading out to watch the German team play in the Euro Cup football games. European football, not American football. I don't understand that game. Come meet us at the Red Parrott. We'll be there in fifteen. P.S. It's an important game. I repeat, the Germans are playing. Auf Wiedersehen.**

I checked the time: 2:00. I debated ignoring Wolf's invitation, if for no other reason than to avoid Bobby, who no doubt would be there, hitting on European women who probably didn't speak English all that well. I knew that these were the types of things I should be going to if I wanted to meet people on this side of cyberspace: friends of friends, smaller groups, specific sporting events. The problem was, I really wanted to go home to my book, a hot shower, and maybe, if I was being honest with myself, a dish of ice cream. This was the typical tug-of-war that I had been fighting with myself since Ben and I broke up. I wasn't twenty-two anymore. Most nights I didn't want to be out in the bars mingling and flirting in the hopes of finding a guy. I wanted to be home in comfy pajamas drinking wine on the couch. The real big problem with this was that I was pretty sure I wasn't going to meet anyone sitting on my couch with a glass of wine, unless of course someone broke into the house and decided to stop and have a glass of Cabernet. Although stranger things have probably happened. This was Rhode Island after all—the criminals were probably more refined.

I thought about what to do as I walked home when my phone rang. I looked at the caller ID and sighed. I loved my mother, I really did, but she didn't make it easy. No matter how good her intentions were, she always managed to make things harder than they needed to be. If the road to hell is really paved with good intentions, my mother will be going on the express bus. *You should answer it,* I said to myself. *You can't hide forever. Answer the phone.*

"Hi, Mom," I said, all of my energy sucked out of my body before she even said a word. That was a skill. The woman could make plants wilt just by entering a room.

"Hi, Abby. How's the beach? You're staying out of the sun, aren't you? You're not a young girl anymore, *and* you're single. You need to wear sunscreen—you have *mature* skin now—really *slather* it on. You can't be too careful, your days of not having to worry about wrinkles are over, I'm sorry to say."

My mother the wordsmith.

My mother had been straddling the line between crazy and clueless her whole life and had no idea how to deliver advice without making you feel like you were smacked with a blunt object. She believed that it was her job to tell you the truth even when you didn't ask for it. It made for difficult teenage years, to say the least.

"Thanks for the tip. Is there a reason you called? Other than to remind me that I'm single and alone?" I should *not* have picked up this phone call.

"We need to talk about the limos for your sister's wedding."

"Why exactly?" I asked. I could think of no reason we needed to discuss that.

"We're going to use the same cars that you were going to use because they're lovely and people should be able to see me getting out of a limo at one of my daughters' weddings, don't you think?"

"I don't know how many times I have to remind you, Mom, that my broken engagement was not my fault and this is not about you!"

"Tell that to all the ladies in my bridge club. Do you know how hard it's been for me to show my face there?"

"Why, did you overdo your lip injections again?"

"Don't talk to your mother like that."

"Don't talk to your daughter like that."

"Can you at least pretend to be happy to hear from me?" she asked, pretending her feelings were hurt, which was impossible since I was pretty sure she didn't have any.

"Sorry. Seriously, what did you want to talk to me about?"

"Do you think I'd look better in a black or a white car?"

I felt like telling her she'd look best lying under one with only her legs sticking out, like the Wicked Witch of the East when the house fell on her, but that probably wasn't a nice thing to say to your mother. Even if she was a witch.

"You called to ask me that?" *Why, why, why did I answer this call?*

"There will be photographers, dear. People will be looking at these pictures for years to come, and you of all people should know that details matter."

"What's that supposed to mean?"

"Oh nothing." Silence. And then she clearly couldn't help herself. "Only, if you had paid more attention to the details in your own life, like the ones that should have alerted you to your fiancé skipping town without you, maybe you could've prevented *that* mess from happening."

"Are you sure I wasn't switched at birth?"

"I'm not answering that. By the way, have you slimmed down at all?"

"I'm not answering that."

"I'll take that as a no. Have you thought about doing one of those juice cleanses before the wedding? Julie Brink's daughter did one and lost about four pounds in just one week. I know that losing the weight has been frustrating for you. Maybe that will be a good jump-start to get you moving in the right direction."

"You want me to pay money to not chew so that I can look presentable in that disgusting pink dress? Are you kidding?"

"Just because the dress is ugly doesn't mean you have to be. It's not an excuse to not look your best. That's all I'm saying."

"Get the black car, Mom." The color of evil.

I hung up and fought back the urge to stand in the middle of the street and scream in frustration. I had been trying for thirty-one years not to let my mother get to me, but had yet to figure out how to make that possible. I stared at my phone for a minute before sending an emergency text to the only other person on earth who really understood how screwed-up my mother was and, like me, was stuck with her until death did them part. Her older—and somehow normal—sister, my aunt Patrice.

Mayday. She's going to drive me crazy Aunt Patrice, she really is.

Sadly she can have that effect on people. Shall I come down to Newport next week? Let's have lunch.

You wouldn't mind? How's next Tuesday?

Great. I'll make a reservation at Castle Hill. Cheer up, whatever she said, she didn't mean it.

Feeling somewhat better that my fairy god-aunt was coming to my rescue, as she always did when my mother pushed me to the brink of hysteria, I decided that I'd join the guys at the bar. I needed a drink, which was completely normal following a conversation with my mother.

I headed over to meet the boys and pretend that I was interested in, or even knew anything, about European football when my phone beeped again. I figured it was Wolf telling me that I was missing the greatest feat of German athleticism ever seen. But no. It was Ben.

Thinking of you

I knew I shouldn't reply. I mentally went over the pros and cons of responding. The con list was seventeen pages long. The pro list was blank. Oh well. I replied:

Thinking of you too.

I didn't know why I couldn't just let him go. The problem was that every time he wrote me I kept hoping that he would have changed his mind, admit that he had made a mistake, and come back. It had been months, and I knew deep down the window for that happening had already closed, but girls behave irrationally when they want something they can't have. Anyone can tell you that.

My phone beeped again.

Sorry, that actually wasn't for you.

So much for that.

I shouldn't have been surprised. Ben was always quite the sweet-talker. I loved when he whispered sweet nothings meant for somebody else into my phone.

Oops. I thought the message was from somebody else.

Good one, Abs, no way he'd see through that.

I was ashamed of myself and the fact that I still gave him the power to upset me from the opposite side of the country. I turned my phone off, something I only did on airplanes, threw it in my bag, and started walking again. If nothing else, at least I would spend happy hour with people who didn't tell their ex-fiancé by mistake that they were thinking of them when they weren't. At this moment, that was all I wanted.

I WALKED INTO THE BAR and scanned it for my new pseudo-friends. Wolf was glued to a TV, wearing a German soccer jersey, and Bobby was holding court at the bar, which from what I knew of him so far wasn't all that surprising. I reluctantly went and stood next to him, happy to have someone to talk to so that I didn't have to stand in the corner by myself or jump into the middle of the European soccer fans and risk being trampled if the refs made a call they didn't like. One thing I knew for sure: you didn't screw around with Europeans and their love of soccer.

"I'll have a martini, filthy, extra olives," Bobby said to the bartender as I dropped my bag on the floor next to his feet. He immediately looked up at me and smiled. "Well, look who it is. What's up, Abby?"

"Filthy? What kind of way is that to order a drink?" I asked. I was never a martini drinker myself, so I was unsure of the protocol for ordering one, but I was pretty sure saying you wanted a drink made filthy was not in the bartender's manual.

"It just means extra dirty, like not just a dirty martini, a filthy dirty martini. That's the way I like my cocktails. And my women. Nice to see you, by the way."

They should study this guy's brain for science.

"I've never met anyone who could turn ordering a cocktail into a sexually explicit event. Why can't you just be normal?" I heard myself ask the question and then realized how silly it sounded. He had a Y chromosome. What chance of normalcy did he really ever have?

"You know, if you think about it, you should be able to order your cocktails in more, shall we say, diverse ways. I should be able to order a dirty, filthy, slut martini without *someone* making a comment," he said, completely serious.

"And I'd like to order a man who's half-normal and only half-bat-shit-crazy, but that doesn't seem to be possible either, so I guess you and I will just have to suffer through our mutual disappointment."

"I'd like a really slutty martini on the rocks, hold the olives. How does that sound? Maybe I'll invent new cocktail names. Do you think there's any money in that?" he asked.

"I doubt it. But you're not working anyway and there's no money in that either, so if you want to be entrepreneurial, who am I to stop you? Maybe you could go on *The Apprentice* and see what Donald Trump thinks of your idea. He could sell it in the bars in some of his hotels. I'm sure his super-wealthy clientele in their thousand-dollar suits would be more than willing to drop twenty bucks on a drink called a Slutty Martini."

"See, now you're talking."

"I was kidding."

"I bet you someone thought that a cocktail called Sex on the Beach wouldn't be a hit either and look how fast that took off."

He actually had a point. There was also a drink called the Fuzzy Navel. I wouldn't have thought that would be popular either, and yet college kids all over the country were probably licking them off girls' stomachs in bars as we spoke. Bobby would probably invent the next big thing, become a gazillionaire, and spend the rest of his life trolling for girls in the bars all over the Eastern Seaboard with the tagline "I invented the Slutty Martini."

There's simply no justice in this world sometimes.

I ordered a beer, and when I turned back around, Bobby was still standing there, munching on an olive.

"Don't you have someone to hit on?" I asked.

"There's no rush. I'd rather talk to you right now. Besides, I'm sure I'll find someone. It's still early!"

"Lucky me."

"I talked to Grace before. Unlike you, she actually enjoys talking to me."

"There's no accounting for taste. And anyway, I think her taste in men is quite obviously flawed, no?"

"Ahh, that jackass of a boyfriend of hers. Though I don't know if I can really call him a jackass anymore. It sounds like he's making some real efforts lately. She seems happy for the first time in a while where he's concerned."

"I guess. I want her to be happy, but then again, I think she deserves so much better. I hate watching her go through this. Part of me wants them to break up because I think it'd be better for her in the long run, but I feel bad saying that. It's like, if it happened, I'd be sorry I wasn't sorry, you know what I mean?"

"You women are complicated creatures. Do you hear yourself?"

"Yeah, I know. Anyway, guess what?" I said, my excitement audible in my voice.

"You're going to tell me why your last relationship blew up? Was it another guy? Another woman? Wait, did you have another woman?"

"Sorry to disappoint you, but none of the above. I did, however, get the job. And the funny thing is, I know the owner from high school."

"Is it a guy?" he asked.

"No, why?"

"Because the only thing better than trying to pick up girls while they're at work is picking up a colleague *at* work," he answered flatly.

"I bet Grace would have some opinions on that topic. Dating in the workplace, bad idea."

"True. If you do and you find out you're just some dude's slam piece, you're screwed."

"Grace is not his slam piece! Don't talk about her like that, especially since I have no idea what a slam piece is."

Bobby laughed and placed his pornographic cocktail on the bar. "Okay, see I just learned something new about you. You're ferociously loyal. That's a good quality. I'm sorry. I wasn't trying to insult Grace, and I'll make sure I never do that in front of you again."

"I think that's a good idea." My mind started to drift, and for a second I completely checked out of the conversation we were having.

"Why don't you tell me what's really on your mind, Abby?" he asked as he waved his hand in front of my face to get me to refocus on the present.

"It's nothing." I sighed. It was the truth. It was nothing, and yet at the same time it was everything.

"It's pretty obvious it's something. I'm standing right here. Why don't you tell me whatever it is that has you so preoccupied."

"If you really want to know, I'm trying to figure out why the guys you want to stay around never do, and the ones you want to get rid of stick like pissed-off mice in glue traps. Why is that?" I asked. As hard as I tried to push thoughts about Ben to the back of my mind, they refused to stay there. There were so many of them bouncing around inside my head, I was surprised I could hear myself think at all.

"Am I supposed to be the mouse in this scenario?" he asked, confused.

"What? No. You're not the mouse," I answered, still distracted.

"Because I'm trying to be your friend here. I don't think comparing me to a rodent is the basis on which healthy friendships are started."

"I was thinking about all guys, guys in general. Not just you."

"Ahh, okay then. Well, maybe we're gluttons for punishment. Or maybe we like a challenge, so the girls who tell us to get lost are the ones we become most interested in."

"It can't be that simple."

"Guys are simple creatures. It's the girls who are crazy and complicated. Chew on that for a while, and when you're ready to admit that it actually might be that simple, you know where to find me," he said with a wink as he grabbed his martini and ambled over to a crowd of people on the other side of the bar.

I fished my phone out of my bag, hoping no one would notice it was turned off and I was only pretending to check it to appear busy, when someone over my shoulder said, "The scary thing is, that dirty slut martini might actually take off."

I turned and saw a stocky, friendly-looking guy with shaggy blond hair and dark eyes standing next to me. He was drinking a draft beer and smiling broadly, revealing a dimple in his left cheek.

"Believe me, I know. He'll probably end up having a bar named after him or be inducted into some kind of liquor hall of fame."

"Still, I don't know that I'd ever order a cocktail like that in front of a lady. Especially one I just met. With my luck, she wouldn't hear me correctly, would think I just called her a filthy slut, and throw a drink in my face."

"Do people still do that? Throw drinks in guys' faces?" I asked, sincerely interested. I figured that move went out with hair-twirling.

"I have a friend who gets it at least one a month."

"He must have a way with the ladies."

"A way to piss them off, yeah, definitely," he joked.

I smiled a genuine smile. This guy seemed nice, and as far as I could tell, he didn't have a forked tail or cloven hooves, so talking to him seemed harmless enough.

"I'm Abby," I said.

"Ryan," he replied as he shook my hand. "Are you from around here?"

"I'm from Boston, but I'm spending the summer here. You?"

"Yes and no."

"Consider me intrigued," I said as I took a sip of my drink. It was the best flirting move I could come up with on the fly now that I knew that straw-sucking wasn't an option.

"I just moved here from New York, so technically I'm from around here, yes, but I don't know anything about the area. I usually spend my summers in the Hamptons, so this is new for me."

"How does it compare so far?"

"So far they're pretty similar. There are fewer fedoras here, and it's nice to be able to walk places instead of dropping fifty bucks on cabs every night. It seems like a good time. So do you, by the way." Well, blond Ryan wasn't shy, that was for sure.

"And what makes you think that?" I asked, still trying to be flirty. No one who knew me would accuse me of being a good time. Not lately anyway.

I looked up and caught Bobby eyeing us from across the bar and making lewd gestures with his beer bottle. It was a wonder no one had snatched him off the market yet.

"Can I get you a drink?" Ryan asked as he gestured to the bartender.

"Anything except a filthy whore martini."

"How about a glass of wine?"

"Sure. I'll have a Sauvignon Blanc, please."

"You got it." This was going surprisingly well considering I had no idea how old he was, what his last name was, what he did for a living, or why he was talking to me. As soon as I had those details figured out, I was pretty sure that I was still going to think that this was going well. As long as he didn't tell me he moved to Boston because he broke up with his fiancée in New York City and wanted to travel.

He handed me a glass of wine. "So, I don't mean to be nosy, but that guy you were talking to, is he your boyfriend or something?"

I almost spit my wine all over the bar. Not exactly something you want to do in front of a guy unless you've been on at least three dates with him. "No, not at all. We have a mutual friend, but we just met over Memorial Day."

"Okay. I just wanted to make sure I'm not stepping on his toes."

"Rest assured, you're fine." *Interesting,* I thought. *Maybe there is such a thing as a guy code after all.*

"Good. In that case, do you mind if I ask if you're seeing anyone?"

There it was. The harmless question that hurt like a bitch. I'd have rather he'd asked me something less torturous, like, if I had ever had any venereal diseases.

"No, I'm not." And that was 100 percent true. I hadn't seen Ben in months. Had he asked me if I sometimes talked to my ex-fiancé, I'd have answered the question differently. Semantics matter.

"Well, I don't know a whole lot of people here, and I'm going to be back and forth on the weekends. Would you mind if I got your cell number? Maybe you'd like to get a drink sometime."

"I'd like that," I said, and it surprised me to realize that I meant it. *Look at me, I'm dating!* I thought to myself. *Grace would be so proud.* My dating project was only just started, and I was already kicking ass.

"Great, so let's have it." He took his iPhone from the pocket of his cargo shorts and programmed my number into it. I leaned against the bar, tucked a frizzy lock of hair behind my ear, and continued to have the first adult conversation I ever had with a guy who potentially wanted to date me. We spoke for a half-hour that felt like three minutes before he excused himself to go say hi to his friends who were crowded in the corner. Not long after he walked away, Bobby returned to order another drink and, apparently, to poke fun at me.

"So now you're going after guys who highlight their hair at home with Garnier Nutrisse or whatever hair care product Sarah Jessica Parker is hocking on TV?" he asked as he eyed Ryan off in the corner.

"First of all, those highlights are real, and second of all, it worries me that you can not only reference women's home hair color products but also their spokespeople. I wouldn't advertise that."

"I'm out of work at the moment. I watch a lot of TV."

"What channel, Lifetime? Because I doubt they're paying to advertise that particular product on ESPN."

"I fancy myself a Renaissance man, Abby."

"I fancy you a metrosexual, Bobby."

"I'm secure in my manhood."

"That makes one of us."

He laughed, the glint in his eye reminding me that he liked a challenge and that he enjoyed our combative conversations. If only Ben had been half as tenacious, maybe things would've worked out differently.

"See you later, Abby. Stay sassy," Bobby said as he knocked twice on the bar before turning to leave.

"Count on it," I replied as he sauntered away, his shoulder blades poking through the back of his dark green T-shirt. I felt myself smile for a second. If nothing else, Bobby was amusing, and there was nothing wrong with that. Especially these days.

CHAPTER 9

The Bitch Stole My Snack Pack

MY MOTHER WAS homecoming queen of her high school. I know this because she tells anyone who will listen. Even the checkout girl at the grocery store knows she was the head cheerleader, the most beautiful girl in town, and the one voted "Most Likely to Succeed." She was undeniably pretty and knew it—she used it to manipulate everyone around her into giving her what she wanted. One thing she was not voted was "Most Likely to Get Knocked Up by Her Boyfriend Senior Year of College." She married my father and had me a few months later, her twenty-two-year-old waist suddenly a distant memory, just like full nights of sleep and her dreams of being a newscaster and making her own money. Unlike most babies, I didn't come into this world as a joyous monument to my mother's future. I came into it as the reason for the sudden destruction of her past. A past she was by no means ready to let go of.

I was seven and my sister just five when my mother's unflinching vanity and immaturity finally became too much for my father to take, but I knew something was wrong long before that. I didn't have a difficult childhood, but I remember there being tension and sitting at the dinner table with no one speaking. I remember my father reading the newspaper and my mother microwaving Lean Cuisines, two people in the same room but in entirely different worlds. Some kids have memories of their parents fighting, of things breaking, of arguments so volatile the neighbors could hear them. I don't remember that. I remember silence. I remember my parents not even caring enough about each other to yell. I remember my mother being very good at pretending everything was fine. I think she's been pretending ever since.

Oddly enough, the yearbook didn't have a "Most Likely to Be Divorced with Two Kids by Thirty" either. Go figure.

After my dad left, she fixated on making him wish he'd never left her and proving that she was still the fairest in the land. After all, she was the envy of every girl in town when she was growing up, and she'd be damned if she was going to let him take that away from her. She became even more obsessed with her appearance, and more important, with ours, turning Katie and me into miniature versions of herself. She dressed us to the nines every time we left the house, always in smocked dresses, patterned hair bows, and patent-leather shoes. At home, we ate nothing but frozen diet meals and were forced to watch her do her aerobics video every afternoon before we could put on our cartoons. One year for show-and-tell, having already absorbed my mother's lessons on what was truly important in life, Katie dropped to the floor to show her classmates how to tighten your tush with Jane Fonda's leg lifts. Another time I made the silly mistake of taking a snack from one of the car-pool moms after soccer practice. My mother took one look at me, pudding cup in hand, and recoiled as if I were holding some kind of poisonous insect. She grabbed it from me and said, "A moment on the lips, a lifetime on the hips," as she threw it in the garbage. I was ten. I didn't have hips, and I didn't care. All I knew was that the bitch stole my snack pack.

Our relationship only went south from there.

When I was in high school, I came home from school one day and caught her trying to squeeze into my prom dress, somehow convinced that it was appropriate for a thirty-eight-year-old woman to wear her teenage daughter's dress. For a few minutes I was worried that she was going to try to steal my date. Not exactly the kind of problems normal mothers and daughters have. All I wanted was for her to drive a minivan and watch *Dr. Quinn, Medicine Woman* at night like everyone else's mom. I didn't want to worry about running into her at a keg party. It became very clear that she was never going to give me the kind of sage advice girls rely on their mothers for, unless you consider knowing that women over the age of forty are more likely to be hit by a meteorite than get married useful or accurate information for a teenager to have. It's not like my mother was asking the mirror every night if she was prettier than I was, but I felt like she was competing with me, that she envied me my youth and resented me for unintentionally taking her own. She might not have been a stepmother, but I'd seen enough Disney movies to know I'd be wise to be wary of her. Let's just say that if my mother handed me an apple, I'd think twice before I bit into it.

As an adult, I stopped thinking that my mother was born without the maternal gene that incited most women to bake cookies and read stories and do all the things that my mother could never do, and I accepted the truth. She never recovered from the humiliation of being dumped, and she let it morph her into a different person, one who clung to the past and the dreams she had before real life got in the way. We all fear turning into our mothers as we get older, but I wasn't just afraid, I was terrified. Over the years her narcissism had taken on a life of its own, and like any good fungus left unchecked, it had spread until it infected and ultimately destroyed everything in reach, including our relationship. I was worried that my premarital catastrophe would somehow result in my becoming like her. I knew it wouldn't manifest itself in quite the same way, as evidenced by the fact that I wasn't averse to chewing food as of yet, but the parallels were there. Fine, I'd never steal my kid's snack pack, but I was beginning to understand her, just a little, and I realized it was time for a very serious reality check.

The following week I waited for my aunt in one of the dining rooms at Castle Hill, a mansion on the bluffs that had been converted into an expensive hotel. I sat at a small table by the window overlooking the water and listened to the sounds of silverware clinking on china plates, diners engaged in pleasant conversations, and, eventually, the swish of my aunt's dress as she approached. She was a slight woman, only five-one, but she had an enormous personality and, more important, a healthy attitude about life. Her dark hair was swept back off her face, her dress was cinched snugly around her waist with a wide leather belt, and a scarf was draped around her shoulders. Aunt Patrice was everything my mother was not, and she had served as a surrogate mother for me for as long as I could remember. When my father passed away when I was in fourth grade, her husband, my uncle Mac, stepped in to fill the void, and now the two of them were basically my parents. They weren't able to have kids of their own, and I know it was hard for both of them, because they were naturals as parents. Instead, they became the best aunt and uncle a girl could ever ask for, and my aunt had taken over as the main role model in my life, always guiding me with her wisdom, humor, and love. I imagined that was what a normal mother would do, one who wasn't too busy telling a prepubescent child to worry about her hips or informing her that carrots have a deceptively high sugar content.

Aunt Patrice hugged me and planted a kiss on my cheek before taking a seat across from me. "So, let's save the pleasantries for later. What happened? Are you and your mother at it again?" she asked as she removed her scarf and hung it over the back of the chair.

I mindlessly traced circles on the tablecloth with my finger. "Not really. It's just more of the same stuff, you know? More of Mom being Mom."

"Your mother simply being your mother wouldn't have spurred you to text me, and certainly wouldn't have brought me down here for lunch. Did something happen? No one knows your mother better than I do. Whatever it is, I'll understand."

I grabbed the ends of my hair and twisted them, trying to quell my brimming tears. I was used to my mother's incapacity to love me the way a normal mother would. That wasn't what was bothering me. What was bothering me was my realization that history might be repeating itself.

I folded my hands in front of me as I spoke. "I'm so scared of becoming her, you know? I've spent my whole life trying not to be her, and all of a sudden I find myself being bitter and angry and skeptical of men and of life in general. What if I end up like her? Thinking that if I spend enough time loving myself I won't notice that no one else does?"

"You're being crazy. Lots of people love you, and lots of people love your mother. She's just a little selfish, and her brain is wired differently. She doesn't see the world the same way you and I do. I know sometimes she says and does things that are a little, how do I phrase this, unorthodox, but she doesn't mean to hurt you. Her heart is in the right place. It's her mouth that gets her into trouble."

"I know. What's bothering me is that I'm noticing some similarities these days. She never got over Dad leaving, and certainly not him dying. If he had stayed around, maybe she'd be different. If Ben had stayed, I'd be different too. For starters, I wouldn't be living in elastic pants. I look at her and I feel like I'm seeing myself in twenty years, and it terrifies me."

"Women get divorced every day. Your mother isn't the way she is because she's divorced—she's divorced because of the way she is. Your mother has spent her entire life refusing to grow up. Even after she had you guys, she was always selfish. Ultimately that's what ran your father off, God rest his soul. You didn't chase Ben away. He ran on his own because he's a coward who's not good enough for you. He never was."

"What if people start to say that about me?" I asked. " 'Once upon a time Abby was cute and fun and pulled together, but after Ben left she went to hell with herself and now she needs a crane to get out of her house.' It's not a far stretch. I'm just so scared that I'm going to spend all of my energy pretending that I'm fine to the point where I start to believe I really am. That's what happened to her. She drank her own Kool-Aid."

"Cut your mother some slack. She went through hell trying to figure out how to raise you girls on her own. Being a single parent isn't easy, and your mother did the best she could. You didn't see how scared she was. I don't defend some of the coping mechanisms she developed to deal with her divorce, but you have to at least try to understand her. Anyway, you don't have to worry about repeating her mistakes. When you're ready to move on, you will. I'm not worried about you," she said forcefully as she rested her elbows on the table, sunlight dancing off the gold bracelets on her wrist.

"What if the choice isn't mine to make? I've been thinking a lot about that kind of stuff lately," I admitted. It felt good to say it out loud.

"What stuff?" she asked.

"How life can surprise you. When you're little, you just assume that everything will work out. You think one day you'll look up and there'll be your Prince Charming on a white horse with a full head of hair and a dazzling white smile."

"There's a reason those fairy tales are geared toward little girls and not grown women who know better," she said with the authority of a woman who was wise enough to have relinquished the concept of perfection a long time ago. "In real life that hair is a toupee and that smile is a veneer. And for the record, the princess in that story is wearing Spanx and a Wonderbra. That's why those stories are called fairy tales and are not the headlines on the six o'clock news."

"I know, but now look at me. At my age, finding a guy who hasn't gone prematurely bald is like hitting the dating jackpot."

"You know, baldness never bothered me," Aunt Patrice said, tapping her manicured nail on the tablecloth. "At least you know what you're buying. What's infuriating is when you marry a guy who's in great shape and then ten years later he can't even see his toes. I knew I married a bald man. I had no idea there was a fat man hidden in that bald-headed body. Good thing I never loved your uncle Mac for his pecs," she said.

"You're missing my point," I said with a smile. "I can't help but feel like this fairy-tale nonsense that society beat into my brain when I was younger is partially responsible for my problems now."

"A cartoon didn't make Ben leave, Abby," she reminded me. Just in case I needed a reminder.

"No, not that. I'm just realizing that I'm so quick to judge people, you know? It's easy to find flaws in real live guys when you constantly compare them to the animated characters you watched when you were five."

"Right, just like guys have problems dealing with real live women after they spend three hours looking at *Playboy*. Fantasy isn't reality. You need to keep those two things separate or life is only going to get uglier from here. Stop being afraid of everyone. Stop looking for reasons to not try to be open to new relationships. You can't lock yourself in a tower because you're too afraid to live in the outside world."

"Maybe that's what all those princesses were doing. Maybe they decided they'd rather live on the far side of a moat and let their hair grow down to their asses than go on dates."

"I don't think that's what Walt had in mind."

"I hate Walt Disney. He completely fucked me up."

"Abigail, do you hear yourself? You're now blaming a man whose head is cryogenically frozen for your problems. Get out there and start dating. You might have some fun along the way. Did you ever think of that?"

"I'm trying," I said. "I actually gave my number to a guy I met last week. I haven't heard from him yet."

"That's fantastic! Does he have hair?" she said with a wink.

"Very funny."

"Just trying to lighten this lunch up a bit."

"The sad thing is that I was actually proud of myself for doing that, like giving out my cell number was some huge sign of progress. Do you know how pathetic that is?"

"Why's that pathetic? That's the first step toward meeting someone."

"Maybe, but I'm still going to be dateless for Katie's wedding. That's not going to do much for my self-esteem. As if this extra weight hasn't done enough damage."

"Listen, it's okay to be really pissed off by the timing of the wedding. It doesn't make you a bad person if you're struggling with it."

"I'm trying not to think about it," I said. "My mother reminding me that I'm fat doesn't help with that."

"You're not fat. And I doubt your mother meant to call you fat either. She's probably just trying to motivate you in her own way. She thinks you'll feel better about everything if you feel fit and beautiful. Anyway, I'm here to tell you, don't worry about it. A lot of people put on a few after they have bad breakups. I certainly did back before I met Mac."

"I guess."

"I'd rather you focus on fixing the you on the *inside.* Once you do that, I think you'll be surprised to realize that the weight will take care of itself. Get back out there and meet some people, at least try to. You might not find a Prince Charming, but it can still be fun to kiss some frogs. You know what I'm saying?"

"I do. I know you're right." She always was.

"Let's order. I'm starving," she said, opening her menu.

"Me too," I sighed, looking down at my thighs. "I guess I'll just get a salad."

I stared at the bread basket, resisting the urge to devour a roll. I wasn't about to do a juice cleanse, but it wouldn't kill me to lay off the carbs for the next few weeks either. Aunt Patrice read my mind and, as usual, said exactly what I needed to hear.

"Life's too short, Abby. Eat the goddamn bread."

CHAPTER 10

I Put Her in My Phone as Crosby, Stills, and Nash

THE FOLLOWING MORNING I reported for my first day of work. I spent the entire morning unloading boxes in the storage room, and the afternoon affixing price tags to the bottom of various pitchers, platters, and boxes of wine charms. Lara stayed in the front of the store working the register and dealing with customers, leaving me alone in the back, but I didn't mind. It felt nice to have a purpose without the pressure of having to make small talk. It was just me and my box cutter, and I couldn't have been happier.

I realized that working two days a week was turning out to be a perfect summer gig. It was great to finally have a routine, and for some reason going to work in Lara's little store gave a much-needed boost to my self-esteem. It was now the middle of June, and Newport was starting to feel like home. I didn't get lost when I ran, I didn't wake up in the morning feeling like I was in a strange bed, and I didn't feel like

I was still in the "getting to know you" phase with the guys. They were now officially my friends, and I hoped that once I was allowed out of the stockroom, Lara would become one as well.

I figured if Ryan had called me right after we met, that would have seemed too forward, and I was convinced that after the first week had passed I'd hear from him. I had been cautiously optimistic on Monday, hopeful on Tuesday, confused on Thursday. Then I started checking the personals to make sure that Ben hadn't taken out an ad declaring me a man-eater and telling guys to stay away.

"Hey, Abby, did you ever hear from the blond guy you met at the bar last week? What was his name? Ryan?" Grace asked as she smoothed moisturizer over her legs on Friday night while sitting on our couch. Bobby was rummaging through our cabinets, trying to block out the girl talk and find himself something to eat, while I stood at the stove and tried to make dinner for us, which wasn't saying a lot. The only thing I knew how to make was pasta. I figured if I threw some basil and tomatoes into the mix, it would at least be edible. I hadn't been to Bobby's house yet—there was no reason to since he spent most of his time at ours—but I was pretty sure his cabinets contained nothing but packs of cigarettes and mouse traps.

The first thing Grace asked about now every time we spoke was for an update on Ryan. It had only been two weeks since I'd begun trying to date again, but meeting Ryan made me believe that maybe there was someone else out there for me. It was the best I remembered feeling in a long time, so I didn't mind being patient, but he was beginning to push it a little.

"Not yet," I admitted as I rummaged through a kitchen drawer looking for a spoon with a handle long enough to shove into the pot of water without burning my hand.

"Did you give him your number or your email?" she asked.

"My number actually. I don't want to hide behind email. I figured it was more mature to encourage an actual conversation. Aren't you impressed?"

"I am. The teacher gives you an A plus."

"Why, thank you. I'm trying to be positive, but I'm starting to get a little paranoid. Is it possible I'm being rejected by people I don't even know? Is that what I've been reduced to?"

"Nah, I'm sure you'll hear from him. He's probably just busy or something," Grace said as she examined her thoroughly moisturized legs. "Can I help?" she offered as she made her way into the kitchen. I handed her a container of cherry tomatoes I had picked up at the grocery store when I went on what seemed like my thousandth beer run.

"Sure, cut these, I guess," I said as she took the container from me and began to slice them in half.

"He's not busy. You won't hear from him," Bobby said as he removed a can of Budweiser from our refrigerator. If he didn't stop drinking our beer, I was going to start charging him. He was at our house all the time and spent most of it eating and drinking anything that wasn't toxic.

"Why in God's name would you say that?" I asked, surprised that he had the nerve to weigh in on something that didn't concern him, while drinking one of our beers, no less.

"Because if you're wondering why a guy hasn't called, it's because he's not going to call. You so clearly need my help with this, it's ridiculous. What did you ever do before you met me?"

"Slept better at night for starters, and made fewer trips to the grocery store," I said as I took a box of pasta from the cabinet and dumped spaghetti into boiling water, causing the scalding liquid to splash all over the stove. How some people could find cooking enjoyable was beyond me. "And you know what? I'm firing you and Wolf as wingmen. He said he was going to set me up with his friend Paul and never did. Why offer to help if you're going to flake out?"

"Relax! I'm sure he's working on it. Just keep your fingers crossed that this guy doesn't highlight his hair like the dude at the bar," Bobby said from the stool at the kitchen counter. I really wished I could find some way to keep him quiet, but sadly, short of stabbing him, I wouldn't be able to shut him up with anything less than duct tape or a muzzle, neither of which was handy at the moment.

"He does not highlight his hair!" I said, not sure why I felt the need to defend him.

"Okay, sure. Grown men over the age of thirty are still natural platinum blonds, right. Just like Grace over here is tan all year long without weekly appointments at the fake-and-bake salon."

"I have no idea what you're talking about," Grace said as she finished chopping the tomatoes.

"Why can't you just admit that some people, obviously not you, swam in the deep end of the gene pool instead of wading in the kiddie pool like you did?" I asked Bobby.

"No, no. That's fine. We will stick with male Barbie being au naturel. I'd bet if I saw him in the locker room, I could prove your theory wrong, but I'm on your side, so I'll let this one go."

"I hate you," I said.

"Whatever. Now, here is the million-dollar question: did you Google-stalk him?"

I wrinkled my brow in confusion, not understanding what he was getting at in the slightest. "No. Why would I do that?"

"He's Google-stalked you, I assure you."

"So what? I don't think anything comes up if you Google me."

"Wait, you're telling me you've never Googled yourself?" Bobby asked.

"No. Why would I? I know me. I don't need the Internet to tell me about myself."

"Well, for starters, every guy you've ever met has Googled you. You have no interest in knowing what they find when they do?"

"I'm boring. I'm a teacher, not Paris Hilton. I'm not all that concerned about someone finding a sex tape on the Internet."

"That's the first thing someone does after meeting you. I guarantee it," he said.

"So I'm being screened basically? Is that what you're saying?" I admit I Internet-stalked Ben, but it never occurred to me that maybe cyber-stalking was a two-way street. Again, maybe I am that stupid.

"Absolutely. Which is why you need to make sure when you Google your name no absolute freaks show up. If the first few options for 'Abigail Wilkes' are all train wrecks, he won't even keep looking. He'll just fold his cards, forfeit the hand, and you will never hear from him again. I guarantee that's what happened. He's gone."

"That's insane. You know how many people out there probably have the same name as I do?"

"Great point! Let's see what comes up when we Google you, Abby." Bobby grabbed my iPad off the counter. "Is it weird that I'm excited to do this?"

"Yes," Grace and I replied simultaneously.

I watched as Bobby entered my name into the search engine and felt the color drain from my face when he began laughing uncontrollably.

"What?" I asked as I lunged for the iPad. "What are you laughing at?"

"You were on the debate team in junior high?" he asked as he scrolled through the article he was reading. "Oh, this is amazing. It explains so much, now that I think about it. You are unusually good at verbal sparring."

"So what? I was trying to broaden my résumé so that I could get into a good college. I don't apologize for that!"

"Not only were you on the debate team, you were the captain of the debate team! This is bad enough, because it screams geek squad, but this picture—Abby, this picture is just fantastic," Bobby said sarcastically.

I finally managed to snatch the iPad away from him and froze in horror at the image staring back at me. There I was, front and center in the picture of our debate team, right after we won the district championship. I was smiling broadly with the gold medal hanging around my neck, which in and of itself would've been okay. The real problem was that eighth grade wasn't exactly kind to me. I had full-blown acne, braces, and frizzy hair that resulted from a misguided attempt to home-perm my hair one afternoon when I decided I wanted to look like Bernadette Peters for reasons that still escape me. It was awful. It was the reason I avoided mirrors for a solid six months that year and the reason my mother canceled our charge account at the local drugstore. And now this picture was on the Internet, for all eternity. It was official: I was going to die alone.

"That is so not fair, I'm twelve years old in that picture! I'd love to see what you looked like at that age. No normal guy would ever use that picture as a reason to not contact a grown woman!" I cried, hoping that what I was saying was true.

"I agree with you, but here's what we learned from this little Internet search: one, you're smart and not afraid to argue with people, and two, you were probably tormented in junior high and in all likelihood have deep-seated insecurities as a result. See? Now I have a better idea of who I'm dealing with."

"Well what do you suggest I do? Petition Google to remove any pictures of me taken before high school? I cannot stand that this is what the world has been reduced to. This type of information should only be revealed to someone once you're in a serious relationship. It shouldn't be common knowledge for any shallow moron to see."

"That's why Facebook is the single best thing to happen to the dating world. You can control what pictures you put up there. You can control what information you release for all the shallow morons to see. If you know one person in common, you can weed out all the randoms and find the exact person you're looking for, so you're positive before you email that you're not writing a muppet with a unibrow or adult acne. You see what I'm saying? Facebook shall set you free," he said flatly.

"I'm not on Facebook anymore. In fact, Mark Zuckerberg is lucky I don't sue him for aiding and abetting an asshole." I now hated Facebook the way most people hated telemarketers. The day I deactivated my account I swore I would never visit the site again. Now, once again, Facebook was biting me in the ass like it was mad at me. Which is odd, because I swear I never did anything to it.

"Which is why you won't hear from him. He's assuming that any girl who's not on Facebook, or worse, who's on it but won't post any pictures, is ugly. He thinks you look like Shrek. Unless you get back on there and post a hot picture of yourself, never plan on hearing from any prospective blind dates, ever," he replied.

"It's not blind. I met him at the bar, remember? You were there!"

"That's a technicality. The bar was dark, he was drunk, and he had probably hit on twenty girls throughout the course of the night, and the only things he remembers seeing—at best—are your ass and your profile. Trust me, he has no clue what you look like. He was just tossing a wide net, well aware he'd be throwing back the bottom-feeders. He probably didn't even put you in his phone under your real name."

"What's that supposed to mean? How else would he have programmed me in there?" I asked.

"He looked up your real name on Facebook and then reprogrammed your number in his phone under any number of useful mnemonic devices to help keep the chick catalog straight in his head. I mean, Grace has been calling him The Guy from the Bird Bar. Maybe you're in there as Bird Bitch. Who knows? Guys who are actively dating will rarely use real names. It's way too hard to keep all the girls straight, and if you accidentally mix up stories or names you look like a womanizer, and there's no coming back from that. It's just easier this way. I met a girl named Tara Crosby once, or was it Tina? Anyway, I put her in my phone as Crosby, Stills, and Nash. I wonder what happened to her now that I think about it," he said.

"And that was how you remembered who she was?" I asked, shocked that guys in their thirties adopted such immature tactics.

"Yup. If she drunk-dialed me a month later, I wouldn't have remembered who Tara was. But Crosby, Stills, and Nash, that would've rung a bell. I once put a girl in my phone who was only visiting for a weekend as LN, which stood for Last Night. I doubt Blondie came up with anything that clever, but you get the gist."

I was really beginning to despise modern technology.

"You guys are all pigs," Grace said as she hopped up off her chair, removed a bottle of wine from the rack, and began fishing through the kitchen drawers for the corkscrew.

Before I could probe Bobby further as to how common this practice was, Wolf returned from a run and popped into our living room, his earphones hanging around his sweaty neck like a scarf.

"Hey, guys. What are we talking about?" he asked as he went straight to the kitchen and removed a bottle of coconut water from the fridge. *That's it,* I thought. *I'm padlocking the refrigerator.*

"Abby being ditched by a guy who highlights his hair," Bobby said.

"Would you shut up about that?" I yelled. "Wolf, I thought you were going to set me up with Paul. What happened to that?"

"Oh, I forgot to tell you that I talked to him on Monday. He wants to meet you, little Abs! You're set for next week. Saturday night, okay?"

"And here you were ready to fire poor Wolf when he's been working so hard to find you a man."

"I don't want to be fired!" Wolf said. "Fired from what?"

"Don't worry about it, Wolf. Thanks so much for setting this up! I'm looking forward to it. Ignore Bobby. He's an idiot."

"Okeydokey," Wolf said with a shrug.

"What are you mad at me for?" Bobby asked.

"I'm not mad. I'm still shocked that you use memory devices for girls in your phone. I mean, how many girls can you possibly date at one time? Crosby, Stills, and Nash? Seriously?"

"Yep. I thought it sounded cooler than putting her in there as Bing Crosby, don't you think? And to be clear here, these aren't girls I was actually dating. They're just girls I met. Half of them I never saw again."

"Who's Bing Crosby?" Wolf asked, understandably confused after walking into the middle of this ridiculous conversation. Though it was equally unnerving to find out there was someone on this planet who didn't know who Bing Crosby was.

"Almost a nickname for a girl I met once," Bobby replied nonchalantly.

"I don't get it," Wolf said.

"My thoughts exactly," I said. At least someone else in this room was normal. It seemed the foreign national and myself were the only people who weren't aware that this was common practice. I wasn't sure what to think about that.

"American girls are weird," Wolf added as he shook his head, perplexed.

"No, we're not," I said in defense of girls everywhere, which really wasn't a fair assessment. I knew some who should be wearing straitjackets for sure.

"Oh yes, you are," Bobby said as he stretched his arms above his head.

"Well, look at what we're dealing with. If you're the prime example of today's man, no wonder some of us have gone a bit batty. You are the poster child for dysfunction," I teased. If we were going to have this conversation, then I was going to have a drink. I motioned to Grace to pour me a glass too.

"I'm a shining example of what a normal, red-blooded American male is thinking. I told you, you should use me a resource," Bobby reminded me.

"I think the saltwater has damaged your brain," I said, still reeling from the possibility that Ryan had saved my number in his phone under something other than "Abby." I was beginning to understand why some girls stole phones and searched them. Maybe they weren't that crazy after all.

"Fine, whatever, don't listen to me, but you're only hurting yourself. Why aren't you on Facebook anyway? I looked you up after Grace said you were staying in the house. You're the only girl I know who doesn't have an active profile."

I refused to answer his question. I was not about to tell Bobby what had led me down the road to deactivation. So I lied. "For that exact reason. I don't want guys like you making predetermined judgments about me before you even meet me. And besides, every girl I know uses that stupid thing to spy on people or just be nosy (myself included). No thanks. I'd rather not subject myself to that. I value my privacy."

"Well, if Grace hadn't promised me you weren't a troll, I might have thought twice about hanging with you all summer. I'm telling you, it matters."

"Gee, thanks. You sure do know how to give a compliment," I said, poking the pasta with the spoon to see if it was still crunchy.

"Look, we can solve your problems right now. Go put your bikini back on and go sit on the deck with a cocktail, and I'll take your picture. Better yet, only put on the bottom and I'll take your picture. Then we'll set your profile up again and wait for the floodgates to open."

"Okay, that is ridiculous," Grace said in my defense as she sipped her wine. "No guy is that shallow. She could get fired for doing something like that. I'd imagine the nuns at her school prefer their teachers to keep their clothes on."

"We are *all* that shallow," Bobby deadpanned.

"See, this is the problem with dating," I said as I turned my focus solely on Bobby because he was the only American-born male in the room and therefore the only worthy recipient of my wrath. "Do you realize how stupid this has all become?"

"What?" he asked, defensively.

"You think I'm crazy for not allowing myself to be cyber-stalked by strangers, because that's your idea of how to date. It's just so lazy! No one picks up the phone and calls a girl anymore to ask her out. First, he does a complete background check and then writes something on her Facebook wall. How is that going to get a girl excited to date you? Don't feel like chatting? Send a text. Send an email. Send an IM. Don't feel like making the effort to get off the couch, but your laziness is about to send your would-be girlfriend over the edge of reason? Skype. Face-time. No problem. Modern technology has made it possible for guys to not have to do anything, or even be physically present, and still think they're dating! Our generation's idea of a love letter is a late-night drunk text asking if you have any more beer in the fridge. You heard it here first, kids. Romance is dead."

"Speaking of, do you have any more beer in your fridge?" Bobby asked as he stood up from the couch with his hands up, as if he were surrendering to authorities.

"Grace, help me out here. You know I'm right." I looked at her, but she just shrugged.

"I don't really know. Johnny calls me all the time, plus I see him at work every day. I never had these problems, so I can't help you," she said. Since their fight over Memorial Day, things seemed to have improved between them.

"I'm just giving you the guy perspective," Bobby added, as if he was the only guy on earth I had to talk to. That might very well have been true, but he didn't have to be so smug about it. "I'm trying to help you, but if you don't want to listen to me, that's fine. Just keep in mind that I have lots of girlfriends, and well, you're getting negged by strange dudes simply because you're not on Facebook."

"If you think not being on Facebook is the reason why I never heard from Ryan, you're wrong. You have no idea what you're talking about," I declared with defiance, even though there was a very small part of my brain that was wondering if he was right.

"You have a better explanation?"

"Maybe he's dead."

"You're right. Death is a way better alternative."

"I refuse to believe that that's the reason. I just won't. And I am not going to start using Facebook again. No way."

"Suit yourself. And enjoy waiting for your phone to ring." He pulled open the screen door and went to sit on one of the chairs outside. For someone who barely knew me, he clearly had no problem telling me what he thought of me, my life, and my current social situation. And yet, I oddly enjoyed talking to him. I really was a lightning rod for the deranged.

My phone didn't stay silent for long. When I was straining the now-overcooked pasta into a colander, I did get a message, just not from anyone I wanted to hear from.

Hey you. How's Newport?

It was Ben.

It's good. How's it going there?

I waited and waited and with each passing moment hated myself more for caring, and worse, for letting him know that I cared. Five minutes later he responded. I wanted him to tell me he was lonely. I wanted him to tell me he was bored. I wanted him to tell me he had fallen into a canyon and was in traction. Not exactly.

Not bad, actually. They have these outdoor movies here, they're great, you'd love them. Now there's something you can't do all year round in Boston. I'm running out to see one now. Have fun.

I shook my head in disgust and tried to not let myself care that Ben had just told me he was going on yet another date. Whatever, he was someone else's problem now, and as I looked around the kitchen at my new friends I told myself, whoever she was, she could have him. Wolf pulled plates out of the cabinet, and I poured the pasta into a large serving bowl and tossed it with some basil leaves, Grace's tomatoes, and cheese. "Looks yummy," Wolf said as he grabbed the bowl and took it outside to the table on the deck. Grace gathered the wine and the silverware, and I took the plates and a basket of bread, and we all headed outside to have dinner.

"Abby," Bobby asked from the other side of the table as he grabbed a piece of bread from the basket. "Do you want to see my Facebook page? Maybe I can throw some pictures from the summer up there and tag you in them so your ex can see you having fun with a handsome stranger. That would be fun, wouldn't it?" He laughed to himself, and I couldn't help but smile. It would be kind of fun, but I didn't care enough anymore to even try and make Ben mad. He could live his life, and I would live mine, thousands of miles away, at the beach, with my new friends, and maybe, just maybe, a new guy in my life. I clung to this thought all through dinner—that Ryan was just playing a little too hard to get, but would eventually reach out like he said he would. Later that night, I crawled into bed with my phone, willing it to ring, but knowing deep down that it never would.

I AGREED TO MEET WOLF'S friend Paul the following Saturday at a Thai restaurant with outdoor seating and a killer selection of dumplings. Wolf showed me a picture of him he had on his phone so I would recognize him, and truth be told, I liked what I saw. He had a tall muscular build and, more important, dark hair that clearly had never seen the inside of a peroxide bottle, which made him one of the most normal guys I had met all summer. I spotted him immediately when I entered the bar, and without hesitation, I walked up to him and confidently tapped him on the shoulder. "Hi, are you Paul?" I asked. He turned and smiled at me, immediately making me feel comfortable—or at least I would have been if I wasn't distracted by the blisters that were covering his bottom lip.

"I am! You must be Abby. Wolf told me a lot about you, it's great to meet you!" he said, seeming at once friendly, easygoing, and, in all likelihood, contagious.

"He told me a lot about you too," I said, which wasn't exactly true. He did tell me that his name was Paul, but he failed to mention that Paul might or might not have some form of herpes.

"Do you want to get a drink? Pull up a stool," he said, motioning to the seat next to him. I sat down and smiled nervously before ordering a very stiff vodka tonic. "So Wolf told me that you're a teacher, is that right?" he asked.

"Yes," I replied. "I teach kindergarten. I love it, but it does leave me a good bit of spare time. I'm working at a little store down the street two days a week this summer to stay busy."

"You're lucky. I work in advertising, so I'm pretty busy all the time. I'd love some time off to concentrate on other things."

"It's one of the perks, that's for sure," I said. I didn't know what to do. Did I ask about the mouth blisters to make him feel at ease? Or would that be considered rude? Was I supposed to pretend that I didn't notice them? These were so not normal questions to ask oneself on a first date. I realized that the next time I felt unfit to be seen in public because I had a zit I should probably reconsider, since there were way worse ailments running around this island.

"What do you like to do in your spare time?" he asked. I wanted so badly to not be grossed out by the blisters he had all over his mouth, but I couldn't help it. I wasn't a shallow person, but did guys these days think that mouth sores didn't even warrant an explanation? I thought about asking if he'd had an allergic reaction to something, but I didn't know the protocol for handling uncomfortable and potentially contagious medical conditions. If there was one thing I had learned from my mother over the years it was that sometimes honesty is really not the best policy.

"I read a fair amount," I lied. Unless he considered the weekly tabloids or the latest edition of *Coastal Living* reading material, I hadn't read anything in ages. "What about you? What would you do if you had more spare time?"

"Actually, I'm a beekeeper. I'd do it full-time if it paid the bills, but sadly, it's just a hobby," he replied, as if that was the most normal thing in the world to say.

"I'm sorry, I don't think I understand. What do you mean you're a beekeeper?" I asked, completely convinced that I hadn't heard him correctly. I was pretty sure I still had water in my ears from my morning at the beach.

"I have honeycombs in my backyard. Have you ever tasted really fresh honey? It will blow your mind. I've been doing it for years. I absolutely love it."

"No, I get my honey from the plastic bear-shaped containers sold in the grocery store. I guess I'm a wimp that way. To be honest, bees scare me. I don't even like Honey Nut Cheerios." This was by far, one of the strangest hobbies I had ever heard of in my life. I wondered if maybe he was allergic to the bees, which would at least explain the blisters. *It might be time to get a new hobby, Paul,* I thought.

"You're missing out! Few people appreciate how beautiful bees are. There's so much more to them than most people understand," he said, staring dreamily into space as if it made him happy to just think about his insect friends. I was going to kill Wolf.

"Really? Like what?" I asked in what turned out to be a very, very stupid decision.

"I'm so glad you asked! I'd be happy to teach you a few things," he said. And he did. For the next hour and a half, I listened to him wax poetic about his love of bees and realized that Paul might have been a very nice guy, but he was oh so definitely not for me.

CHAPTER 11

A Lobster Named Snappy

WHEEZE, COUGH, WHEEZE, COUGH. My lungs once again battled through their oxygen assault as I trotted down Spring Street Sunday morning, dodging churchgoers leaving Sunday morning mass. I wasn't as out of shape as I used to be, my jogs not only had gotten longer but didn't feel quite as torturous as they used to, and I liked being able to actually clock the progress I was making in a tangible way. If only everything in life could be measured so easily. I had forgotten how much I loved the endorphin surge I got from exercising, one of many things I'd let Ben make me forget I enjoyed. Though I had a long way to go before I was back to pre-breakup fitness levels, I refused to let it frustrate me. There was a time not too long ago when I didn't even know where my running shoes were. The fact that they were now on my feet and being put to use was something to be proud of; the fact that I'd just managed to pass the two-mile mark without seeing spots was something worth freakin' celebrating. *Baby steps, Abby,* I told myself as I slowed and waited for my pulse to come down to levels that probably wouldn't set off any alarms at a cardiologist's office. *Baby steps.*

When I finished jogging, I walked down to the piers, where I quietly people-watched and enjoyed being inside my own head without wishing there was an escape hatch. Around noon, Grace, Bobby, and I grabbed our beach bags and headed over to the beach, dragging chairs and the essential cooler of beers with us. We were strolling along the sand, looking for a spot to set up for the next few hours, when I recognized the somewhat gaunt-looking woman walking toward us. It was Lara, flip-flops in hand and her mind somewhere else entirely, as evidenced by the fact that she almost ran directly into me before she realized who I was.

"Hey there!" I said as I stopped and gave her shoulder a quick squeeze hello. She wore a loose white tunic and sunglasses and was rubbing a stone I assumed she had picked up on the beach somewhere along the way. I turned to Grace and Bobby to introduce her and caught Bobby glancing at her left hand to see if she was someone he could hit on. He was visibly disappointed to discover she wasn't. "Guys, this is Lara, my new boss. Lara, these are my friends Grace and Bobby."

"Nice to meet you," Lara said. She was trying to be polite, but I got the feeling that she wasn't much interested in making small talk. Sometimes there's nothing worse than running into people when you had planned on being alone. I once ran into a friend of my mother's in the ice cream aisle, and I would have climbed inside one of the frozen food cases to get away from her.

"Hi!" Bobby and Grace said in unison.

"Did you have a nice weekend?" I asked.

"Kind of. I had to go to bridal shower just outside Providence last night, and I had to drive back here after it was over. I was so exhausted that I called my mom and begged her to work for me today so I could take the day off. One late night and I need about fifteen hours of sleep to make up for it. I feel like I'm getting old," she said as she glanced at the sand, at the parking lot, anywhere except at me, as if I might be able to read her mind or something.

"You're not old, you're tired! They're not the same thing. Besides, you deserve a day off, you can't work seven days a week, I'm pretty sure that's against labor laws."

"If it's not, it should be," Bobby added. "I should look into that."

"We're going to lie out for a while if you'd like to join us," I offered, even though I suspected she'd have rather drowned herself.

"Thanks, but I just came down here for a nice long walk. I'm going to head home, take a shower, and read for a bit. It was good to see you, though. Enjoy the beach and I'll see you later," she said as she walked away quickly.

"Okay, bye!" I called after her, unsure if she even heard me.

The three of us walked a few feet farther before we dropped our bags and set our towels down.

"Abby, what happened with Paul last night?" Bobby asked. "Was it as good as I think it was?"

"What's that supposed to mean? And no, it wasn't. He had blisters or something all over his mouth. He never even mentioned them, but I think it was herpes. Anyway, it doesn't matter. We have nothing in common. He's a beekeeper, and I have no interest in getting to know him or his bees—who have names, by the way—any better. We had two drinks, and then I left. I don't mean to sound like a bitch, but mouth sores and bees? Really? That's Wolf's idea of a good setup?"

"Well, someone didn't mind the sores or the bees. Wolf said he saw him on the Walk of Shame site this morning wearing a wrinkled button-down shirt and a big smile. No one wears long-sleeve dress shirts during the day at the beach, so clearly the guy never went home."

"Are you telling me that after our date he met someone else and went home with her?" I asked, horrified not only that he went out with another girl after me but that, whoever she was, she was willing to risk getting a sexually transmitted disease rather than go home alone.

"It seems that way. I guess the guy's got game."

"Guy's got the herp, Bobby!" I said, shocked that there were girls out there who didn't seem to think that was a problem.

"They were probably sun blisters from fishing, not herpes. Are you always this judgmental?" Bobby asked, as if I were being overly picky by passing on a guy with open sores on his mouth.

"You've got to be kidding me! I'm not being judgmental, I'm being hygienic!"

"Can we talk about something else, please?" Grace asked. "This conversation is grossing me out, and I'm tired of listening to you two bicker."

"Sure, what do you want to talk about?" I asked, relieved to change the topic.

"How about the fact that I am so over bridal showers it's a joke," Grace said. "It's like, yeah I get it, you're getting married, congrats. The world does not stop spinning for the rest of us who have better things to do than watch you sit in a pink tulle–covered chair and open toaster ovens." To anyone passing by, Grace might have sounded a little bitter, but the reality was, no one particularly enjoys going to showers of any kind unless they're the one receiving the gifts, and even then, showers can still be pretty painful. The two of us had probably attended about three hundred bridal showers—or more accurately, the same exact bridal shower three hundred times. Eventually, they get old for everyone. Then again, so does dating.

Bobby was used to getting stuck in the middle of girlie conversations, but I was pretty sure he didn't mind at all. He might have tried to hide it, but the truth was, Bobby was more in touch with his feminine side than he liked to admit. "I'm sorry," he said as he rubbed sunblock on his nose. "I think the whole concept is just stupid. Registries and all that stuff. Why should anyone have to buy you supplies for the life choice you made? I became a lawyer; I didn't ask anyone to buy me crystal beer mugs. Though now that I think about it, maybe I should have."

I laughed. Bobby had a way of phrasing the most obvious things that you never bothered to think about (and would probably never say out loud). "I agree," I said as I smoothed suntan lotion over my legs. "Do you have any idea how much money I've spent on other people getting married? Engagement gifts, shower gifts, bachelorette gifts, wedding gifts. The whole system is rigged. You get married, so I have to buy you All-Clad pots? How does that work?" I was trying to be supportive of Grace's frustrations, but I was lying through my teeth. I had loved registering. You really don't know power until you're set free in a department store with a registry scanning gun and allowed to zap anything your heart desires. To know that kind of power and then have it suddenly snatched away from you—it was simply too horrible to relive. It was like coming in last place in the appliance Olympics.

I figured that if I checked the wedding rulebook, it'd say that you're not officially engaged until you've had a bridal shower. And since I didn't make it that far, I was allowed to make fun of all the things that I never got to do. Kind of like a parting gift of sorts.

"Right?" Grace said as she mindlessly thumbed through a magazine. "I'm supposed to buy you top-of-the-line stuff when I can't afford it for myself, but you and your husband's combined income will now probably mean you can afford to buy a second home. Single people are fucked."

I laughed so hard I got a cramp. "Totally! And meanwhile, I'm still living in a miniature apartment drinking wine out of Solo cups and mugs from various airports, but I'm so glad I spent three hundred dollars to buy you Waterford wine goblets. I guess only married people deserve stemware."

"And don't forget, when they buy that second home, you'll be required to buy them more presents when you go to their housewarming to celebrate them being richer than you are," Grace added.

Even Bobby laughed at that. "I don't believe in those. If you buy a house and invite me to come see it, I don't think I'm required to bring you something. If I am, then I'd prefer to just not be invited. I really don't care what the wallpaper in the kitchen looks like, you know?"

Grace said, "By the way, I totally get that married people would call us bitter, but I think it's just being rational. And economical."

Bobby turned to face Grace. "So what do you consider to be the craziest gift you ever bought off a registry?"

She giggled. "I once got a girl a panini press. Do you believe that? Who eats enough sandwiches to need a panini press?"

"Actually, that sounds awesome," Bobby said. "I want one."

"Abby, back me up here," Grace said as she adjusted the strap on her suit. "Tell Bobby that it's ridiculous to ask someone to buy you a sandwich maker."

"Let's just say it's not a necessity," I admitted. I meant for it to sound like I was agreeing with Grace, but the truth was, I was so jealous I could barely breathe. I didn't think registering for that panini press was stupid in the slightest. Everyone knows you can't make a good grilled cheese without a really expensive sandwich press. I had registered for one myself, a top-of-the-line, shiny, grilled-cheese-making wonder-machine. I hadn't thought about it in a very long time. It hurt too much to remember the sandwiches that might have been.

"Well anyway, that's what I got her, and the truth is, hers wasn't anywhere near as crazy as some of the registries I've seen. I mean, I know girls who registered for $500 ice cream machines when I knew full well that they barely knew how to use their microwaves."

An ice cream machine! Why didn't I zap one of those? I thought.

Grace wasn't finished with her appliance tirade. "Or how about the crazy expensive coffee machines! Thanks for inviting me to your shower, and I know you like cappuccino, but that doesn't mean you need a professional machine in your apartment. News flash: there's a Dunkin' Donuts on every corner in the city."

"I had no idea that you could get all of that stuff when you get married," Bobby added. "Can people register for barbecues?"

"You can register for anything you want. It doesn't mean people will buy it for you, but sure," I answered. "Why are you asking?"

"If I ever get engaged, and I can't believe I'm going to say this, but I'm definitely going with my girlfriend when she registers. I could probably get a beer fridge, some barbecue tools, maybe even a cool recliner or something. Can you register at Home Depot?"

"Sure, and then you can be the subject of countless conversations like this one where people make fun of you for expecting them to buy you a recliner or bathroom tiles because of the life choice you made."

"Laugh away. You think I'll care while I'm reclining in my Barcalounger?" he asked.

We read our magazines and lay in silence for a few minutes, soaking up the sun and the quiet. Then Grace spoke.

"Your bag is ringing," she said. I had almost fallen asleep and didn't hear it. I reached over and dug my phone out of the plastic ziplock bag I kept it in when we went to the beach to keep sand from clogging the keys. I shielded my eyes to make out the number displayed on the caller ID. It was Wolf.

"What's up, Wolfie? How was golf?" I asked as I lowered the back of my chair a rung to get more sun on my face.

"Uh, hi there, little Abs," he said in his thick German accent. I loved that he called me "little Abs." It made me feel skinny. "You guys better maybe come back to your house now."

He sounded both happy and concerned. I didn't really care. The only reason I could find worthy of dragging myself off the beach during peak tanning hours was if the barbecue had exploded and the deck was on fire. Even then, he should be calling the fire department, not me.

"Why? I really don't see myself packing up and driving back there right now. I'm quite comfy."

"Well, uhh, see, I came over to borrow your headphones, and one thing led to other things, and right now there are about a dozen live lobsters crawling around your bathtub."

Clearly, he was joking. Or his English once again had hit an idiomatic snag. "I doubt that, Wolf. What are you talking about?"

"This box came addressed to Gracie. It said to open immediately because the contents were alive. So I opened the box, since no one was here, and there were twelve lobsters in there. They look very yummy. I didn't know what to do with them, so I put them in the bathtub, but I don't think you girls would like that very much, so maybe someone can come back here and tell me where the lobsters should live until I boil them for dinner. I think they'd go nicely with one of my bottles of Chardonnay, no?"

I sat upright in my chair and looked quizzically at Grace, who had now removed her sunglasses to peer at me directly, and Bobby, who was still busying himself with digging a giant hole in the sand for reasons unknown.

"Who are they from?" I asked, incredulous. "Who in God's name would send a dozen live lobsters to someone's beach rental?"

"It says from JF. I don't know who that is, but I like JF."

Well, I didn't see that coming. "We'll be right there," I said before hanging up. I turned to Grace. "Your deranged boyfriend sent us a box of lobsters!" I squealed. I don't really know what I expected him to do to show Grace that he was working toward ending his marriage and legitimizing their relationship, but I wasn't expecting shellfish. I saw a smile creep onto her face. It's amazing what makes girls happy.

"Aww, that's sweet!" Grace said. "Where did Wolf put them?"

"Right now there are a dozen sea cockroaches crawling around our bathtub. That's one of the most bizarre gestures I've ever heard of in my life!"

"It's nice!" she continued, defending her boyfriend.

"I think it's fantastic!" Bobby gushed. "I'll date this dude if he'll send me lobsters on a regular basis."

"Maybe you're right," I sighed, not wanting to deflate Grace's happiness. "I give him points for getting creative, that's for sure. It's been a long time since a guy bought me presents. Maybe this is what people are doing now. Remind me to pick up a copy of *In Style* later," I added.

"Again, I'll remember this. Jewelry is out, lobsters are in. That's a gift worth giving." Bobby laughed.

"Umm, Abby," Grace said as she stood and picked up her towel, "I hate to bring this up, but considering that until recently you were having a freakin' mental love affair with your ex via laptop, that's not all that surprising. The only thing you get from that Arizona asshole is an increase in your Wi-Fi bill. First, let's find you a good guy. The presents will follow."

"Fair point," I admitted.

We gathered up our bags, chairs, and the cooler still full of Coronas and reluctantly trudged our way across the scorching hot sand back to the parking lot. I wasn't happy about leaving the beach ahead of schedule, but I was even less happy to leave Wolf and a dozen lobsters unsupervised in our house. As soon as we hit the parking lot Grace pulled her phone from her bag and began dialing.

"What are you doing?" Bobby asked Grace as we made our way back to the car.

"I'm calling him to say, 'Thank you'! I want him to know how much I appreciate the gesture."

"If I were you, I'd wait. Call him later or even tomorrow morning. Don't chomp at the bit right away," Bobby suggested.

"I think it's a little late to start playing hard to get."

"That makes no sense to me either," I admitted, though I was curious as to why Bobby seemed to think that calling Johnny was a bad idea.

"I'm just saying that maybe let him sweat it out a little. That's all. You do what you want, but the last thing you want him to think is that you're some kind of shellfish slut," Bobby said.

"A shellfish slut?" I asked.

"Yeah. You don't want him to think that you'll give it up for a box of lobsters, Grace. You've been waiting a long time for him to do right by you. It's cool he sent you something, but you don't want him to think lobsters are an alternative to leaving his wife. Why don't you try holding the cards for once? That's all I'm saying."

"And women are supposed to be the ones who play games?" I asked.

"Maybe I've been hanging out with you guys too much. I need Wolf. I'm starting to think like a chick," he admitted as we trudged through the parking lot.

"No, you're right! I'm no lobster lush," Grace replied, forcefully.

"You're most certainly not. You're better than that. At least hold out for a box of Omaha steaks or something," Bobby suggested. I was beginning to see his motivation. He wanted to see what else JF would send us to eat.

"Or the wine of the month club," I added. It wasn't the worst idea I'd ever heard.

"Now you're talking," Bobby said. "Is there such a thing as the bacon of the month club? Can you register for that?"

I wrapped my arm around Grace's shoulder as we walked. "I'm really happy for you, Grace, but be careful. I know how hard this has been for you, and I know you've been through hell. I just think you need to tell him his time is up. He needs to leave his wife, or you're going to walk."

"That will be tricky since I work in the neighboring office."

"I didn't say that plan was perfect."

We drove the five minutes back to the house, brushed sand off our feet at the bottom of the stairs, and walked upstairs to the deck. Wolf was sitting on a lounge chair with his mirrored sunglasses on, sipping a glass of wine and listening to European techno music on the speaker dock.

"So, umm, was there a card?" Grace asked Wolf as she approached him.

"Oh, he could have attached a really cool love note," Bobby mused. " 'Roses are red, live lobsters are blue, come back to Boston, so I can bang you,' " he sang.

"That's touching," I said, smacking his bare shoulder with my magazine. "Move over, Shakespeare."

"Not bad for an on-the-spot poem, huh?" Bobby asked.

"Yeah, there was a card. It's over there," Wolf said as he gestured to the table. "It said something like, 'The best is yet to come, love JF.' Who's JF?"

"Her boyfriend," I said, once again feeling funny calling him that when he was someone else's husband.

"The one with the wife?" Wolf asked, surprised.

"The one with the soon-to-be-ex-wife," Grace clarified with a smile. "He's ready to divorce her, I know it. *I can feel it.*"

"Don't get ahead of yourself," Bobby said. "This is what I'm talking about, Grace. It's just a box of fish. It's not divorce papers."

"Must you rain on my parade?" Grace asked. "It's going to happen," she said.

"I don't care if he has three other wives, please don't ever break up with the lobster guy, okay? I like him!" Wolf exclaimed.

"You never met him," I pointed out.

"I met his lobsters and I like them," Wolf said. "Here, come see!" Wolf was so excited, you'd have thought someone had just air-dropped forty pounds of schnitzel from the motherland onto our deck and not a few lobsters that had probably been dredged out of the Atlantic a few miles away. Funny what gets guys going.

We followed him into the house and made our way to the hallway bathroom. Bobby pushed in from behind, basically knocking me into the wall as he made his way into the center of the room. You'd think he'd never seen live lobsters before. In a tub. In our house.

"Here they are!" Wolf said proudly as he slid the clear plastic shower curtain over to reveal a dozen ugly blue lobsters crawling all over each other. Thankfully, giant rubber bands were clamping their humungous claws shut. "I named them. See, this one is Snappy, this one is Claw, that's Fang, and the little one over there I call Travis." Grace and I stared, trying to process what we were looking at and wondering if any of us could ever bring ourselves to step foot in that shower again. It was like Red Lobster was using our bathroom to store its inventory. I had a flashback to the fish store my mom used to take me to when I was little. I used to look at those disgusting lobsters in the tank—lying all over each other, wiry antennae and claws and tails intertwined as if they were having some sick and twisted lobster orgy in a glass case for all the world to see.

How anyone figured out that these disgusting-looking things actually tasted good I will never understand.

"Why would you name them?" I asked.

"I thought we should try to get to know them before I throw them in boiling water and eat their tails with garlic butter. Back in Germany, we had a farm with chickens. I used to name them when I was little. So, I figured, why not name the lobsters too?"

We shrugged. Trying to explain to Wolf that naming animals you were going to eat a few hours later was creepy seemed as futile as trying to explain what it meant to shoot fish in a barrel.

"I think I'm going to go up to the store right now and get some butter for them and, what do you think, some corn?"

"This is going to be awesome," Bobby said as he reached into the tub and grabbed a lobster, holding it up to his face as if he wanted to meet it before he ate it.

"I'm so happy, I'm in heaven number seven," Wolf said as he smiled wide.

"You mean seventh heaven?" Grace asked as she stifled a giggle.

"How does anyone speak your language?" he asked. He shook his head as he shuffled out of the bathroom, grabbed his car keys, and headed into town, leaving us alone to stare at the lobsters crawling around our porcelain tub.

FOUR HOURS LATER WE SAT at the table on our deck with bottles of wine, citronella candles, paper plates, rolls of paper towels, bowls of garlic butter, and lobsters with claws the size of Rhode Island splayed out all over the place. For most people, lobsters are a high-priced luxury item: leave it to us to trash them up by not even using napkins or real silverware to eat them.

The boys had thoroughly enjoyed making dinner. Wolf took control of the cooking process, his European sense of refinement clearly making him the most qualified guy for the job. As he dropped lobsters into the enormous pot of boiling water, Bobby stood at his side making the screeching noise from *Psycho* and pretending to stab the crustaceans to death before Wolf closed the lid on them. Bobby then went outside and leaned against the railing, smoking cigarettes and barking orders from the deck. "Turn up the flame, use the other burner, only cook two lobsters at a time." Grace and I sat outside and listened to music, wanting no part in the great lobster massacre. Now that it was time to eat I stared down at my plate and felt strange for two reasons: one, I hated to somehow benefit from Johnny's psychological warfare against my best friend; and two, I was pretty sure I was about to eat a lobster named Snappy.

Wolf raised his red Solo cup to toast. "To Gracie, and her awesome boyfriend who sent us these lobsters. I like this guy. I think you should be keeping him." Apparently, the way to a man's heart really is through his stomach.

Bobby leaned over to talk to Grace and me at the end of the table. "You know, if you guys ever do get married, you can register for those little lobster forks," he laughed. "We could use some of those right about now."

"I promise you, if I ever get to register, I'll throw some lobster forks on there and give them to you for Christmas," Grace said.

"Awesome," he replied as he attacked the tail, squirting lobster juice all over me.

I playfully tossed a wadded-up paper towel at Bobby and said a silent apology to Snappy—before ripping his giant right claw off his body with my bare hands.

CHAPTER 12

Beware of Guys Who Say You Look Like a Celebrity . . . They're Either Lying or Have Cataracts

THE FOLLOWING WEDNESDAY I went into work and discovered that it was going to be a painfully slow day. Thankfully, late in the afternoon Lara appeared, and I ran down the street to get us iced coffees in the hopes of making the afternoon pass a little faster.

I liked talking to Lara because she was a fantastic listener. I was beginning to find it slightly odd, though, that she never talked about her husband or her own personal life. I considered her a friend, but I really didn't know the first thing about her, which, when I thought about it, was kind of a strange position to be in. Anyway, I wasn't letting it bother me. June was quickly approaching its end, and the beginning of July didn't mean only the height of the summer and an increase in temperature were approaching—it also meant Katie's wedding was just a month away. I needed to talk to someone about how I was feeling, and I felt like I had exhausted Grace so much over the last few months I couldn't ask her to listen to me complain about anything else. Lara, on the other hand, was always asking how I was doing, what was new, and what I was up to, so I didn't feel like I was bugging her by telling her what was on my mind.

The bell over the door rang when I reentered the store, and I found Lara sitting exactly where I had left her, behind the register staring into space. I handed her the iced coffee, tucked my purse away in the closet in the back, and then sat next to her. Lara's thin blue dress was probably a size 0 but was still too big for her, and she looked tired. Way too tired for someone her age who was living at the beach and got off work every day at 6:00 P.M.

"I'm dreading this wedding," I admitted as we sat behind the register drinking coffee and waiting for customers. "I feel awful about it, I mean she's my only sister. I should be thrilled to see her this happy, but the thought of having to go to her wedding makes me want to stick my head in the oven. What kind of person does that make me?"

"It makes you normal. You had a bad breakup, everyone struggles with some irrational emotions after they go through something traumatizing, and a wedding is the complete opposite of that. It's not strange that you'd be conflicted over it."

"Maybe it's normal, I don't know. I think what kills me is that now that she's on such bridal autopilot she's acting like nothing happened to me, like everything is just fine. I don't think she appreciates how hard it is for me to have had my engagement canceled and then have to jump into being her maid of honor. It's such a mind-fuck. She doesn't get it."

Lara stared at me, stunned, and then tried to busy herself with the previous day's receipts to make the moment less awkward. I hadn't meant to tell her, I really hadn't. It just slipped out. Katie's wedding made it impossible for me to think about anything else.

"I didn't realize you were engaged, Abby. I'm really sorry."

"Yeah," I said as I tried to pretend it was no big deal. "It was a while ago, and I'm doing much better now, but all this dating stuff is hard. And apparently I suck at it."

"I'm sure that's not true. I hated dating and wanted so badly to be off the singles circuit, and I was only in my twenties. I'm sure it's been frustrating for you to have to get back out there," Lara said in a tone so laced with sympathy it was hard for me to hear it. She was right, though. Accepting what had happened meant being able to attend other people's weddings and not want to go cry in a corner somewhere. Life goes on.

"It's been interesting, that much I can tell you," I joked. "Anyway, I don't know what I'm doing anymore. I'll get through the wedding, and hopefully I'll be able to locate the normal emotions that I should be feeling and actually find myself happy for her. But enough about me. How long have you been married?" I asked, hoping to steer the conversation away from myself and my demons and give Lara an opportunity to open up.

"Three years," she said as she spun her watch around her impossibly thin wrist. I realized that I never really saw Lara eat anything, not that I didn't snack enough for both of us. Still, it wouldn't kill her to knock back a milkshake, or six.

"That's great, I'm jealous. I'd love to meet him. Will he be down here this weekend? He should swing by and say hello." I knew I was in dangerous territory. Lara never mentioned her husband, and while I had no idea what was going on with her marriage, I didn't want her to feel like I was prying. Still, it was strange to pretend I didn't notice, or worse, to have her think I didn't care.

She sighed and waved me off. "No. He doesn't come down here on the weekends. He works a ton, so he's staying in Boston for the summer. I used to joke that he was cheating on me with his job. All work and no play," she said as she once again fidgeted with her rings. She spun them so frequently I wondered if she had left a permanent groove in her skin. I figured maybe her husband was busy, not that he was living in another state. What kind of married woman lived apart from her husband for an entire summer? The obvious answer was, an unhappy one.

"So do you have any plans for the Fourth?" I asked, trying to turn the conversation back to neutral ground and finally beginning to understand why Lara was so eager to listen to me complain about my personal life—it distracted her from her own.

"No, I'm not doing anything special. I'll watch the fireworks on TV at home. What about you?"

"My friends and I are going to some party down on the beach. Why don't you come with us? It's silly for you to watch the fireworks on the news when they'll be setting some off a few blocks away. Come on, they're nice people, you'll like them." I didn't know who Lara spent her downtime with, but I was becoming more and more suspicious that when she wasn't at the store she was home alone, or with her parents, and I wanted her to feel like she had friends in town. I wanted her to know that whatever was going on, she didn't have to go through it by herself.

Lara hesitated a moment before she answered, as if she was afraid to commit to anything, even a party on the beach. "Maybe I'll join you. Are you sure that'd be okay?"

"Definitely. It will be fun. It's hard to believe June is almost over, isn't it?"

"It is. Hopefully things will pick up in July," Lara added, referring to sales, but I couldn't help but hope the same was true for my dating project.

"I'm sure they will," I said, believing myself for a change.

Lara smiled as she grabbed her bag off the floor. "It's pretty quiet and I have a screaming headache. Do you mind if I cut out of here early? Can you handle the afternoon by yourself?"

"Of course." I nodded and squeezed her shoulder. "Feel better, I'll see you next week."

"Great, thanks," she said as she walked slowly out of the store and left me alone at the counter. I reached into the bottom drawer that I had turned into my personal vending machine and removed a bag of animal crackers. Not exactly healthy, but not a pint of ice cream either. I'd take my victories wherever I could find them.

I kept myself busy for the rest of the afternoon. I dusted the shelves in the store and sold a few trinkets to ladies who were in need of a hostess gift for a friend. Then I began to organize the top drawer behind the counter. When I finished that, I planned on rearranging the window display so that the lamp with the driftwood base would be more visible to passersby. I heard the bell ring from behind the register.

I smiled at the guy who had just entered, a stereotypical preppy New England guy who had no idea what he was doing in a store like ours. Like most men, it was pretty clear he needed help.

"Can I help you with something?" I said politely, without leaving the register. There was nothing worse than pushy salespeople, so I made it a point not to approach any of the customers more than once unless they asked for something specific. Even the cute ones.

"I'm okay for now, thanks," he said as he roamed the displays in the store window, most of them containing picture frames covered with various sizes of seashells and kitchen towels etched with anchors. I nodded and continued to organize the receipts from the day before. Then I heard the little bell over the door ring again. When I looked up, Bobby was walking toward me.

"What's wrong?" I asked. Bobby had never come to visit me at work, and for a minute I was worried he was going to tell me that Wolf was in some kind of accident, or worse, that my sister had shown up at the house.

"Nothing." He smirked and put his hands in the pockets of his board shorts as if he was trying to decide what to say. "Why does something have to be wrong? I just came in to say hi. You're closing soon, right?"

I looked at my watch and realized it was almost six. "Yeah, probably after this customer leaves." Bobby and I both glanced at the guy who was still roaming aimlessly around the front of the store, casting glances back toward us every few minutes. For a second I wondered if he was some kind of preppy shoplifting bandit.

"Okay, why don't we go into town and get a drink after this? I'm getting antsy sitting around at home, plus it's hot as hell and the ceiling fans aren't doing jack to cool off the house."

"My house or your house?"

"Both of them, actually. Come on, my treat."

Apparently having found what he was looking for, the preppy guy walked up to the counter. Bobby stepped to the side and leaned against a large china cabinet that held stacks of colorful ice cream bowls and water pitchers.

"I'll take this, please," he said as he placed the giant cheese board with the three-dimensional boat on it on the counter.

"Great, is it a gift? I can wrap it for you," I offered.

"Uhh no, you don't have to. Well, yes, I mean, it's a gift, but you don't have to wrap it."

"Are you sure? I don't mind."

"Umm, yeah. Thanks, and you know what? I'll take one of these too," he said as he reached over and pulled a small wooden sign that said I'D RATHER BE FISHING off a hook on the wall. Bobby raised a lone eyebrow as he looked at the guy strangely.

"Sure, not a problem," I said as I began to peel the price tag off the back. "Do you fish?" I asked as I continued to pick at the tag like it was a scab.

"Oh no. I don't," he replied, still looking a little nervous and jittery.

"Smooth," Bobby muttered under his breath as he turned and walked toward the door to wait for me to finish up.

"Oh, well . . . it's still a nice little accessory for someone." I placed the cheese board and the sign in a shopping bag and swiped his credit card. When it went through, I handed him his card and smiled at him again. I know I didn't know a lot about the way people flirt with each other, but if he wasn't going to knock over the store, then the only other logical explanation for his behavior was that he was stalling to talk to me. If that was the case, I wanted to show him a little encouragement, let him know that I wouldn't be against talking to him. I wanted to prove to myself and to

Bobby that I had learned a few things over the past month, even if I hadn't managed to actually go on any real dates yet. "Here you go, . . ." I said as I gave him his bag and scanned his credit card receipt for his name, ". . . Tom. Thanks for coming in. I hope you'll come back again soon."

"Umm, yeah. Okay, bye," he said as he turned and left the store, forcing Bobby to step out of his way and onto a basket of needlepoint throw pillows.

I eyed Bobby suspiciously. He and I had never gone out in public alone together, but I had to admit that the concept of getting out of the house wasn't a bad one. "Okay, Bobby," I said, "you're on. Wait for me outside while I lock up."

"Cool," he replied as he headed outside, leaned against a street sign, and smoked a cigarette while he waited for me. I locked the register, turned off the light in the storage room in the back, made sure that all the receipts were tucked away in the bottom drawer behind the counter, and closed up the shop for the night.

Bobby and I walked a few blocks to the Landing, which had become our regular watering hole, headed to the corner of the bar where we usually congregated, and grabbed two stools. We flagged down Jane, the pretty blond bartender who had become friendly with our group and now knew our drink orders by heart, and settled in at the waterfront bar that was easily one of my favorite spots in town.

"So this is overdue," he said as he slugged the beer Jane put in front of him. "You and I have never gone out solo before," he said.

"I think that's because we're afraid we'll kill each other."

"Could be. I think it's a bit silly, though, don't you? You and I aren't all that different, you know."

Well, that was an odd thing to say, since I couldn't really think of anything we had in common other than our friendship with Grace. "You don't think so?" I said. "For starters, I'm looking for someone special, and from what I can tell, that's the furthest thing from your mind, so I don't think our going out together makes a whole lot of sense."

"How do you know I'm not looking for anyone?" he asked, pretending to be offended.

"You've told me," I said.

"When have I done that?"

"Maybe not in so many words, but I can tell. You're not serious about finding anyone, and don't get me wrong, that's fine. You're a young guy, you have plenty of time. I just don't feel like being single anymore. I was used to being in a relationship. It's what I'm good at. I miss it."

"How can you miss being in a relationship with a guy who did God knows what to you? And I mean that, because no one will tell me what the hell happened, so now I'm imagining the worst. Like, was there bondage or something involved?" he asked, the glint in his eye still visible beneath the brim of his baseball hat.

"You're sick. No."

"Did he want you to move to a commune Waco-style and live with him and seven other wives?"

"You're terrible at this game," I joked as I playfully smacked his arm.

"Then tell me. Come on, it's just us girls here." He leaned his chin on his hand and smiled shyly while he batted his eyelashes.

"I really don't want to get into it, it's nothing I want to relive and . . ." Before I could say another word, a portly, middle-aged man entered the bar, glanced in our direction, and veered our way, stopping between Bobby and me to order a drink and taking a moment to stare at Bobby and his batting eyelashes in confusion. The strange man ordered a beer before he turned to me and flashed a smile that only a mother could love. I shot Bobby a disgusted look, and he returned it with one of bemusement.

"I'm Victor," the guy said, as if I had bothered to ask his name. "My friends call me Vic."

"In that case, hello, Victor," I said. Bobby flashed a quick smile, but Victor didn't pick up on my subtle insult. In fact, I don't think this guy would pick up on anything less subtle than a cartoon-style frying pan to the head.

"Are you from the area? Or just here for the summer?" he asked as he angled himself so that his back was turned toward Bobby, almost boxing him out of the conversation entirely. Every guy I'd met this summer had used some version of that as his opening line. Someone really needed to come up with better material than "Are you from around here?" or "Come here often?"

"Just for the summer. What about you?" I glanced at Bobby. At least now he'd fully understand my unique ability to attract weirdos.

"I live here year-round. I'm a postal delivery professional."

"Oh, that's nice," I said, trying to be polite. I couldn't have cared less if he owned half the mansions in town. He was creeping me out big time.

"Has anyone ever told you that if you had brown hair you'd look like a cross between Sophia Loren, Rachael Ray, and J Lo?" He smiled wide, genuinely impressed with himself for coming up with what he perceived to be a staggering compliment. He probably expected me to stand and tell him to take me home at once, because lines like that actually worked once upon a time. Bobby choked on his drink and raised his eyebrows while Victor continued to pretend he didn't exist.

"No, Victor. I can honestly say that no one has ever told me that before," I replied, still trying to be polite but starting to fail. I briefly wondered if there was a difference between being told you looked like J Lo, Jenny from the Block, or Jennifer Lopez. I was pretty sure in one of those versions you had to wear velour sweat suits and hang off Ben Affleck like a hood ornament. I made a mental note to check the Internet when I got home to see which one was which.

"Well, it's true. You should know that."

"I don't think she can cook, though," Bobby chimed in. "She ruined pasta the other night, so maybe she could do thirty-hour meals, but thirty-minute meals is out of the question unless you just want her to boil water."

Victor shot a glance at Bobby, letting him know he didn't appreciate the interference, which was hysterical since he was the one who had interrupted us to begin with. I was beginning to wonder if this guy was playing with a full stack of envelopes.

"Thank you, that's a nice compliment." *In a parallel universe where it makes sense that you and I are even having this conversation.*

"How about you let me show you the island?" he asked, flashing his creepy, yellow-toothed smile for the second time in as many minutes.

"I've been showing her around actually," Bobby said. It was kind of fun feeling like two guys were fighting over me, even if I wasn't interested in either of them.

"On land?" Victor asked.

"Yeah, my seaplane's in the shop, and she left her magic flying broom in the city," Bobby shot back, proving that his wits were sharper than most.

"I have a boat, and I'd be happy to take you out on the water and show you the island that way. It's pretty amazing," Victor said.

"I don't think so," I said curtly.

"Are you sure? It's going to be a gorgeous weekend."

Before I could tell Victor to go drown himself, Wolf bounded into the bar, and Bobby immediately waved him over. Victor stepped back as Wolf approached, clearly more intimidated by him than he was by Bobby, not that I could blame him. A six-five German will evoke a different reaction than a scrawny American any day.

"Hey, guys," Wolf said as he patted both of our backs. "Who's your friend?" he asked, staring at Victor.

"Oh, this is Victor, we just met him. Victor, this is our friend Wolf, and I don't think you actually met Bobby either." I took the opportunity to point out that Bobby and I were in fact together because I didn't like the way this complete stranger was disrespecting him. He was a mailman, for God's sake. Not the mayor.

"Hey," Bobby said as he shook Victor's hand.

"Nice to meet you," Wolf added as he ordered a glass of wine on our tab.

"Uhh, well, I won't interrupt you guys anymore. Enjoy your evening. And here's my number," Victor said as he removed a pen from his breast pocket and scribbled on a napkin. "If you change your mind about coming out on my boat, let me know."

"A boat?" Wolf said, wide-eyed, not realizing that that trip would probably end with my appendages sawed off and packed in a cooler.

"We'll talk about it later, Wolf, okay?" I asked, hoping that Victor wouldn't mistake Wolf's enthusiasm as an extension of my own.

"Cool!" Wolf replied, as happy as ever. "I'm going to go say hi to some people in the back. Talk to you guys later." Wolf grabbed his wine and headed toward a group of girls at the back of the bar. I wished that I had one-tenth of his courage. It would make dating a whole lot easier.

"Bye, Victor," I said as I shook his hand and turned my back to let him know in no uncertain terms that this conversation was over. He should consider himself lucky. Sophia Loren would've thrown his ass in the Arno ten minutes ago.

He nodded as he walked away, and I giggled as I shrugged my shoulders at Bobby. "You see? That's what's out there."

"That's the second time this summer that some guy hit on you right in front of me."

"Maybe he knew he could take you. Or maybe we don't give off that relationship vibe. We don't really look like we are all that enamored with each other."

"I repeat, guy code. You just don't do that," he said, seemingly genuinely confused as to why no one else adhered to his code of ethics.

"I think you're the only one following this alleged guy code. You do realize that, right?"

"It's very real, and it should be respected."

"Are you jealous of a fifty-year-old mailman?"

He laughed. "I'm going to give you a little tip. Beware of guys who compare you to a celebrity . . . they're either lying or have cataracts. In this case, I think we can lean toward cataracts, but that was even more ridiculous because he compared you to three. That guy has clearly licked too many stamps."

"How do you know who Rachael Ray is, by the way?" I asked, curious as all of a sudden I remembered his reference to thirty-minute meals.

"I told you, I'm a Renaissance man."

I sighed. "You know what's the worst part about being hit on by a guy like that?"

"Imagining him naked?" Bobby suggested.

"Okay, until this second, no, and now I think I may go blind from that mental image."

"Sorry. My bad. What's the worst thing?"

I hesitated. I didn't want to hear myself say it out loud, but the truth was, well, it was the truth. "Every time someone like that hits on me, someone much older, or just, you know, not to be snobby, but . . ."

"Not in your league?"

"Well, yeah." I was grateful Bobby said it for me. If someone else says it, it's a compliment. If you say it about yourself, you're a narcissist with an entirely too high opinion of yourself, and I'd already noticed one too many similarities between my mother and me this summer.

"He doesn't think you're in his league—which, by the way, you're not. You were a Hail Mary pass."

"What's that exactly?" I asked, not sure what religion had to do with anything.

"Guys do it all the time. They find a girl they expect will reject them and they figure, why not? Maybe just one time I catch a girl who is wasted, or so miserable she'd go home with a circus midget, or even better, a wasted, angry girl who wants to piss off her boyfriend or ex-boyfriend by going home with anything with a pulse. He realized that you weren't any of those things, so he moved on. Don't think for one second that that's what you should be dating. It's so far from the truth it's a joke."

Bobby reached out and patted my knee. Not in a creepy way, he didn't squeeze it or anything, but a nice friendly pat. It felt normal. Comfortable. It was the most comfortable I had felt with a guy in a very long time. And I didn't even like him. God, I was screwed up.

"Thanks, Bobby," I said as I put my hand on his forearm. "I appreciate it. I know I give you a hard time, but you're not so bad, truth be told."

"Did that hurt you to admit?" he asked.

"A little bit," I said with a smile.

"Thank you. You're not too bad either. I'm sorry I was so forward with you when we met on Memorial Day. Grace mentioned that you were going through some stuff, and I just wanted you to have a good time. I'm not really good with the whole kid gloves thing. My heart was in the right place, though."

"I know. And I'm glad you suggested we get out of the house tonight too. I need someone to push me to get out. It's hard for me to force myself to do it."

"Out where?"

"Out in the dating world. There are mass murderers, and rapists, and guys who will ask you to spend Saturday nights listening to them relive their high school years as they jam with their bands."

"You have a problem with *Wayne's World?*"

"Hey, I like *Wayne's World* as much as the next girl, but I have no interest in dating either Wayne or Garth. Besides, it's such a huge waste of time. Once you hit thirty, your odds of meeting someone through the normal course of life decreases by, like, fifty percent."

"Where the hell did you get that statistic from?"

"My mother."

"I'm beginning to understand you a little better. She sounds delusional."

"Just because she's evil doesn't mean she's wrong."

"And you won't do the whole Internet dating thing why exactly?"

"Because of my fear of murderers, rapists, and Wayne."

"Right. So at the ripe old age of thirty-one you decided that you don't want to date. What do you do with all of your free time then? I mean, if you're not going out and being social, then what do you do all day? Sit on your ass and eat ice cream?"

"Grace told you?"

"She might have mentioned it."

"Remind me to kill her."

"Seriously. What have you been doing with your time in isolation?"

"Well, I joined a club. I meet with a bunch of other women once a week during the school year." As soon as I said it I wished I hadn't. A guy would never understand. Especially a guy like Bobby.

"What sort of club? It's not some male-bashing joyless luck club type thing, is it?" he asked.

"No. It's not related to men in any way, shape, or form." I hesitated, biting my lip before I answered, knowing that he'd have something to say about my answer. "It's a knitting club."

"I'm sorry, a what?" he asked as he leaned toward me in case he had misheard.

"A knitting club. See, once a week we . . ."

"Shhhh," he said as he suddenly covered my mouth with his hand. "You cannot ever say that out loud in a public place ever again, do you hear me? If someone hears you say that, you won't have to worry about what's out there on the dating circuit because guys will cross the street to stay away from you."

"What's so bad about a knitting club? It's therapeutic." Sheesh. Apparently I couldn't do anything right.

"What the hell are you even knitting? An afghan like all the other octogenarians in the Northeast?"

"Of course not. I'm not good enough for that yet," I admitted.

"Then what? An ice cream cozy?"

"No! Though that's really not a bad idea now that I think about it." Bobby's shock registered all over his face for reasons I didn't fully understand. There were way worse things than a single thirty-one-year-old girl in a knitting club. If I thought long and hard enough, I was sure I'd come up with something eventually.

"What? Tell me. Please tell me what you're knitting."

"Pot-holders," I said defiantly. "But so far I only have one. I hope to finish the set by Christmas."

"Okay. The first thing you're going to do is drop out of that knitting club, pronto," Bobby ordered, seeming to forget that so far I hadn't listened to anything he'd said to me.

"Why? I'm a few months away from having a matching set!"

"It's just too sad for me to even explain the reasons why. If you listen to one single piece of advice I give you, listen to this: you, Abby Wilkes, should not be spending Friday nights sitting in a living room with knitting needles. I'm sorry, I won't allow it."

I sighed and laughed a little. He was right. It was yet another hideout, and I knew it. "Okay, I will. I promise. What about you? How come you aren't dating anyone?"

"I haven't found anyone special, I guess. Believe it or not, I'm not really into casual dating, and I hate rejecting people. I'll meet girls and have a good time with them, but unless I find someone I think I could spend a serious amount of time with, I'm fine staying unattached. It's easier that way. Besides, it's not high on my list of priorities right now. I need a job, not a girlfriend."

"I find that to be really sweet, actually," I said, seeing that there was a lot more to Bobby than I realized.

"Don't go telling people that. I don't want word to get out that I'm actually a romantic at heart."

"Your secret is safe with me."

The bartender returned and placed two more Belgian beers in front of us. Bobby held out his glass and gently clinked the rims together. "Out with the old and in with the new, Abby. I think you're going to be just fine." I was beginning to believe that myself.

We sat at the bar for another two hours, talking about life, unemployment, our friends, and our families. It was the kind of basic, easy conversation that seemed impossible to find with any of the other guys I had met so far this summer. I realized that had this been a date, it would have been one of the best first dates I'd ever had in my life. Maybe the best one, period. If nothing else, my night out with Bobby proved that it was possible for me to have pure, unadulterated fun with a guy again, and that was definitely a step in the right direction.

I was just surprised at who was responsible for it.

CHAPTER 13

The Clam Jam

THE FOURTH OF JULY holiday is always fun no matter where you live (as long as it's in the United States). Few things make people happier than long weekends, especially people with full-time jobs. I returned from an afternoon jog and had a voicemail from Grace, who sounded especially cheerful. I assumed it was because she was going to have an extra day to work on her tan and the weather forecast was for clear skies for the foreseeable future. She said she was on her way.

I entered the kitchen and found Bobby flipping through the newspaper and drinking a diet iced tea, probably the first time since we had met that I'd seen him consume a nonalcoholic beverage. I opened the cabinet and removed a bag of chips as I sat down next to him and began to read over his shoulder, chomping in his ear.

"That's not at all annoying," he said as he continued to read.

"Sorry," I said, even though I enjoyed bothering Bobby for sport more than I enjoyed just about anything else.

Just then we heard Grace running up the deck stairs, her flip-flops flapping. She burst through the door and threw herself on me. "You guys will never believe what happened!" she squealed, with a look on her face I'd never seen before.

"What happened?" I asked, as she continued to hug me so tightly I could barely breathe. "Did you win the Lotto or something? Because we made that pact in high school that if one of us won, we'd split the winnings, and as far as I'm concerned that agreement is still in effect."

"Better!" she screamed.

"The suspense is killing me," Bobby said.

"He did it. He told his wife it's over. He's leaving her!"

Bobby and I didn't move, stunned into silence. If it was true, then everything I thought about Johnny was wrong. If it was true, then Grace hadn't been wasting all of her time on someone who could never be with her. If it was true, I had to seriously start putting money on the long shots at the track. "He did it? He's filing for divorce?" I asked.

"Yup. He told her this morning, and then he left the house. He's crashing at a hotel right now. I invited him to come here for the weekend, but he needs to call lawyers and deal with everything. Do you believe this is actually happening? We can finally be together." She ran her hands through her hair and grabbed her skull, like she couldn't believe it herself.

"I don't know what to say! I'm shocked. I mean, I'm really happy for you, but I'm shocked. I didn't think he'd ever do it," I admitted. I guess some people did get their happy endings.

"I know you didn't, but I did. I knew in my soul this was meant to be. I know it's complicated, and the road was . . . what's the word I'm looking for?"

"Untraditional?" Bobby offered. I was impressed with his diplomacy.

"Yes, good one! Untraditional. But it's over. I don't have to live a lie anymore. I feel like I'm going to explode."

"Grace, congratulations. You went through hell, and I worried about what you were doing and how this would end, and I'm really happy you're finally going to have this all legitimized," I said, relieved.

"It's a very, very good day. And I'm beyond pumped about the party tonight."

"I am too," I admitted. And I was. I only hoped it wasn't too good to be true.

A FEW HOURS LATER, when Grace and I agreed that we were both perfectly accessorized, we headed over to the beach party otherwise known as the clam jam. Wolf and Bobby bounded through the parking lot toward the sand, already a bit buzzed from the beers they'd drunk at the house while Grace and I were primping. We discussed the fact that I had to head back to the city the following week for Katie's final dress fitting and checked out our reflections in each other's sunglasses to make sure that our hair remained straight after the hour we had spent using flat irons. As we approached the beach and the crowd came into view, I almost keeled over with shock. It was packed with people, all of them drinking, laughing, and having fun. I had found the motherland.

My phone rang right as we were about to join the party. I checked the caller ID. It was Katie, and since her wedding was only a few weeks away, I knew I had to answer it. I stopped at the foot of the stairs. "I'll meet up with you down there, go ahead."

"Okay!" they yelled in unison as they sped off in front of me, kicking their shoes into the pile of sandals that had accumulated on the sand.

"What's up?" I asked as I watched my friends disappear into the crowd.

"Hey, Abby! How's it going?" a happy Katie chirped in my ear.

"Pretty good, but I'm at a party, so talk fast," I said, jamming my finger in my ear so I could block out the noise from the party and the breeze.

"I need a favor. Can you pick up my wedding undies and bring them to my fitting next week? I'm swamped, and I won't have time to get them."

"I'm sorry, did you say wedding undies? I don't know what those are."

"You know, the underwear with BRIDE written across the butt in rhinestones for my wedding day. I have them on hold at Intimacy in the Back Bay. Can you grab them for me?"

"Sure," I said, hoping the sudden sadness I felt didn't resonate in my voice. "I'm coming home on Wednesday, so I'll pick them up on the way."

"Great! I don't mean to be a pain, but please, please, don't forget. I will just die if I don't have them."

"Why? It's just underwear. It's not your dress." I didn't mean to sound snippy. I just could not believe that I was now reduced to picking up her underwear. How the mighty had fallen. And hard.

"You'll understand someday, Abby," she said, the words stinging like I had been attacked by a swarm of jellyfish. I was aware of how important the little things were to brides. What I didn't understand was why she thought this was a normal thing to ask me to do from across state lines.

"I'll bring your underwear, Katie. I'll see you next week." I hung up on her and felt my mood begin to turn. I had been really looking forward to this party, and now Katie's reminder that the wedding was fast approaching and that I wasn't the bride, only the maid of honor who had to fetch underwear, was depressing.

I walked past the crowd of people gathered around various kegs and grills and wandered aimlessly off down the beach, my little sister's request still ringing in my ears. I wasn't sure why I was having such a strong reaction to her phone call, but I had had enough mood swings over the past year to know that sometimes they came when you least expected them and that when they did, it was better to work through them alone.

When I was far enough away that I could hear myself think, I sat down on the sand and threw my head back to stare at the stars. I said out loud to the waves as they crashed against the beach, "Fuck my life." I meant it. This was not how I wanted this night to go.

"And here I was hoping that you were going to tell me that you were still in a good mood," Bobby joked. "What are you doing? I saw you walking down the beach looking like someone had stolen your lollipop. Are you okay?"

I shrugged. "Yeah, I'm fine." He sat down and handed me one of the two red Solo cups he was carrying. "Thank you," I said with a weak smile. I placed the cup on the hard sand in front of me. I struggled to make small talk and force my feelings back into my emotional basement where they belonged. "Have you been to this thing before?"

"No," he replied. "It's . . . uhh . . . not really my scene. There are at least three different guys over there named Chad, did you know that?" He pointed back to the Polo-clad guys surrounding the keg, looking like a walking pack of Starbursts.

"I didn't know that, actually. I haven't been in there yet. I got a phone call from my sister and decided I needed a few minutes alone before I joined everyone."

"Sorry to spoil your alone time."

I shrugged again. "It's fine." He tilted his red cup toward mine, and we clanked them together, spilling beer foam onto my hand. He produced a napkin from his pocket and handed it to me.

"Thanks," I said.

"No problem. But since I did bring you this beer, free of charge I might add, are you going to tell me why you want to fuck your life?"

"Oh, you know, just the usual nonsense that seems to follow me everywhere I go."

"Like what? More wedding stuff?"

I didn't answer. It *was* wedding stuff, but I guess it was a little more than that too.

"Come on. You owe me," he said.

"Fine. Yeah, the wedding stuff. I won't get into all the details, but for a lot of reasons my little sister's wedding has me in a funk. It's kind of held a magnifying glass up to my own life and made me look at where I am. It's not where I thought I'd be, believe me."

"You're at a party on one of the prettiest beaches in the country. Where else would you rather be? A lot of people would kill to be you."

"If you knew the full story, I think you'd retract that statement."

"Do you want to tell me?"

"Let's just say it was a bad breakup and leave it at that."

"Okay. Just so you know, I'm going to keep trying until I catch you at a weak moment and you tell me the full story."

He really didn't know who he was dealing with. I'd wire my jaw shut before I'd tell him what had happened. It wouldn't even be a big deal. If I couldn't lose these extra pounds before the wedding, it might come to that anyway.

"Look," he continued, "I'm thirty-three, single, and currently in between jobs. Do you think when I graduated law school this is where I thought I'd be? You can't plan everything in life. Stop looking at what's gone wrong and start appreciating what you've done right. To people who don't know that you're a walking basket case, you seem like you've got it all together. I mean it."

I laughed. "I'm so not together it's a joke. And now I have to go to my sister's alone, not to mention the fact that I have to get her wedding underwear."

"You have to get your sister underwear?" he asked, confused.

"Yup."

"Girls are weird."

"I'm leaving on Wednesday for her dress fitting. I'm going to need Xanax to get through this."

"I have some if you want them."

"What are you, a dealer now? Or do you just offer narcotics to chicks to get them stoned so they'll go out with you?" I joked. I looked at Bobby sitting next to me, just trying to be a good friend. I realized how badly I had misjudged him.

"We've come a long way since we first met, huh?" I asked him as I bumped his shoulder with mine. "You're not nearly as big a jerk as I thought you were."

He rested his forearms on his knees as he buried his feet in the sand. "Aww shucks. Thanks . . . you weren't the friendliest person when we first met either, you know."

"Fine. But you came on a little strong, don't you think? I wasn't in the right frame of mind to handle you being so . . . you."

"I get that a lot. People either love me or hate me. I thought you were a cool girl, so I guess I messed with you more than I should have considering I really didn't know you. I wanted us to be friends, and I guess I thought it'd be okay if I ripped on you, sort of like an older brother or something. Sorry if I took it a little too far."

"It's not a big deal. I kind of like it. But does this mean that you'll stop making fun of me now?"

"No way. It's just too easy most of the time."

"Thanks."

"I liked you off the bat, for what it's worth. Even if I thought you were a humungous pain in the ass with way too many defensive mechanisms, and I had no romantic interest in you whatsoever . . ."

"Sweet-talker."

"You know what I mean. But I get it, you've been through the ringer. Do you want my advice?" he asked.

"I've already told you, I don't."

"As a general rule, I think long-distance relationships are a bad idea."

"And you apparently still don't care." I sighed.

"How could someone who hates modern technology, won't get on Facebook, won't use Twitter, detests all of that stuff—hell, you'd still have a rotary phone or a walkie-talkie if you could find one—think that dating long-distance is a good idea? With Ben, of all guys? Didn't he move away and leave you here by choice?"

"I don't want to talk about him. It's complicated."

"Maybe so, but from what I've heard through the grapevine . . ."

"You mean Grace?"

"I cannot reveal my sources."

"Okay, Brian Williams."

"It sounds like your ex was way too much like you in a lot of ways. It never would've worked. So it doesn't matter how it ended, because it had an expiration date."

"What are you talking about? You don't even know him!"

"I don't need to. I know his type."

"Be careful here, Bobby," I warned. I wasn't about to let him completely degrade my almost-but-not-really-husband. Is nothing sacred anymore?

"You should seek out someone opposite to you. A yin to the yang, if you will."

"Oh God, now you've gone Far Eastern on me. I appreciate it, but I really don't want to talk about it, okay?"

"Okay. Anyway, don't let it get you down. You're doing great. You're a whole different person than the one I met Memorial Day."

"Do you mean that?" For some reason, it made me feel better if he actually meant it. Maybe it was because I knew Bobby would never hand out empty praise, or maybe it was because I had grown to actually value his opinion. Just a little bit.

"Sure," he said as he stood and brushed the sand off his calves. "Are you ready to go join the party? Or are you going to stand over here by yourself to contemplate how much you hate your life and leave me alone with all the Chads?" He smiled a crooked grin, almost goofy, but somehow still . . . cute.

"I think you can take them," I joked. I grabbed his hand, and he pulled me up from the sand.

"That's what I'm afraid of. Can't you just see the headlines on the news? 'Crazy Unemployed Lawyer Kills Multiple Chads in Newport Beach Brawl.' "

"You're right. I wouldn't want to be responsible for that. Let's go."

We walked back toward the reggae band and the large bonfire that was burning about a hundred yards away. "I'll leave you to find Grace," he said. "Cheer up. It's just underwear."

I laughed out loud. Indeed it was. "Thanks for the beer and for the chat. I actually feel much better."

"Don't sweat it, and don't waste your time worrying about the wedding and all that girl stuff. It's a Saturday on the beach. You're supposed to be having a good time."

"I am. I promise." I might have even meant it. I wasn't sure.

I wove through the crowd looking for Lara and Grace, digging through my clutch for my phone. When I checked it, I discovered that I had two text messages from Ben. I refused to check them. Instead, I silenced my ringer and threw it back in my purse. I felt better after talking to Bobby and was determined to enjoy this party. I didn't see Lara anywhere and realized that she'd opted to stay home rather than join us for the party. I knew better than anyone that if she wanted to be alone, there was nothing anyone could do to force her out, but I figured at least I had tried. Sometimes that's all you can do.

I gazed into the crowd, trying to locate Grace, and before I knew what happened a guy who was apparently chasing a wayward football knocked me on my ass. So much for that.

"What the hell?" I said as I tried to get my bearings. This was getting ridiculous. Now strangers at parties were physically assaulting me. People wouldn't believe this if I told them.

"Oh Jesus, I'm so sorry, I wasn't paying attention to where I was going," the guy said as he helped me up. "Are you okay?" he asked as he awkwardly tried to brush sand off my legs.

"No, I'm fine. It was my fault. I wasn't paying attention either," I said as I shook out my hair.

"I'm Pete," he said with a smile, revealing a slightly crooked left incisor. I caught myself wondering if he would be adverse to Invisalign braces to fix his snaggletooth.

It was becoming painfully obvious that I really needed to rewire my brain.

"I'm Abby," I said shyly. I pushed my hypercritical thoughts to the back of my mind where they belonged. If he was looking at me the same way I was examining him, I was screwed. I'd missed my last lip wax appointment, so he was probably wondering if I was planning on auditioning for the role of the bearded lady in the circus. I had to try to get to know this guy, see if we had anything in common, figure out if he was a serial killer before I eliminated him as an option.

"Listen," he said as he awkwardly scratched the nape of his neck. "The least I can do is buy you a beer after I mowed you over like that. Care to accompany me to the keg?"

"Sure, why not?" I said, realizing that the beer Bobby had given me was gone. I smiled nervously at Pete, turned, and walked with him toward the keg. There was no reason not to. This is what dating was, right? Having beers with a strange guy who levels you on the beach. It's almost poetic. A weird, tragic, bizarre poem, but poetic nonetheless. He was cute, not traditionally good-looking, but definitely not bad. His shirt was open, revealing a chest that was so hairy it looked like he was wearing a fur vest in summer, but then again, I was trying not to be too judgmental of people these days, so I decided to let it go. If this ever went anywhere, I figured I could just get him really drunk and wax it in his sleep.

I fancy myself quite the problem-solver.

We started chatting as the sun began to set over the water, a sight that despite living on the Eastern Seaboard my entire life has never ceased to impress me. So far, Pete seemed like a guy with real potential, if for no other reason than he made me laugh. I realized that while throwing myself into the ocean might have been a bit extreme, allowing someone to physically knock me over on the beach wasn't the worst way to meet a guy.

"So, do you have any interest in grabbing dinner next weekend? It's the least I can do to apologize."

"I thought this beer was your way of apologizing?" He was asking me out, I realized. And this time Bobby couldn't claim that he was drunk and didn't remember what I looked like.

"That was before I knew you. Now that I do, I think dinner is in order. How about we go to the Black Pearl next week? I'll make a reservation and prove to you that I'm actually much more polite than our initial meeting would have you believe."

"Okay. I'd like that," I said with a stupid smile more appropriately found on fourteen-year-old girls.

"Great. Want to say eight o'clock?"

"Eight o'clock it is." And just like that, I was booked.

We continued to make small talk until I felt a light tap at the back of my head and turned to find Bobby, grinning widely.

"Hey, I'm Bobby," he said. "I don't think I've seen you around this summer. Do you guys know each other?" he asked Pete, knowing full well that we didn't know each other at all.

"Not exactly. I accidentally knocked her over. I figured the best way to make it up to her was to get her a drink," Pete said, smiling politely at Bobby.

"Get out, you actually knocked her down?" he asked. "That's great. I mean, I don't know how many love stories begin with physical violence, but you never know."

"It was an accident," I said in Pete's defense. I didn't want this potentially good guy to be known as a violent offender before we even had dinner.

"Okay," Pete said cheerfully. "I'm going to go find my friends. Abby, it was really great to meet you. I'll see you next Saturday at eight, okay?"

"Great. I'm looking forward to it."

"Nice to meet you," he said to Bobby as he shook his hand before leaving.

"Hey, it was great to meet you, man. Maybe I'll see you around."

Pete waved as he walked away, and Bobby huddled next to me, like we were going to gossip like girlfriends.

"Guess who has a date?" I sang as I watched Pete disappear into the crowd. "One that I got all by myself."

"I picked up on that! That's great! Aww, see! I told you things would turn around. Our little girl is all grown up."

"Thank you," I said as I clinked my cup against his.

"One word of caution, though. He was a little furry. If that's what his chest looks like, I don't even want to know what is going on with the rest of him."

"Oh, would you stop! He seems very nice!"

"Good, I hope he is. Come on, Wolf's wondering where you've been. Let's go find the crew."

"Sounds like a plan," I said as Bobby wrapped his arm around my neck and escorted me back to the party.

A few hours and more than a few drinks later, we walked home singing Bob Marley songs in the kind of cheap-beer drunken haze I hadn't felt in ages. It was the first time in a long time that Grace and I had both been genuinely happy. Neither one of us was being weighed down by relationship baggage. We were the girls we used to be: carefree and optimistic about the future. Bobby fell into step with me as Grace gushed to Wolf about Johnny finally being hers.

"I'm keeping my fingers crossed for you that this one has real potential. I want you to know that," Bobby said. "His chest hair can keep you warm during our long Bostonian winters."

"Very funny."

"I thought so. Can I come to dinner with you? Where are you guys going? I'll just sit at the bar, I won't say a word, I promise."

"Sorry, I don't think I want a chaperone. Thanks for offering, though," I said as I poked him in the ribs.

"Things are looking up for us, Abs," Grace mused as she winked at me.

"It's about time!" I answered. And that was the truth.

I spent the next hour before bed laughing with my friends on the deck, looking forward to a legitimate date with a nice, albeit hairy, guy and thoroughly enjoying the company I was keeping.

CHAPTER 14

Vodka Is Everyone's Favorite Orphan

Months had passed, but I dreaded going back to Vera Wang the way I dreaded calling the pizza place down the street once they started to recognize my voice. I really shouldn't have complained about Katie wanting me to do this one maid of honor task for her, especially since I hadn't really done a single thing to help her plan her wedding. I figured as long as her fiancé showed up at the church, there wasn't really anything for her to worry about. Katie took my disinterest to mean that I was jealous and resentful of her for getting married before me, which was partially true, but it wasn't the only reason why I didn't want to sit with her while she tasted thirty versions of chocolate cake. At the time, I had been busy. Really. I was. I had a lonely carton of Cherry Garcia in my freezer probably going through some epic separation anxiety.

The second week of July I walked down to Newbury Street and paused in front of the bridal salon. *Hello, old friend,* I thought as I peered in the window. *I never meant for things to end this way.* I was trying to be a good maid of honor, and more important, a good sister, so I made sure that I had left with enough time to stop by the lingerie store, aptly named "Intimacy," and pick up Katie's bridal underwear for her like she asked. I knew picking up my little sister's bridal undies would be painful, but I was ready for it. I was prepared. What I was not prepared for was for the salesgirl to mistake me for the bride, stare at my rear end, inform me that the size small would most likely not fit, and suggest that I buy a full-coverage granny panty instead. There was nothing quite like the unique humiliation of having to explain that I was not the bride, but only the fatter, older, jilted sister of the bride, so the size small panty would be just fine for my size small sister and her size small ass. That was nothing short of excruciating.

I took a deep breath as I prepared to enter Vera Wang, when Grace called. I figured she was calling to reassure me that my return to Vera wouldn't be as mentally torturous as I was expecting it to be. Not exactly.

"Thank God you called," I said. "I need a pep talk before I go back into this store. I think I'm breaking out in hives or something." I scratched at the skin on the back of my neck. I knew it was going to mess with my head being back in Vera Wang. I didn't think it would mess with my skin too, but it felt like my neck was on fire.

"Abby, I need you to help me," Grace said as she sobbed into the phone with such choking spasms I had a hard time understanding her. "You have no idea what just happened to me."

"Are you okay? What's wrong?" I froze as I waited for her to answer, terrified that she had been in some kind of accident or that someone had died. I glanced at my watch and realized I was already fifteen minutes late for Katie's appointment. It didn't matter. She'd have to wait.

"His wife just called me at the office," she whispered, and I could hear the panic and the fear in her voice despite the fact that I could barely hear her at all.

"Oh my God. What did she say?" I said calmly, hoping somehow that this wasn't as bad as I knew it was.

"She told me to stay away from her husband and called me a home-wrecker. She asked me if I knew he had a wife and kids at home and said only an evil woman would come between a man and his family." Grace was hysterical.

"I don't know what to say." I didn't. Neither of us had any experience with this type of situation. It was complicated, and Grace may not have made the best decisions where Johnny was concerned, but it crushed me to hear her this upset. We had known that if she had an affair with a married man, she was going to have to deal with the fallout, but deep down we were hoping it wouldn't happen. I wanted to be with her, and I glanced at the bridal store and wished that I didn't have to go inside. I would have stayed on that corner and talked to her forever if she wanted me to, the same way she had talked to me when I needed her. That's what friends are for. The problem was, I had a sister in a wedding dress who needed me too. "What did you say?"

"Nothing. I listened to her scream at me, and then she hung up. What could I even say? I've never felt this bad in my life," she wailed. "How did I end up here?"

Then I repeated the words she had said to me months ago. "I wish there was something I could say here to make you feel better. I know you're a good person, but this sucks. Are you sure this is what you really want?"

"What do you mean?"

"I know that he told her he's going to leave her, and that's what you wanted, and I'm happy that he's finally doing what he needs to do to be with you, but that's not going to change the fact that this woman hates you and is going to make it her life's mission to ruin you."

"I love him. I know the timing was horrible and I did things I'm not proud of, and I have to live with that. But I love him and I want to be with him. Why does it have to be so goddamn hard? Why couldn't I have fallen in love with someone who was single like normal people?"

"Because love isn't rational, and sometimes you can't choose it. It chooses you." I glanced up at the store window again and realized that so many people associated bridal salons with the happiest times in their lives. I associated them with one of the worst in mine, and now in Grace's too. It was clear that for some reason this store had very bad mojo. I decided I'd try to avoid walking by it going forward.

"I can't believe this is happening."

"How'd she get your number?" I asked.

"I don't know. I don't even know how she found out about me."

"She's not stupid, Grace. When he told her he was leaving her, she probably went through his phone or something. Men rarely leave their wives unless there's someone else for them to go to. They can't be alone. Ben might have stayed with me as long as he did simply because he didn't know how to work his washing machine. Eventually she had to find out about you if you guys are going to be together."

"I was prepared for eventually. I wasn't prepared for today."

"I know, babe. I know. I think you need to get out of there. Can you go home?" I asked, checking my watch again and watching the minutes tick by.

"I already left. I'm on my way home now, except I walked the wrong way. I feel like I'm spinning in circles."

"Go home, take a hot shower, and curl up on the couch. I'll be over as soon as I can."

"Don't tell anyone, please. No one else understands the way you do. I'm so ashamed."

"I won't, I promise. Everything will be okay." I tried to sound soothing. I don't think it worked.

"Hurry up. I don't want to be alone right now," she cried, so desperately I actually winced.

"I will. Just sit tight, I'm coming."

She hung up, and I threw my phone in my bag as I mentally switched gears and hurried into the salon. My heart broke for her, and I was nervous about leaving her alone when she was so hysterical, but there was no way I could miss Katie's appointment. Grace had single-handedly nursed me back to sufficient mental health, and now when she needed me most I had to make her wait. Why did everything always happen at once?

I stared at the floor as I walked to the back of the room and met my mother, sitting in a chair, looking at herself in a compact mirror, fixing the makeup she probably applied with a spatula. My mother had apparently been doing some maintenance on herself in preparation for the wedding. She looked like a wax figure that escaped from Madame Tussauds.

"Hey," I said as I slouched down next to her in my long black cotton dress, baseball hat, and dark sunglasses. I gave her a peck on her Restylane–filled cheek "How are you?"

My mother eyed me curiously. "Why do you look like you're about to rob a bank or something?" she asked.

"I'm afraid the salesgirls will recognize me. I'm pretty sure I'm banned for life from this store. I probably could be arrested."

"You could be arrested for walking around looking like a homeless person, that's for sure. You would feel so much better about everything if you dressed nicely and got a new haircut or something. It's been months, Abby. When are you going to start taking care of yourself again?"

"Not today, Mom. Definitely not today." I sat on the chair that Grace had occupied eons ago, only I didn't have the luxury of slugging champagne like she had. I was too embarrassed to even look at the salesladies, never mind ask for a cocktail. If I'd been smart I'd have packed a flask.

"Did you take my advice and look into ordering a juice cleanse?" my mother asked. "I don't want to upset you by asking, but you never call home and tell me anything so you leave me no choice."

I'm trying to save money, and long-distance calls to the underworld are pricey, I thought.

"No. But I started running again. That should help," I said. I heard my aunt Patrice in my head, reminding me that my mother was trying to help me, and tried very hard to keep my composure.

"Well, if you don't want to do a cleanse, why don't you do what I did and become vegan?"

"I don't even know what that is." *And I don't care,* I thought.

"It's simple, really. You eat mostly vegetables and soy products. You can't consume anything that once had a mother and a father."

"Lucky for you vodka is everyone's favorite orphan," I said flatly. Bye-bye, composure.

"What's with the attitude?"

"Honestly, I'm trying to lose the weight, but you constantly reminding me that I'm fatter than usual isn't helping. And really, who cares? No one will be looking at me."

My mother shrugged, finally acquiescing. "Okay, suit yourself. We'll just buy you some extra Spanx, maybe a full body shaper. I'm sure we'll find something that'll help."

"Gee, you're the best mom in the whole world."

"I know you're being sarcastic, but let me remind you that I am your mother. It's not my job to make you feel better about yourself. It's my job to tell you the truth."

The sick thing is, she actually believed that.

"I'm almost ready!" Katie chirped from behind her velvet curtain. "I can't wait for you guys to see how amazing this dress is!" I found it hysterical that Katie got herself a designer gown and threw me in a giant pink garbage bag. Just in case I wasn't self-conscious enough as it was. Bobby was right. Bridesmaids probably were supremely easy targets.

"What are you wearing to the wedding anyway?" I asked my mom, trying to change the topic of conversation.

"I'm not telling anyone. I want it to be a surprise."

"Why? You're not the bride. Don't you think keeping your dress a secret is a little bizarre?"

"Abby, I've been working hard to look my best for this wedding because I'm planning on actually being able to walk down the aisle this time, and I care what people think of me. I want to dazzle everyone!"

"You're right. How insensitive of me. I'm so sorry that my fiancé broke up with me and denied you the chance to waltz down the aisle."

"Oh, stop being ridiculous. It's not about me," she said. "I do want to ask you, though, how do I look? I haven't seen you in over a month, and I've been getting these resurfacing facials. They're supposed to take years off your complexion. What do you think? Don't you see a difference?" She spun around and placed one hand on her hip like she was posing for some geriatric pageant judges. My mother's obsession with youth was going to bankrupt her. She had had her entire body nipped, tucked, sucked, and pinned so tightly it was a wonder she could move. If she knew where to find one of those hyperbaric sleeping chambers Michael Jackson had, she'd probably put one in the living room.

"You can definitely see a difference, Mom. You always look great," I replied without even looking at her. I knew it was what she wanted to hear, and because I loved her despite all her flaws, I wanted to give her an honest compliment. I only wished that just once she could bring herself to return the favor.

"Thank you, Abby. That's nice to hear," she said as she turned to face the mirror.

"Okay, are you guys ready?" Katie asked, thankfully putting an end to our conversation.

"We're ready. Come on out, Katie," I said. *Hold it together when you see her,* I ordered myself. *You're her older sister, and it's your job to hold it together.* I would not allow myself to ruin this experience for her. I would not allow Ben to turn me into a horrible sister on top of everything else.

She threw the curtains aside, and my mouth dropped at the sight of her. She smoothed the skirt over her midsection and held her arms straight out to the side as she turned so we could see the intricately sewn satin-covered buttons running down the back. It was beautiful. It was perfect. It was stunning.

It was mine.

"So what do you guys think? It's just gorgeous, isn't it? I can't wait for Charlie to see me in this!"

My mother eyed her critically. "The dress is beautiful, Katie. I'm just wondering, are you sure you're tall enough for a train that long?" she asked.

"Yes! It's exactly what I've always wanted," Katie squealed with the kind of joy only impending brides can feel.

"And you don't think it makes you look like a giant marshmallow? The skirt is rather full, darling, and the last thing a woman needs is extra fabric around the hips."

"It's a wedding dress, Mom. The skirt's supposed to be full," Katie replied, gritting her newly bleached teeth.

"Turn around," my mother ordered as Katie turned to reveal the satin buttons running down the length of the dress. "It's a lovely dress, but if you want to wear strapless, I think you should start doing some exercises for your back and your shoulders. You know, girls forget that when they're on the altar everyone will be staring at their back, and you don't want those little rolls to be spilling over the top," Mommy Dearest said.

"Do you think it would be *possible* for you to just say something nice for once in your life without the added criticism? Can't you just say, 'The dress is lovely,' and then shut your mouth?" Katie snapped.

"Why my daughters have to be so mean to me, I just don't understand. I'm only trying to help."

"Abby, what do you think? Say something," Katie said as she turned to me, hoping that I'd be the relative who'd tell her how unequivocally beautiful she looked in her dress.

Unfortunately, today was just not her day.

"Take it off. Take it off right now," I said, feeling beads of sweat run down my back.

"Huh?" she asked, understandably confused.

"What part of 'Take it off' is hard for you to understand? Take it off, now."

"Why? Is there something wrong with it?" she asked nervously as she turned to make sure there wasn't some kind of flaw on the train.

"What's wrong with it is that it's *my* dress," I said, the same way a three-year-old does when another kid takes her pail in the sandbox.

"I don't get it," Katie said, shaking her head, still confused.

"That's my wedding dress," I informed her.

"Umm, last time I checked you never got married, so you never had a wedding dress," she snapped.

That was low, I thought. *It was accurate, but it was still low.*

"That's the dress I was going to buy. That's the dress I was wearing when Ben broke up with me. You are not wearing that dress. You can wear any other dress in this entire store, in the entire world, but you cannot wear that one."

"Oh my God. This is the dress you were going to buy? I never got a chance to see it," Katie said as she placed her hand over her heart. For a second, I hoped she'd feel some compassion and immediately agree that she should buy something else.

"Well, now you have, and I'm sorry, but it's just too . . . painful to see you in that. You can't wear it."

"So, I'm basically . . . you?"

"Yes. Take it off," I repeated. I could not for the life of me understand why, despite the fact that I had told her to ditch the dress multiple times, she was still wearing it.

"Don't you think it's kind of poetic? I fell in love with this dress the second I saw it. Maybe that's why! Maybe that sisterly bond we have was telling me that if you couldn't wear it, then I should. To *honor* you."

"On what Earth do you think this is honoring me? This is not honoring me, this is torturing me! I moved past you buying the same sweater I had when we were in high school, and the same exact boots that I got when I was a freshman in college, but I draw the line here. You are not going to copy my wedding dress. Take it off. Now."

"I absolutely will not. You're insane."

Yup. I most certainly was. And I couldn't have cared less. So much for sisterly compassion.

"I will not let you impersonate me! That's my Vera, and if I'm not going to wear it, you sure as hell aren't!" I shrieked as I lunged at her and tried to force her to spin around so that I could undo the zipper.

"Oh my God! Get off of me! What the hell is the matter with you?" she yelled as she tried to swat my hands away. I didn't let go of her (correction: *my*) dress as we screamed loudly enough for people outside the fitting room to hear us. If there had been any doubt that I was no longer welcome in this store, it was gone.

"Mom, do something! She's gone totally mad!" Katie screamed as she tried to pry my hands off the dress.

"Girls, stop that," my mom said as she moved a single piece of hair off her forehead and tucked it behind her ear. "You're causing a scene. People can hear you!"

Katie pushed me, and I stumbled backward until I bounced off the wall behind me. Oddly enough, the dressing rooms weren't large enough for physical altercations with loved ones while trying on designer gowns. You'd think no one had ever got into a fistfight in Vera Wang before. I lunged at her again, grabbed the back of the dress, and before I knew what happened, I had pulled her down on the floor, and we were wrestling as I literally tried to rip the clothes off her annoyingly skinny body.

"Girls," my mother hissed. "Stop it! You're embarrassing me."

Then we heard a noise that froze both of us instantly: the undeniable sound of fabric ripping. It's a noise every woman knows and never wants to hear, especially when she's wearing a wedding dress.

"Oh my God," Katie said as she turned as white as the satin she was lying in.

"Okay, maybe it's not that bad. I'm sure it's nothing. Just a little snag," I said, trying to catch my breath and hoping that if I spoke calmly, Katie wouldn't go completely ballistic.

I slowly helped Katie to her feet and gasped when I realized that the skirt had been partially ripped from the bodice.

"Is everything okay in there?" a saleslady asked from outside the fitting room.

"Yes, fine, fine," our mother said airily. "Just a minor sisterly squabble."

"I realize this might look bad," I said as Katie stared in horror at the dress wreckage. At that moment, she was a real-life Cinderella, right after the crazy stepsisters ripped her to shreds. At least I felt bad about it. I wasn't a total bitch.

"What the hell is wrong with both of you?" Katie screeched as she burst into tears. "My only sister just attacked me and tore a hole in my wedding dress, and all my mother cares about is that the salespeople might hear us? We are the most dysfunctional family in America!"

"Relax, sweetheart," my mother said. "If the dress was going to rip, it's best it happened here. There are seamstresses everywhere."

"You ruined my dress," Katie said through clenched teeth as she took a step toward me. I backed away so that my back was against the wall. Literally and figuratively.

"Hey, I didn't ruin it," I said, coming back to earth from my momentary trip to crazy town. "This is so very, very fixable."

"My own sister just tackled me in my wedding dress."

"I admit that may have been a bit extreme. I just . . . I don't know . . . I saw it . . . and what are the odds of you. . . ." I didn't see the smack coming, but I felt it when she cracked the right side of my face. Hard. Tears automatically filled my eyes, and my cheek burned from the impact. My first instinct was to hit her back, but I figured I had done enough damage to our relationship for one afternoon.

"You're my maid of honor," she cried. She was stunned, and embarrassed, and crying. I had felt pretty bad about myself for most of the last year, but it was nothing compared to how I felt now, standing next to my sister in that dressing room. At that moment, I didn't just feel bad about myself, I actually hated myself, and I couldn't blame Katie for hating me too.

"I think we need some help in here," I called out into the salon. We desperately needed help. We needed a team of psychiatrists and anger management specialists. But for starters, a seamstress would have to do.

"Oh my God, what happened here?" the seamstress asked as she examined the gaping hole, the skirt attached to the bodice by mere threads. Apparently, the seamstress and the saleswoman had been lingering outside the dressing room as they materialized the instant I called for help.

"My ill-mannered daughters mistook your dressing room for the WWF ring. That's what happened. Honestly, girls, it's as if no one taught you how to behave in public. Can I have some more champagne, sweetie?" my mom said, holding out her glass to the understandably shocked sales associate.

"I think maybe I should go," I whispered, the realization of what I had just been reduced to, and what I had done to my sister, finally sinking in.

"I'll never forgive you for this, Abby. Not for as long as I live."

"That makes two of us, Katie," I said. And for the second and hopefully last time, I left Vera Wang in tears.

I went directly to the grocery store and bought some ice cream to bring to Grace. We sat on the couch for hours as she cried and talked about how important her relationship with Johnny really was to her, trying to rationalize what had happened and make peace with the fact that the road to getting what she wanted had left some casualties along the way. As hard as it is when you're the one who ends up hurt, it's even worse when you realize that you're the one hurting other people. I lay on the couch with her and tried to cheer her up while knowing that I had just hit my own personal rock bottom. There was no way I could possibly have felt worse about myself than I did sitting on Grace's couch with a swollen face and a heavy heart.

Hours later I went home and stared out the window, trying to figure out why both Grace and I faced such challenges in the love department. I was too ashamed to tell Grace what I had done, and I felt so badly about myself, I decided to do the smart thing and make myself feel even worse.

You around?

Hey you. How was your day?

Traumatizing. Katie got my wedding dress. She's going to be married in the dress I was going to be married in . . . assuming they can fix it.

I'm sorry. I'm sure you'd have looked better in it.

Especially considering I attacked her and ripped it, yeah, probably.

You ripped it?

What have you done to me?

I don't get it.

That doesn't surprise me. You never did.

I had felt pretty bad for most of the last year, but when I crawled into bed that night, I felt like the worst person on earth. It was time to stop playing the "poor pitiful me" card. After today, it was pretty clear that I deserved everything I got.

CHAPTER 15

Real Men Wear Pink

I WENT BACK to the beach and tried to figure out how to handle the fact that I freaked out on my innocent sister and her even more innocent dress. It took a lot of apologizing to Katie's voicemail and begging for forgiveness to get her to speak to me again, not to mention two bouquets of flowers and a gift certificate for a pre-wedding facial. I didn't blame her for being angry with me—hell, I would probably never have spoken to me again—but I had one thing working in my favor, and she and I both knew it. She needed me to control our mother on the quickly approaching wedding day. Granted, that was nearly impossible, but someone had to at least try. And for that, she'd forgive me for just about anything.

Meanwhile, I spent a few days trying to get myself mentally prepared for my date. It was the second week of July, and I was ready for this little project to finally start to produce results. I couldn't decide what to wear and had gone through the contents of my entire closet twice before I admitted that I needed some reinforcement.

"What do you think?" I asked Lara as I did one last spin in front of the mirror. "Does this dress cover my love handles or do I look fat?" Lara had stopped by on her way home from work to wish me luck and give me final outfit approval. I was so happy that I had Lara to hang out with while Grace spent the workweek in the city. Without her, I'd have had to ask Bobby or Wolf what they thought of my outfit, and since Wolf thought that it was hot if a girl wore a dirndl and Bobby adhered to the less-is-more mentality, I doubted that either of them would have been of much help.

"I think you look cute. I don't really know what girls wear on dates anymore, but I like it."

"Did you used to freak out about this stuff when you were dating your husband?" I asked.

She ran her hand through her hair and tucked it behind her ear. "I used to freak out about everything. I thought my husband was the most handsome man in the world when we were dating. I used to worry that if I didn't look perfect or act perfect or be the perfect girlfriend, he'd break up with me or something. It wasn't normal. Just remember that the guys you want to be with are supposed to make you feel comfortable, not crazy. Trust me when I tell you I learned that one the hard way." She began to spin her rings, as per usual, but now I wondered if she did it out of endearment or habit, or because she felt like her finger was wearing a handcuff she wished she could remove.

"That's a good rule! You're right. It's just dinner. How bad could it be?" I realized that Lara always seemed sad and a bit disillusioned, except for the few times I'd seen her talk about her husband. Then she just seemed seriously pissed off.

"It'll be fine," she said. "My idea of an exciting night these days consists of ice cream and a romance novel. I'll be lucky if I'm awake at ten."

"Ice cream and a book sound pretty good to me," I admitted,

smoothing wayward frizz along my hairline. "Part of me wishes I was doing that too." I thought fondly of many cozy nights with my friends from the freezer.

"No, you don't," she said as she stared at my reflection in the full-length mirror. "I admire you, Abby. I think it's great you're dating. You're out of your rut. That's not easy to do."

"I don't think I'm quite out of it yet, but this is a good start."

"Can I ask you a stupid question?" she asked as she handed me a stack of bracelets.

"Shoot."

"Do people make out on first dates these days? I mean, this isn't college where you leave a keg party bombed at 2:30 A.M. How do dates even end? Are you going to shake his hand or something?"

"I hadn't thought about it. But thank you for sufficiently freaking me out," I said.

"Carrie Bradshaw never shook anyone's hand, I don't think," Lara said. I couldn't tell if she was remembering her dating years fondly or cursing fate for some of the decisions she had made along the way—most likely the ones that landed her in Rhode Island and her husband of three years in Massachusetts for months at a clip.

"Carrie Bradshaw also lived in Chanel couture despite making three cents a word at a newspaper people used to line their birdcages. I don't think she should be my role model. The real world is a little different. I think."

"So then what's the answer?" Lara asked. Despite my efforts to go on dates, I realized I didn't spend a whole lot of time thinking about what that actually meant. Shit.

"I won't shake his hand. But maybe I'll give him a high-five or something," I said, only partially kidding.

"Interesting. You're right. Maybe that's better," she said, nodding.

We were educated women in our early thirties, and we were debating the merits of high-fiving a guy at the end of a date. Something was seriously wrong with us.

"Have fun," she said as I did one last check to make sure my body shaper wasn't showing. "I'm going to stop at the grocery store, cook dinner, and go to bed, so no matter what happens, you'll have a better night than I will. Think of it that way."

"Are you sure you're okay?" I asked, hoping that maybe Lara would open up if I just gave her the opportunity. "If you ever want to talk about anything, I'm here for you."

"I'm fine!" she said with way too much enthusiasm. "Go, get out of here, don't worry about us boring married ladies."

We walked out to the driveway, and I waited for her to buckle herself into the front seat of her car. "Have fun tonight. Call me tomorrow and let me know if he's a good hand-shaker," she joked.

"You got it! Have a good night," I said as she pulled out of the driveway and I headed into town for my very first date in a very long time. I had just hit the sidewalk when my phone beeped.

I had a pretty brutal day and could use a laugh. You around?

Sorry, gotta run. I have a date.

I stared at the message I sent just to make sure that I actually wrote what I thought I just wrote. *Ha!* I said out loud to my phone as if Ben could somehow hear me. *I don't need you and I don't want you! I have a hot date with a hot guy at a hot restaurant. How do you like me now?* I was so proud of myself when I put my phone back in my bag that I actually began to strut. The truth was, I was happy he had a bad day, and even happier that I couldn't help him even if I'd wanted to. I had somewhere to be. I had a date.

Damn, that felt good to say. And even better to actually mean it.

The Black Pearl was one of Newport's most popular restaurants. The food was great, the crowd was lively, and it was located on the pier near the water. So far as date spots go, it was a no-brainer. I entered the restaurant and found Pete waiting at the bar. He was drinking a draft beer, wearing a blue golf shirt, pink pants, and a whale-patterned belt. I stopped in my tracks at the door, taking in the sight of him and his very, very pink pants and reminded myself that I was not going to be hypercritical of him because of his wardrobe. Real men wear pink, and every girl knew that once you started dating a guy you could change all of his clothes. So I figured I could handle it for now and then burn his pants and any item of clothing with fish stitched into the fabric when the timing was right. Like date number two. Besides, I already knew what I needed to know to make him an acceptable dating candidate: he was nice, he was funny, he was an architect, and he actually followed through on making dinner reservations. Those were not bad qualities in a guy.

I tapped him lightly on the shoulder and waved hello. "Hey there," I said with a smile, trying to sound effortlessly friendly and not at all nervous that my Spanx suit was riding up.

"Hey," he said as he pecked me awkwardly on the cheek. "You look very nice."

"Thanks, so do you." And he did. The pink pants were growing on me.

"Are you ready to sit? I think our table's ready."

"Absolutely. I haven't eaten here yet. I hear the food is amazing."

"Best clam chowder in the world," he said confidently.

"Careful, I'm from Boston. Those are fighting words."

He smiled and grabbed his beer off the bar before he stood, leaning over to pick something up off the floor. "Here," he said sheepishly. "These are for you."

He thrust a bouquet of roses at me. Bright, vivid purple roses. I didn't know roses came in that particular shade of, well, Barney-the-dinosaur purple. I felt awkward holding them, like some kind of pageant contestant, but I reminded myself to appreciate the gesture. Grace was right, I had to stop finding flaws in guys who were too nice. These were the first flowers I had received in years, and I was pretty sure that the guys who bring you flowers are supposed to be considered the good ones. Even if they do have questionable taste in said flowers. And pants.

"Thank you. They're beautiful," I said as I held them up to my nose to smell them.

"I'm glad you like them. I wasn't sure guys still gave flowers on dates. Did I overdo it?" he asked shyly.

"Not at all. It's a really sweet gesture."

"Good. Let's sit," he said. "I'm starved."

We followed the hostess to a small wooden table in the back by the windows that overlooked the wharf. I gently placed the flowers on the floor and prayed that I wouldn't forget they were there and accidentally crush them with my chair during dinner.

He passed me the wine list and asked, "Do you prefer red or white?"

"It's kind of hot out, so I'd prefer white, but I'm fine with anything."

"Great. So am I, so why don't you pick a bottle?"

"Sure," I said as I glanced at the list. I didn't know a whole lot about wine, so I found a reasonably priced bottle of Sauvignon Blanc and pointed to the number as the waitress looked over my shoulder.

"I'll be right back to take your order," the waitress said as she left to get our wine.

Once she was gone, Pete wasted no time diving into the topic I had been praying he'd avoid. Bobby.

"So, Bobby seems like a funny guy."

"Yeah, I'm sorry about him. He's cool, but he has an offbeat sense of humor. I wasn't sure how I felt about him when we first met, but he's a good friend."

"He seemed to like embarrassing you."

"I guess. He's harmless, I promise."

"Was he drunk?"

"Sadly, no. That was him dead sober. You can imagine what he's like after a few cocktails."

"You seemed to handle yourself pretty well. You were actually pretty funny too. A lot of girls probably would've started to cry."

"Thanks, I try."

"I like that about you. I like girls with a little fight in them. It was a nice surprise."

If this was what dating was like, I had been worried for nothing. It wasn't so scary after all. Truth be told, talking to Pete was easier than talking to Ben had been for the last few months of our relationship. Maybe I would have noticed that if I'd had something to compare it to. The waitress took our orders, and we continued to have the kind of easy conversation I had thought was impossible for first dates. My heart fluttered in my chest when he spoke, a feeling I had long since forgotten and feared was gone forever. Just like that, it was back, and I felt Ben's hold on me loosen a bit more.

After a fantastic lobster dinner, the waitress cleared our plates and brought us a dessert menu, which I politely pushed to the side. I thought the date was going great, but I didn't want to assume that Pete wanted the night to continue. I also couldn't afford to eat dessert with the wedding only a week away.

"Do you want dessert?" he asked as he scanned the menu.

"No, I'm okay. I don't have much of a sweet tooth," I lied. I wasn't one of those girls who didn't eat on dates, but I also didn't need to be one who licked ice cream off a plate either.

"I'm not in the mood for dessert, but I thought the wine you picked was pretty great. Would you be up for ordering another bottle? If you want to get home, I understand, but I don't think I'm ready for the night to end yet. I hope that doesn't sound creepy."

I smiled wide. "I think another bottle is a great idea. I'm having a nice time."

"Me too," he agreed as he waved the waitress over and ordered another bottle, and my insides continued to flutter, just a little, at the potential and possibility of Pete.

An hour later I stomped up the stairs to the deck cursing and bashing anything within reach with the newly decapitated beauty queen flowers. I was reeling from shock. And embarrassment. And confusion. I was planning on throwing the flower stems in the garbage, myself on the couch, and my optimism out the window. Unfortunately, fate once again had other plans for me.

"She's back!" Bobby yelled from a chair on the deck. He was almost invisible in the darkness, save for the orange glow of his cigarette. "How'd it go?"

"Don't you ever go home?" I asked, embarrassed that I was going to have to relive this for him. Once was way more than enough.

"We don't have any food at our place. Plus, I was waiting for you to get back. I feel like a proud papa sending my little girl out on her first big girl date."

"I don't think I can talk about it. It's too ridiculous." I sighed in frustration.

"Oh, stop exaggerating. What happened? Did he refuse to give you his varsity jacket or something?"

"Bobby, I just had one of the worst dates ever. I mean it."

"Okay, again, I'm sure you're exaggerating, but I'll bite. Tell me what happened," Bobby said as he battled a yawn.

I began to pace back and forth across the splintered deck in front of the grill, my anger making it impossible for me to stand still. "I can't believe that just happened," I said.

"You realize I'm still waiting for you to tell me, right?" Bobby sighed under his breath as he finished his beer and fished another one from the partially melted ice in the cooler at his feet. Finally, he noticed the remains of the flowers I was still holding in my hands.

"What happened to those flowers?" he asked.

"I beat them against a lamppost on the way home. Anyway . . ."

Bobby interrupted me. "Wait." He laughed. "Are you seriously telling me that a date that started with dinner at the Black Pearl and roses went so badly that you had to destroy them on the three-block walk home? I give up. You might actually be beyond repair."

"Oh please. They're fucking purple. His pants were pink, and his flowers were purple. I should've known something was off."

"So the guy has bad taste in flowers, and apparently in pants, but I'm still not seeing the big problem here. Unless he was gay. Was he?" Bobby asked.

"No, and I was fine with his penchant for pastels. I really was. Everything was going great, and then the check came."

"Oh God. Tell me he made you split the bill," Bobby asked, placing his beer on the table as he waited for my answer.

"No. Worse," I said, slowly, delaying telling him the story for as long as possible.

"Did he ask you to leave the tip? That's not the worst thing in the world. I know a lot of guys who do that, and a lot of girls who like to do it. Some empowerment bullshit or something."

"Worse," I replied.

"He made you pay for the entire dinner? That's unacceptable. There's absolutely no excuse for that."

"Worse."

"I can't really think of anything worse than a guy making a girl pay for dinner on the first date, unless of course he went to the bathroom when the check came and climbed out the window. He didn't climb out the window, Abby, did he?"

"You have no idea. The bill came, and his entire demeanor changed. It was like someone flipped a switch and turned him into a crazy person. He basically snarled at me!"

"Did you order a ten-pound lobster or something? Maybe I should've pointed out that most girls don't really eat much on first dates. I'm not sure why. Someone must have told them that guys think it's hot if they think their date has an eating disorder or something."

"Hardly. He looked at the bill and started yelling. He said he was going to have to take out a second mortgage on his apartment to pay for it. Now, at first I thought he was kidding, and I actually thought it was funny because that meant that he owns his apartment and being invested in real estate is not a bad thing."

"That's what you thought about? The fact that he owned his own apartment?" Bobby shook his head.

"That was my way of trying to find the silver lining."

"There's no silver lining to a man yelling at a woman he doesn't know over a dinner bill."

"Yeah, I'm aware."

"This is great. I wish I had popcorn." He laughed as he crossed his arms over his chest and threw his feet up on the table.

"He complained that I picked out a bottle of wine that was way too expensive, and that I had some nerve to assume he wanted to spend that much on a girl he didn't even know."

"What? How much was the bottle?"

"Forty dollars!" I finally collapsed in a chair. Reliving the embarrassment made me want a beer from the cooler.

"Oh, come on. This guy is an architect and he was complaining about a forty-dollar bottle of wine in a restaurant? What kind of wine can you even get for less than that during high season at the Black Pearl? Something that comes in a box?"

"I have no idea what the hell he expected me to order, or why he didn't just order it himself if he was going to be such a price whore. That's not even the worst of it. Then he signed the check, crumpled up the receipt, and threw it into the candle on the middle of the table."

"I'm sorry, what?" he asked, his face contorting from trying to stifle his laughter.

"Bobby, he lit the check on fire. I had to throw my water on it to put it out."

"You're lying," Bobby said as he burst into hysterics, finding humor in my misery like the good friend he'd become.

"Like I could make this up."

"What a dick move. You should have hit him with the flowers instead of hitting the lamppost."

"I couldn't because before I knew what was happening, he just up and left. He left me sitting at the table trying to put out the embers. All of the waiters were staring at me. It was completely mortifying. I swear to God this doesn't happen to anyone except me."

"Oh relax. It absolutely does," he said. "I bet you a million women across the country had bad dates this week. It's not your fault he's a cheap asshole."

"I have endured my fair share of ridiculous in the dating world, Bobby. Don't I deserve to have a few nights here and there go smoothly? What is wrong with me?"

"There's nothing wrong with you. And I'd like to point out that I didn't go anywhere near the restaurant, as promised, and instead have been sitting on your porch drinking your beer for the last two hours, of no help to you at all. If you had let me come chaperone your date, I'd have thrown him through the window the second he torched your check. See, my offer to come with you doesn't seem so silly now, does it?"

"This isn't funny!" I squealed, even though I realized it sort of was.

"It's a little funny. You have to see that."

"Why couldn't he just be normal? We didn't need to get married or anything, but why couldn't he at least be a normal human being? Is that too much to ask for?"

"I have no idea why Scrooge McArchitect couldn't spring for a nice bottle of wine. Unfortunately that is a question I can't answer for you, lover girl."

"I've been trying to stay positive, I really have. And I followed your advice and tried to go for the opposite of what I'm typically attracted to. Well, I'm sorry. The purple-flower-buying, pink-pants-wearing architect was as opposite as I could possibly get, and I was pretty sure he had potential. I'm done trying. I've accepted my future as a cat lady."

"Jesus, will you listen to yourself? Go take a shower, have a drink, and chill out," he said. "Maybe in the morning you'll realize how completely ridiculous you sound. You had a bad date. You can't let it keep you from ever wanting to date again. I've had plenty of bad dates. Believe me, you'll get over it."

"No. I won't." I took a long swig from my beer and buried my hands in my now-crunchy beach hair. "I can't do this. All that nights like this do is remind me that I'm better off at home alone on the couch with ice cream in one hand and my remote control in the other."

"That's not going to help you. If you keep that attitude and start housing sugar again, you're going to end up with either an appearance on *The Biggest Loser* or type two diabetes. Whichever comes first. Just shrug it off and move on. Don't dwell on it."

"Sure. That'll be easy," I said as I went inside to take a scalding hot shower in the hopes I'd wash the night off me.

I didn't even have time to dwell on it, though, since the next stop on the "things I'd rather drink bleach than do" tour was coming up. It was time to face the wedding music.

CHAPTER 16

The Overfed Flamingo

THE ALLIED FORCES spent less time preparing for D-Day than my sister did for her wedding, which I couldn't understand for the life of me. We got dressed at my mom's house and waited in the foyer for the florist to arrive, while Katie barked orders and fanned herself with a dinner napkin. I ran around like a lunatic trying to calm Katie's nerves and earn some goodwill after tackling her in the dress salon. I was doing my best to suck up to her when, for once in her life, my mother finally did something to help me out. She pissed off Katie even more than I had.

"Ladies! What do you think? How do I look?" she called from the top of the curving staircase that led to the foyer. "Isn't this stunning?"

My sister and I looked up the stairs to marvel at our mother, perched on the top step, with one hand in the air and the other on her hip. She wore a long, satin, cream-colored gown, complete with beading at the bust and crystals covering the skirt. Oh God. She was wearing a wedding dress.

Katie opened her mouth, but couldn't speak. There she was, at the bottom of the stairs, in her fully mended satin wedding gown, and there was my mother, at the top of the stairs, in hers. It was like looking through a sick and twisted magic mirror. I looked at Katie, unable to breathe, let alone speak, and finally my big sisterly instincts kicked in. No one disrespects my sister on her wedding day. Especially not our clueless mother.

"Take it off," I said, having a flashback to the bridal salon. Why was I constantly telling the women in my family to change?

"She . . . that . . . it's . . ." Katie stuttered, still staring at herself twenty-five years in the future.

I stood frozen, alternating staring at the present-day Katie and the future Katie, unsure of what to do. *Damn you, Emily Post,* I thought. *Why do you refuse to address any of my bridal problems?* "You can't wear that, Mom. You just can't," I said, still utterly flabbergasted.

"What's the problem? This gown is gorgeous, and look at all the details!" she said as she turned to display the long satin train. Now I understood why she had suggested that Katie's train might be too long. She didn't want it to be longer than her own. I finally realized why my mother had been so obsessed with looking her best for this wedding: in her mind, it was the chance to have the wedding she'd always wanted. The one where she got to wear an elegant gown and have everyone think she was beautiful, instead of the one she actually had, pregnant in a polyester suit at city hall. For a moment, I felt bad for her, and so sad that this stunt was actually her pathetic and misguided attempt to recapture a moment of her youth that she hadn't been allowed to have.

Then I got over it.

I moaned in complete frustration. "You can't wear a long white dress to the wedding! You're the mother of the bride, not the bride! You're going to make a fool out of yourself!" That was saying something considering this was coming from someone who looked like an overfed flamingo.

"Don't be ridiculous. First of all, this isn't white, it's cream, and second of all, as the mother of the bride, I can wear anything I want."

"I honestly don't know how your mind works. What were you thinking?" I hissed as my mother slowly descended the stairs.

"What do you mean? You can't possibly say you have a problem with this. I told you about this, Abby," my mother said nonchalantly as she swished past me. Five seconds later her train followed.

"You knew about this?" Katie screamed, turning her fury on me now. Any goodwill I had incurred was gone.

"No, you did not! I specifically asked you what you were wearing, and you said you wanted to surprise us!" I said, still in shock. "I knew nothing about this!"

"We spoke on the phone about it over a month ago," my mother replied innocently.

"No, we spoke about what color *car* would be best. A car, not a dress. And I said black. Has all that Botox seeped into your brain?"

"Oh, calm down. What's the big deal? I want to make sure that everyone knows that I am the mother of the bride. That's all. It's not like I'm wearing a veil or anything!"

Oh my God, I thought. My mom was one of those T-shirt-wearing chicks from the bachelorette party. I should probably consider myself lucky she didn't have a tiara perched on top of her lacquered bob.

"This isn't happening," Katie whispered. The Wilkes sisters were apparently wedding-cursed. At least I'd finally found something we had in common.

"Don't worry," I said to Katie, realizing that we were going to lose this battle. "Just stand next to me all night. Look at the bright side: now you have an excuse not to go anywhere near her."

"Abby, she . . . I think I saw that dress in Vera Wang."

"It's not that bad. You make a way prettier bride than she does, I swear." I could not believe I just said that.

"Why don't you just tackle her and rip it so she has to change?" Katie sobbed.

"Okay, it's your day, so I'm going to let that go," I replied, trying to keep the very tenuous peace agreement between us intact.

"I'm not kidding, Abby. *Do it,*" Katie ordered. I thought about it for a second. My mother wasn't anywhere near as strong as Katie was, and I was pretty sure I could take her.

The doorbell rang, and I ran to answer it, happy to buy some time so I could figure out a way to persuade my mother to change. When the small, stocky woman appeared on the doorstep with our bouquets, my sister grabbed mine and stared at it like she had never seen a peony before. My fear had been realized. My mother wearing a long white dress had finally caused Katie to have a psychotic breakdown.

"These are completely hideous!" she wailed to the poor woman who didn't realize she was delivering flowers to a Bridezilla in the midst of a nervous breakdown. "What the hell are these?"

"They're peonies, and they're fine," I said flatly. Katie's nerves and adrenaline were quickly turning her into a lunatic. Of course, Mom's dress didn't help with that either.

"These are awful!" Katie wailed, throwing the bouquet back in the box with such force that random petals actually exploded from the box and showered the floor.

What the hell is happening? I thought.

"I specifically said I wanted cotton candy–colored flowers. What the hell would you call these?" she asked me as she stared at the bouquet.

"I'd call them pink," I said, my own nerves beginning to fray.

"This is nowhere near the color I asked for. These are raspberry."

"They're pink, Katie. No one is going to notice the difference, I promise." That was true. For the first time in the history of weddings, no one would be looking at the bride because they'd be too busy gawking at her older sister, a shrew dressed head to toe in a color that *definitely* couldn't be called pink, standing next to her mother, who was also clad in a wedding dress.

Next time I was so going to elope.

"They're too pink! They don't work!" She actually stamped her foot the way she used to when she was little and didn't get her way. I forgot how much it bugged me.

"Who the hell are you, Goldilocks? You're getting married, Katie. Who cares if your attendants' flowers are two shades darker than you thought they'd be?"

"Who would be caught dead carrying flowers this color? They're vile!"

"This coming from the girl who picked this gem out for me?" I asked, grabbing the sides of my skirt like I was about to curtsy to the captain of the Good Ship Lollipop. "I look like a walking Pepto-Bismol bottle."

"I thought that color would look nice on you!" she lied.

"This color wouldn't look nice coating a doughnut and covered with sprinkles!" I screamed, regretting the words the second they escaped my lips.

"I'm not letting you ruin this for me. This is *my* day," she said defiantly.

"Are you sure? Then why are you wearing *my* dress?" Unfortunately, the truce was over.

"Girls, stop it!" our mother screamed as she ran over to keep us from getting into another wrestling match. "Katie, the flowers are fine, relax. Abby, zip it. Not another word out of you. Today is supposed to be the happiest day of *my life,* and you're both ruining it for me!" she scolded.

My sister and I finally stopped arguing with each other and turned to stare at her.

God, my family was screwed up.

I made a mental note to remind Aunt Patrice to shove gum in my mother's mouth when it came time to say the vows to make sure she didn't shout "I do" and accidentally end up marrying Katie's fiancé. Thankfully, there was no more time to argue. It was time to walk the plank.

When the organ music started, I exited the church vestibule, clutching my flowers like a security blanket and feeling as if everyone in the room was staring at me. Not that that made me any different from any other maid of honor in any other wedding on planet Earth, but the attention made my knees shake so badly I was worried that I might actually fall in the middle of the aisle. As bad as that humiliation would have been, I wasn't entirely sure that Katie would wait for me to get up before she began her procession, and I'd most likely end up a giant pink speed bump on her way to the altar.

I tried to bury the emotions that were brimming with each step I took. I knew it wasn't meant to be for me, not yet at least, but it didn't make attending my first post-breakup wedding any easier. I stood at the altar next to her, holding her bouquet, fluffing her dress, watching her float past me in this important stage of life. It was like I was being left behind all over again and forced to watch every moment of what could have been in slow motion, with a smile plastered on my face. When the priest asked if anyone objected to the marriage, I realized that maybe I was lucky that Ben had called off the wedding when he did. The only thing worse than canceling our engagement on Facebook would have been if he had objected to his own nuptials from the altar. If that had happened, I'd have had to spend the summer somewhere much farther away than Newport to rebuild my emotional switchboard. Like Guam or something. I guess I was trying to find the silver lining here too.

After the ceremony and innumerable pictures, most of which involved my mother attempting to stand in front of the bride and groom, we headed to the reception at the Boston Public Library, the venue I had booked for my wedding. I had attended dozens of weddings over the years, and no one had had their reception at the historic Boston site. It was one of the things I loved about it. It was different, it was original, it was going to make my wedding one that everyone would remember. In my dreams it was going to be perfect. Of course, in my dreams I was also skinny and wearing the white dress. It's funny how things turn out sometimes.

We entered the reception hall, and I stopped in my tracks. The long rectangular tables were covered with white damask tablecloths and dotted with huge topiaries of roses and hydrangeas. Candles covered every surface in sight, and the high vaulted ceilings and dramatic paned windows made you feel like you had walked into a veritable wedding wonderland. On a table off to the side was a dramatic four-tiered wedding cake, covered with vanilla buttercream and adorned with pink and white sugar flowers. I didn't have to wait for the cake to be cut to know that it was red velvet, Katie's favorite. At the very least, provided I was able to stomach it, I knew I'd enjoy dessert.

I took a glass of champagne from one of the trays and turned to say hello to some of the guests. I was approached right away by Charlie, my brand-new brother-in-law.

"Hey, Abby," he said as he leaned down and kissed my cheek. "You look beautiful, you really do. Have you lost weight?" he asked. Katie had clearly trained him well.

"Thanks, a little, yeah. I've been trying to at least," I said as I reached up and straightened his boutonniere. "Let the record show that you're officially my favorite brother-in-law."

"Listen, I hope you don't mind my saying this, but I just want to say that I think it's really great how cool you've been about this whole thing. I know it's been hard. For what it's worth, it's been hard on Katie too," he said with a strained smile.

"What do you mean hard on her? She seems fine." I caught sight of my sister out of the corner of my eye, playing the part of the perfect bride. You'd never guess that we had been mere minutes from a full-blown fistfight just a little while ago.

"You know, getting married so soon after everything happened to you. Ben's an asshole, by the way. It's his loss."

"Yeah, I've figured that out already," I answered, though hearing Ben's name in this setting made my stomach churn.

"She loves you so much, and she's been so torn up about this whole thing. I feel like I'm responsible. If I had known what had happened,

I would've waited to propose. I'm sorry that the timing of this sucks so badly for you." Charlie stared at the floor as he spoke. I realized he felt guilty, something he shouldn't feel on his wedding day. No one in this room was to blame for what had happened, not even me. I think I believed that.

"It's not your fault. And I'm happy you didn't wait to ask her to marry you. That wouldn't have been right either," I said.

"I just love her so much, and I want both of you guys to enjoy today."

"You do, don't you? Love her," I asked, looking at the expression on Charlie's boyish face. It was one I'd never seen on Ben's, not once in the ten years I was with him.

"I can't imagine my life without her."

"Me neither," I said honestly. "Now go mingle. You don't need to spend your cocktail hour over here talking to your new sister-in-law. We have years for that."

"Okay. Promise me you'll at least try and have fun," he said as he hugged me.

"I will." I meant it. I think.

Charlie smiled sheepishly as he walked away, and I smiled in spite of myself. I had been dreading this day since I found out Katie was engaged, and the truth was, this had nothing to do with me. Apparently, life did not stand still for everyone else just because my own world stopped spinning, and that's exactly how it should have been. Now if only someone could explain that to my mother, we'd be all set.

Before I was able to sample an appetizer, Katie grabbed me and forced me to follow her into the ladies' room. "I can't get this comb out of my hair, and I want to take my veil off for the reception. Can you pull it out for me?" she asked. She sat down on one of the overstuffed chairs and tilted her blond head back so that I could remove the comb that held her fingertip-length veil in place. For some reason she had styled her hair in one of those bad hairdos you expect to see in your parents' prom pictures from the fifties. Dozens of bobby pins were entangled in her ornate hairstyle, blond curls piled en masse on top of her head.

I tossed my bouquet of pink (fruit-punch pink, not raspberry) peonies down on the chair next to her enormous bouquet of white something or other and placed my glass of champagne on the small table next to her chair. I began to delicately move her hair out of the way of the comb to try to figure out which pins were catching, but there was no way to tell. She had enough metal in her hair to prevent her from getting through security at Logan Airport, and trying to identify the pins that were causing the problem was an exercise in futility.

"Can't we cut the veil off the comb from the bottom and just leave the comb in your hair? It's pretty, I don't think it will look funny, and then we don't need to worry about ruining your . . ." I searched for the words for what to call this look she had so carefully orchestrated. "Bird's nest" came to mind, but I didn't think that was what a bride wanted to hear on her wedding day. ". . . Curls?" I tried. Much better.

I gazed at our reflections in the mirror, and her eyes looked like they were about to explode out their sockets. She gasped and wailed in horror, "Cut my veil? I'd think that was a joke if you didn't have a history of ruining my wedding attire. I cannot believe you just said that." Her shoulders hunched forward as if I had somehow managed to suck all of the bridal bliss out of her body by suggesting I ruin her veil. I yanked on the comb a little harder than I should have, and her face tensed in pain.

"Oww! Abby!" she squealed. Tears welled in her eyes, and she began fluttering her hands in front of her face while looking up at the ceiling lest her falling tears ruin her eye makeup. Okay, making the bride cry was probably something I should have tried to avoid. Now I felt bad. I hated when that happened.

"Katie, I'm sorry. Just sit still a minute! I'll get the comb out without ruining the veil or your hair, I promise."

"Forgive me if I don't believe you," she snorted.

"Do you want to argue with me, or do you want to get back to your cocktail hour?"

The mention of her party immediately cheered her up, and her eyes grew wide with excitement. "You're right. Let's just take care of this so we can get back out there. By the way, did you see the scallops? They looked really good. We have mini-grilled cheeses too."

"You do?" I began to work diligently on the curls and the pins with renewed urgency. "Why didn't you say that to begin with? I would have had this out already," I laughed.

Katie reached back and put her hand on my wrist. I looked at our reflections again in the mirror. My sister in her Vera Wang gown and crystal-encrusted bridal panty, and me in my horrendous pink dress and cotton Fruit of the Looms. No matter how often I saw the two of us together, I still could not shake the thought that one of us must have been switched at birth. How two such totally different people could be born from the same woman was really mind-boggling. Then again, she looked like my mother, and if I wasn't really my parents' child, my mother would've returned me by now. So I guess we would have to chalk it up to a medical mystery and the wonders of the human genome.

"I'm sorry I snapped at you," she said quietly. "I'm really glad that you're my maid of honor. I wish you had decided to bring a guest. It would be more fun for you."

"It's fine," I said reluctantly. "There isn't really anyone I would have brought with me anyway."

"Have you met anyone at the beach? What about that guy you've been hanging out with? You talk about him a lot. What's his story anyway?"

I held pins in her hair with my right hand while gently pulling at the comb with my left. The sooner I freed this comb, the sooner I could revisit the bar. "Sort of," I sighed. "There isn't much to tell about Bobby. He's a nice guy who likes to make fun of me. We've had some interesting moments so far this summer. We get on each other's nerves more than anything."

"You and Ben started off that way, remember? You used to say he drove you crazy and not in a good way."

"Exactly. And look how that ended," I sighed.

She picked up her bouquet and spun it in her hands, checking the blossoms to make sure they weren't starting to wilt. "Well, I hope you're starting to realize how crazy he made you. I mean, you attacked me in a bridal salon. It was like you were possessed. He's turned you into a nut. You know that, right?"

"I do. That wasn't one of my prouder moments," I admitted.

"I blame him for most of it. I mean, don't get me wrong, I blame you too. But mostly him. You weren't acting like yourself. And the dress, I didn't know, Abby. I swear I didn't."

"I know," I said.

"I wouldn't have bought it if I'd had any idea."

"Do you mean that?"

"I don't know. I would have at least talked to you about it instead of having you find out the way you did. I would have asked for your blessing."

"You have it. It was meant for you."

"Thanks. You look great by the way. Whatever you're doing down in Newport, keep it up. I haven't seen you look this alive in a very long time."

"I'm trying to go back to being the old me."

"Is it working?"

"It might be, actually."

"Good," she said, and smiled at me.

One final pull and the comb slipped out. I placed it on the chair next to me, letting the tulle fall in a tangled ball on the floor like a giant ballerina car wreck. "There," I said as I tried to smooth the wayward hairs back into place. She exhaled, incredibly relieved that I hadn't destroyed her precious bridal hair. I picked up my champagne and took a long swig.

"Can you do the bustle for me?" she asked sweetly as she turned her back to me.

I dropped to the floor and ran my hands around the inside hem of her dress, looking for the small fabric loops fastened to the inner layer of her gown. I attached them all to the buttons and then I fluffed the hem of her gown so that it fell gently around her.

"That should do it," I said as I sat back on my heels and looked up at her from the floor.

She smiled wide at her reflection. "Time to join my party!" she chirped, grabbing her bouquet off the chair and floating out of the room like a giant, mobile cream puff, leaving me alone on the floor with my flowers and a pile of tulle, just like Cinderella after she helped the evil stepsisters get ready for the ball. Plus the champagne flute. Minus the mice.

I spent most of the cocktail hour slamming mini-grilled cheeses and washing them down with additional flutes of bubbly. I caught sight of my mother in the corner of the room, showing her guests her intricately beaded gown, and wondered if she had even the slightest clue as to how absolutely nuts people thought she was. Other than Katie, myself, and Aunt Patrice, I don't think anyone really had a full appreciation for how crazy she was, but wearing a wedding dress to her daughter's wedding certainly gave people a pretty good idea.

When the cocktail hour ended, waiters escorted us into the main dining room. I sat down at my table by myself, looking at all the couples on the dance floor, and realized there was only going to be one way to get through this event alone. I stood and once again smoothed my bubblegum dress over my thighs, then returned to the bar, the only place where a single girl could hide from the couples in plain sight. I was going to take my very full flute and disappear into the ladies' room while I pretended to fix my makeup again when Aunt Patrice strolled up and lightly hip-bumped me.

"Hey there!" she said cheerily as she patted me on my ass. "How're you doing?" She leaned her hand on the bar. Her martini sloshed back and forth in her glass, two olives nestled in the bottom of the liquid. We clinked our glasses together and both took large sips.

"I'm great!" I sang as I threw my non-flute-holding hand up in the air over my head like I was holding a pom-pom.

"Well, you look great. Have you been working on being more social like we talked about at lunch?"

"I've been trying."

"Any luck?"

"So far just a whole lot of frogs."

She bobbed her olive skewer up and down in her vodka and olive juice. I wondered if Bobby would call that a filthy whore or just a dirty slut martini. "Well, that's okay. Like I said, the frogs can be fun too. What are you doing over here?"

"Hiding," I admitted. "Not that that's possible in this dress, but I'm trying my best." I realized that hiding from anyone became impossible the second I left the house. The days of embarrassing moments living only on the pages of family photo albums were long gone, and I had no doubt that thanks to Katie's Facebook- and MySpace-obsessed friends, pictures of me in this dress were already splashed all over the Internet for any cyber-stalker to see. It was only a matter of time before some guy Googled me, discovered a picture of me in this dress, and understandably ran for his life.

"You know, no one likes a lady alone at a bar. It looks desperate."

I shrugged. "Ordinarily I'd agree with you, but I don't think that sitting alone in the bathroom looks particularly great either. I'm thirty-one years old, and my fiancé ditched me. I look desperate just by virtue of leaving the house."

"And why are those your only two options? How do you know there aren't cute single boys in the ballroom? Do you know how many people meet their husbands at weddings? It's a perfect social situation: it's a romantic happy occasion, everyone is already prescreened by nature of being invited, and there's free alcohol. It's a single girl's dream! So why aren't you mingling? she asked. "I thought you were going to try to improve your attitude this summer. You promised me," she added.

"I've been trying. I've been trying to meet people and be less negative and go on dates this summer, and every guy I meet has some tragic flaw that I can't seem to get past. I'm not being too picky either. I'm telling you, some of the guys are moat monsters."

"Let me ask you this: are you still hung up on Ben? Maybe that's part of your problem."

"I really don't think I am. I think I'm finally at the point where I'm over him. Still, I don't love the idea of starting over. It's hard, Aunt Patrice. And exhausting. I'm mad at myself for wasting as much time on Ben as I did, and now I'm worried it might be too late for me."

"Oh, that's ridiculous. You're thirty-one, not sixty-five. Things happen when you least expect it. Relax. I'm not worried about you."

"My mother is," I said flatly.

"Your mother is having some kind of midlife crisis. I caught her staring at her reflection in a butter knife before. And don't get me started on her dress. For the life of me I can't figure out what she was thinking. Katie must have wanted to kill her."

"It crossed both of our minds. More than once. There was nothing I could do, though."

"Well, there's something I can do."

"What are you talking about?" I asked.

She smiled mischievously. "I may or may not have accidentally drizzled some pinot noir all over the back of her dress. To be honest, I felt bad about it, but this time she deserves it. I imagine the neighbors will hear her screaming when she gets home and realizes she waltzed around here looking like Lady Macbeth all night."

"You didn't!" I said as I laughed wide-eyed and clutched Aunt Patrice's free hand.

"You bet I did. You're never too old to have your big sister teach you a lesson. I justified my actions by telling myself that it was sort of a wedding gift to your sister."

"Thanks," I said. "You have no idea how much we appreciate it."

"No problem. Now listen, I know it's hard for girls like you. You have high expectations, and you're smart and beautiful and funny, and a lot of guys who are insecure don't have the confidence to handle you. If they can't play knight in shining armor, a lot of them will run. You just need to find someone who isn't afraid of the whole package. Girls like you send out a signal without realizing it."

"What kind of signal? I didn't send Ben a signal. It wasn't my fault," I said. I was starting to believe that more.

"I know it wasn't, darling. But you do. You give off the 'don't try to pull the wool over my eyes' signal. But those aren't the types of guys you want to be with anyway! Eventually, you'll meet someone, and everything will just click. Until then, think of all these dates as good practice."

"Everyone keeps saying that, but I've had years of practice. That should be enough," I growled. "It's just so unfair."

"Abby, you need to let it go. It's over. You're holding on to something that's not there anymore. Stop being sad and get pissed."

"I am," I said as I squeezed her shoulder. "I swear I am."

"That's my girl. In the meantime, my favorite niece does not hide in the ladies' room, okay?"

She put her hand on my waist and walked me back into the party, her martini still sloshing and her high heels clacking on the hardwood floor. I took my seat at the dreaded singles table and shook hands with the guy sitting on my right. His name was Larry, and he was an aspiring artist who liked to spend his free time partaking in jousting competitions at medieval times events. That was all I needed to know about Larry. On my left was Kyle. Kyle was a thirty-four-year-old student who had a later start in the grad school game because it had taken him six years to get out of college and he had spent the next few years traveling the world in search of himself. Maybe my aunt was right. Maybe it was unacceptable for me to hide in the ladies' room, but she was wrong about something too: there was absolutely, positively no way in hell that I was going to meet anyone at this wedding. And I really couldn't have cared less.

Three hours and countless glasses of alcohol later, Katie asked me to help her change into her departure outfit. She swished in front of me down the hall and into the lounge, and I scurried after her, knowing that this was going to be my final duty as maid of honor, the last time it was going to be my job to take care of her. As soon as we entered the lounge she collapsed on the chaise and let out a shriek. "Abby, do you believe I'm married?"

"I kind of don't. It was hard to tell you and Mom apart. You were the one on the altar, right?"

"That's so not funny," she said with a smile. She hesitated for a moment before she asked the same question I had been asking myself for a while. "Abby, do you think she'd be different if Dad were still alive?"

"I don't know. I do know that Dad would have loved to be with us today, and that he would never have let her wear that dress. That's for sure."

"Someday I think I'll laugh about it. Just not anytime soon," she said.

"Me too. Someday years from now, we will find it funny. I feel that way about a lot of things."

She turned her back to me again, this time so I could unhook and unbutton the elaborate mechanisms that held up her gown. When they had all been unfastened, I gently slid the dress down her tiny frame and let her lean her weight on my shoulder as she stepped out of the dress, now pooled around her on the floor like a satin puddle. I helped her lower her short white cocktail dress over her head, taking care, once again, to not disrupt her curls. She reapplied her lip gloss and turned to me one last time before departing for Hawaii.

"I'm happy, Abby. I hope you know that. And I hope you're happy for me."

"I am," I said. I surprised myself, because I meant it.

"You were a really great maid of honor. I'm sorry if I made things harder on you than they already are."

She reached over, and we hugged tightly, something she and I had not done for a very long time. Weddings really do bring out the sap in people.

I released myself from her embrace and fixed one stray curl that had fallen down behind her ear. "Go, have a great time on your honeymoon. Call me when you get back. I want to hear all about it."

"I will, I promise," she said as she once again left me alone in the ladies' lounge, surrounded by the white remnants of her wedding day.

I picked her dress up off the floor and put it in the garment bag we'd brought from home. I folded the bag, fastened the buckles, and handed it to my mother in the vestibule by the doors.

"Can you take this home, please?" I asked. "It needs to go to the dry cleaner, and I'm heading back to the beach on Monday morning."

My mother took the bag from me, but clearly had a problem with that. I imagined I would've been able to see the shock on her face if her face was able to register any type of expression whatsoever.

"What do you want me to do with this until I leave? I can't just stand here holding a travel bag. I look like an out-of-town guest," she said.

"Don't worry, Mom. There's not a person here tonight who doesn't know who you are. Give it to one of the waiters to stash somewhere if you don't want to hold on to it, but I can't take it home with me." I turned and headed back to the lounge to make sure Katie hadn't left anything else behind.

"Abby," I heard my mother call from behind me. She came up to me and for the first time in a very long time wrapped her arms around me. "I know today was hard for you, and I'm proud of you for the way you handled yourself."

"Really? Thank you. That means a lot," I said. I squeezed her tightly. We may have had more differences than I could count, but I loved her and deep down still hoped that one day we could mend our fractured relationship.

"You're welcome. And I want you to know that nobody could have pulled off that dress, but you came damn close."

That day would not be today.

I decided that it was time for me to leave.

CHAPTER 17

Princess Leia Was a Whore

I WAS ABLE to get a cab as soon as I got outside, and once I was nestled in the backseat I immediately kicked off my shoes to rescue my throbbing feet and knees. I couldn't wait to get home, ditch the dress, peel off my Spanx, and pour myself a glass of Cabernet. I got out on the corner and walked barefoot down the dirty, dusty street toward my building, staring at the ground as I walked. When I looked up, I found Bobby sitting on my stoop, smoking a cigarette and playing a game on his iPhone.

"Always a bridesmaid, huh?" he said as he blew a steady stream of smoke into the night air. "Why are you carrying your shoes?" he asked, eyeing the chunky pink shoes in my hand. "You'll need a tetanus shot if you're not careful."

"What are you doing here?" I asked, embarrassed to be seen in this get-up. He smirked at me, the freckles on his nose invisible in the dark. He smiled, enjoying his successful attempt to ambush me, and placed his pack of cigarettes in his pocket.

"That's some dress. What does one even call that shade of pink?"

"I don't even think the people at Crayola know what to call this shade of pink."

"You look like you just escaped from a cotton candy machine."

"Bobby, it's been a long night. Did you come here just to make fun of me?" I asked. "I don't need you to tell me I look ridiculous any more than I need you to tell me I'm actually a brunette and still slightly overweight," I moaned. "Please be nice to me."

"I'm sorry," he sighed. "I didn't come here to make fun of you. I knew that you weren't exactly thrilled about going to your sister's wedding, and I happened to be in the city because I just found out I have a job interview on Monday. I figured the wedding would be over by midnight and you'd be coming home alone and would maybe want some company. So I took up residence on your stoop about a half-hour ago, and here you are."

That was actually sweet. I appreciated Bobby going out of his way to help cheer me up, even if his methods were, as usual, a little strange. "It actually ended up being okay. Nowhere near as bad as I thought it was going to be," I admitted.

"Good. Can we can go inside now?" he asked as he took the ugly pink satin pig shoes from my hand.

"Who said you were coming inside?" I asked.

"You're not going to invite me in after I sat out here playing Words with Friends while I waited to check on you?" he countered.

"You're right, where are my manners?" I said as I climbed the stoop to my front door. "I was planning on opening a bottle of wine. Do you want to come up and have a glass?"

"What kind of gentleman would I be if I made you drink alone?"

"You're no gentleman," I teased.

"Here I thought weddings were supposed to make girls all sappy and romantic. Typical, it turns you into a bubblegum-colored Rambo. Is there anything normal about you? Do you hate puppies?"

"Very funny." I glanced down and noticed a zipped-up gym bag sitting at his feet. "What's in the bag?" I asked.

"Something that's going to make you feel very bad for just saying that I was an asshole."

"I didn't say that. I said you weren't a gentleman. They're not the same thing."

"Sounds like it from where I'm standing."

"Speaking of where you're standing, can you please move so I can open the door? I really need to change. Come on up, even though you called me ugly."

"Good God, woman, I did not say you were ugly. I said the dress was ugly. They're not the same thing."

"Sounds like it from where I'm standing," I said as he grabbed the door and held it open for me. We walked up the three flights of stairs to my apartment. On the landing of the second floor, he held my pink shoes with their four-inch heels up to his face and examined them closely. "I will never understand how you guys walk in these things."

"One of many sacrifices women must make," I said.

"For who? Podiatrists and orthopedic surgeons?"

"Among others." I threw open the door to my apartment and walked down the small hallway into the den.

"So this is where you live," Bobby said as he followed me inside.

I suddenly felt very self-conscious about my apartment and the fact that I had done nothing to prepare for company. I noticed everything that was wrong with the place: the counters were dusty, the green-and-white throw pillows on the couch were jammed into one corner where I had been lying on them last night, stacks of old magazines littered the coffee table. For a second, I thought about suggesting we go to a bar around the corner, but since he was already inside, throwing him out so he didn't notice that the towels in my bathroom hadn't been washed seemed a bit silly. Especially since he had seen me with wet hair and no makeup for most of the time we had known each other.

This must be what being married is like.

I tossed my bag on my navy blue couch and dropped keys in a small dish on a console in the hall. Bobby followed me into the kitchen and placed the mystery bag on the floor as I flicked the light switch on the wall. I reached up into one of the wooden cabinets over the Formica counter and removed two heavy wineglasses, then turned to remove the bottle of wine from the rack in the corner by the utility closet.

"I hope you don't mind red," I said. "It's all I have, and before you go raiding my fridge like you do at the beach, let me assure you, I don't have any Budweiser." He stared at me smiling, but didn't say anything. "What? Seriously what?" I asked, looking down at myself. One thing I knew for sure: pink taffeta was not see-through. So at least I had that going for me.

"Let me finish my statement before you freak out, okay?"

"Oh, sweet Jesus, I just wanted a drink," I said as I tilted my head toward the heavens (or in my case, the floor of the apartment above me). "Why, God? Why will you not even give me the simple things I ask for? I'm ready to admit there might be some master plan I'm unaware of that has me enduring the idiots you parade through my life like show ponies, but a drink in my own apartment? That's too much to ask for without being tormented by a member of the opposite sex?"

I've been known to have a flair for the dramatic.

"So much for you letting me finish. You didn't even let me start, you drama queen."

"Fine. Start. Whatever," I replied, curious as to what was about to come out of his mouth.

"What I was going to say was, you look nice tonight, outfit aside. I hate when girls go to weddings and do something crazy to themselves. They think they look prettier if they paint their faces with clown makeup and break out the curlers and stuff. There's nothing scarier than a pretty girl who looks like an alien version of herself."

"Thank you. I will send your regards to the highly skilled hair and makeup professionals who worked on me for three hours this morning."

"Stop," he said, almost as if he was slightly irritated. "You do that a lot, you know that?"

"Do what?" I asked, genuinely confused.

"Deflect compliments with self-deprecating humor."

I exhaled, as that was nowhere near the top of the list of offensive things I thought he was going to say. I shrugged my shoulders and replied, "I'm sorry. It's force of habit. What should I have said?"

He tilted his head to the side as he thought. "I don't know. 'Thank you' would have sufficed."

"Okay, thank you."

"There. Was that so hard?"

This wasn't the first time someone had pointed out to me that I did that. Ben used to point it out to me all the time. Maybe it was insecurity; maybe it was nerves. Maybe I really did have hair and makeup people work on me for three hours before they deemed me worthy of leaving the salon. Was that really so hard to believe?

"Thank you. Really."

"You're welcome. Now that that's out of the way, why don't you let me get the drinks? You go get out of that thing and put on some normal clothes."

"Good idea," I said with a smile as I handed him the bottle. "There's a corkscrew in the top drawer next to the stove. I'll be right back."

I walked down the hall past the front door and the bathroom and into my bedroom. When I closed the door, I found myself wondering if maybe what I had been looking for had been here the entire time. Maybe the concept of Bobby and me wasn't completely crazy. We got along great, we both appreciated verbal sparring and combative banter, and we both agreed that Dark 'n' Stormys are one of the most underrated cocktails on planet Earth. Since when can those things not be considered a sufficient basis for forming a relationship? *What are you, crazy?* I thought as I immediately pushed the idea from my mind. My friendship with Bobby was by far the healthiest relationship I'd ever had with a guy, and I refused to ruin it by developing feelings for him. I shook my head and reminded myself that I was just trying to feel a little less lonely after the wedding, and that the concept of ever getting romantically involved with Bobby was a train wreck waiting to happen. Besides, he was a better dresser than I was, and I had no interest in dating a man with a better wardrobe than I had. Now that I thought about it, I wasn't entirely sure he wasn't gay and just didn't know it yet.

I unzipped my dress, kicked it off into the corner of the room, and changed into some much-welcome sweats. Before I had time to take the earrings out of my ears, I heard banging in my kitchen, and then the unmistakable sound of a cocktail shaker in action.

When I went back to the kitchen, the mystery bag was open, and the bottle of wine was sitting on the counter. Next to it was a bottle of tequila, a bottle of triple sec, a box of salt, and a container of lime juice that had apparently been squeezed before being packed into Bobby's portable Mexican cocktail kit. He was shaking a metal shaker like a maraca when I entered.

"What the hell are you doing?" I asked.

"Forgive me, but I didn't think wine was going to be strong enough for you," he said as he danced and shook his money-maker around my kitchen. "You had a rough week, so I thought I'd bring over a proper cocktail. How do you like your margaritas? I probably should know that by now."

"On the rocks," I said. It was appropriate when I thought about it. On the rocks: my cocktails, my personal life, my mental state. If I had a car I'd make that my vanity plate.

"On the rocks it is," he said as he popped ice cubes out of the tray he had removed from my freezer. He dropped cubes into the wineglasses and filled them with the now properly chilled cocktail, and handed me one. "Voilà," he said as he handed me the glass. "Listen, I don't mean to kick you when you're down, but I couldn't help but notice what you have in your freezer."

"I had a rough breakup, I told you."

"Do you actually have all thirty-one Baskin-Robbins flavors in there? Is every Girl Scout troop in Boston coming over to make sundaes? Or is that actually all for you?"

"I plead the fifth."

"Ah, lawyering the lawyer. Okay, be that way. I don't think you really need all that comfort food anymore considering how much better you're doing since you met me. Maybe it's time to throw them away . . . toss them right down the garbage chute with that dress."

"I'll think about it," I said. Cleaning out my ice cream stash would be like getting rid of old friends. I pushed the thought from my mind. That would be tomorrow's horror.

"Don't think about it. Do it," he said he collapsed on my couch. I followed him, stopping to grab the stereo remote control off my oval wooden coffee table. I hit Play, and the CD player came on.

"Ella Fitzgerald, huh?" he asked.

"Yeah, I love her."

"Doesn't it make you feel like you live in a Pottery Barn or something?"

"Not until this moment, no. Anyway, you listen to the Beastie Boys at the beach. You cannot judge my choice in music."

"I'm not judging. I actually like jazz a lot. There's a club in the Back Bay I go to sometimes on Saturday nights. They have an awesome jazz band. You should check it out sometime."

I should check it out. Sure, Bobby, that's what I should do. Go sit in a dark bar where people aren't allowed to speak, alone. That's the way to meet someone. Thanks for that.

"How was the wedding? Did you have fun?"

"It was okay," I muttered. "Going alone was kind of a buzz-kill, but otherwise it was fun."

"Why didn't you bring a date?"

"What? Are you serious? You've had a front-row seat to my dating catastrophes this summer. Who should I have brought with me? The pink-pants-wearing architect was out of the question because I couldn't fit a fire extinguisher in my purse."

"I don't know. You could've brought a friend or something."

A friend? What, like you? Did he just ask me why I didn't bring him to the wedding? Am I in Oz?

"Nah, I didn't want to bring a friend to a family event like that where I'd be preoccupied tending to my sister half the night. Works out well for you, though. If I had, I might have gone out somewhere afterward, and you'd have packed your boozy travel kit for nothing."

"Good point."

"Wanna see what's on TV?" I asked as I switched off the CD player and turned on the Sony flat screen hanging on the wall facing my couch. I sat down next to him and flipped through the channel guide. *Pretty Woman* was playing. Jackpot.

"What is it with girls and this movie?" he asked with genuine interest as he shifted his weight to turn toward me. "Every girl I know has seen it about a thousand times and is still perfectly content to watch it every single time it's on. It must be like how geeks feel about *Star Trek.*"

"We prefer the term 'Trekkie.' Thanks."

"You were a space geek? I should've known. I was more of a *Star Wars* guy, for obvious reasons. I bet you rocked some nice Princess Leia braids."

"Nah. Princess Leia was a whore. Everyone knows that."

He laughed. "Seriously, though. What's with the female obsession with this movie?"

"I don't know," I said as I genuinely thought about it. "I guess it's like the ultimate Cinderella story."

Yes. I did just hear the words that came out of my mouth. I hate myself.

"It's about a hooker who keeps her rent money in her toilet tank. Are you mental?"

"No, it's not really about her being a hooker. It's about a fairy tale. She says so in the movie. It's about being rescued, and overcoming obstacles, and meeting Prince Charming. It's about hope and about finding love in strange places. It probably doesn't seem like it on the surface, but it is." I sighed. "You know what they say: when you're not looking, you'll find it. This is the quintessential example of that."

"Well, whatever. I don't care, really. I like the movie. Mostly because Julia Roberts is a complete babe."

He took our empty glasses off the table and returned to the kitchen to whip up another batch of what was admittedly a damn good margarita, as "King of Wishful Thinking" played over the opening credits. *Wishful thinking indeed.*

"So, can I ask you a question?" he asked as he returned with our refills and resumed his position on the opposite end of the couch.

"Sure."

"What happened with the guy, what's his name? Biff?"

"His name's Ben. And you knew that," I growled.

"Seriously, the mystery of what happened to you guys is killing me. Why did you guys break up? Just tell me."

I paused before I spoke, but the wedding had made me more self-reflective than usual, and the truth was, I wanted to talk. I was tired of carrying it around with me. So very, very tired. "I know it sounds crazy, but I swear to God I don't even really know. That's the worst part, the fact that he left me so utterly confused."

"I'm not defending the guy, but people break up with their girlfriends in all sorts of weird ways. We aren't really into the emotional nonsense, you know?"

I hesitated before I said it, not sure if I wanted to let Bobby into this part of my life. What was I now, a pushover for a guy with a sense of humor and a margarita kit?

Yup.

"Fine. You win. The thing is, I wasn't his girlfriend," I said as I stared at him, waiting for my words to register.

"I don't get it," he said. So much for that.

"He was my fiancé," I admitted, cringing from having to say that out loud.

"Whoa. Get the fuck out of here. You were engaged to that guy?" The look on Bobby's face was one I won't forget for as long as I live. It was a combination of his usual impishness, mixed with shock, awe, and I think a little regret that he had been pushing me so hard to tell him what happened. I quite enjoyed seeing it.

"Was. Briefly. Yes."

"I honestly don't know what to say about this."

"That makes you no different than anyone else in my life. There's nothing to say."

"I think you should be happy about it. He doesn't even live here anymore."

"I know. I'm finally at the point where I'm okay with everything," I said as I yawned and curled into a ball in the corner of the couch. My eyes were heavy.

"I know you don't want to talk about it, but let me just add that talking to him won't help you move on. Maybe that's why you've been having a hard time with your little dating project. You can go out with as many guys as you want, but if your head's not in the game, it's just a waste of time. He's probably got a full-blown girlfriend out there already and is just stringing you along for if and when he has to come back east. You know, some girl who trims cacti for a living or something. Who knows? But you don't deserve that."

I barely heard the last part, or the conversation that Viv has with the salesgirls in the snobby store when she tells them that they made a big mistake (big, huge!) not waiting on her. I fell asleep with the lights and the TV on, and with Bobby nestled in the corner of the couch at my feet.

Like a dog.

I woke at 10:30 A.M. with multiple layers of wedding makeup smeared all over my face and, sadly, all over my couch cushions. The TV was off, the glasses were gone, and so was Bobby. I rubbed my hand against my forehead to brush the hair out of my eyes and felt something odd. I reached up and removed a blue Post-it note taken from a pad I kept in my kitchen. I examined it.

You fell asleep and missed the part where a smoking hot Vivian in the black dress shoots the snail across the restaurant. One of the best parts. Hope you slept well. And p.s. you snore.

Not exactly a love letter, but it was still written on actual paper before he stuck it to my forehead. It was the first handwritten communication I had received from a guy in a very, very long time. Maybe, truth be told, ever.

CHAPTER 18

Wheel of Fortune for Single Girls

THE OPPRESSIVE JULY HEAT rolled on toward August, and I began to long for the cool New England fall days that were just a month away. For reasons I can attribute only to a tear in the universe, the frequency of Ben's messages had increased. For reasons I can only attribute to the fact that my brain was no longer severely miswired, I refused to read them. I didn't want him back. Why would anyone want to invite the cause of her virtual destruction back into her life right after she finished repairing the damage? It'd be like calling an exterminator and then holding open the door so the ants could crawl right back in. The only thing dumber I could think of would have been to shave off my own eyebrows with a Daisy disposable razor, and I liked to think I'd progressed some since the fourth grade.

I took the train back to Newport, reported for duty at the shop on Wednesday, and was looking forward to a nice quiet night at home. Now that Katie's wedding had come and gone, I felt like I had lost ten pounds (figuratively, not literally). I didn't fully feel like myself, but it was the best I had felt in a very long time. Now if I could only do something about the cellulite on my legs, I'd be downright chipper.

I was folding laundry when Bobby called my cell.

"Hey, how are you? How was your interview?" I asked.

"I think it went pretty well, actually."

"That's great. When do you think you'll hear from them?"

"Who knows? Summer isn't exactly the best time to be looking for a job. Half the people responsible for making hiring decisions are on vacation this month, so it's probably going to be a slow process. We'll see."

"Good luck. Keep me posted."

"Will do. So a friend of mine from law school is having a birthday party at one of the bars on Friday night. You guys should come. It will be good networking for me and good man-hunting for you."

"I don't like to think of it as hunting. I like to think of it as competing in some kind of modern game show. It makes it sound less desperate. I'm *not* desperate."

"Oh, I know you're not. But are you honestly telling me you're starring in your very own island dating game in your mind?"

"I've been thinking of it more like *Wheel of Fortune* for single girls."

"I'm all for whatever gets you out there, sister. I'll probably head over about 9:30, so you can meet me there any time after that."

"Okay. I have to work on Friday. I told Lara I'd help her catalog some of the inventory for fall. Then I want to work out and I have to run a few errands, but I should be ready by ten at the latest."

"What exactly takes you guys so long to get ready? Seriously, I can walk into my house, shower, change, and leave for the bars in fifteen minutes flat. What the hell do you guys do to yourselves?"

"It takes time to be pretty. We have to straighten our hair, curl our eyelashes, that kind of stuff."

"Don't you think it's strange that you waste all that time straightening what's naturally curly and curling what's naturally straight?"

"I'd never thought about it like that before."

"I'll never understand your kind. Gotta go, talk to you later."

And with that, he was gone.

I RACED HOME FROM WORK on Friday and got in the shower. I decided to leave my hair curly to prove to Bobby that I wasn't as nuts as he thought I was, and then took a deep breath and began what has become one of the most timeless and universal wars that women have been waging since the dawn of civilization: woman versus denim. These were pre-Ben jeans that I hadn't dared try on since I gained my breakup weight, but my summer at the beach had separated me from my freezer, gotten me back into a regular workout routine, and helped me drop some weight, so the time had come to see if I could zip up the jeans without ripping them up the ass. I sucked in as much as I could as I struggled to pull up the zipper. Much to my surprise, my old friends fit better than I thought they would. They were definitely tight, but I was pretty sure they wouldn't rip if I didn't do any squats or side lunges. Few things will make a girl happier than losing enough weight to once again fit into her old jeans.

Score: Woman, one. Denim, zero.

Grace and I left the house around a quarter to ten. We entered the Cook House, yet another popular bar on the pier, and were told to head downstairs to join the other members of the "Happy Birthday [Insert Random Guy's Name Here]" group. We were no more than two feet inside the door when Grace realized she needed cash and left to run back out to find an ATM. I headed downstairs alone and entered a large room filled with low couches and even lower cocktail tables, and with a long bar that wrapped around the perimeter. I walked the length of the bar and was surprised to find Lara sitting alone on a stool talking to a guy who was wearing a tight black T-shirt and a diamond stud in one ear. I made my way over to her and squeezed into the space between

Lara and the man in the extra-small shirt. Over the years I'd found that the size of a man's shirt is inversely correlated to the opinion he has of himself. The smaller the shirt, the bigger the ego.

"Oh, what a small world!" she squealed, revealing that she had had more than a few cocktails since I'd left her. It was sort of a silly thing to say. Of course it was a small world. It's Rhode Island, not China. "I'm so happy to see you. I was having dinner upstairs, and this guy I was talking to invited me to come join the party. I figured why not, right? This is Sal," she said as she gestured to the guy who looked like he belonged in the cast of *Jersey Shore* and nowhere near Newport, Rhode Island.

I turned my attention to the man with the large diamond earring and the shaved head.

"Hi," I said curiously.

" 'Sup," he answered.

"Sal works here," Lara said. "He's a promoter."

He turned and smiled at me, revealing gold front teeth. He handed me a business card. "Nice to meet you. If I can ever do anything for you ladies, you just let me know."

"Thanks. We will." I planned to throw his card in the garbage as soon as he slithered away and started bugging someone else. But it was not polite to be rude to someone's face. Even if the face is of a Cro-Magnon man.

Sal said good-bye and shook Lara's hand, then proceeded to work the crowd at the opposite end of the bar. I ordered an Amstel from the bartender, and when he handed it to me, he leaned in and looked curiously at Lara. "Look," he said quietly. "It's none of my business, but you look like nice ladies. I would steer clear of Sal if I were you."

"How come?" I asked. "He said he's a promoter here." I looked at the business card, which I admit was a bit strange. It said SAL, followed by a beeper number. It might as well have said, FOR A GOOD TIME, CALL. . . . Oddly enough, I doubted Sal was much of a good time unless you were under the influence of heavy narcotics and suffered from night blindness.

"A promoter?" The bartender laughed. "Girls, he's a drug dealer.

He's shady, and judging from the looks of you two, I don't think you're really into his scene."

Lara squealed in horror like he had just told her that Sal was a Bosnian war criminal. "A drug dealer?"

"Thanks." I shook the bartender's hand and gave him the card to throw away. I always thought drug dealers hung out in alleys somewhere. It never occurred to me that they circulated among the rest of the world, like normal people, in bars full of preppy guys and girls who thought that wearing Lilly Pulitzer was some kind of religious sacrament. But then again, I also knew for a fact that there were a lot of normal-looking people out there who turned out to be complete psychos, so it kind of made sense. "What brings you out?" I asked.

"After I locked up, I decided I needed a drink, so I came down here for dinner. I only got here a few minutes before you did."

"You've been at this party for all of five minutes and you befriend the leader of a drug cartel. Well done," I joked.

"It was fifteen minutes, and I did no such thing. How was I supposed to know?"

"The gold teeth might have given it away," I suggested.

She sighed, disappointed that her judgment had betrayed her, and then said innocently, "I thought maybe he was a boxer."

Well, she had a point there.

Grace arrived ten minutes later, a pack of cigarettes for Bobby in hand. "Hey," she said to the bartender, waving her hand to get his attention. "Vodka soda, please?" She squeezed a lime in her drink, removed the straw, and threw it on the bar before taking a large gulp. "What did I miss?"

"Lara spent her first fifteen minutes here talking to a drug dealer, but other than that, you missed nothing," I said.

Grace seemed completely unfazed by this. "Oh good, I'd have hated to miss all the fun. I don't see Bobby anywhere," she added as she stood on her toes and scanned the crowd. "Oh wait, there he is. He's actually talking to some guys I know from work. I'll be right back. I want to go say hello." She wove her way through the throngs of partygoers to one of the couches in the corner of the room where a large group of guys were getting very drunk, very quickly. Paying $300 for a bottle of Stoli and the luxury of being able to actually sit down in a bar seemed really stupid to me. Especially when you consider that this was the beach and the bar stools were free.

Lara's eyes followed Grace to the table, where she planted a kiss on Bobby's cheek and shook hands with the rest of the guys in the group.

I pulled my iPhone out of my clutch and checked to see if I had any messages. There was one from Ben. I deleted it without reading it and immediately felt confident. Funny, all you have to do is take the power back from one asshole in your life and it does more for your self-esteem than a year spent in therapy or a salon-worthy hair day. Go figure.

I looked up and realized there was a very cute blond staring in our direction. The old me would've worried that I had something stuck in my teeth or one of my boobs had popped out of my shirt Janet Jackson Super Bowl style. Not the new me. The new me smiled and remembered that she was a babe. She was single. She had just deleted her ex's text message. Ain't nothing gonna break her stride. He smiled a toothy, perfectly straight grin and made his way over toward us. Lara was continuing to assure the bartender that she was not the type of girl who would court a drug dealer, not that he cared in the slightest, and was completely oblivious to the conversation that was about to start up directly next to her. This was probably better. I was rusty enough in this arena. Throwing Lara in the mix was like making a Molotov cocktail of lunacy.

"Hey," he said as he slid up next to me. "Tom Marsh," he said as he extended his hand.

"Abby Wilkes," I said, feeling my face blush either from insecurity, booze, or, most likely, both.

"You look familiar, have I seen you around?"

"Didn't that line go out in the nineties?" I figured it best to just throw the sarcasm Frisbee and see if he'd fetch; if not, there was no point in continuing this conversation. If I was going to take this dating experiment seriously, then it was important that I examine compatibility factors off the bat.

"Call me old-fashioned."

Not bad, Tom. Good boy. He deserved a Scooby snack.

"Well, I'm from Boston, and this summer is my first time in Newport, so in all seriousness, I doubt it."

"No, I mean it. I've seen you in one of the stores in town. I went in to get a gift for my mom once, and you were working the counter. I thought about trying to talk to you, but I chickened out. I ended up buying one of those ridiculous signs you hang on doorknobs while I tried to build up my courage."

"Really? That's funny, and flattering." I looked up at him and realized that I did recognize him. He was the guy who bought the I'D RATHER BE FISHING sign. The one who I thought seemed interested, but then left without even so much as asking my name. And now, a few beers in, he had no problem talking to me. Maybe I should suggest that Lara sell cocktails in the store to make sure that nothing like this ever happened again. I found it oddly cute that he could place me from his brief visit to the shop. This guy was either hugely attentive or a complete psychotic stalker. I decided to go with attentive until he displayed some other sign of needing to be locked up in a high-security prison wearing a face mask. "Oh yeah," I said as I broke into a wide grin. "I do remember you. I'm sorry it took me a few minutes to place you."

"Don't be sorry. Is that what you do for a living? Work in that store?"

"No, I'm helping the owner part-time this summer. I'm actually a kindergarten teacher in Boston during the year."

"Really, that's great. It must be rewarding working with kids. At least you feel like you contribute something to the world."

"And you don't contribute?"

"I work in the accounts department of an ad agency. Let's just say that if I drop dead tomorrow, no, I won't feel like I have left my mark on society in any real way, you know what I mean?"

Cute, employed, and civic-minded. *Keep up the good work, Tom,* I silently instructed.

"I think these days everyone is trying to figure out how to make their lives more meaningful, but I'm sure the accounts department is happy to have you," I said, so impressed with how far my ability to flirt had progressed over the last two months.

"Thanks. You must love being out here during the week when the town isn't being overloaded with people."

"Yeah, it's been nice. You weekend people cramp my style."

"I'm sorry to hear that. We aren't all that bad, though, you know."

"Hmm. Sorry, I have no evidence to support that statement."

"Well, if you're up for it, why don't you meet up with us next weekend when I'm back? I'm meeting a few friends tonight, who I actually just saw come in, so I should go join them."

"Oh, okay," I said, preparing myself for a brush-off.

"But I'm serious," he said. "Let's meet up next weekend if you're around. Can I get your number?"

I was shocked. Was my aunt Patrice right? Had I been flashing some kind of DO NOT DISTURB sign this whole time like some bitter woman bat signal?

"Sure," I said. I was about to give him my number when I had a thought. "I should probably mention that I'm not on Facebook. That's been an issue for me in the past."

"That's fine. I never check it anyway," he said.

Marry me.

He removed his phone from his back pocket and programmed my number into it. I hadn't been this hopeful about anything in a very long time, and for once, I didn't have to worry about Facebook sabotaging me. He squeezed my shoulder briefly as he said good-bye. "Nice to meet you, Abby. I'll be in touch with you sometime this week."

"Sounds good. Talk to you later. It was nice to meet you."

I was giddy, and I couldn't wait to tell Bobby about my progress. At least I now recognized when I was being hit on.

"There are some cute guys over there," Lara said, surprised, as she strained her neck to see through the crowd. "Does Grace work with cute guys?"

I looked over at the table, but it was dark and half of the group had their backs to us, so the only thing I could tell from where we were standing was which ones were going to bald prematurely. By my count, at least three.

Lara was contorting her upper body so badly I was afraid she'd throw her back out. "You should hang out with her work crew. Lawyers are smart," she reminded me. She tapped her index finger on the side of her temple to illustrate, just in case I didn't know what smart meant. "Smart means successful. Successful is good."

"Smart could also mean they're huge nerds," I said. "You could spend the rest of your life watching your husband play Dungeons and Dragons on your computer. Is that the kind of life you want? I sure don't." I could handle a lot of things, but a man who played computer games to have a good time was completely unacceptable.

The bartender reappeared, holding a bottle of champagne. He popped the cork, spilling a stream of fizzy bubbles on the floor, and set flutes on the bar in front of us. "This is for you guys. Compliments of the gentleman in the orange shirt at the back table over there." He pointed to the table where Grace was gabbing with her fellow lawyers. The bar was dark and deciphering a shirt color was nearly impossible, so I was having a hard time figuring out which one of the crew had sent over the bottle of champagne. Not that I cared. I'd take a free bottle of champagne from Lucifer if he offered it to me.

"Oh, there's the guy," Lara said as I strained to follow her gaze. The champagne sender had originally had his back to us, but now he stood facing us, wearing a very orange polo shirt and khaki shorts. He smiled slightly and waved. "He's cute, actually, isn't he?" Lara asked.

I felt the color drain from my face and heat prickled the nape of my neck. I swallowed hard and grasped the bar, hoping a firm grip would keep me upright. Apparently, my first instinct was wrong. I would not, in fact, take a free bottle of champagne from Lucifer.

I grabbed Lara's flute out of her hand and poured our drinks down the bar sink.

"What the hell is wrong with you?" Lara watched in horror as the bubbles fizzed and dissipated.

"The guy . . . that's Ben," I said, my voice quivering despite my best efforts to stop it.

"Is the bottle bad?" the bartender asked.

"The bottle is fine. It's the sender who's bad." I grabbed a dry cocktail napkin from the stack on the bar, borrowed a pen from the bartender, and furiously scribbled a note. I asked a waitress to deliver it for me.

"You've got to be kidding me," Lara gasped. "That's Ben? Live and in the flesh? Shouldn't he be going through a desert on a horse with no name or something? What's he doing back east?" she asked, but my brain was having a hard time processing her oh so many unanswerable questions.

"I don't know. I didn't even know he was in this time zone, but he's been texting me a lot lately and I've ignored them. Maybe that's what he wanted to tell me."

"You've been ignoring him? I'm so proud of you!" she said.

"Thanks. I apparently picked a great time to get over him. Those were messages I maybe should've answered."

"Of all the bars in all the world, he had to walk into yours," Lara mused.

"Yeah, well, this is some seriously fucked-up version of *Casablanca.* Leave it to me to corrupt a classic."

"I can't believe he has the balls to send you a bottle of champagne as, what, a peace offering? What does he want from you?" Lara was angry, and she wasn't alone.

Grace returned to the bar after saying hello to the rest of the legal eagles and wrapped her arm around my waist. "Abby, you need to get out of here. Now." She turned around and scanned the group again, her eyes almost bulging out of their sockets. She slammed her fist on the bar. "I don't want to have to tell you this, but . . ."

"I saw him," I said, trying hard to keep my eyes from gravitating back to where he was standing. "I don't know what to do! I'll look pathetic if I leave. I don't want him to think I'm still so hung up on him that I can't even be in the same room as him. I want him to think I've moved on."

"What the fuck is he doing here?" Grace screamed. "You're doing so well, and I told him that if he thought he was going to win you back he could forget it. I told him you were single and loving it and you'd rather be alone forever than spend one more night with him."

"Please tell me you're kidding!" I wailed. It's amazing how the good intentions of friends can sometimes make you want to kill them. "I want him to think that I'm seeing someone. I want him to think that I'm dating half of Newport. I don't want him to know I'm alone!" I hissed, mortified as we all turned and watched the waitress hand Ben the napkin note.

"No offense, Abby, but that's ridiculous. He knows you're not seeing anyone. You've been talking to him! I've seen his name in your phone."

"You've checked my phone? What are you, a jealous boyfriend?" I asked.

"No, a concerned friend, and phone-checking is completely within my rights. I also saw that lately you've been ignoring him. Good girl."

I made a mental note to add a password, and possibly a padlock, to my iPhone.

"I didn't know he was coming home, but since I also didn't know that he didn't want to marry me, that's not all that surprising. It's probably on his Facebook page."

The three of us watched as Ben read the note and laughed. Apparently, he thought it was a joke. Apparently, he thought I was a joke. And that was more than I could stand for one evening.

"He's not cute at all now that I get a better look at him," Lara scoffed in a failed attempt to make me feel better.

"What did you write on that napkin?" Grace asked.

"I told him I would sooner drink from a toilet than from that bottle. Not my best work, but I had no time to prepare."

"Abby, I don't think he took the hint," Lara said as she nodded in his direction. "He's coming over here."

It's funny. I'd been thinking about what I would say to him if I ever had the chance to speak to him in person instead of hiding behind my computer screen. For some reason, I was much braver in the scenarios where I was envisioning seeing him than I was now that the opportunity was actually real. Instead of having any of the dozen conversations I had rehearsed in my head, I decided to take a slightly different route.

I turned and ran for the exit like the bar was on fire.

CHAPTER 19

Cupid Clearly Hates Me

I WOVE MY WAY back through the crowd and exited onto the pier by the street. I couldn't for the life of me understand why some girls had it so easy and the good Lord chose to make my path so fucking hard. I mean, I had finally felt better. I had felt confident. I had felt empowered, and yes, I had felt skinny. And then, He decided to send Ben down on me like a thunderbolt just to remind me that my road to happiness was currently closed for construction. And he decided to do it on the one night when I didn't even bother to blow-dry my hair.

"Abby, wait," Ben called from behind me. Maybe I needed a refresher course at jilted fiancée obedience school, but I was pretty sure telling me to "wait" wasn't going to do jack shit. Not anymore at least.

"Leave me alone, Ben," I said, quickly spinning around to see how much distance there was between the two of us. Funny, not too long ago I felt like two time zones was way too much. Now he was closing in on me from a half-block away. I thought I caught someone else coming out of the bar when I turned around. I hoped it was Grace, getting ready to crack a bottle over his head like she promised she'd do if she ever saw him again.

"I tried to tell you I was coming to see you. I didn't want to sneak up on you like this, but you didn't give me a choice," he yelled. "I sent you texts telling you I needed to talk to you, but you never answered and you haven't logged on."

"You should have taken the hint. We don't need to talk. It's way too late for that," I said, walking as fast as was humanly possible in platform wedges and jeans that were dangerously close to ripping.

"I know that, but I had to at least try. I thought maybe it could be kind of romantic—you know, my coming to find you."

"Romantic? Are you kidding me? How is ambushing your ex-fiancée in a bar romantic? You know, I realized you had a severely fucked-up way of communicating with me when you broke up with me on Facebook, but this is a stretch even for you."

"Maybe that wasn't the best idea in retrospect," he admitted sheepishly.

"Considering this isn't a bad romantic comedy, yeah, I'd say that's a safe bet."

First the ring in the soufflé, now this. Maybe he was a closet Jennifer Aniston freak.

He had annoyingly long legs and caught up to me much faster than I expected him to. The streets were crowded with laughing, drunk groups of friends all out on the town for a night of harmless fun, and then there was me: a walking, talking dating apocalypse.

"I understand that you're mad," he said, rationally, as if he was trying to calm me down because he was an hour late for a dinner reservation instead of a year late for our wedding.

"Mad? What gave you that idea? How'd you even know where to find me? What, did you hire someone to follow me around or something, you sick fuck?"

"It wasn't exactly difficult. I just checked Grace's Facebook page. She's constantly posting where she's going. It's probably so that that guy Johnny what's-his-name knows where she is at all times. Are they still together?" he asked, as if it was perfectly normal for him to be making small talk.

I was going to kill Grace. Somehow she had failed to realize that alerting everyone to what she was up to on Facebook also told everyone what I was up to. And now she had enabled Ben to find me by simply reading a wall post. Facebook must be a nightmare for the marshals in witness protection.

"Get away from me, Ben, before I scream that you're trying to attack me and have every good guy in a ten-block radius pummel you to bits."

"I deserve that," he said, although I don't think he meant it.

"You deserve to have your balls put through a meat grinder," I said, and I definitely meant it.

"That seems extreme," he replied as he reflexively put his hand over his crotch to make sure they were still there. I was wondering that myself, since all evidence pointed to him not having any whatsoever.

"Oh, you think so? What do you think is an appropriate response to you asking me to marry you and then ditching me with no warning and no explanation?"

"Can you please let me explain?" he begged.

That actually made me laugh. "There is no possible viable explanation for what you did, and even if there was, it's too late. Why do you want to explain now? Is this some sort of twelve-step process for assholes where you have to try to make peace with those you have wronged? Am I step ten or something? Right before you see the light and become a born-again evangelical and start traveling the desert in search of the meaning of life? Because I'm all for that as long as that means you'll be denied access to Wi-Fi."

He reached out and touched my shoulder, and while part of me shuddered with disgust, I was ashamed to admit that part of me shuddered from something else—that physical reaction that can only be induced by someone who you loved so thoroughly, for so long, and who for whatever reason would always be able to get under your skin and stay there.

Which I guess makes him sort of like a rash or something.

"I'm not saying it's one you want to hear, but I know I owe you one."

"You owe me a refund on the save-the-dates is what you owe me."

He motioned to a small iron bench just behind a nearby streetlight. This was not how I had played this out in my head. This was not how this conversation was supposed to go down. I was supposed to scream, yell, hurl insults I had been working on for the last nine months, and walk away with my head held high, making him wish he had never let me go. I was not supposed to be sitting next to him on a park bench illuminated by moonlight. All we needed was for someone to start spontaneously playing a violin and this horror show would be complete. Cupid clearly hates me.

He rubbed the stubble on his face, his five o'clock shadow as familiar to me as the sound of his voice or the look he would give me when he was bored at a dinner party. I sat in the corner of the bench, my hands clenched together in my lap. I had dated actively for almost two months now, and who had I met? A cheap, pink-pants-wearing pyromaniac masquerading as a walking prehistoric Wooly Mammoth, a guy who liked to go to Renaissance faires and do jousting competitions for kicks, a guy with alleged sun blisters but probably mouth herpes, a drug dealer with gold teeth, a geriatric mailman, a hair highlighter, and Bobby. And I'd rather have been with any one of them than sitting on this bench with Ben. Why couldn't I be here with Tom Marsh? Why'd he have to wait so damn long to get up the nerve to talk to me?

I waited for Ben to speak, staring at the cobblestones, tracing the outline of a brick with my left toe. I couldn't believe he'd thought that coming here was a good idea. Then again, he also thought that I'd want my engagement ring covered in chocolate sludge, so clearly he didn't know the first thing about me.

"I'm not proud of what I did," he said.

"Okay, I'm glad we had this talk. Have a safe trip home, happy trails, and all that stuff," I replied, hoping he'd let me leave, but deep down knowing better.

"I panicked. I didn't have the guts to tell you I wasn't ready to get married myself. I couldn't stand the thought of how badly it would hurt you, and how I'd have to live with the memory of your face in that moment for the rest of my life. So I took the easy way out, and I ran."

"That's attractive. That's exactly what a woman wants. A man who bolts like a skittish puppy when things get difficult. I think I'm falling in love with you all over again."

"It's a pathetic excuse, but it's the truth. I think I wanted to make you so angry with me that you'd never want to come back. I wanted better for you than what I could give you."

"Then you can rest easy. I agree with you. I want better for me too. So now that that's all cleared up, you can head back to the Wild Wild West and get off Grace's Facebook page. We're done here." I stood and took two steps away from the bench. Then, feeling like the newly empowered woman I'd become over the last two months, I decided I wasn't going to run from him. He was the one who ran from difficult conversations, not me.

"You know what?" I said as I turned and stood over him while he remained on the bench. "When exactly did you decide that I deserved better than you? Do you think maybe you could have decided this when we were in college or something, so that I didn't waste my twenties thinking that we both wanted the same thing? Or if that was too much of a stretch, do you think you could have decided before you proposed? Because I don't know about you, but I operate under the assumption that engagements are serious, that you actually intend to end up with the person forever when you pop the question. I mean, I get that Elizabeth Taylor was married like, twelve times, but I was planning on only doing it once. I didn't think you were one of those people who just give away engagement rings the way I give away hair elastics. So when did you have this epiphany exactly?"

"I don't know," he said as he stared into my eyes. For the first time, he looked at me and actually saw me the way I was now. Not the girl who sat crying on his couch in his apartment almost a year ago, trying to convince him to stay. The girl who was over him.

"I see. Well, this has been enlightening, and since I don't particularly like desert heat all that much, I'm glad you found somewhere to call home that I have no interest in ever visiting. I wish you had stayed there." He grabbed the hem of my shirt and pulled me back down to the bench. So I sat, because I didn't care enough to run. "Fine, Ben. Say whatever it is you came to say and get it over with."

"I came home for a reason. I need to talk to you."

"I already returned the engagement gifts, so if you're in need of a toaster oven, I can't help you."

"That's not what I'm talking about and you know it." I did. He wouldn't know a toaster oven if one went flying toward him while he was sitting in a bathtub.

Not that I'd envisioned that or anything.

"Then what?" I demanded. This had already gone on too long. All of it.

"I'm thinking of moving home."

I felt like I had been hit with a blunt object. I knew I shouldn't care, but I did. I didn't want him back in town. I heard my subconscious saying to me over and over and over again, *You don't care, you don't care, you don't care.* Then I realized that, this time, I agreed with her. I felt her relax for the first time in a year. Poor thing must have been exhausted.

"What happened to the girl you were seeing?" I asked.

"How did you know?" he asked, genuinely surprised that I was able to crack his oh so complicated email cipher.

"Oh, don't insult me. You made it very clear you were dating someone else without actually having to say the words. I'm not stupid, so answer the question. What happened to her? Or are you running out on her the same way you ran out on me?" I waited for him to answer. He really ought to be careful if he was pulling one of his disappearing acts on an unsuspecting girl in Arizona. Gun laws are way more liberal out there than they are in New England. If he pissed off the wrong girl, he could end up getting shot in the crotch with a six-shooter.

"She left me." He sighed.

I chuckled. I wish I knew her name so I could send her a thank-you note. "Wow, Ben, I wish I could say I was sorry, but the truth is, I really don't care."

"For a landscaper."

"Not sure why I needed that piece of information," I said.

"I'm completely alone out there. I don't know what happened to me, but I managed to blow up my entire life in a year. I left you, I left my job, I left my friends. It's like I had an early midlife crisis or something, and I want my old life back."

"I don't care what people say, Ben, but in your case, you can't go home again."

"I'm so lonely, Abby."

"Get a dog."

"I did."

"He didn't help?"

"He's great, but I'd rather have a woman in my bed than a dog."

So the only reason he dated me for as long as he did was because his building didn't allow pets. *Awesome.*

"Take out an ad in the personals. What do you want me to tell you?"

"I was hoping you'd tell me you'd be willing to give us another chance. Even though I know I don't deserve it. I've changed, I'm not the selfish guy I was a year ago. I don't even know who that guy was," he said flatly.

"You can't be serious."

"I'm very serious," he replied, proving that even after a year apart, he still didn't understand me in the slightest.

"You thought I'd take you back because you showed up here and told me that your girlfriend broke up with you and you'd rather sleep with me than your dog. Is that the gist of this conversation?" I said as I folded my hands in front of my chest and tried so very, very hard to understand why I let this loser destroy me for the better part of a year. He looked at the sidewalk, and finally, finally, I saw what everyone else saw. I not only removed the rose-colored glasses, I pulverized them into rose-colored dust.

"That's not what I meant either. Stop twisting my words."

I laughed as I cracked the knuckles on my left hand and stared at my naked ring finger, for the first time thanking God that it was unadorned.

"Ben, I've been trying to figure out what you mean for so long now. It's basically been a full-time job, trying to understand why you did what you did, wondering if I missed signs that things weren't right, what went through your mind when you baked a diamond ring in a cake. And you know what? I don't care anymore. I don't care what you mean. I don't care if you're alone, or lonely, or homesick. You said that we always agreed on everything. Well, here's something we won't agree on. I don't ever want to see you again. From this moment on, Benjamin, you don't exist. Don't call, don't write, don't email, don't text, don't iChat, don't tweet, don't Facebook, which I know will be hard for you considering how much you love to do that. Don't attempt to communicate with me in any way. Go back to Arizona and date your dog, or move to Boston and restart your life. Just make sure that your life never intersects with mine ever again, or else your dog won't be the only thing on all fours licking his balls."

I turned and left him sitting there stunned, speechless. The old Abby, the one he knew, would never have talked to him that way. And I realized that I didn't like that girl very much.

As I walked home I exhaled deeply and smiled in smug satisfaction, happy to be the one doing the leaving this time. The last time. I continued to walk through town sensing that someone was following me. I could feel the figure behind me, keeping enough distance to not encroach on my space, but just close enough so that I could tell it was there. Normally, this kind of sensation of being followed, call it intuition, makes women run screaming through the streets. I wasn't worried at all, because I knew without ever looking behind me that it was Bobby, my self-proclaimed wingman, silently escorting me home.

CHAPTER 20

The Other Woman's Other Woman

THE FOLLOWING MORNING the boys mercifully decided to go on a fishing trip, leaving Lara, Grace, and me alone for some much-needed girl time. Few guys will understand the way a girl feels after finally being able to tell off the guy who broke her heart, and none of them can listen to you tell the story about how you told him to go kill himself over and over again without telling you you're acting like a crazy person and to shut up. Times like these are when you really need your girlfriends to assure you that you did the right thing and that you're not psychotic.

We decided to skip the beach and instead planned on bringing in greasy food from one of the bars in town and watching movies on the couch all day. As Lara and Grace made pitchers of Bloody Marys and tried to figure out how to work the DVD player, I headed into town to pick up ribs, fries, and anything else that girls shouldn't eat while wearing bathing suits in the presence of guys. I waited at the bar for the bartender to bring me my order, which in retrospect was big enough to feed the entire defensive line of the Patriots, and looked around at the guys downing beers and watching the afternoon baseball game. I glanced at a table in the corner and suddenly someone caught my eye. Well, not so much someone, as the bleached-white hair atop that someone's head. It was Ryan, the guy who said he'd call me and then disappeared a month ago for reasons unknown. The guy responsible for Bobby thinking that he was the walking vaccine for all of my dating diseases. The guy who was about to have a very interesting conversation with a girl who demanded some freakin' answers.

I sauntered over to where he was standing and tapped him on the shoulder. "Hi, remember me?" I asked.

He smiled an awkward smile, "Yeah, of course. How are you?" he stuttered, pretending that he actually remembered me. I couldn't remember what he did for a living, but I knew for sure he wasn't an actor.

"No, you don't. You have no clue who I am. Just admit it. I won't cry," I said with a shrug. And while the old me might have once again let her mood be spontaneously altered by a moron, the new me was done with that.

"Excuse me?" he said, understandably confused as to why a snarky stranger was interrupting the Red Sox game for him.

"I'm sorry, I maybe should have told you that this is going to be one of the most painfully honest conversations you've ever had with a female in your entire life. And in keeping with that honesty, why don't you just tell the truth and admit that you don't remember me."

"Okay, fine. I'm sorry, I don't. Are you sure you don't have me confused with someone else? I'm, um, surprised I don't remember you," he said with a smile, hoping that would somehow sugar-coat the fact that he found me entirely forgettable.

"Yeah, I'm sure. We met at the Red Parrot back in June. You asked if I wanted to meet up for drinks, and I said sure, and I gave you my number, but I never heard from you again, and I was wondering why that was."

"Are you serious?" he asked. Like most guys, he didn't know how to deal with girls who didn't care about embarrassing themselves. Sadly for him, he was about to find out.

"You bet your highlighted hair I am," I said as I put my hands in my back pockets and rocked onto my heels, the way Bobby did when he antagonized me. It felt nice to be the one doing the taunting for once.

"What are you talking about? My hair isn't highlighted," he insisted as he ran his hand through it to make sure it was still there.

"Oh please, Billy Idol would think your hair is too blond, but I'm not here to discuss your effeminate cosmetic habits." His eyes darted nervously around the bar, looking for his friends, and I can't say that I blamed him, but it was time for guys everywhere to own up to acting like assholes when they acted like assholes. I was making it my personal crusade, and I was starting with him.

"What the hell is wrong with you?" he yelled, apparently done with the pretending to be nice to me part of this conversation.

"Me? Oh, no, there's absolutely nothing wrong with me. I get that usually girls act like it's no big deal that you said you were going to call them and then disappeared, or they ignore it altogether for fear of looking crazy. The thing is, I don't really care if you think I'm crazy. I've spent way too much time worrying about what guys will think of me and letting that dictate my every move, and the reality is, you should be worried about what we think of you and your entire gender, because I'm fairly certain, if my sample set is correct, that girls think you guys are all demented. So I'm liberated by not caring that you're going to go home and tell your buddies what some psychotic chick said to you in the bar. All I care about is you telling me what I want to know, and that is why you never fucking called me?" He said nothing, at least not out loud. I'm pretty sure if there had been a thought balloon over his head there'd have been enough expletives running through it to make George Carlin blush. I felt he needed a bit of prodding. "It's okay. Don't be shy. Speak up."

"I don't remember why. I think I went to look you up and couldn't find you," he said with a shrug.

"Look me up where? The yellow pages?"

"No, on Facebook. Your name's Abby, right? I tried to find you on Facebook, and you weren't on there. I guess after that I just moved on."

Bobby was right. Good God, there'd be no living with him now.

"You moved on," I said, still trying to process the fact that Bobby's Facebook theory was true, "to someone who was on Facebook. That's how you decide who you're going to go out with and who you're going to blow off? Am I getting this right?"

"Well, yeah. It's just an easier way to talk to people, plus you can tell from the kind of pictures girls post what their personalities are like. You can see if you have mutual friends, stuff like that."

"Oh, you can? So if I had posted pictures of myself half-naked, you'd have assumed I was a slut, or if there were pictures of me with a dozen cats crawling all over me, you'd have assumed I was crazy. Is that right?" I didn't let him answer. "So what did my not having any pictures at all tell you? That I'm afraid of flash photography? What?"

"No, I assumed that you were super-shy or something."

"Yeah, well, you read that wrong," I scoffed. Maybe I used to be, to be fair, but not anymore. Shy Abby was so June.

"You've made that clear. I'd have thought you were less crazy if you had the cat pictures up there to be honest. Are we done here?"

"Yeah, we're done. I'm sorry if I took up too much of your time. I'm sure you have a very hot date with a bottle of peroxide or a girl to investigate on Facebook and I wouldn't want to keep you from that."

"I'm sorry if my not calling you made you . . . I don't know, nuts."

"Oh, don't you worry, it didn't. You don't have to run home and check your stove to make sure that your bunny's not boiling. See, since we're being so honest with each other here, I should let you know that I don't give a shit about you [true], and I never gave a shit about you [partially true]. I was just wondering if there was a reason why you never called when you said you would. And now that I know for certain that Facebook is out to get me, I'll sleep much better tonight, so thank you."

"You're not normal, you know that?" he said, dismissing me.

"Yeah, I've known that for a long time, but thanks for weighing in."

I grabbed the food off the bar and all but skipped out of there.

THE WORLD IS COMING TO an end, Bobby was right," I said as I placed the plastic bags on the floor in the kitchen.

"Please don't tell me that," Grace said from her perch on the end of the armchair. "He's been weighing in on my life too, and if it turns out that he actually knows what he's talking about, I'm going to have to kill myself."

"Why?" Lara asked as she flipped through the channel guide on the TV.

"Grace has some problems with her boyfriend. The timing is off," I said diplomatically. It wasn't my place to tell Lara anything about Grace's situation. One thing I had learned over the last few months was the importance of privacy and the knowledge that your friends will keep their mouths shut when they're supposed to.

"I'm sorry," Lara said, finally finding something on the cooking channel and tossing the remote back on the table. "Do you want to talk about it?"

"Not really. But Abby is being polite. To say it's bad timing to fall in love with a married man is kind of a huge understatement. Let's just leave it at that."

"I'm sorry, what?" Lara asked, understandably confused and, well, appalled.

Grace sighed and dropped the newspaper she was reading on the floor. "Long story short, Lara, my boyfriend was married, now he's separated, she didn't take it well, and she called me at the office and ripped me to pieces. Not one of my finer moments, but I've made my peace with it. The things we do for love, huh?" Grace had gone from being horridly depressed after that phone call to just numb. I understood that it was her way of handling the reality that her actions had deeply hurt another woman, but to someone who hadn't been along for the entire roller-coaster ride of her relationship, I guess she sounded a little nonchalant about the whole thing. I knew that wasn't the case, but everyone has their defense mechanisms.

"Your boyfriend is married?" Lara asked, shocked. I suddenly felt the mood in the room change, and not for the better. This was not how I wanted this girl bonding session to start. I needed a lovefest. I needed to reenact the part where I told him never to contact me again, and add in all the other things I could have said if I had thought of them.

"Yup. Lucky me, huh?" Grace sighed.

"How could you be okay with that?"

"He made a mistake that he's most likely going to be paying for one way or another for the rest of his life, and so will I. Believe me, I'm not okay with it in the slightest, but when you love someone, you forgive just about anything."

"It's disgusting. It's wrong. It's immoral," Lara said. I looked up and half-expected her to be dousing Grace with Holy Water or hanging cloves of garlic around her neck. This was not good.

"The guy knows he fucked up, believe me," Grace said.

"My problem isn't with him. It's with you," Lara said, pointing her finger dangerously close to Grace's face.

Didn't see that one coming. I stopped unloading the ribs and stood frozen in the kitchen.

Uh-oh.

"Me?" Grace asked.

"Do you have so little respect for the institution of marriage that you have no problem coming between a man and his wife?" Lara's voice had elevated, and now she was actually screaming.

Uh-oh.

"She knew the marriage was over long before I entered the picture.

Now that he's told her it's really over, she's not taking it well. Not that I blame her, but at this point their marriage is just a piece of paper. Wait, why am I even answering this question?" Grace asked, switching from defense to offense.

Uh-oh.

"It's not just a piece of paper." Lara stood and stared Grace down. I guess I should've realized that, as a married woman, she'd have some pretty strong opinions on the subject, but I underestimated her passion, her vehemence, and, well, her balls to weigh in so heavily on someone else's personal life. Especially someone she barely knew. It was clear that this was very, very bad. Like *Exxon Valdez* bad. Like Chernobyl bad. Like *Buffy the Vampire Slayer* bad.

"I really don't think this is any of your business, Lara. I don't even know your last name, so who are you to preach to me about my morals? The only reason you're here is because Abby invited you over to hang out, not to give me an ethics lesson."

So much for my quiet afternoon with fattening food. This was quickly going the way of *Jerry Springer,* and I really didn't want them to start cracking chairs over each other's heads. I was counting on getting our security deposit back.

"Did you ever stop to think that maybe that woman has feelings? That she's sitting at home trying to make a nice life for him and raise his children, and you have the gall to bitch about the fact that the timing's been bad for *you?*"

"Yes, I've thought about it. It's all I've been thinking about lately." Grace's voice rose as she tried to defend herself. "You don't even know me. Why the hell do you care?"

"You guys, let's not get into this now. We've all done things in life we regret." It was my best attempt to restore order from the kitchen. Pathetic, I know.

"I care on behalf of married women everywhere," Lara yelled, putting her bony hands on her even bonier hips.

"So you're the spokeswoman for married people now?" Grace asked.

"Yes, for women who have had their marriages ruined by women like you. My personal life is a mess . . . and it's your fault!"

Uh-oh. I didn't see that coming either. Or have the slightest idea of what she was talking about.

"I'm sorry, what?" Grace asked, understandably wondering if Lara was having some kind of out-of-body experience or seeing things. Or more accurately, people.

"I'd like to go on the record here as saying that I'm only aware of Grace having one affair, and it's not with your husband," I said.

God that sounded stupid.

"I can't believe you knew about this, Abby. How could you possibly support this? This whole time you've been telling me how hurt you were in your breakup and you're still friends with someone who is putting someone else through hell?".

"Grace is my best friend. Of course I knew about it. And what does this have to do with me? I'm alone, remember?" For once that was actually going to come in handy.

"She's my best friend, she's supposed to be supportive, yes," Grace snapped.

"There's a name for girls like you, you know," Lara said.

I really didn't like where this was going.

"Oh, is there? Girls like me, huh? Okay, I didn't realize you were the fucking Virgin Mary over there," Grace said as she stood to face her.

"Does anyone want nachos?" I asked, holding up a container of salsa. I hoped fattening food would comfort them, the way it had me for most of the last year. I found there were few things that empty calories couldn't fix.

"No, I'm not pretending to be the Virgin Mary, but I do understand the scorned wife pretty well. My husband left me for his secretary. You'll have to forgive me if I don't feel sorry that you don't get to see him on Friday nights."

Okay, I might have just found one. Nachos weren't going to cut it. All of a sudden I had a flashback to Lara's comment about how she used to joke that her husband was all work and no play. She must have wanted to die when she realized that he had found a way to combine the two and that it wasn't his paperwork keeping him late at the office.

"Guacamole? Anyone?" I asked.

"Enough, Abby!" Grace yelled.

"Lara, I'm so sorry. I had no idea things were that bad." I sighed. "I can't believe I've been bothering you with my pointless problems when you've been dealing with the end of your marriage. You must have wanted to smack me. I feel so stupid," I admitted as I gave up hope that nachos would be the answer to all of our oh so serious problems. I had so wanted us all to be friends, and now I was pretty sure they were going to kill each other.

"Well, now that you do, what does that do to your view of what she's doing?"

"I don't really want to get involved in this," I said.

"It's too late for that, Abby. You're already involved in this," Lara said.

"Huh? How'd that happen? All I did was pick up the ribs." Which were getting cold, but I didn't think it was appropriate to start eating lunch when a catfight was about to bust out in the living room. I was not good at mediation, and I knew it. Where was Bobby when you needed him?

I couldn't believe I just thought that.

"Abby, you're friends with the other woman!" Lara squawked, like being Grace's friend was some kind of crime.

"I usually refer to her as Grace," I joked. No one laughed.

"That makes you almost as bad. You're the . . . other woman's other woman."

"I'm no one's woman!" I yelled in exasperation. Again, odd that that'd be a bonus point.

"Leave her out of this," Grace snapped. "You think you're going to turn her against me? Do you have any idea how good a friend I've been to her? Do you think other people would have listened to her bitch and moan and cry for the better part of the year the way I did? I should get a medal for being the best friend on earth, which you would know if you actually bothered to get to know someone before you passed judgment on them."

"That's true," I admitted, hoping Lara would realize that Grace's one bad decision didn't define her. "Without Grace, I don't know how I would've gotten over everything that happened. I was getting dangerously close to outgrowing my fat pants."

"I just can't believe that you've had the nerve to complain about your situation, like you're the victim in this whole thing! How could you actually expect us to have sympathy for you?" Lara screamed.

"I made a mistake. I don't think that means I should be dragged out back and flogged."

"Everyone makes mistakes," I whispered, staring at the wilting nachos, trying to figure out how to rescue them from their now-soggy state and how to restore peace between my friends.

But mostly I wanted to fix the nachos. I didn't want anything to do with this argument.

"That's what you have to say? 'Everyone makes mistakes'? We women are supposed to stick together. I thought you appreciated that more than anyone, Abby. I can't believe either of you. I'm sorry, I have to go." Lara jammed her feet into her flip-flops and headed for the door.

"Lara, wait. I know this is awkward, and I don't blame you for being upset, but Grace isn't your husband's secretary."

"I'm no one's secretary, I'm a lawyer," Grace said smugly. It was bad enough Lara was attacking her character, she wasn't about to let her disbar her as well.

"Not now, Grace," I hissed.

"You don't get it. You haven't been married, so you can't understand," Lara snapped. Here we go again, playing the married card. I was waiting for the day when it was "you haven't been married, so you don't know how to clean out closets," or, "you haven't been married, you don't know how to cook a chicken." The fact that I actually don't know how to cook a chicken is completely irrelevant.

"I'm so sorry for what happened to you," I said, hoping that my understanding (even though I'd never been married) would somehow keep Lara from having the nervous breakdown she was clearly heading toward. "I think it's amazing that you had the strength to walk away and start over and rebuild your life. You've done everything I've had such a hard time doing."

"Too bad Johnny's wife isn't more like you," Grace added. "My life would be a hell of a lot easier."

"Not now, Grace!" I snapped.

"And I'm sure that's what his wife is worried about. How to make your life easier."

Lara blew through the front door with such force I was afraid she'd ripped a hole in the screen. Grace and I stared at each other in shock. I felt awful for Lara and understood her rage, but Grace was my friend, and I wasn't going to abandon her for being stupid. If she'd done that to me, I'd have lost her long ago. Before either of us said a word, Wolf and Bobby walked into the living room, holding a large plastic bag of freshly filleted striped bass. "Hey, girls," Wolf said as he threw the bag in the fridge. "We had an amazing time on the water. I caught spotted bass!"

"Striped bass," Bobby said. "If you'd caught spotted bass, we'd have to call the FDA."

"Oh, sorry, right," Wolf said. "Anyway, they're going to be yummy."

Bobby popped a beer and collapsed on the couch in the same place where Lara had been sitting before she ran out of there like Grace and I were chairwomen of the "Destroy the First Wives" Club.

"So what did we miss?"

CHAPTER 21

Holy Rollers Sit to the Right

I WOKE UP the next morning and knew that even though I wasn't scheduled to work, I needed to talk to Lara. I hesitated as I entered the store. Lara was behind the register, flipping through receipts. The argument had gotten so heated so quickly the day before that I wasn't even sure what happened, and I had no idea what to expect when I showed up at the store unannounced. I didn't know if we were still friends, or even if I still had a job. I couldn't blame her for being angry at Grace, or at her husband, or at life in general, but being mad at me seemed like a bit of a stretch. I mean, I considered it a victory if I talked to a guy in a bar. It was a very long leap from that to adultery.

"How's it going?" I asked as I faced her across the counter, tracing a groove in the counter surface with my finger. There were boxes of cheese plates and ceramic lobster pitchers stacked on the floor next to her. I picked up one of the boxes and began to remove the contents, figuring that if I could be productive she'd be less likely to fire me for being friends with the enemy.

"I've been better," she said flatly, still staring at the receipts, though not seeming to read them. She was apparently deep in thought. Most likely bad ones.

"Sorry, Lara. I didn't know anything about what happened to you, and it's none of my business. I don't want to pry, but if you want to talk about anything, I'm here to listen."

"It's stupid," she said, finally peeling her gaze from the small stack of paper in front of her and taking a sip from a bottle of iced tea.

"I doubt that. Getting divorced isn't a small thing. Getting divorced for these reasons has got to be awful."

She stared down at her hand as she drummed her fingers on the counter, and I realized that her left hand was naked. She rubbed her ring finger, now twisting an invisible band, an act I'm sure she had done millions of times over the last few years, and you know what they say about bad habits dying hard. Like Bobby and his smoking, or Grace and Johnny, or me and too many things to list at the moment. She noticed me looking at her hand. She said, "After yesterday's meltdown, I finally decided it was time to take them off. I put them in a drawer. Poetic, don't you think? Those rings were supposed to symbolize the most important commitment I'd ever make in my life, and now they're in a drawer next to my underwear."

"I know how hard it was to remove my engagement ring, so I get it, at least a little bit. But I think it's a big step. It's not your fault that this happened, and for what it's worth, I think you're being really brave about moving on. A lot of women would have stuck around because they were too afraid to be alone and start over. You should feel good about that. I admire you."

"He didn't really leave me much choice. I should've taken my rings off the day I found out he was cheating on me."

I thought back to when Ben had told me that he thought I'd be happy to know the reason for him leaving had nothing to do with another woman. I remembered thinking at the time that it somehow made things worse, that it hurt more knowing I was being left for no real reason at all. Now I realized it didn't make a difference. Being left behind sucks no matter the reason, although I'd bet knowing it was for your husband's secretary packs a pretty bitter punch.

"I had no idea your husband cheated on you. If I'd known, I would've done something differently. I don't know what, but something. I'm sorry that whole argument happened."

"I'm sorry too. I know I went a little crazy. I shouldn't have yelled at you like that."

"It's okay, I think you've earned the right to yell a little bit. How'd you find out? Did he tell you?"

"Oh, hell no. He would have continued cheating on me forever if he could. I found a picture she sent him on his phone. She was wearing a leopard bra and nothing else. Not exactly what I thought I'd find when I went to download photos from his birthday party."

"Then it's better you found out when you did."

"He actually blamed *me.* He said I wasn't fun anymore, that I never wanted to do anything, that I wasn't as *social* as I used to be. Well, forgive me! Living in a strange city with a husband who travels all the time tends to mess with one's social calendar. I should've seen it coming the second he started wearing cologne."

"I'm sorry, Lara. I really am."

"What did you do with your engagement ring?" she asked. "Is yours in your underwear drawer too?" Maybe she was wondering if there was some kind of protocol we jilted girls were supposed to follow regarding rings that had been rendered useless.

"I weaponized it." That was probably not the answer she was expecting.

"What?" she asked, cracking an almost imperceptible smile.

"I threw it at him. Last I saw it, it was on the floor under a table.

I shouldn't have done that, in retrospect. I should have sold it for the cash."

"I'm not even strong enough to do that," she said with a shrug. "It feels strange not wearing them, like I just went back in time or something. I'm officially not taken."

"You've been officially not taken since the day you found pictures of another girl in a leopard bra in his phone. The rings are just stupid metal and stones. They don't mean anything."

"Yeah, stupid, beautiful, D color, high-quality diamonds set in platinum that I will never wear again. I just can't believe this is how it ended. When he proposed, I thought he worshiped me. Everything was perfect. I thought things would stay that way forever."

"Funny, my first clue that something wasn't right was the way Ben proposed."

"What do you mean? How did he screw up your proposal?" she asked.

"Well, it's not that he screwed it up so much as he didn't do it in a way that I would've really expected. It was so . . . not me. I mean, come on, how much thought goes into hiding a ring in a soufflé at a fancy restaurant? It just wasn't me."

"That's awkward, especially if you don't really like attention."

"I don't! Even worse, I detest soufflés."

Lara laughed so hard that tea came out her nose. "I'm sorry, I don't mean to laugh."

"Nah, it's okay. So I should've known something was off. But you choose to ignore a multitude of sins when someone's about to slip a ring on your finger. Even if you do have to brush chocolate sludge off it before you can actually put it on."

"Makes one hell of a story, though."

"Yeah, I've got a lot of stories, that's for sure. You know what I think is crazy?"

"Trusting that my husband was actually working late with his twenty-two-year-old assistant while I was home ironing his shirts?"

"Okay, maybe in retrospect you could have used that iron to burn every shirt he owned to cinders, but no, that's not what I was going to say."

"What then?" she asked, turning her glassy, dazed eyes to look at me.

"That you can know the entire pedigree of a ring you wear, and yet know nothing about the guy giving it to you. If you ask me, guys should come with authenticity papers, like diamonds."

"Interesting idea," Lara said. "If my husband was as high-quality as my ring, I wouldn't be in this mess."

"Think of all the stress you could've saved yourself if you'd known that. VS1: very screwed up. VVS1, very very screwed up. If the guy gets a grade of A to C, you know he's a guy you want. D to F is acceptable, but not without concerns, and anything below F is run for your life before he rips you apart like the sales rack at Saks. I think this is genius."

"You're funny. Seriously, where do you come up with this stuff? You know a lot for someone with limited dating experience."

"Trying to understand the inner workings of my brain is an exercise in futility. That said, I've always been mature for my age. Maybe that's the problem. It would explain why I hit spinsterhood at the ripe old age of thirty-one."

She chuckled, just a little. I was proud. I felt like if I managed to make her laugh for even just one second while she was going through this mess, that was something. I realized that while my own near-marriage collapse wasn't exactly pleasant, it was nowhere near as bad as this.

"Well, I think you're great. You don't have any baggage, you're funny, you're a nice person, and even you can't find a guy to be normal to you. I mean, your last date lit your check on fire. Maybe there aren't any normal ones out there."

I didn't have the heart to tell her that if my social experiment was any indication, then no, there definitely weren't.

"Yes, there are. You'll meet someone, I'm sure of it."

"I've been listening to you tell me about your dating stories, and I'm worse off than you are. I haven't dated in over fifteen years. I don't even know how to do it at this point. Things have changed a lot. Like what the hell is speed dating? I heard some southern belles talking about it in Atlanta, and I thought it sounded awful. Have you ever tried that?"

"If you count talking to a guy for three minutes before I decided that he was a complete and utter loser as a speed date, then yeah, thousands of them."

"I'm serious Abby," she said as she grabbed my hand from across the counter. "I don't know the first thing about anything. I'm not ready for all of this."

"Lara, you only removed your wedding rings a few hours ago. I don't think you need to be ready for speed dating, online dating, or dating of any kind. But you aren't out of the game entirely. When the time is right for you to reenter the murky, diseased waters of the dating pool, you'll know. Though I strongly advise against speed dating or giving anyone your phone number who compares your looks to that of a celebrity. Trust me on that one."

I squeezed her hand quickly when the bell over the door rang, and a customer entered the store. I recognized him instantly, even though he was now wearing board shorts and a backward baseball cap, but it was definitely Tom Marsh, holding a plastic bag from the convenience store across the street.

"Hey, Abby!" Tom said as he kissed me on the cheek hello. "I was hoping I'd find you here."

He was still so very cute, but I was a little unsure as to why he was looking for me. I had just given him my phone number. He knew how to get ahold of me. Unless, of course, he had programmed me in his phone under a memory device and couldn't remember which one I was. If there was one thing I'd learned it was that sometimes Bobby actually knew what he was talking about.

"Hey. How was the rest of your weekend?" I caught Lara looking at us out of the corner of her eye while pretending to be busy behind the register.

"It was good, but it got a little crazy, and I lost my phone."

"Oh, that's too bad. I went through a phase where I lost three phones in as many months. There's nothing worse."

"Well, it's not so much lost as destroyed. My buddies and I were on a boat yesterday, and I ended up getting thrown overboard with it still in my pocket. It's toast."

"Boating hazard, I guess."

"Which is exactly why I was never big into fishing."

"Though the sign you bought would suggest otherwise."

He laughed and glanced at an I'D RATHER BE FISHING sign on display, a mate to the sign he had bought when he was trying, and failing, to work up the nerve to talk to me. "Exactly. Anyway, I obviously don't have your number anymore, and the end of summer can get a little crazy, so I wanted to come by and see if I could convince you to give it to me again. I've decided no more water sports for the rest of this summer, so I should be able to hold on to it."

I was just about to give him my number for the second time in three days when I had a thought. "You know what? Why don't you give me yours? *I'll* call *you.*" It was time I took some of the power back. I didn't have to sit around and wait for people to reach out to me. If I wanted to talk to someone, I could just as easily call them.

"Okay, sure. I'd like that," he said, seemingly intrigued by my suggestion.

I pulled out my phone and stored his number under his real name. I may have understood the male of the species a little better by the end of the summer in Newport, but that didn't mean I wanted to play their games.

"Great. So, I'll call you," I said. "And thanks for coming by to tell me you lost your phone. I'm glad you did."

"Me too. I'll let you get back to work, but hopefully we can catch up soon."

I waved good-bye as he left, and I felt so empowered I had to resist the urge to jump on the counter and start singing "I Am Woman."

"He's cute!" Lara said after he had passed the store window and was out of sight. "Like super-cute!"

"He is, yeah. And now I have his number, so whether or not I see him is entirely up to me."

"Well, they say things happen when you least expect it, and I sincerely doubt you were expecting that!"

The truth was, with the craziness of the last two days, I had forgotten about meeting Tom, so no, I definitely wasn't expecting that. But I was definitely happy it happened.

"Not at all, so we'll see what happens. Anyway, are you going to be okay?" I asked, getting back to the conversation that had been interrupted when Tom came in.

"I think so, yeah. I owe Grace an apology, though. I'm so embarrassed at how I acted."

"It was awkward for both of you. I'm sure she'll understand." Although I had no idea if Grace would understand. Grace could be brutally stubborn sometimes, especially where Johnny was concerned, but Lara didn't need to know that right now. "We're going to be at the beach later for happy hour. Why don't you come meet us after you close the store? We'll be there until 7:00 at least. It's nice to be down there for the sunset."

"I don't know. I don't even know what I'd say, and I don't really feel like being social."

"I'm going to say to you what Grace said to me when Ben left. You can't sit home by yourself all the time. It's not going to help you get over it."

"Grace said that?"

"She did. See, she's not the anti-Christ. Come on, it'll be fun. Six o'clock okay?"

"Okay," she sighed. "I'll come."

"Don't worry," I assured her. "It will get better." I have no idea why I managed to be so upbeat about other people's lives and yet could never muster the same positive thinking when it came to my own. I wanted Lara and Grace to make peace with each other because I had enough stress in my life to deal with and I really didn't feel like playing referee to any more arguments between them. I decided not to tell Grace that Lara was going to come to the beach and meet us for two reasons: one, I wasn't sure that Lara was actually going to show, and two, if Grace knew Lara was coming, I had no doubt that Grace wouldn't.

At around 6:00 p.m., Grace and I dragged our things to our usual spot on the beach and set up our chairs on the sand. We unpacked the wine and cheese we had brought with us for happy hour as I filled her in on what happened when Tom entered the store and how badly Lara felt about the things she had said. Grace didn't seem to want to talk about Lara at all. In fact, as far as she was concerned, she never wanted to see Lara again. I also think part of Grace felt badly about some of the things she said to Lara, but she would never admit it. I thought that one of the reasons Grace was so upset was that deep down she agreed with some of the things Lara had said.

I glanced toward the parking lot and caught sight of Lara walking toward us. Now was as good a time as any to let Grace know she was coming.

"Oh, by the way, I invited Lara to join us," I said casually, bracing for her reaction.

"Are you fucking kidding me, Abby? After what she said to me? Whose side are you on?"

"I'm not on a side. I'm trying to be impartial, but come on, Grace. From where she sits, it's hard to be sympathetic toward your cause. Just hear her out, okay?"

Before Grace could answer, Lara approached us and waved shyly. "Hi, guys," she said.

Grace pushed her large Chanel sunglasses up onto the top of her head and stared at Lara, letting her know without question that she was less than thrilled to see her. "This is the home-wrecking section of the beach," Grace said as she dropped her shades back on her face. "The holy rollers sit to the right."

Okay, so it was off to a rocky start.

"I'm sorry, Grace," Lara said as she stood in front of her. "I shouldn't have been so hard on you. I might not agree with everything you're doing, but I basically blamed you for my husband cheating on me. It wasn't fair."

"No kidding it wasn't fair. You don't know what it's been like for me either. I'm sorry about what happened to you, but that doesn't mean that I have to listen to you insult me. I didn't do anything to you, or your marriage, and so you should keep your opinions to yourself."

"You're right," Lara said.

"I know I'm right," Grace replied, a bit surprised by how easily Lara conceded. Today she was a very different person from the one screaming for married women's rights everywhere yesterday.

"I shouldn't have judged you the way I did. Your relationship is none of my business."

"You've got that right," Grace said, still miffed. She sat in her chair and wiggled her toes in the sand, not saying anything more. I sat quietly and tried in vain to untangle the cord on my headphones. I figured if I pretended to be busy, they wouldn't mind having this conversation in front of me.

"I'm sorry. I really am," Lara repeated.

"What do you want me to say?" Grace asked.

"I guess nothing really," Lara said. "All I wanted to do is apologize. I'm not proud of myself for yelling at you like that. It's kind of ironic, huh? You and I being on opposite sides of the same coin."

"This coin sucks," Grace sighed.

"Believe me, I know."

"Does that make me the creamy filling in this bitter woman Oreo or what?" I asked from my seat between them.

Lara and Grace both turned to stare at me, but neither of them spoke. Apparently, it was still too early for humor. Noted.

"For what it's worth," Grace said quietly, "if I could do it over again, I'd do things differently. I guess at this stage it's easier for me to be in the position I'm in if I don't put a name or a face to the woman at home. You kind of made that impossible. It's a lot to think about."

"I guarantee you she's put a face to you. And has probably thrown darts at it."

"Interesting. And I guess I deserve that."

Lara shrugged. "Regardless, it has nothing to do with me, and I'm really sorry. I'd like to be friends if you'll forgive me."

"I don't know if the woman scorned and the woman who scorns can really ever be friends. It's like cats and dogs sleeping together. It's unnatural."

Lara laughed. "I'd like to try, if for no other reason than I'd love to hear more about Abby's dating project. I think she's exaggerating some of this stuff."

"Is that so?" I asked, not sure I wanted them to unite and join forces against me. This may have been a very bad idea.

"You know," Grace said, warming a little, "if you really want to know about her dating project, you should ask Bobby. He'll sing like a canary."

I lay back on my giant yellow beach chair and felt every muscle in my body relax. I removed my sunglasses, closed my eyes, and enjoyed doing absolutely nothing. "That's true, for some reason that I don't yet fully understand, making fun of me is one of Bobby's favorite pastimes."

"Maybe he likes you," Lara said. Grace and I turned to stare at her.

"What? What on earth would make you say that?" I asked.

"Maybe teasing you is his way of showing you he likes you. There's this little boy I see at the park in town all the time, and he's constantly kicking this one poor girl. I think he has a crush on her. Not that beating her up is a good thing, but it's typical kid behavior. Maybe Bobby's a shin-kicker."

"He's not a shin-kicker. That's ridiculous," I said.

"Maybe Lara's right, Abby. Don't get me wrong, Bobby drives a lot of people crazy for fun, but maybe him picking on you is his way of flirting."

"I liked it much better when you two hated each other," I joked.

"Oh, stop," Grace said. "I'll admit that his methods are immature for a grown man, but regardless, it's flirting. You teach kindergarten. You should be familiar with this kind of behavior. Of course, when five-year-olds do it, it makes sense. When a thirty-three-year-old does, it's like learning about a new species on the Discovery Channel."

"We're just friends. Is that so hard to believe?" They didn't respond, like it was actually that hard to believe. This was pointless. "Can we talk about something else, please?" I begged.

"Okay," Lara said as she turned to leave. "I should get going anyway. I just wanted to apologize, Grace. Maybe we can get drinks sometime."

Grace stood and dropped her sunglasses on her towel. "I have a better idea. It's way too nice a day to leave the beach. Stay for the sunset. I'm going to take a dip. Do you want to come?"

"Are you going to try and drown me?" Lara asked.

"Shouldn't I be asking you that question?"

"Awww, this is great. Everyone is friends again, I wish I had a camera," I said, surprising myself at how much like Bobby I sounded.

They turned and headed toward the water, and I breathed a sigh of relief that they were able to make amends. If poking fun at me and Bobby was what helped bridge their differences, then that was a small price to pay.

CHAPTER 22

Let's Go Hammer Ourselves

I NEVER THANKED Bobby for following me home the night Ben surprised me at the bar, or even acknowledged that I knew he was there. Instead, I stopped complaining about him raiding our fridge and picked up extra packs of cigarettes for him when I was in town. These were small gestures that, like him walking me home, I hoped said things better than words ever could.

A few weeks later, on a particularly hot August Thursday, the boys and I spent the morning paddle-surfing—or more accurately, Wolf and Bobby paddle-surfed while I tried in vain for the better part of an hour to pull myself onto the board. Water sports were never my thing, but I still figured that counted as exercise for the day. You'd be surprising how strenuous it is to suck at surfing.

After a few hours we left the beach, and Wolf went home and took a nap. Bobby and I were sitting on the couch, talking about the pros and cons of men using hair gel, when Grace appeared at the screen door, her eyes bloodshot, her hair mussed, and her nails bitten down to the quick. You didn't need a crystal ball to know who was responsible.

"I broke up with him. It's over. This time it's really over. I just put in for every vacation day I have for the rest of the year and got the hell out of Boston. I need a drink," she said as she barged in, slamming the screen door so hard that it ricocheted against the wall before shutting.

I knew I'd never forget where I was when I heard this news, like my mother felt about Kennedy being shot, and Bobby felt about *The Girls Next Door* being canceled. Everyone has those defining moments in his life.

I grabbed her elbow and led her over to the couch, trying not to be surprised that she was here in the middle of the workweek or that she was able to drive down from Boston when she was such a wreck. Bobby, partially in an attempt to help his distraught friend and partially to keep himself busy so as to avoid the very girlie conversation that was about to take place, immediately poured vodka and a disproportionately small amount of club soda over ice and handed it to her. He slowly sat down on the edge of one of the wicker chairs adjacent to the couch, almost afraid to move.

"What happened?" I rubbed her back as she put her head between her knees in order to calm her breathing. Everyone had known it would end this way. Truthfully, I think she had known too.

"I did something really stupid."

"You mean, like dating a married guy?" Bobby joked. I shot him a death stare. This was not the best time for sarcasm.

"I went to send him an email, telling him how much fun I had with him last night and how much I loved him."

"What was last night?" I asked.

"He came over. We had dinner and watched a movie and talked about where we were going to live when we moved in together." Grace had a sense of urgency in her voice I hadn't heard in years. The last time she sounded this panicked was after she'd been thrown in the clink during college for having an open container of Pabst Blue Ribbon on the sidewalk. "Okay. Why's that a problem?"

"I accidentally sent it to the entire team," she said as she once again burst into sobs.

"Oh God. Please tell me it was a normal message and not some X-rated thing. You didn't send him naked pictures, did you?" It seemed like a ridiculous question to have to ask, but "sexting," as the kids were calling it these days, had become an ever-increasing phenomenon. It was one that I found profoundly stupid, but again, technology had changed courtship so much that it was as commonplace to shoot off inappropriate pictures to people as it was to ask about the weather. I really missed the old days, you know, when someone had to actually be in your presence in order to see you naked. I doubted that girls had sent nude Polaroids of themselves through the mail in the eighties. But the eighties had also been a crazy time, so maybe I'm naive.

"I really don't think I want to know the answer to this," Bobby said as he stood and headed for the door, deflecting my question regarding Grace's potentially X-rated email. "I think I hear my mom calling me. I have to go."

"Your mom lives in Florida," I said.

"I know. She must be really mad."

"Sit your ass down and shut up," I said. He hung his head and returned to his seat on the wicker chair. If only boyfriends were so obedient.

"It wasn't an X-rated message, but I went on and on about how much I loved him and how much I wanted to be with him. How could I make such a stupid mistake? I just announced to anyone with an IP address that I'm in love with a colleague. What the hell am I going to do?"

"How'd you manage to confuse his email address with a distribution list for your entire team? I don't even know how that's possible." I felt horrible for Grace. This would cause her so much embarrassment at the office. She certainly wasn't the first one to have a relationship blow up because of the Internet. In this room alone I knew for a fact she was at least the second, and there were only three of us present.

"I don't know. I wasn't thinking."

"Can you recall it? Or pull the plug on the network? Or infect the place with some kind of virus?" My brain was spinning, trying to think of something to say to make this less of a disaster. It was pointless.

"No, Abby, believe it or not, I'm not technologically savvy enough to know how to crash the network of a major law firm. Thanks for that staggeringly helpful suggestion."

"Okay," I said, ignoring her sarcasm. "This is not the worst thing in the world. Do you know how many emails I ignore on a regular basis? I doubt that many people will even see it."

"It gets worse," she said, her entire upper body heaving.

Oh God. Grace backed into a corner was never a pretty sight.

"What did you do, Grace?" My question was met with silence. "Answer me."

"The only thing I could do. He was out of the office at a client meeting, so I dug the spare key out of his secretary's desk and broke into his office to delete it from his inbox."

"Please tell me you're kidding. Grace, you can be fired for breaking into your boss's office and going through his emails! You can be fired for a lot of things you're doing at that firm. Do you really need to add breaking and entering to your résumé?"

"This coming from the person who just suggested infecting the firm's entire network with a virus!"

"I don't think breaking into his office was a good alternative."

"I figured I'd just pull up his email and delete it. No big deal."

"Sorry to point out the obvious, but I'd bet he had his BlackBerry on him. Deleting something from his computer wasn't really going to solve your problem."

"That's great, Abby. Freak me out even more than I already am."

"Sorry. But for the record, these are problems girls didn't have before email. I mean, how many people would accidentally address, stamp, and mail an envelope to the wrong person?"

"Please not now, Abby," she snapped. "I can't listen to another diatribe on how much you hate modern technology. It's not helping."

Sheesh, fine. I decided that I'd stop talking about it, but I made a mental note to silently crusade for the return of actual handwritten love letters. Romeo and Juliet might have both ended up dead, but it wasn't because of a misdirected email.

"Did you get caught?" I asked, almost afraid to hear the answer.

"No, but I saw something else on his computer. He left an instant chat on his Google account on his screen. He was talking to his wife."

"Well, they're still married, so talking isn't all that strange," I said, trying to find some encouraging words for her. "Especially if they've started divorce proceedings, they're going to have to talk to each other."

"It wasn't that they were talking. It was the content of the conversation."

"You read it?" I asked. I don't know why this surprised me.

"Of course I read it."

Okay, I thought to myself. *Add electronic mail fraud to Grace's list of legal violations for the day.* Good thing she worked at a law firm. She was going need a hell of an attorney to get her out of this.

"And?"

"And he was telling her how much he loved her and how much he was looking forward to reconnecting during their weekend in Bar Harbor. He's not leaving her, he's taking her away for the weekend! Why would he come over last night and say all the things he did if he was then going away with his wife for the weekend? He told me it was over. He told me we were going to be together. He sent me lobsters!" she wailed. "It's not even like she doesn't know about me. We spoke on the fucking phone!" The sight of Grace crying unnerved me. It didn't happen often. In fact, for most of high school I wondered if she even had functional tear ducts, or if she just lived in a perpetual state of dehydration.

"I'm so confused," I admitted, feeling stupid for being surprised again. I had hoped Johnny was finally going to live an honest life. I had given him the benefit of the doubt, and once again, he had made a fool out of my best friend. I wanted him shot.

Bobby shook his head and leaned forward in his chair. "Grace, this has to be enough. He's lying to you and he's lying to her. I don't believe a word that comes out of that guy's mouth, and I honestly can't believe you do at this point."

Grace was too smart to be acting like this, but love will make you do insanely stupid things, not the least among them, breaking into your boss's office to delete damning email evidence.

"I know. This was the last straw. After everything he put me through, after how awful I've felt about myself dealing with this whole thing, I'm not going to do this to myself anymore. I waited for him to get back, and then I went into his office and I told him point-blank that I was tired of being an afterthought and that I'd never forgive him for making me think he was leaving his wife when he wasn't."

"Good for you. It was long overdue, Grace. I'm sorry to say it, but it's true," I said as I got up to hug her. "I had hoped things would change, but they won't. You deserve so much better than this."

"I know. I told him that it was over and to leave me alone. I'm tired of being strung along." Grace was shaking so badly I thought she was going to throw up. "How did I end up here? He's been stringing me along for two years. Two years of my life, gone."

"Listen, I know you don't want to hear this, but this is a good thing. You weren't going to be able to get out of this on your own. Maybe this is what you needed to make the change. I hate to bring this up now, but do you think while you're taking your mental health leave slash fake vacation you could poke around at other firms and see what's out there?"

I wasn't sure if this was the right time to throw further upheaval into the life of a notorious control freak, but sometimes it's better to just rip the Band-Aid off. Of course, if I was wrong, she was about to have a meltdown the likes of which couldn't be solved with every bottle of Smirnoff on the island.

"I don't know. I don't think anyone will be interested in even speaking to me if they find out the circumstances surrounding why I want to leave. It's a big black mark on my résumé."

"Your personal life shouldn't make a difference. You're a good lawyer. That's what people will care about." Theoretically, this should be true. I doubt Lara's husband had a hard time replacing his secretary after his affair became public.

Just then Wolf walked into the house, took one look at us, and with his inborn German attention to detail, knew instantly that something was wrong. "Why's everyone so sad? It's such a beautiful day!"

"Grace broke up with her boyfriend," I said.

"The lobster guy?" he asked, incredulous. "Why would you ever break up with the lobster guy?"

That was *so* not a normal way to describe someone's boyfriend.

"What am I going to do?" Grace sobbed.

"Oh no, I'm so sorry, little Gracie," Wolf said sympathetically. "Let's go hammer ourselves! That will help," he suggested.

"The term is 'get hammered,' not 'hammer yourself,' " Bobby said. "Saying 'hammering yourself' means you're going to beat yourself with an actual hammer."

"I see," Wolf said with a nod. "And to say 'get hammered' means to drink lots of booze?" he asked.

"Yes," we said in unison. I looked at Grace as she downed her vodka. She was well on her way to hammering herself. I couldn't blame her.

Wolf reached into his pocket, retrieved his phone, and proceeded to type something. "What are you doing?" I asked.

"I keep a list of all the idioms I mix up so that I can learn them. The Apple people should probably look into this. American idioms, there's not an app for that."

Grace stood without saying a word and grabbed her purse. "I don't care what you want to call it, but yes. Let's go hammer ourselves."

It seemed rude to say no.

WE HAD BEEN IN 41 NORTH for all of three minutes when Grace broke away from us and beelined for the bar, or more specifically, for the drinks that would be found at said bar. She was newly single, heartbroken, and determined to make everyone believe that she didn't give a damn about either.

"Is she going to be okay?" Wolf asked. The bar was packed with a bunch of Navy guys who were stationed at the base in Newport, and Grace was holding court in the middle of them.

"She will be. I think," I said.

"Okay, if you say so. Do you guys want to dance?" Wolf asked.

"I'm going to get a drink first," I said. I decided I needed a few more drinks in me before I was ready to hit the dance floor.

"Yeah, I'll come with you," Bobby yelled over the noise of the crowd as the two of us made our way over to the bar. Since my meet-and-greet with Ben, I felt like Bobby was being slightly protective of me in a big-brotherly sort of way. I liked it. I never had a big brother, and lately, I'd wished I had one. At least I wouldn't have had to worry about a big brother stealing my wedding dress.

"How do you really think Grace is doing?" he asked as we ordered drinks. "Do we need to worry about her keeling over from alcohol poisoning tonight or what?"

Truth be told, I wasn't sure. I glanced over at her working the room like she was competing for the Ms. Newport pageant. "I think she's fine. You know, faking it like only a good woman can."

"I'm going to pretend you didn't say that."

"Suit yourself," I said with a smile.

"You could single-handedly undo about fifteen years of praise with your quips, you realize that?"

"Fifteen, huh? That would mean that you were . . ."

"Do you want to play this game?"

"No, not particularly." I had learned a few things over the course of the summer. Bobby was as good a verbal boxer as any.

"Didn't think so."

"So what's the latest and greatest? Any update on the job front?"

"Hah, job hunt. The last one I was interviewing for fell through, unfortunately. I imagine things will be pretty slow now until after Labor Day."

"Hmmm. Labor Day," I sighed, realizing that summer was lumbering toward its close. Soon I'd be heading back to Boston and my little apartment and my new class of bright-eyed five-year-olds. I wasn't looking forward to leaving the beach, but at the same time I couldn't wait to get back to my old life and actually live it again.

"You were right," I said to Bobby as we jostled with other people trying to get the bartender's attention. "I wasn't going to tell you, but you were, so I guess there's no harm in my admitting it. You were right, I was wrong."

"That's not surprising. I'm always right. What exactly was I right about?" he asked.

"That guy from the Red Parrott, the one who never called me."

"He *did* highlight his hair! I knew it," Bobby said as he swayed to the music.

"No, I'm talking about why he never called me, although yeah, you were probably right about the dye job too."

"How'd you find out? What, did you come out and ask him or something?"

"Yup," I said.

"I was kidding. Did you really ask him?" He laughed, his eyes wide.

"Yeah. I mean, what do I care at this point? I ran into him, and he admitted that he couldn't find me on Facebook, so he ran. I probably didn't do much to make him think he made a bad decision by yelling at him in the middle of a bar, but whatever."

"You're hysterical sometimes. Crazy, but hysterical. Anyway, who cares? I repeat: that guy was a loser."

"I guess I just didn't want to think that guys were that shallow. I know better now, thanks to you."

"You didn't think he was shallow? Abby, he *highlights* his hair."

"I guess," I said as I took a sip of my beer. "Thanks for helping to show me the ropes. I wouldn't be doing as well as I am right now without you."

He blushed and flashed an awkward grin as he ran his hands through his dark hair. I wasn't trying to embarrass him, but I was pretty sure that was what I had just done. Apparently, I couldn't even give praise to a member of the opposite sex without eliciting some sort of adverse reaction. I should come with a warning label and an epi-pen.

"Well, he was a tool anyway," he said. "You can do better. You know, like the mailman."

"Yeah, Ryan never told me I looked like J Lo for starters."

"And that should be the standard against which all future guys are measured. I'm glad I was there to witness that. You really do attract some gems, don't you?"

"It's a unique talent."

"At least he didn't light anything on fire."

"No, but there's no saying he wouldn't have hacked me to bits on his boat."

"Good point."

"Thanks."

We turned away from the band and surveyed the crowd. The music was blaring, and people were dancing frenetically—singly, in pairs, in groups. It was a mob scene. My head started to throb, and I realized I was turning into one of those people who hate really loud music, no doubt yet another sign that I was getting old. Next I'd be clipping coupons from the PennySaver and chasing kids away with baseball bats for making too much noise at 8:00 P.M.. There was something to look forward to. Like my first colonoscopy.

When I opened my mouth to speak again, Bobby was waving to someone on the dance floor. Bobby's latest target was easily in her mid-forties and sucking on her straw in a way that no lady should ever suck a cocktail straw. Then again, no lady would ever be gyrating alone on a dance floor in a Lycra dress, flirting with a strange guy at least a decade younger than she was. So clearly, this lady was a tramp.

"What do you think of her?" Bobby asked under his breath.

"What do I think of her? I think she looks like a very nice old lady. She probably makes really delicious chocolate chip cookies and tells good bedtime stories. What do you mean, what do I think of her?"

"Do you think she's hot?" he asked without taking his eyes off her.

"I think she's having hot flashes, if that's what you're asking."

"I'm going to go dance with her," he said as he cracked the knuckles on his left hand.

"She's old enough to be your mother!" I squealed in shock.

"She's eyeing me, and she looks like she's a good time. You chill here. I'm going to go test the waters."

"You must be joking."

"No, I'm not." He looked at me with a straight face. "See, Abs, older women can be a great time. They don't want anything from you. They're not thinking that maybe you're the future father of their children, or if you can afford to buy them a nice house in the 'burbs, or even if you're going to call them tomorrow. They just want to have fun."

It was an interesting point. It must be a lot easier to have fun with guys when the pressure is gone. I wondered if I could find some way to make that possible at my age, like electroshock therapy or hypnosis or something.

"Why aren't you ever worried about being rejected? I could never do what you do because I'd be too afraid of being snubbed. It'd kill my confidence."

"That's the difference between guys are girls. Girls, if rejected, will wonder what's wrong with them. Guys, if rejected, will wonder what's wrong with the girl who isn't interested. You need to think more like a guy."

"It must be so nice to be that delusional."

"Sweetheart, you have no idea."

"Fine, go ahead. Leave me here to fend for myself."

"You'll be fine. You wait here for Mr. Right, or even Mr. Kind-of-Acceptable-if-You-Only-Hang-with-Him-in-Rooms-Where-the-Bulbs-Are-on-Dimmers, and watch me show that there lady how it's done."

"You are the whitest white man I've ever met. What makes you think you can dance?"

"I watch *Dancing with the Stars.*"

"Part of your being well rounded again?"

"I repeat: Renaissance man."

I watched Bobby weave his way through the crowd and start dancing with the woman in the red Lycra dress. Bobby couldn't dance, but that wasn't really what I noticed. I noticed that he didn't care. He was out there having fun, not concerned with who was watching, or what he looked like, or where the night was going. And it made me feel like dancin'.

I wove through the crowd on the dance floor and saw Grace in her bright yellow sundress out of the corner of my eye, still talking to a bunch of Navy guys who were more than happy to supply her with an endless stream of cocktails. She smiled when she saw me and immediately reached into her clutch and pulled out her cell phone.

"Here," she screamed so I could hear her over the music, already so buzzed her eyes were starting to glaze over. "Take this."

I took the phone from her and threw it in my bag. "Okay. Why?"

"Because I don't trust myself to not drunk-dial Johnny later, and if I do that I'll have to kill myself. I'm being proactive here. Don't give it back to me no matter what I say, promise?"

I was impressed she had the foresight to keep herself from doing something stupid in her drunken stupor. Why hadn't I thought of that back in the day? It would have cut the number of death threats I had sent Ben by at least half. "You got it. I won't return this to you tonight under any circumstances."

"Perfect. Come on, let's dance!"

I joined Grace and the Navy guys on the dance floor and happily accepted a tequila shot from one of the sailors. I made eye contact with Bobby as I held my shot glass up in the air, and he smiled as he nodded approvingly. For the next two hours, I danced like the whitest white girl on the planet, one who had never seen a single episode of *Dancing with the Stars* and couldn't have cared less. I may have looked like a complete idiot, but fast music and alcohol will make you worry about that, well, not at all. We stayed on the dance floor until last call, swaying and jumping and sliding and covered with sweat, and when the lights came on, Grace was nowhere to be found.

"We lost her!" I yelled to the boys as people filed out of the bar and into the street by the piers.

"Gracie dancie!" Wolf sang as he grabbed me and spun me around.

"She's a big girl. She'll be fine," Bobby said. "You looked good out there!"

"You think so?" I asked, continuing to dance toward home.

"No! Not at all, but you looked like you were having fun, so who cares."

"I was. I don't think I'm going to be able to walk tomorrow, my feet are so sore."

"Another benefit of being at the beach. Shoes are optional."

"You're a genius," I yelled as I twirled on the sidewalk.

I took my shoes off as we walked home in a drunken haze, singing and laughing, enjoying the perfect night air and one another. When we got back to the house, we sat on the porch with more beer, a bag of Tostitos, a jar of salsa, and a pack of cigarettes for Bobby. We stayed there for a few more hours, having so much fun that none of us wanted the night to end—so much fun that none of us thought twice about the fact that Grace never came home at all.

CHAPTER 23

It Doesn't Count if You Have to Blow Them Up or Pay Them by the Hour

I WOKE THE NEXT MORNING still in my clothes, lying on top of the covers on my bed. I reached for my bag on the nightstand, checking to make sure my credit cards and driver's license made it home with me. I found both my cell phone and Grace's and tried desperately to remember how I had gotten home. No dice.

I begrudgingly dragged myself out of bed and outside to the porch, where Bobby was drinking coffee and reading an article on his iPad. I had no idea why he was here so early, but I was happy to see him. I was hoping he could piece together the night for me.

"Hey," I said quietly as I sat down next to him and threw both cell phones on the table. My queasy stomach and pounding head made it hard to even blink my eyes. I was too old to be hungover like this. One of the other side effects of getting older was that hangovers seemed to get exponentially worse.

Bobby slid his iPad out of the way and pushed his coffee mug across the table. I took a sip and immediately felt my stomach lurch. Adding caffeine to the copious amounts of alcohol no doubt still sloshing around in my stomach was probably not a good idea, but my headache couldn't have cared less if the coffee came from the head of the Colombian drug cartel—it wasn't turning it down. "How are you feeling?" he asked, his sunglasses making it impossible to determine if he was actually looking at me or not.

"Okay," I said as I continued to drink his too-strong coffee. "I don't remember getting home last night, to be honest. What did we do to ourselves?"

"Yeah, you were pretty blitzed by the end there, not that I was sober at that point either. I think we might have overdone it a little."

"We're old," I said sheepishly. "I can't drink the way I used to."

"Speak for yourself. I feel great."

"Seriously?"

"No, I actually feel like shit. My headache woke me up. I came over here because Wolf was listening to European techno music and I couldn't stand it. But a little hangover is a small price to pay for a great night out."

"I'll have to get back to you on that," I said as I rested my head on the table. "Where's Grace?" I asked, hoping to turn the conversation away from me and my drunken activities from the night before.

"Haven't seen her. We lost her in the bar last night. I called her before we left, but then your bag started ringing and I realized you had her cell. There was nothing else I could do."

"So we just left her there?"

"Or she left us. I looked all over for her, but I couldn't find her anywhere, and she looked like Big Bird in that bright yellow dress. I think I would've spotted her if she was there. Don't worry, I'm sure she's fine."

I sighed. I was sure she was too, but I didn't like the idea of her not having her phone on her. Newport wasn't exactly a high-crime town, but still, there are some things that a drunk girl shouldn't be without. A cell phone topped that list. Pepper spray was right below it, provided you weren't well versed in how to use nunchucks.

"Well, I'm relieved I made it home in one piece and managed not to lose a shoe or my bag or something. Though I'm not sure why I slept in my clothes."

"You're welcome."

"Huh?"

"I put you into bed last night. You were hysterical. You couldn't walk a straight line, and you kept singing 'Anchors Away' to a bunch of the sailors on the sidewalk. You can't sing, by the way."

"The least of my problems," I moaned.

"No arguments there. Anyway, I figured it was better to leave you in your clothes. I have a rule: I don't undress drunk girls for any reason."

"You, my friend, are one of the last true gentlemen."

"Don't I know it."

"I'm sorry. I appreciate it." Then small flashes of the night before started to play through my mind. There was a dance floor incident. There were shots. There was a woman in a red dress that had gone out of style sometime around the *Flashdance* era. Slowly, pieces of the puzzle seemed to fall into place. Grace was doing shots with a bunch of sailors, and then she was gone.

"No problem," he said. "What are friends for?"

We sat in silence for a few minutes as he returned his focus to his iPad. I checked my watch—it was 11:00 A.M. I was starting to get worried about Grace. I stood to stretch my arms over my head, leaned over the railing of the deck, and immediately cracked up laughing, which I wished I could stop because it exacerbated my headache. But there was no way to not laugh at what I was looking at.

"Let me guess, it's Grace in her Big Bird dress?" Bobby said.

"How did you know?" I asked as I stared out at the street at the disheveled, wrinkled girl in a yellow dress who looked an awful lot like

Grace—or at least what I imagine Grace would look like after waking up under a tree somewhere. She walked slowly, her sandals dangling from one hand.

"Because she got busted on the Walk of Shame site! Her picture was posted ten minutes ago!" Bobby laughed as he showed me his iPad. Grace's embarrassing picture was front and center for everyone in Newport to see. This was so not good.

As Grace approached the house, Bobby stood and started applauding. She staggered up the stairs to the deck and collapsed in one of the chairs. "Next time I tell you to take my phone, don't do it," she said as she picked up her cell and checked for messages. "You have no idea how badly I needed that thing this morning, and I was completely incommunicado. I just walked two miles home. Never again. My feet are destroyed."

"What happened?" I asked her as Bobby went inside and poured her some coffee. He returned and placed the mug in front of her and leaned against the railing.

"You look like hell, Grace," he said with a smirk. "If it's any consolation, you look worse in person than you did in the picture I saw on the Walk of Shame site!"

"Are you kidding me? Someone took a picture of me walking home this morning and posted it already? I didn't see anyone. What does he use, a telephoto lens?"

"Yup. If I had seen it earlier, I'd have come looking for you. Sorry," Bobby said.

"I swear to God I will find out who is behind this stupid website and I will kill him. I will murder him with my own fucking hands! It should be illegal!"

"How do you figure that? He didn't take a picture of you in the shower. You were walking down the street."

"But everyone will think that I, you know, I . . ." Grace yelled.

"Forget the stupid website. It'll be on to the next victim by tomorrow. What happened?" I asked again. "Are you okay?"

"Theoretically, yeah. I ended up back at some guy's house. One of the ones I was talking to in the bar. They were having a late-night party, so I figured, why not, right? I'm single now. That's what single girls in their thirties do. They go to house parties and hook up with random dudes."

"Not *all* single girls in their thirties. Abby doesn't, though not for lack of effort," Bobby said.

"Thanks for that," I said as I shielded my eyes from the sun.

"I don't know what happened," Grace continued. "One minute we were playing cups on the back deck, and the next thing I know I woke up in a bed all by myself, and the whole house was empty. He left me there. The guy just got up and went to the beach or wherever with his buddies and left me asleep in a strange house."

"Maybe he thought you needed some beauty rest," I offered, trying to make her feel better.

"Maybe he took one look at you this morning and realized he'd rather gnaw his own arm off than have to do the awkward morning-after conversation, so he just ditched and said a prayer you'd find your way out," Bobby offered as an alternative suggestion.

Grace and I stared at him, shocked once again at his utterly blunt and heinous assessment of the situation. I crossed lawyers off the list of professions I'd ever entertain the notion of dating. They have absolutely no bedside manner, and worse, you're all but guaranteed to never win an argument.

"The worst part," Grace continued, "is that I really had to pee, but was so humiliated that I ran out before I used the bathroom. I ended up copping a squat in the bushes on the way home, and I used leaves as toilet paper, and now I'm worried I just gave myself poison ivy in places no girl should ever have poison ivy."

"That's not good," I said as Bobby burst out laughing. "That sure as hell won't help your new single social life."

"Look at me! I break up with Johnny, and this is what I have to deal with? I refuse to do this. I won't be like you, Abby, running around trying to date anything in pants to avoid being alone. I can't. It's simply not an option."

"Whoa, what did you just say?" I was sure she didn't mean for that to come out the way it did. Why would my best friend say that I was pathetic? She wouldn't. *Would she?*

"I'm going to call him. I'm going to force him to make a choice. It's me or her, he can't have both. And he has to decide now."

"I'm confused," I said. "He already made his decision. And you already broke up with him. Quite dramatically, I might add." I wondered if I had been hallucinating when we had that conversation.

"I'm going to take it back. I'll apologize, and everything will be fine," she said, irrationally panicked.

"Grace, you're just upset," I said, trying to talk her out of making an epically bad decision. I knew this look of desperation. I'd been there. And if you're allowed to act on that emotion, regret always follows.

"I know," Grace said in a small voice, tears welling in her eyes. "Rationally, I know. But the heart wants what the heart wants."

Grace's phone buzzed. She snatched it off the table.

"Thank God, it's him," Grace said. I grabbed her free hand and stared into her eyes.

"What happened to you being done with this? Grace, please just tell him to go kill himself and get on with your life before you waste another two years."

"We work together," she said. "I can't just pretend he doesn't exist."

"*I* can't stand to watch you do this to yourself anymore. Turn it off," I said as I reached over and took the phone from her hand. "Bobby, help me out here. Say something."

"I want no part of this. Pretend I'm not here," he said, apparently deciding for the first time since I met him that silence was golden. As usual, his timing was perfect.

"Give me my phone, Abby," she hissed, not appreciating my take-charge attitude.

"Why? I thought you wanted me to take your phone from you to keep you from talking to him. That was just a few hours ago. Is that all you have in you? A few hours before you go running back?" I was aiming for tough love. I missed.

"I don't have to defend myself to you. Give me my phone back, Abby. I mean it," she demanded.

I underestimated the degree of Grace's frustration, or maybe I overestimated my capacity for self-righteous indignation since I had told Ben to leave me alone for the last time. Whatever it was, it was something, and things quickly erupted.

"Fine. Let him keep you as a concubine. Whatever you want, but I think it's pathetic."

"Says the girl who begged her fiancé not to leave her, and what was it you said, Abby? That you'd wear cowboy boots under your wedding dress if he wanted? Excuse me if I don't feel like taking advice from you. I don't know where you think you get off judging anyone, all things considered." Apparently, the gloves were off. Now it was war.

"Okay, sure. Here," I said as I handed her the phone. Grace and I didn't fight often, but when we did, it could get ugly. "I'm not judging," I said as I held my hands up in the air. "You do whatever makes you happy. Hey, now that I think about it, don't even bother texting him back. Here's a thought: why don't you just post your whereabouts on Facebook so that he can keep you under his thumb while he sits at his wife's breakfast table?"

"I've always been a big Facebook person, and you know it! Let me remind you that if I hadn't been on Facebook, you'd probably think you were still engaged!"

"I'm pretty sure I would've figured that out on my own. So going forward, do you think you could do me a favor and *not* post where we are at all times? Some of us don't want our exes knowing where to find us, you know."

"Don't blame me for that. If he wanted to find you, all he had to do was start hanging out next to the ice cream case at the grocery store and you would've shown up eventually!" she screamed. Bobby just sat there, like a spectator at a tennis match, watching us fight with each other, looking too scared to move.

"Did you just call me fat? That's so out of bounds!" Now we were standing on opposite sides of the table, screaming like crazy people.

"If the elastic waist pants fit . . ." she said smugly.

"Guys," Bobby said. "Both of you, stop. Unless you're going to strip down and go all Gorgeous Ladies of Wrestling on me—in which case, well, as you were."

"Shut up, Bobby," we yelled simultaneously.

"First of all," I said as I pointed my finger in her face, "we both know that I've gotten past that stage, and the fat jokes at this point are just mean. Second, what are you getting mad at me for? I'm trying to *help* you!"

"You should understand this better than anyone, Abby. It's not easy to just cut all ties. You still talked to Ben after you broke up, and that was way worse. I mean, what did that guy have to do for you to walk away from him? Call off your wedding? Oh, wait . . ."

"That was low."

"It's the truth. Not my fault if it hurts."

"You both are nuts, you know that?" Bobby said.

"Stay out of this, Bobby," Grace snapped.

"No, I won't. I'm sick of listening to both of you bitch and moan about your relationships. You guys are like a reality show! You should both just relax and get over yourselves."

"Get over myself?" Grace hissed.

"Yeah, what's that supposed to mean?" I asked. I wasn't sure why I was snapping at Bobby, other than I was too tired to differentiate emotions.

"You're both so paranoid about being alone, it's all you think about. You should just chill the hell out. Besides, neither one of you will ever be alone. Abby will have the spinsters in her knitting club, and Grace will probably have a dozen lobsters to keep her company."

This had officially turned into one of the craziest conversations I had ever had. And considering some of the doozies I had had with my mother, that was saying something.

"And what will you have? A fridge full of Budweisers and a collection of porn?"

"I'm dating plenty of girls," he replied.

"It doesn't count if you have to blow them up or pay them by the hour," Grace snapped.

Touché. Apparently no one was safe. Grace was intent on attacking Bobby too. There were no teams, it was every man for himself.

"Hey, you can criticize me all you want, but at least I've never gotten up in the morning and left some random chick passed out in a strange house by herself. That guy is either a moron or so not into you he'd risk you stealing his stuff."

"So, is that why you wake them up and kick them out early? Because you're worried they're going to steal your boxers?" I asked.

"Is that so crazy? After hanging out with you two all summer, I don't put anything past your kind anymore!" The vein in his neck was visibly pulsing, and a red flush was spreading to his earlobes. That was new.

No wonder none of us had managed to find a healthy relationship—we were all taking advice from equally demented human beings. What was even funnier was that from where I was standing, I was in the best shape of the three of us. It had been a long time since that was the case.

"Can we all please just calm down?" I pleaded, not only because I didn't want to fight, but also because my head felt like it was about to explode. "All I'm trying to say here, Grace, is that you deserve better. I'm trying to help you."

"You're the last person on earth who should be offering to help. Look at yourself. It's a joke what you're doing. Finding a boyfriend has been your highest priority all summer! You think you're completely worthless unless you're in a relationship. Aren't you a little worried that the big flashing desperate sign above your head is going to scare guys away?"

I had had enough, and I lost it. I took off my shoe and hurled it at her head. I wish I'd looked closely at where I was throwing, because maybe I would have seen Wolf walk up the stairs and been able to avoid cracking him in the face with a flying flip-flop. The shoe ricocheted off his cheek and landed on the deck with a thud. The whole summer I'd been wondering what it would take to wipe that perpetual smile off Wolf's face.

Looked like I'd found it.

He stared at the three of us, red-faced and visibly shocked, and I was too afraid to speak. Poor Wolf was the only one who hadn't done anything wrong, and he was the one who got physically assaulted. "Okay, I'm going to be going now," he said as he turned, clomped down the steps, and all but took off down the street back to Bobby's house.

"Nice one, Abby," Bobby said.

I ignored him, figuring that I'd apologize to Wolf later. "Fine, Grace. Go running back because you had one bad night. That makes sense."

"It's my life, Abby. And if you have a problem with that, then you don't have to be a part of it anymore."

"Well, that's dramatic," I said. And I should know. No one is more dramatic than me.

"I mean it. I'm going to take a steaming hot shower, and then I'm out of here." She turned and stormed into the house, while Bobby and I sat in uncomfortable silence. I suddenly felt like the walls were closing in on me, which was odd since we were outdoors.

Bobby spoke first. "Man, you girls can be mean. For the record, the way you guys are acting right now is a perfect example of why sometimes it's fun to hang out with older women. If there's one thing I've learned from you two this summer, it's that girls our age are psychotic. Plain and simple."

I'll admit he had some fair points, and that I was probably in the wrong on this one, but I wasn't ready to admit defeat yet. "What's that supposed to mean?"

"Were you not just here for the argument that went down? You're both nuts. If I had kept dancing with Melinda last night instead of hanging out with you, I could have avoided this enormous display of crazy."

"Fuck you, Bobby."

"So now you're going to be bitchy to me too?" he asked.

"You started it when you insulted my knitting club, unprovoked I might add. I'm just saying that you looked ridiculous dancing with that woman. Just because you dance with Mrs. Robinson doesn't make you Dustin Hoffman."

"You know what?" Bobby said as he picked up his newspaper. "I don't need this bullshit." He sounded angry, frustrated, and worst of all, indifferent, all at the same time. Before I had a chance to respond, he was down the stairs and gone, leaving me alone on the deck.

TRUE TO GRACE'S WORD, half an hour later she stormed out of the house carrying all of her clothes in a huge ball. She threw them into the backseat of her car and left. She didn't say a word to me, and I truly didn't care, because I was mad at her too. Friends fight, that was fine, but you weren't supposed to use their biggest weaknesses against them, and she had crossed the line the second she called me fat.

And desperate. But mostly fat.

I sat alone on the deck staring into space for the rest of the afternoon, trying to understand what had caused all of us to blow up on each other so suddenly. Maybe it was a summer's worth of frustrations, maybe it was the heat, maybe we were all hungover and our nerves were shot.

When 8:00 P.M. rolled around and I still hadn't heard from anyone, I realized how serious this was. I heard footsteps on the stairs and looked up, hoping that Grace had come back and wasn't really dumping me as a friend. I'd been dumped enough for the time being.

"How are you doing?" Wolf asked as he sat down next to me, a small, red mark visible on his cheek.

"I've been better," I said. "I guess you heard what happened."

"Yeah." He sighed.

"I'm sorry I hit you with my shoe," I said. I couldn't believe I actually had to say those words.

"That's okay. I'm happy it was an accident. And that you throw like a girl."

"I don't know what happened. One minute we were talking, and the next we were attacking each other. I think we've all lost our minds," I said as I stared out into the road, hoping Bobby or Grace or both of them would return and want to be my friend again.

"Friends fight sometimes. This one sounded like a big one. I could hear you guys from down the street." He shook his head in sadness.

"This is a disaster. Everyone is mad at everyone, Grace left, and I have no idea where Bobby is. I don't know what to do."

"Bobby's at the Landing," he said casually.

"Shocker."

"He came home talking about how of all the times he imagined you and Grace getting into a girl fight, that was nothing like what he expected."

"I can't believe she left. I thought she'd drive around for a bit and come back."

"It will be okay, little Abby. You will make up. I need to apologize to her too."

"Huh? Why do you have to apologize? Did you take an extra coconut water out of the fridge or something? Don't worry about it. We forgive you," I said.

"No, it's not that. Although, ya, I did do that too, but that's not what I'm talking about. I have a confession to say."

"A confession? What could you possibly have to confess? You're the only one who hasn't done anything wrong."

"Yes, I have. See, the truth is . . . well, I'm the Walk of Shame guy," he said, staring at the slats on the wooden deck.

"I'm sorry, I don't understand what you're talking about."

"I'm the guy running the Walk of Shame website."

"What? Why? How?" I asked, my brain trying to understand how he could be responsible for the website without any of us knowing about it.

"The guys around here are always talking about what they're planning on doing at night in front of me, when they golf. They talk like no one else is listening, which is strange, because I'm standing right next to them holding their putters. So one day, after one guy wasn't that nice to me, and didn't tip me either, I decided that I would get even by putting his picture on a website. One thing led to another, and then everyone was talking about it, so it sort of became my hobby. I want to be the Perez Hilton of Newport. Maybe one day I can sell the site and make a million dollars. That's the American dream, right?"

"You did that all by yourself?" I asked, still stunned that Wolf was savvy enough to run a covert tech operation off his iPhone.

"I too am a marvel of German engineering!" he said proudly.

"But you put Grace on there! Why did you do that?" I asked.

"That might be why I should apologize. I didn't want to, but she looked so funny in her yellow dress, and I thought maybe I'd be helping her. You know, maybe Johnny would leave her alone if he saw that she was out having fun without him. I'm thinking now that that wasn't the best idea."

"You think? Wolf, she's going to destroy you."

"I was trying to help. But maybe I didn't do that. What's the saying? The road to hell is paved with good intentions?"

Sure, that one he got right. At least now I didn't have to worry about being the sole target of Grace's anger. She was going to pummel Wolf within an inch of his life when she found out about this. With any luck, she'd forget why she was mad at me altogether.

"I have to say, I'm oddly impressed. I guess when I think about it, you sort of disappeared at random times and then magically resurfaced when something was going on. It actually makes perfect sense. You were kind of hiding in plain sight the whole time, you know what I mean?" I asked.

"No. I have no idea what that means," he answered.

"Never mind."

"Well, I'll talk to little Gracie when she comes back here. Don't worry, she'll forgive you, and hopefully me too."

"I hope so, or else we just ended a twenty-year friendship over nothing. Literally."

"No way. You guys are such good friends. It's not easy to have friends like that. It's like finding hay in a needle stack."

I smiled. I didn't need to correct him. I knew exactly what he meant.

"Like I said, Bobby's at the Landing. Just saying. Maybe start there. I'm going to go take a nap. When I wake up, I hope I have my friends back, and that no one is throwing shoes."

He patted my head as he stood and left.

I TOOK A SHOWER AND changed before I went into town to find Bobby and begin my apology spree. I knew I had pushed him too far and had taken my own issues out on him simply because he was there. I walked the few blocks to the Landing and found him sitting alone in our usual spot at the end of the bar, drinking a beer and eating peanuts, their shells littering the space in front of him.

"Wolf has a big mouth," he said as he stared at one of the TVs above the bar.

"I forced it out of him," I lied, not wanting him to get mad at Wolf now too.

"What'd you do, throw your other shoe at his head?"

"Something like that," I said sheepishly as I slid onto the stool next to him. "Anyway, I'll have you know, I wasn't even looking for you."

"Then why are you here?"

"I like the bar nuts," I said.

"You're a bar nut," he replied, tossing a peanut shell at me.

"Listen, I don't really know what happened back there, but I'm sorry. You were right. I had no reason to say anything about that woman, Melinda. It was none of my business. I'm not sure what happened to me, but I'm really sorry."

"I think you were jealous," he teased.

"Don't push your luck."

"Yeah, yeah. I'm sorry I aimed a little below the belt there with the knitting needles. That wasn't cool."

"No biggie. It's over and done with. Friends again?"

"Are you done being psychotic?"

"I think so."

"Then yeah, we're friends again. Get a beer." I ordered a beer and shifted on my stool next to him. "You and Grace went at it pretty good," he said. "I wasn't expecting that from either of you."

"Me neither," I admitted. I wasn't proud of what had happened.

"I'm kind of pissed we didn't have a mud pit handy."

"We haven't fought like that in a very long time, and I haven't heard from her."

"She's going through some stuff, she'll come around."

"I was pretty mean to her."

"Yeah, but she called you fat. You're even."

"Good point."

"I knew guys could drive girls crazy, but I've never seen anything like the two of you. It got me thinking."

"About what?"

"Do you think I've done things that made sane girls act the way you guys just did?"

"You probably have, yeah."

"Jesus. I have to start being more careful. I don't want to fuck people up the way you guys got fucked up."

"I think that's admirable. And potentially insulting. I'm not sure yet."

"No seriously, you guys are like, completely crazy. Like straitjacket crazy. And let me tell you, you're both so much better than Johnny and Ben, it's a joke. I don't get why you let them do this to you. They're losers."

"Love makes smart girls do stupid things . . . until it doesn't." I sighed.

"Do you realize that if either Ben or Johnny cared about you guys the way you care about each other, you both might actually be normal?"

It was one of the smartest points anyone had ever made. "Yeah," I said as I finished my beer. "I think I finally get that."

I went home and got into bed early, but I had a hard time falling asleep. I wanted so badly to call Grace, but I knew she wouldn't answer. She needed to cool down, and I needed to let her, but still I hated feeling like I couldn't call. In that way, all relationships share a common reality: it makes no difference if it's a guy or a girl on the other end of the line, there's nothing worse than wanting to talk to someone and being unable to dial. It occurred to me that I might not be the only person who felt that way. So I dialed.

"Hey, Mom," I said when she answered.

"Abby! Is everything okay? You never call me. You didn't get arrested, did you?"

"No, I didn't get arrested. I'm just calling to talk." There was stunned silence on the other end of the line, and I wasn't surprised. I don't think I had called my mother just to talk in ten years, and I didn't mind the extra time to collect my thoughts. This was new territory for both of us. "I got into a fight with Grace," I admitted.

"Oh," she said quietly, still unsure how to handle this friendly phone call. "Well, that will happen. You two are like sisters. You'll get over it."

"I don't know, Mom. It was pretty bad. I said some things I shouldn't have."

"You didn't attack her, did you?" my mother asked. It would have been a ridiculous question under normal circumstances, but considering my track record that summer, sadly, it wasn't out of the realm of possibility.

"Not physically, no. Do you think I'm pathetic, Mom?" It hurt to say the words out loud, but I needed to know if what Grace said was true, and if anyone would tell me the truth, it was my mother.

"Pathetic?" she answered, the shock registering in her voice. "I wouldn't use that word to describe you in a million years. Actually, I admire you and how you've picked yourself up over the last few months."

"Really?" This was not the answer I was expecting. "You do? I thought you told me I had let myself go, that I wasn't doing anything to help myself."

She sighed, as if hearing me repeat her own words back to her was somehow painful. Now she knew how I felt. "Abby, I know I don't always say the right things. I know I don't always do the right things, and I'm probably not going to win any 'mother of the year' awards for some of the parenting techniques I've used over the years. But I was only trying to give you a kick to get you going. I didn't know what else to do. I was trying to be protective of you, and I wanted you to show everyone how strong you are. How no man could destroy the confident, beautiful woman I raised. If I messed it up, I messed it up, but you know what? You don't see how far you've come the last few months. You've got your smile back. I like to think my tough love tactics helped put it there. I tried my very best with you girls."

"I know you did. You always meant well."

"Thank you. I really appreciate you saying that."

"Listen, I'm going to be home soon. Maybe we can get dinner one night after work. Just the two of us."

"I'd like that," she said, though I could sense her hesitation.

"We can go somewhere vegan if you want," I added, offering one final olive branch.

"Great!" she said. "You'll love it, Abby. It's really not bad at all. Just try to keep an open mind."

"I've been trying to do that all summer."

"Keep it up, it's working. And don't worry about Grace. Just say you're sorry. Sometimes those two little words go a very long way."

"Thanks, Mom. I'll call you next week, okay?"

"Good night, Abby. Get some rest. At your age, they say that a woman needs. . . ." She stopped herself, and I waited for her to finish her sentence and tell me that mature skin requires eight to ten hours of sleep a night to keep from looking like a baseball mitt. She took a deep breath and continued. ". . . Absolutely nothing. A woman your age is just perfect the way she is."

I smiled as I hung up, knowing that my mother didn't actually believe a word she had just said, but happy that she finally realized that sometimes a girl just wants her mother to lie to her.

MY ALARM WENT OFF AT 9:00 A.M., and I rolled over to turn it off, realizing that something was sitting on my feet. Odd, since last I checked I didn't have a dog.

"Hey," a very tired-looking Grace said from the edge of my bed.

"Hey. How long have you been there?" I asked, rubbing the sleep from my eyes.

"About half an hour. I brought breakfast. Are you hungry?"

"A little. I'm really sorry, Grace," I said.

"Me too," she answered.

I hugged Grace as I struggled to get out from under the covers. It felt like the two of us had been through everything together, and my one night not speaking to her was enough to know that I never wanted to have another one. I had thought the same thing about Ben once upon a time, but I was wrong. When you really love someone, you don't let more than a day go by before you say you're sorry, and if you're really smart, you bring food with you when you do.

"Did you call him?" I asked. *Please, God, please spare at least one of us from ourselves.*

"No," she replied.

"What made you change your mind?" *Thank you, thank you, thank you.*

"You."

"Since when have I been able to convince you to do anything? That's a first."

"You were able to get rid of Ben, and you guys were engaged, for God's sake. If you can do that, then I can get rid of a married guy who I know, deep down, will never be mine."

I didn't say anything because there was simply nothing left to say. She continued. "Well, it looks like we're both single. That hasn't happened in a very long time, huh?"

"How do you feel about it?" I asked.

"Like eating." She looked pensive, sad. "How'd we get so fucked up, Abby?" she asked.

"I can blame my mother. I don't know who you can blame. I'm not sure what went wrong with you."

"We're still pretty great, though." Grace had apparently been doing her daily affirmations in the mirror again.

"I like to think so."

"Someday some poor schmucks will be lucky to have us."

"Do you want to go out with the pyromaniac? You can have him," I offered, figuring it was the least I could do.

"I don't think so. Thanks, though."

"Did you really bring breakfast?" I asked, realizing that I hadn't eaten anything the day before and I was starving.

"Sort of." She pulled a pint of ice cream and two spoons out of her purse. "You're right," she said with a smile. "Empty calories really do make you feel better."

"Yes, they do." She crawled into bed next to me as I ripped the cover off the ice cream and grabbed a spoon from her hand. And for the next two hours that was how we stayed, just two best friends, having breakfast in bed at the beach.

CHAPTER 24

Renaissance Man

LABOR DAY STILL means to me what it always has: the return to school. When I was a student, I was one of the few kids who actually welcomed the end of summer and the beginning of a new school year. I loved back-to-school shopping. I loved making textbook covers with brown paper grocery bags. I loved buying new supplies that had that familiar smell that somehow signaled the beginning of a new year rife with possibilities, and I loved getting away from my mother for eight hours at a clip. Even now that I returned to school as the teacher and not the student, I still loved the promise that the beginning of a new year held. For those kids, I'd be part of something they'd always remember, and that feeling, the one that had drawn me to teaching to begin with, was one of the greatest feelings in the world.

We packed up the house, scrubbed the place down, and prepared to return to our real lives back in Boston. Grace, Lara, and I went out to lunch on our last Saturday at the beach to toast the end of summer and each other, not necessarily in that order.

"So, I have an announcement to make," Lara said.

"Do tell," I said as I squeezed lemon into my water.

"I've decided to try online dating," she said proudly. "I'm tired of fighting the inevitable, and I don't want to be afraid of getting back out there. This way I can sit in the comfort of my own home and email people before I meet them. It's a safe first step." Finally, email and Internet dating have actually come in handy. Maybe there was something to it after all.

"I think that's awesome. Just stay away from any guys who mention being in a band," I said.

"Got it. If I need any help or anything, Abby, do you think it would be okay if I call you sometime? I can't thank you enough for all of your help this summer. You were a godsend."

"I didn't do much," I said. "I didn't even know you were separated for most of the summer."

"You kept me company, and you showed me that it's okay to start over."

"You're welcome, and definitely call me anytime. You're going to do great." I reached over and rubbed her shoulder, trying to encourage her one last time before I left.

"Speaking of calling, what are you going to do about the cute guy from the store?" she asked.

I had forgotten all about Tom Marsh, and how I told him I'd call. "Thanks for the reminder," I said as I pulled my phone from my bag and dialed his number.

"You'd never know you spent most of the last year afraid of guys," Grace said as she nodded in approval.

"Voicemail," I said when I heard his recording. I cleared my throat and in a cheery voice said, "Hey, Tom, this is Abby. We're leaving the beach today, so I figured I'd call and tell you it was great meeting you this summer, and if you'd like to get out for a beer back in the city, give me a ring. Have a safe trip back. Bye."

"Smooth," Lara said when I placed my phone back in my bag.

"The bar was low, but I think that officially wins me the most improved award of the summer, don't you guys think?" I asked.

"Definitely," they said. And I agreed with them.

We soaked in the last of the summer sun and the Newport scene as we ate our salads, and when we had finished and paid the bill, I caught myself feeling so very sad to leave the place that had helped bring me back to life. Had I known that this little town in Rhode Island possessed such powerful healing properties, I'd have come a lot sooner.

"Well, Abs, I think it's time we hit the road. Lara, let's get out and troll for guys when you're back in the city," Grace said as we stood and prepared to part ways.

Lara hugged us both good-bye one last time before she hopped in her car and went home. It felt like the last day of college, when you and your friends all went your separate ways and you knew that things would never be the same again. You could only hope that things would get better. That was how I was feeling now—nostalgic and hopeful.

Grace and I walked back to the house, linking arms the way we always did. She asked, "So who do you think had it the worst, me, you, or Lara?"

"Three-way tie."

"That's some tough competition."

"Everyone's got something." I laughed.

"Yeah, well, that's damn true where we're concerned."

I had spent an entire summer trying to fill what I thought was a gap in my life, and if the experience had taught me one thing it was that that was a complete waste of time. None of us had had the fairy-tale ending, at least not yet, and that was perfectly okay.

"Did you have a good time this summer? Are you happy I forced you to do it?" Grace asked.

"Very. I didn't realize how badly I needed it."

"I did. I finally feel like I have the old you back. I missed you."

"I missed me too."

"Are you worried about Ben?"

"Nope. Are you worried about Johnny?"

"A little."

"Well, just remember: they're just lobsters, they're not love."

She elbowed me in the side as we walked up the steps and discovered that the boys were there, sitting on the porch as always, drinking our beer. Summer was over. A new season was starting, and it didn't include Bobby and Wolf living down the block. And that made me sad. I smiled as I turned to say good-bye to them.

"So we will get out for drinks next week maybe?" I said to Wolf as I hugged him.

"Yes. I'll call you, and if you don't feel like drinking, maybe we can play some more Scrabble. I'll use English words this time."

"Better let him win, Abby," Grace warned. "Or else he might take a picture of you in the shower and throw it on his website."

"Gracie, I said sorry!" Wolf said, opening his arms and enveloping her in a giant hug. "Please don't hate me!"

"I don't hate you, Wolf," Grace said. "But from now on, I'm off-limits to you and your website, deal? In return, I won't tell everyone on Facebook that you're the one running the website. I still can't believe that, by the way."

"Deal!" Wolf said, his huge smile making it impossible for Grace to stay mad at him.

"Bye, you pain in the ass," I said to Bobby as I hugged him. "We've come a long way in a few months, haven't we?"

"Well, you enjoy talking to me now, and I actually remember your name, so yeah, definite progress was made."

"When will you be back in Boston?"

"I don't know. Later this month probably. September is the best time down here, after all the summer people leave and the weather's still warm. I'm going to hang here and wait and see what happens on the job front, you know?"

"I'm jealous." I sighed.

"I always knew you were."

"Let me know what happens with the job stuff, and give me a call when you get back to the city."

"Did you just ask me on a date?" he asked.

"No," I replied.

"Do you want to?"

"No," I said, forcefully.

"Okay, well, that was pretty similar to the first conversation we ever had, so it appears we've come full circle."

"Don't be a stranger," I said. I meant it.

"I won't. Drive safely. Don't try and pick up any dudes on the way out."

"Right back at you."

"Couldn't just let me have the last word, could you?"

"Now what fun would that be?"

We waved good-bye as we exited the driveway, turned left onto Thames Street, and headed for home.

TWO DAYS LATER I WAS finishing up the last of my summer laundry, organizing my closet, and mentally preparing to return to work, when my door buzzed. I trembled for a second, afraid it was Ben pulling another surprise guest appearance. I hesitated before I hit the button on the intercom. "Hello?"

"Took you long enough. What are you doing up there?" Bobby asked.

"The better question is, what are you doing down there?"

"Buzz me up, come on." I pressed the button and opened the door, listening to the sprightly footsteps on the stairs as he climbed the three flights.

"What are you doing here?" I asked when Bobby reached my door.

"I think you said the same thing the last time I showed up here."

"That's because you always appear unannounced."

"What, we're not friends?"

"We are. I'm just surprised to see you. I thought you were staying in Newport through September."

"I think it might be time for me to reenter the grown-up world," he said.

"When were you ever a member of the grown-up world?"

"Once upon a time I wore a suit to work and everything."

"I have a hard time picturing that," I said as he followed me into the den.

"Well, hopefully, you'll see it for real soon enough. I have an interview on Thursday. The firm has a great reputation, so I'm hoping it goes well."

"That's great!"

"Yeah. I need to start mentally preparing myself to go back to work, you know?"

"Believe me, I get it." I noticed he didn't have a gym bag with him. "What, no margaritas?"

"Margaritas are like white pants; they're verboten after Labor Day," he quipped.

"Wow, how very metrosexual of you."

"Two words for you . . ."

"Fashion maven?"

"Renaissance man."

"Good Lord." I so should have seen that one coming.

"Can I have a beer?"

"I don't have any. I do still have that bottle of wine from the wedding that I never opened, or I can run down to the corner and get you a six-pack if you want."

"I have a better idea."

"I never liked your ideas."

"Let's go to that jazz club in the Back Bay that I told you about."

"Right now? I'm not really dressed to go out."

"It's not like it's a date, so who cares? Do you have something better to do? You're not knitting, are you?"

"No more knitting. From now on, I'll buy my pot holders like every other woman my age."

"Good. Maybe learn how to cook first. Wait, that reminds me." He went into my kitchen and opened my freezer. "Wow," he said as he nodded at me in approval. "You dismantled the ice cream shrine."

"Yup. All gone. I've lost most of my post-Ben depression weight. I don't want it back."

"Good girl. You look great. I'd like to say you look like your old self, except I don't know what the old you looked like."

"I was starting to forget her too."

"Since you don't have any beer, there's no use in hanging out here. Let's go."

"Wait, there's one thing I want to do before we leave."

"You don't need to primp for me. I've seen you at your worst, believe me."

"That's not true," I said, pretending to be offended.

"In one summer, I've seen you beat flowers to death, hit Wolf in the face with a shoe, and let's not forget that oh so very special pink dress. The jig is up."

He had a point. "That's true, but still, that's not what I meant," I said.

I walked over to my laptop, which was sitting on my kitchen table. Only this time I was going to use it for good and not for evil. I didn't even need to consult my pros and cons list first.

"Come here," I said to Bobby as I pulled out the chair next to me. He sat down as I opened Internet Explorer.

"Oh, Jesus. You've been back for two days. Please don't tell me you've relapsed."

"Just be quiet for once in your freakin' life, would you please?"

"I don't like where this is going," he said as I uploaded Facebook and began to re-create a profile. It had been almost a year since I deactivated my account, and I decided it was time I stopped hiding.

"I thought you hated Facebook. Now you want to put yourself back on there?" Bobby asked. "What happened to the whole 'I won't let strangers stalk me' thing?"

"That was the old me."

"I still don't think I like where this is going. I don't know if I trust this new version."

I re-created my profile and uploaded a picture, a shot Wolf took of the four of us with his phone. We were sitting at our outdoor table, smiling at the camera, surrounded by Johnny's lobsters. I had no idea if Johnny was still Facebook-stalking Grace, but if he was, he'd see the picture, see all of us enjoying our summer, see Grace smiling and happy, and know that he could never, ever have her back. And that would piss him off royally. Finally a reason to be happy that Facebook was created.

"That's a good shot," Bobby said.

"It's a good group," I added.

"Can we go now?"

"One more thing," I said. With a single mouse click, I gave myself a status: single. And I couldn't have been happier. "There," I said as I closed the screen. "Let's go."

Bobby and I left my apartment and strolled down Hancock Street on our way to the jazz show, two friends with no significant others, no baggage, and no agenda. It felt like something I'd never had, but had somehow always been missing.

I'd spent the entire summer trying to fill the void left by Ben, thinking that a boyfriend would make me happy and somehow validate my existence. I didn't find one. And I didn't care. If being married meant that I'd have missed out on spending the summer at the beach with Grace and meeting new guy friends who made me laugh and brought me beer in Solo cups and made me margaritas to cheer me up, then I was happy I wasn't. What I had now was way more important than a boyfriend or a ring. My priorities were finally in order, and for the first time in a long time, having a guy in my life didn't even make the list.

I already had everything that really mattered.

And that was more than enough.

Acknowledgments

Thank you to my family for being patient with me while I wrote this book, and for reassuring me that I would finish it on time.

Thank you to all of my friends. Some of you inadvertently gave me material for this book, and some of you intentionally gave me material for this book, and I can't thank you guys enough.

Once again, thank you to my agent at William Morris, Erin Malone. Your early input and amazing comments were invaluable. Thank you a million times over.

Thank you to my editor, Jennifer Brehl, and the rest of the team at HarperCollins, for all of your hard work, for your wise input, and for publishing my second book!

Last, thanks to my husband, Dan. Thank you for making everything better without even trying.

Much love and many thanks to you all.

P.S.

Insights,
Interviews
& More . . .

About the author

About the book

Read on

Meet Erin Duffy

Elena Seibert

ERIN DUFFY graduated from Georgetown University in 2000 with a BA in English and worked on Wall Street, a career that inspired her first novel, *Bond Girl*. She lives in New York City with her husband (whom she met the old-fashioned way—in a bar) and her twin sons.

Tech and the Single Girl

CONTRARY TO WHAT PEOPLE MIGHT SAY about me, I'm not against modern technology. I swear, I'm not. I love my iPad, Skype, and the fact that the navigation system on my car talks to me when I get lost. I am, however, just a little bit (and I mean a tiny bit) scared of Facebook. I feel about Facebook the way my parents feel about the DVR: it seems like a great idea, but I'm not entirely sure I trust it or understand the full extent of its powers. Sometimes I love it. (Someone posted pictures of her new baby! So cute!) Sometimes I hate it. (Someone posted pictures of "the world's best cinnamon roll"! So pointless!) Call me old-fashioned, but I think Facebook has made us all a little lazy in the way we communicate with our fellow humans, and more important, it has made sharing information so ubiquitous that now people share *everything*. I miss the good old days (read: the 1990s), when if you happened to be humiliated, it was a private matter, the details of which you shared only with your closest girlfriends, your neighborhood bartender, and maybe your therapist. These days someone can harmlessly throw a picture on Facebook and inadvertently destroy your entire personal life with a single mouse click. Am I the only one who thinks that's strange and slightly terrifying?

Allow me to tell you a story.

Once upon a time, a long time ago, I was in a serious relationship with a guy. He was smart, cute, extremely funny, and a massive sports fan. He rarely missed the chance to watch a game, and while I love a New York sporting event as much as the next girl, sometimes I preferred to watch the *America's Next Top Model* marathon rather than ESPN. One Friday night, I stayed home to watch TV alone while my boyfriend went to a downtown bar to watch the Yankees game with his buddies. I was blissfully happy with the way my night was going, until my little cousin innocently posted a picture on Facebook of her and her friends sitting behind third base at Yankee Stadium. There, a few rows behind them, was my boyfriend, holding a beer and kissing another girl on the neck. I stared at the picture, stunned. I examined it from every angle, but it was clearly my boyfriend, who was clearly not at a downtown bar with his buddies, and he was kissing someone who was clearly not me. ▸

Tech and the Single Girl ***(continued)***

The women of my mother's generation had to rely on lipstick on the collar as irrefutable proof that their men were cheating. I had crystal-clear panoramic photos taken at Yankee Stadium and broadcast through social media to anyone with a smartphone. What are the odds of catching your boyfriend cheating on you at one of the largest sporting arenas in the free world because he was accidentally captured in the background of a Facebook post? The really funny part is that my boyfriend and my cousin knew each other quite well, and very easily could have actually laid eyes on each other had he not been too busy sucking some girl's neck, and had she not been too busy posting pictures to Facebook to notice who was sitting twenty feet away. I suddenly found myself faced with that question that has plagued women since the dawn of time, or at least since the dawn of social networking sites: How does one get revenge for accidental public humiliation and a ruined night of TV viewing?

I "liked" my cousin's photo (even though I hated it) and then posted a very simple comment: "What's wrong with this picture?" It took about ten seconds before my friends found my now ex-boyfriend in the photo and began posting some not-so-nice comments on his Facebook wall for all of his friends and family to see. It might not have been the most mature way to handle the situation, but I figured that at the very least there would be no way for him to blame our impending breakup on me and, quite frankly, I felt like Facebook owed me a favor.

A month later, in order to reclaim control of my life and improve my miserable mood, I registered for a charity triathlon. I took the time I would have spent having dinner or going to movies with my boyfriend to train six days a week with a group of New Yorkers who, like me, were trying to improve their bodies and souls through fresh air and exercise and do some good in the process. Ironically, I actually met a guy and we ended up going on a few dates, proving that sometimes good things *can* result from bad situations. Sadly, he turned out to be a sociopath with severe body image issues and a bizarre addiction to energy bars, but that's an entirely different story. Maybe I'll tell you about it someday.

Better yet, maybe I'll post it on Facebook.

Top Ten Ice Cream Flavors to Get You Through a Breakup

1. **Cake Batter**—It's safer than polishing off an entire bowl of actual cake batter. Contracting salmonella will only add to your problems.
2. **Chocolate Therapy**—It's cheaper than paying a shrink and this kind of therapy won't require you to talk about your relationship with your mother.
3. **Candy Bar Pie**—It's a genius way to ingest multiple candy bars without having to look at all the empty wrappers afterward. You feel bad enough as it is.
4. **Chubby Hubby**—A good reminder that most husbands end up fat anyway. Unlike the real thing, when you're done with the carton you can just toss it and try a different one.
5. **Half-Baked**—While drug use is never the answer, this ice cream definitely is.
6. **Strawberry Cheesecake**—Fruit is an important food group and even though you're depressed you still need to eat a balanced diet.
7. **What a Cluster**—Damn, I love ice cream that can read my mind.
8. **Rocky Road**—If you have to travel it then you should be able to eat it.
9. **Dulce de Leche**—You might be nursing a broken heart but you should still keep your brain active. Learn Spanish while you feed your soul.
10. **Rum Raisin**—A socially acceptable way to consume alcohol in the morning is never a bad idea.

Reading Group Discussion Questions

1. Ben's breakup with Abby was unusually abrupt and painful. Why do you think Abby continued to speak to him after the way he treated her? Do you think she would have behaved the same way if she didn't have e-mail and text messaging to rely on for communication?
2. Ben breaks up with Abby via Facebook. How has technology changed the modern dating scene? Have you seen any of this in your own life? Do you think this has been a change for better or for worse? How would Abby see it?
3. Ben breaks up with Abby in order to move out of his comfort zone and build a new life for himself. Although he handles the situation poorly, do you think he has any redeeming qualities?
4. Abby had some difficulties handling her sister Katie's engagement. Do you think she has redeemed herself and repaired her relationship with her sister by the end of the novel? Do you think she was justified in feeling the way she did?
5. Abby has a moment where she realizes that she's more like her mother than she thought, and it results in some very serious soul-searching on her part. Have you ever gone through an experience

that showed you something about yourself you found surprising? How did you address it?

6. Abby has a tumultuous relationship with her mother and her sister. Do you think her relationships with her family change over the course of the novel? How so? What does she learn about family?

7. A year after Ben calls off their engagement he comes back and tells Abby he wants a second chance. Do you think that some people who make bad decisions deserve a second chance? Would you have entertained giving him one?

8. Abby thinks that she has some unrealistic expectations on dating and relationships because of the fairy tales that surrounded her as a child. Do you think that fairy tales play a role in distorting young girls' ideas about how relationships work in the real world? Do you think they can potentially be harmful? Why or why not?

9. Grace's and Lara's lives are both upended by situations involving "the other woman," though Grace is having an affair and Lara has lost her husband to one. Do you think they're both treated sympathetically? How are they ultimately able to find common ground?

10. Toward the end of the novel, Abby finally has a productive conversation with her mother, and says that she's happy that her mother finally understands that "sometimes, a girl just wants her mother to lie to her." What do you think she means by that?

11. Abby and Bobby have a unique relationship, one that ultimately helps her get over Ben once and for all. Why do you think Bobby took it upon himself to help Abby move on with her life? Do you think he really had feelings for her, or was he only trying to be her friend?

12. Grace and Abby seem to think they know what's best for each other, when neither one of them has her own life figured out. Do you think their reliance on each other was more helpful or harmful when it came to dealing with their relationships? Why? ▸

Reading Group Discussion Questions
(continued)

13. What do you think it says about how women define happiness today that all three women ended up alone but happier than they were when they were in their relationships? Do you think that modern women focus as much on love and marriage as they used to?

14. Do you think Abby, Lara, or Grace will find her happy ending, however it is defined, after their summer of self-discovery? Do you think any of them are better positioned to find themselves in healthy relationships? Why or why not?

Have You Read?
More by Erin Duffy

BOND GIRL

While other little girls were fantasizing about becoming doctors or lawyers, Alex Garrett dreamed of conquering the high-powered world of Wall Street. Now she's grown and determined to make it big in bond sales at Cromwell Pierce, one of the Street's most esteemed brokerage firms. Though she's prepared to fight her way into an elitist boys' club, she starts out small, relegated to a kiddie-size folding chair with her new moniker, "Girlie," inscribed in Wite-Out across the back.

Always keeping her eyes on the prize (and ignoring her friends' pleas for her to quit), Alex quickly learns how to roll with the punches, rising from lowly analyst to slightly-less-lowly associate in no time. Suddenly she's being addressed by her real name, and the boys' club has transformed into forty older brothers . . . and one possible boyfriend. But then the apocalypse hits, and Alex is faced with the most difficult choice of her life: to stick with Cromwell Pierce as it teeters on the brink of disaster . . . or kick off her Jimmy Choos and go running for higher ground.